## SEDUCTION WITH THE DUCHESS

The room beyond was dark, lit only by the fire in the fire-place, but as his eyes adjusted, Nicholas could see that it was a bedroom. Emma slipped inside, while Nicholas hesitated on the threshold.

"What's the matter?" she asked, puzzled by his reluctance.

"There must be some mistake. This is not my room."

"There is no mistake, my darling," Emma replied, her voice silky. "This is *my* room. And that is my bed."

"I think perhaps we have had too much to drink."

"I am not drunk," she said indignantly. "If I were drunk, do you think my brothers would have left me alone with you?"

"You were supposed to take me to *my* room," he reminded her gently.

"And so I shall," she said prettily. *"After."*

Books by Tamara Lejeune

SIMPLY SCANDALOUS

SURRENDER TO SIN

RULES FOR BEING A MISTRESS

THE HEIRESS IN HIS BED

CHRISTMAS WITH THE DUCHESS

Published by Kensington Publishing Corporation

# Christmas
## with the Duchess

## TAMARA LEJEUNE

## ZEBRA BOOKS
### KENSINGTON PUBLISHING CORP.
http://www.kensingtonbooks.com

ZEBRA BOOKS are published by

Kensington Publishing Corp.
119 West 40th Street
New York, NY 10018

All Kensington titles, imprints and distributed lines are available at special quantity discounts for bulk purchases for sales promotion, premiums, fund-raising, educational or institutional use.

Special book excerpts or customized printings can also be created to fit specific needs. For details, write or phone the office of the Kensington Special Sales Manager: Kensington Publishing Corp., 119 West 40th Street, New York, NY 10018. Attn. Special Sales Department. Phone: 1-800-221-2647.

Zebra and the Z logo Reg. U.S. Pat. & TM Off.

ISBN-13: 978-1-4201-0873-6
ISBN-10: 1-4201-0873-5

First Printing: October 2010
10 9 8 7 6 5 4 3 2 1

Printed in the United States of America

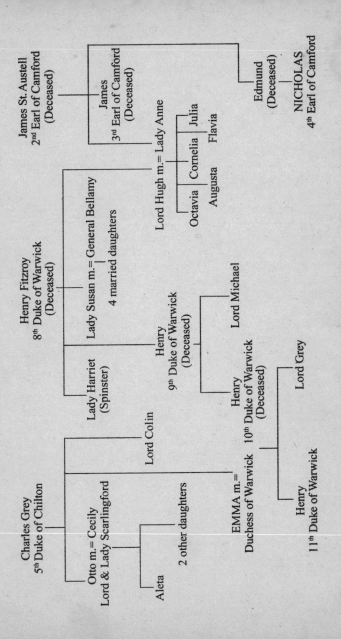

# Chapter One

The iron gates of Warwick Palace stood open all morning, their sharp, gilded spikes gleaming in the winter sun as dozens of heavy traveling carriages rolled up the wide, evergreen avenue to the courtyard of the great house. Emma Grey Fitzroy, Duchess of Warwick, watched the invasion from the window seat of her private sitting room, high above the noise and confusion below.

With her dazzling white skin, steel-blue eyes, and thick, ash-brown hair, Emma was considered one of the great beauties of her time, but men were not drawn to her so much for her angelic appearance as her unbridled sensuality. Born into a life of privilege, Emma had never attempted to govern her passions, had never felt the least need to resist temptation, had never learned to be discreet, or, God forbid, prudent. At twenty-nine, she was as headstrong and impulsive and defiant as she had been as a child. She accepted no criticism of herself. She was, in short, an aristocrat.

"Look at them!" she exclaimed, her eyes flashing with anger. "I should be ashamed to show up at someone's house uninvited."

Seated across the richly appointed room in front of a cozy fire, Cecily, Lady Scarlingford, looked up from the shawl she was knitting. Over the course of her ten-year marriage to Emma's elder brother, Cecily had borne six children, only three of whom had survived infancy, all females. The experience had left her plump, nervous, and worn out. No matter how hard she tried, she always looked rumpled. Her hair was a bushy mess of stubborn brown curls. She was known by smart Londoners as the "unmade marchioness" because of her unfortunate resemblance to an unmade bed.

"Otto will make them go away," she told Emma. "Won't you, Otto?"

Otto Grey, Marquess of Scarlingford, glanced up from his newspaper with eyes more gray than blue. Emma's elder brother was a tall, thin aristocrat with finely chiseled features and black hair streaked with silver. His skin was fashionably pale, and diamonds glittered on his long, elegant fingers.

"It is a truth universally acknowledged that a man's house is never his own at Christmas," he said importantly. "Whatever his thoughts may be on the subject, his family will not be denied their fair share of hospitality. You see, Cecily, how your life will be when I inherit Chilton."

"I'm afraid your husband is right," Emma told her sister-in-law. "The Fitzroys invade Warwick every year; it is a standing engagement. From Stir-up Sunday to Twelfth Night, they look upon my son's estate as quite their own, just as they did when his father was alive. It is quite useless to resist, and even more useless to complain."

"You will do both, however," Otto remarked, folding his newspaper neatly and turning it over. Even this slight, affectionate jab brought a frown from his proud sister. "Is it Uncle Cuthbert?" he asked presently. "Second Cousin Hortensia? Rufus?"

"You are making those names up, Otto," Cecily accused her elegant husband.

He smiled enigmatically. "Am I?" he murmured.

Cecily blinked at him. "Are you?" she asked uncertainly.

"It is nosy, interfering Aunt Susan," Emma interrupted, "and that fat, lecherous, old fool she married. General Bellamy—back from the war and eager to take all the credit for the Allied victory, no doubt. They've brought the whole army with them, too, by the looks of it. Why, the courtyard is perfectly scarlet!"

"Don't exaggerate," said Otto. "Nothing is so common as exaggeration. The Bellamys have four daughters married to officers; a few redcoats are to be expected amongst the party."

"Do I exaggerate, Cecily?" Emma demanded, pointing.

Her sister-in-law set down her knitting. "Oh, how splendid!" she said, coming to the window. "It's like a parade. They must have invited *all* of the officers."

"Quite!" Emma said indignantly.

"You should go down and do the pretty with Aunt Susan, Emma," said Otto.

Emma laughed uproariously. "And let the general pinch my bottom, too, I suppose!"

"I'm perfectly serious," Otto insisted. "You will catch more flies with honey than with vinegar."

"But I do not like flies, brother," she told him.

"You know what I mean," he said sharply. "A little civility will go a long way. It will do you no good to antagonize the Fitzroys—or the Bellamys for that matter. Like it or not, you are related to them by marriage, and connected to them forever by your children."

"It is my *existence* that antagonizes my in-laws," Emma retorted. "In their view, I am nothing more than a worn-out brood mare. Anything I do short of suicide is bound to antagonize them! Doing the pretty in this case would mean jumping off the bloody roof. Besides," she added mischievously, "being a duchess means never having to do the pretty."

She certainly had no intention of going down to greet her in-laws. With few exceptions, she had never liked the Fitzroys, and, since the sudden death of her husband the previous year, she had learned to hate them. The Fitzroys had fought tooth and nail for custody of Emma's two sons, and, after a vicious battle, they had won.

And they had not been gracious in victory. For the first time in her life, Emma did not know where her children were. She had not been permitted to seen them since the moment her husband's uncle, Lord Hugh Fitzroy, had been awarded guardianship of the two boys. Harry, her eldest, had turned thirteen since his mother saw him last. He was now the Duke of Warwick, and essential to the Fitzroys, but Emma feared that Grey, who was just eleven, would not be cared for as assiduously. Keeping him from his mother could only be an act of pure spite.

"They will not keep the boys from their mother at Christmas, surely," Cecily protested.

"Really? Do you believe there is a limit to their cruelty?" said Otto. "Emma? You know them better than anyone. What do you think?"

"I will not go down, Otto," she said fiercely. "I will not crawl to Susan Bellamy or anyone. They would only laugh in my face. I have no leverage, and they have no pity. But the boys will come home for Christmas, and I will see them."

"And then?" said Otto.

"And then we will see," Emma said impatiently.


From the window of another apartment, Captain Lord Ian Monteith stared down at the disorder in the courtyard with a dismay verging on panic. A powerfully built Scotsman with pale green, oddly tilted eyes, he was somehow attractive without being really handsome. His shaggy brown hair fell into his eyes, too long for fashion, but too short to tie back. The younger son of the Marquis of Arranagh, he had been destined for the Army from a young age, and he had not disappointed expectations. At least, he had not disappointed *those* expectations.

"You did not tell me the house would be full of soldiers," he complained to his lover, Lord Colin Grey. "What if I should meet someone I *know?*"

Emma's younger brother was standing at the cheval glass, engrossed in tying his cravat. He and Emma were twins, born just six minutes apart, and the resemblance was undeniable. Like his sister, he was beautiful, spoiled, and reckless. Rumors abounded that the flamboyant younger son of the Duke of Chilton was a homosexual, but, thus far, his rank and wealth had protected him from outright accusation.

"*Is* the house full of soldiers?" Colin asked mildly, studying all aspects of his well-groomed exterior in the mirror. "No one said anything to me."

"Take a look, why bloody don't you!"

Colin calmly strolled over to the window. "My goodness!" he exclaimed, slapping his palms to his cheeks. "A whole camp full of soldiers! Somebody pinch me."

"Oh, shut up!" his friend snapped. "If I'd known about *this,* I would never have agreed to come with you to Warwickshire. You never *think,* sir! You never think."

"On the contrary, I am always thinking," Colin replied, yawning. "Why, I'm practically a philosopher, don't you know. What I do *not* do is worry, Monty. I never worry, and, as you can see, I have no wrinkles to show for it."

"But I *do* worry, sir!" Monty, who was not a day over twenty-one, said angrily. "Unlike you, I am not independent. If it should get back to my father—! If it should get back to my *regiment* that I'm spending Christmas with the infamous Lord Colin Grey, I'd be ruined!"

"Very likely," Colin sweetly agreed. "But *I* happen to think I'm worth it."

Monty was not amused. "My God! Is that General Bellamy?" he moaned. "My colonel plays cards with him."

"We know him as Uncle Susan around here," Colin replied.

"Colin, I must leave here at once."

Colin laughed. "Pull yourself together, Monty! Screw your courage to the sticking place, if you've got one. If anyone inquires into our friendship, tell them you're in love with my sister. Make up to her like nobody's business. Emma won't care three straws if people think you're her latest bedfellow."

Monty seized on the suggestion. "Would that—would that work, do you think?"

"Of course. It's a very neat trick. We've done it before."

Monty frowned at him. "Oh, you have, have you?" he said coldly.

"Lord, yes. Heaps of times."

"*How* many times?" Monty demanded.

"I can't recall. The point is," Colin went on quickly, "people are ready to believe anything about my sister. Now, how do I look? Exquisite or divine? Those are the choices."

Turning in a slow circle, he offered himself up for inspection.

"Oh, I *do* hope Harriet has not botched the arrangements this year," Lady Susan Bellamy, nee Fitzroy, remarked to her husband, as a footman darted forward to open the carriage door for her. He was a perfectly handsome, tall footman, faultlessly turned out in the Duke of Warwick's black and gold livery, but Lady Susan was determined to find a blemish.

"Just once, I should like to come home and find the place in order," she said, lowering her quizzing glass in triumph, having discovered that the footman's eyes were a shade too close together. "Now, is that too much to ask? Heaven knows Harriet has little enough to do. She has no husband, no children, nothing to employ her. Why, I wouldn't know what to do with myself if I had to live here year round," she added mendaciously. "I could never be so lazy."

Still vigorous at sixty, General Bellamy hungrily eyed the other vehicles, the passengers of which were just beginning to disembark. "Good old Harriet," he muttered amiably, even as he searched among the passengers for signs of his mistress, Mrs. Camperdine, the fetching little wife of his quartermaster. In his youth, the general had been a voracious philanderer. Age had narrowed the field for him to just one wife and just one mistress, but he still imagined himself to be a great favorite amongst the ladies.

Lady Susan, herself an aging coquette, bristled at his un-solicited endorsement of Lady Harriet Fitzroy, her elder sister. "I daresay the whole place is in a shambles," she said belligerently. "I daresay our rooms will not be ready for *hours,* and your *good old Harriet* will surely greet us with some ridiculous excuse about my letter going astray!"

"I can reassure you on that head, madam," the general replied. "Since your letters never seem to land where they should, I took it upon myself to scribble a note. *My* letters always manage to get where they are going," he added smugly.

Lady Susan was vexed. She had not actually written any letters to her sister. She preferred to arrive at Warwick unexpectedly, and then complain about her sister's lack of consideration. She thought it very disloyal of the general to go behind her back.

"I'm cold," she complained, hurrying up to the house with the general in tow. "I do hope the fires have been lit. Let us hope the *servants* know what they are about, even if *good old Harriet* does not."

Spotting Mrs. Camperdine at last, the general gave an involuntary grunt of pleasure. "I'm sure you have the right of it, my dear," he said cheerfully to his wife, and they went into the house together.

A tall, thin lady came down the great double staircase to greet them. Although she was ten years older than her sister, Lady Harriet looked ten years younger. Her face was unlined, and her dark eyes were bright with intelligence. Her white hair was cropped short, giving her an odd, almost whimsical appearance. She might otherwise have seemed quite severe.

Lady Susan lifted her quizzing glass, but Lady Harriet retaliated with her lorgnette.

Thirty-odd years before, General Bellamy, then a handsome young captain of the Guards, had jilted Lady Harriet to marry Lady Susan. Lady Harriet had realized very quickly that she was better off without the womanizing George Bellamy, but she had never forgiven her sister's treachery. It gave her malicious satisfaction to see that Susan had grown even fatter since last Christmas. Her beauty was in danger of disappearing altogether amongst the folds of white flesh.

For her part, Lady Harriet looked about the same. But then, *she* had no husband or children to make her fat or give her worry lines, Lady Susan reminded herself, seething with resentment. *Harriet* lived year-round in luxury at Warwick Palace with other people's servants at her beck and call while Susan was forced to spend her own money on her own establishment. So unfair! The quizzing glass was withdrawn.

"I trust the India Suite has been made ready for us," Lady Susan said aloud, in a tone more suitable for addressing one's housekeeper than one's sister.

"You *do* look very tired, Sister," Lady Harriet said with sweet malice. "I know how you like to rest after a journey. However, I fear I cannot oblige you with regards to the India Suite. Her grace occupies it currently, as she always does when she is at home."

Lady Susan was taken aback.

"The duchess is here?" she snarled. "That shameless hussy! That—that Jezebel!"

"Where?" cried the general.

Lady Susan ignored him as he barked at his own little joke. "How could you let this happen, Harriet? You should have sent the hounds after her."

"She has dower rights, Susan," Lady Harriet calmly replied.

"To be sure, she has dower rights," replied Lady Susan. "But that doesn't give her the right to descend upon us any time she pleases!"

"Of course it does, you half-wit," Lady Harriet said impatiently.

"You should have informed me, Sister," Lady Susan insisted. "I would have put a stop to her insolence. I would have sent the strumpet on her way."

Lady Harriet looked innocent. "You mean you didn't get my letter? How strange!"

Lady Susan glared at her, recognizing that her own favorite ploy had been used against her. "Very strange indeed, Sister!"

"You women and your letters!" scoffed General Bellamy. "Will you never learn to address them properly? The postman is not a mind reader, you know."

"Carstairs will show you to your apartment," Lady Harriet said smoothly, beckoning for the butler. "I've put you in Poland."

Lady Susan was incensed. "Poland? Poland! You will not put *me* in Poland, I promise you! Do you hear me, Harriet?" she roared, bustling after her sister as the latter quietly withdrew up the stairs. "I will not be treated like this."

Left to his own devices, General Bellamy scurried off to meet a certain wide-hipped brunette for a quick tryst in the linen cupboard.

\* \* \*

"If you won't listen to my advice, Emma, there's nothing I can do," Otto was saying at that moment in Emma's sitting room. "You refuse to make the slightest effort at civility?"

"I do," Emma said mulishly. "If I had milk for blood, I might do as you ask."

"So be it," Otto said, climbing to his feet. "Well, I certainly don't intend to sit here all day listening to you complain!" he added. "Send for me the instant Lord Hugh arrives."

"Why?" Emma said crossly. "I'm perfectly capable of dealing with him."

"You will do nothing of the sort," he said sharply. "I will deal with him. Cecily, will you come and get me when Lord Hugh arrives? He is expected this afternoon by four o'clock."

"Don't you trust me, Otto?" Emma taunted him.

"No. Cecily?"

"Yes, Otto," Cecily said obediently. "I will come and get you directly he arrives."

When he had gone, Cecily tidied up his newspapers. "Poor Otto!" she said. "You must forgive him, Emma, if he seems a little impatient. He has not been to my bed since Amelia was born. I fear the deprivation has made him . . . irritable."

"Let him be irritable."

Cecily sank into her chair. "But, Emma! I feel so guilty."

"Cecily, it would be a great danger to your health to get pregnant again so soon. You must heed the physician's advice."

"I'm afraid the Duke of Chilton does not care about my health," Cecily said, her voice beginning to tremble.

"My father is an ass," Emma said stoutly.

"If I don't give him a grandson soon, he will force Otto to divorce me and marry someone else. Your father hates me," she added, shivering.

"But my brother loves you," Emma told her firmly. "The

days of my father forcing Otto to do anything are long gone, I can assure you."

"That is what Otto says," Cecily answered, chewing nervously at her bottom lip. "Oh, why can I not have a boy? It's not as though I *mean* to have daughters instead of sons. I don't do it on purpose, as your father seems to think."

"My dear Cecily! You mustn't let my stupid, antiquated father and his stupid, antiquated notions make you so anxious. The surgeons are all agreed that you must have a nice long rest before you try again."

Cecily's round brown eyes filled with tears and the tip of her snub nose turned pink. "Otto has been so kind and patient with me. But, Emma, I fear he will seek the affection of other women."

"No, indeed," Emma scoffed. "Otto is not like other men. He prides himself on being faithful to you. And he has steely self-control. Frightening amounts of self-control. You worry for nothing."

"I don't know how you put up with Warwick's philandering all those years," said Cecily. "It would have destroyed me."

"Ah, but I didn't put up with it," Emma said, with a faint laugh. "I retaliated by taking lovers of my own. When he died, we had not slept in the same bed in years. We had become almost strangers. We had quite a typical Society marriage, in fact—until he fell out of Mary Bellingham's window. *That* was singular, I admit. Can you imagine Otto falling out of a window? Believe me, Cecily, you have nothing to worry about. Otto Grey is a man without fault. I think he must have refused them all at birth, which explains, perhaps, why Colin and I have so many. All the seven deadlies, and a few of our own invention besides."

"He *is* without fault. Oh, I must sound so ungrateful," Cecily fretted. "I know I am fortunate in my husband. If I could just have a *son*—! Then everything would be perfect."

"My dear Cecily—"

"No more," said Cecily, with a resolute smile. "I am done whining. Enough!"

She picked up her knitting. Her needles clicked. The fire crackled. After a moment, Emma took up a book and settled back into the window seat. The cloisonné clock on the mantel began to strike ten, startling the two ladies. At almost the same time, there was a scratching at the door.

"Enter," Emma called out.

"I nearly forgot," said Cecily, setting aside her knitting. "I told Aleta she could play for you after her German lesson. That must be her now." She froze suddenly. "Of, course, if you'd rather not—" she stammered. "If it will remind you too much of Harry and Grey—"

"Nonsense," said Emma. "Harry and Grey are not musical in the least. I should love to hear Aleta play." Climbing to her feet, she closed her book as an austerely clad governess came into the room leading a tall, slender child with a mop of black hair and enormous, dark eyes.

At a nod from her governess, Lady Aleta Grey curtsied. "*Guten Morgen,* Mama. *Guten Morgen, Tante* Emma."

Emma smiled at her warmly. *"Guten Morgen, liebchen."*

The child stared in agonized ignorance as Emma began to question her in German. Her governess sighed in disgust.

"You have not been studying," Emma gently chided Aleta.

"No," Aleta admitted, "but I *have* learned a German song for you," she quickly added, brandishing her sheet music. "A Christmas song. *Die Tannenbaum.*"

"Ah," said Emma, touching the girl's cheek. "Herr Franck's arrangement, I see. One of my favorites. I will open the instrument for you," she added, hurrying over to the pianoforte that stood in one corner of the room.

"I can do it, Aunt Emma," the child said. "Don't fuss over me."

"Aleta!" Cecily protested. "You must not address your aunt in that tone."

"It's all right," said Emma, retreating. "I shall wait over here with your Mama until you are ready. Thank you for bringing her," she told Cecily quietly as they watched the child make her preparations at the pianoforte. "I do not get to see her as much as I would like. She's growing up so fast. Do you think Otto would allow me to take her with me to Paris?" She sighed. "He will probably say it is not wise."

Cecily looked at her, wide-eyed. "You mean to go back to Paris? When?"

"After Christmas, of course," Emma answered. "January. Once the boys are back in school, there is nothing to keep me in England. And now that the Corsican tyrant is safely exiled to Elba, there is nothing to keep me out of France. I have many friends at the French court. And I have bought a splendid little house in the Faubourg de St. Honore."

"Exile!" Cecily said unhappily.

"I'll take Paris over the sanctimonious hypocrisy of London any day," Emma replied. "In Paris I can be at liberty. No one judges me. Why, by Parisian standards, I am a model of virtue!"

"Aunt Emma! Mama!" Aleta called from the pianoforte. "I am ready now."

Cecily and Emma hurried to take their seats as the child began to sing haltingly in German as her fingers limped over the keys. Cecily did not know the words, but Emma gamely joined in singing the old German folk tune.

*Ach Tannenbaum, Ach Tannenbaum,*
*Du bist ein edler Zweig!*
*Du grünest uns den Winter,*
*Die liebe Sommerzeit.*

The musician stayed afterward for twenty minutes—quite twenty times the length of the little song—shyly accepting the praise of her grateful audience. Then her governess whisked her away for her watercolor lesson.

Emma spent the rest of the morning writing letters. After luncheon, she went out for a long walk, returning to the house for tea. To her surprise, Lord Hugh had not yet arrived. The man was usually punctual. He certainly never missed a meal, if he could help it.

As evening dragged into night, Emma became worried, not about Lord Hugh, of course. She could not have cared less about him. Her fears were for Harry and Grey; she could only assume that they were with their great-uncle and guardian. Using her widowhood as an excuse to avoid company, she dined alone in her room, hardly touching her food, much to the dismay of her French chef. Otto and Cecily, Colin and Monty dined with the other guests, but they could discover nothing about Lord Hugh. If he had sent any word to Warwick about a change in his travel plans, Emma was not to be privy to the information.

At ten o'clock, the gates to Warwick were closed, and the guards released the mastiffs to patrol the grounds. Emma lay in bed for hours, restless and uneasy, before drifting off to sleep.

# Chapter Two

*Sunday, December 11, 1814*

Nicholas St. Austell sat in the swaying carriage, squeezed between Lord Hugh and Lady Anne Fitzroy, while five young ladies, daughters of Lord Hugh and Lady Anne, sat packed together on the opposite seat. Wearing a brown George wig and a greatcoat with half a dozen capes, Lord Hugh looked the prosperous, well-fed gentleman. His wife, by comparison, was a thin, faded lady with frightened, watery blue eyes. More often than not, she seemed bewildered by the world around her. They were as unlikely a couple, Nicholas supposed, as the brilliantly colored peacock and his lackluster peahen.

Until very recently, the young naval officer had not been aware of the existence of the Fitzroys at all, but now he was to understand that Lord Hugh and Lady Anne were his uncle and aunt—the lady being the elder sister of Nicholas's dead father—and the five young ladies, whom he could scarcely tell apart, were his cousins. Together, they comprised all the family he had in the world, or so they claimed.

All seven of these Fitzroys had been waiting for him on the dock at Plymouth on the day his ship arrived in the harbor. They had been searching the world over for him, they said, and they seemed genuinely delighted to have found him, safe and sound, aboard the H.M.S. *Gorgon*. Before Nicholas quite knew what was happening, his aunt and uncle had claimed him, and he was in a carriage on his way to someplace called Warwick Palace.

It felt like he was being kidnapped. *They are my family,* he often had to remind himself. *They are not kidnaping me. They simply are taking me home with them for Christmas.*

Their delight in him continued unabated, but two days of travel had been more than enough to weary Nicholas of his companions. Lord Hugh—or Uncle Hugh, as he demanded to be called—had quickly revealed himself as a blustering bully. He shouted and snarled at his wife and daughters continuously, while Nicholas never received anything but smiles and platitudes from the man. As for the young ladies, they seemed to do little more than preen and giggle. Nicholas did his best to ignore them, but he was sure that their inane giggling would haunt his dreams for years to come. Lady Anne—Aunt Anne—was the only one among them for whom Nicholas had any feelings, and her he merely pitied.

As darkness fell around them on the third day, the carriage fell silent. Lord Hugh's head fell onto Nicholas's shoulder, and he began to snore, eliciting sleepy giggles from some one or other of his daughters. Suddenly, the carriage ground to a halt. Lord Hugh was pitched forward, his wig falling into Nicholas's lap. Cursing, Lord Hugh let down the window and barked at the driver.

"We are at the gates," Lord Hugh announced presently, closing the window against the cold night air. "Thank you, Nephew," he added gruffly as Nicholas passed him his wig. "We will be at the house in two shakes," he went on, clapping the hairpiece to his skull. "I've sent word ahead to my sister, and the keepers are holding the dogs."

"If we had not stopped to help those stranded people, we

would be there now," one of the girls said resentfully. "I've missed my dinner!"

"We have all missed dinner," one of the older girls told her sharply.

"A broken axle on a lonely road is no joke," Nicholas said, nettled by the girls' lack of charity. "It was our Christian duty to help the vicar and his wife."

"Oh, someone else would have come along to help them," said Lord Hugh. "I suppose at sea one is obliged to help all sorts of people clinging to shipwreck and all that sort of thing, but it's really not necessary in a civilized country. You're not in the Royal Navy anymore, you know."

"But, sir, the lady was with child!" Nicholas protested.

"Shameless the way these clergyman breed," said Lord Hugh, shaking his head. "Ah, well! What's done is done. We'll be in our beds soon enough."

"I'm so tired! I'm cold! I'm hungry!" the girls complained.

"Then you should have eaten the sandwiches that were offered you," Nicholas told them curtly. "And I can't imagine why you'd be tired," he went on angrily. "You've done nothing but sleep and giggle for three days. If there's any work to be done, you fob it off on your mama."

Lady Anne's hand crept to touch his arm. "Do forgive them, Nicholas," she pleaded. "They're just tired and cross, that's all. They don't mean to complain. There's no complaining in the Royal Navy, I'm sure," she added.

Nicholas instantly felt ashamed. In the navy, malcontents routinely were flogged, but, he realized, young ladies ought not to be treated so harshly. "It is I who am cross, Aunt Anne," he said contritely. "Forgive me, ladies. I am not used to traveling in a closed carriage. I am used to the open seas. I am used to dealing with men. I'm afraid my temper got the better of me. I apologize."

"We forgive you, Cousin Nicholas," they said in unison,

reminding him, rather horribly of the verse from the Gospel of Mark: "My name is Legion, for we are many."

"You see, Nicholas?" said Lady Anne. "They are good girls."

"I hope we are not inconveniencing your sister too much, Lord Hugh," said Nicholas, after a short pause. "It is very late. Why, it must be past midnight."

"But Harriet is a spinster," Lord Hugh said, dismissing Nicholas's concerns.

The drive from the gate to the house was surprisingly long. From time to time, Nicholas caught glimpses of shadowy figures outside, men with broken guns moving in the torchlight, men holding back huge, vicious-looking mastiffs. Their breath hanging in visible clouds around their muzzles.

At last the carriage came to a stop.

A sleepy footman opened the door and let down the steps. Lord Hugh climbed out first. "This is not how I wanted to show Warwick to you," he told Nicholas, as the young ladies left the carriage. "But you can get an idea of the size and the grandeur of the place. I will give you the grand tour tomorrow personally."

Nicholas did not reply. Lady Anne remained in the carriage, and he was shocked to see how little her family respected her. Her daughters seemed to think no more of her than the carriage rug they had left lying on the seat. When he was not bullying her, her husband ignored her completely. Nicholas's protective instincts were aroused. Climbing out of the carriage, he offered Lady Anne his arm.

The door was opened briefly to admit them. Nicholas guided his aunt into the hall. Two footmen were lighting candles, but the room still seemed vast and dark. The sharp, fresh scent of balsam hung in the cool air.

"There was no one outside to greet us, Sister," Lord Hugh was complaining to a tall, elderly lady in a nightgown and lace cap.

"Everyone is asleep, Hugh," Lady Harriet told her younger brother. "*I* was asleep."

"A poor excuse!" said Hugh, sneezing. "What is that smell?" he demanded, sneezing again. "It stinks of the outdoors."

"It's balsam," Nicholas said happily, "and holly. It's all over the room. It smells like a forest. It smells like Christmas."

Holding aloft a branch of candles, Lady Harriet looked at Nicholas curiously. He was a good-looking young man with brown skin and bright blue eyes. His features were strong and clear-cut. His sun-bleached hair grew in a good line. He wore it long, but tied back neatly in a queue.

Lord Hugh, meanwhile, glared around him, squinting into the dimly lit corners of the great hall. The beautiful wreaths and garlands ornamented with gilded fruits and velvet ribbon that had been hung about the room did not meet with his approval. "By God, you're right! It *does* smell like a bloody forest in here. What is the meaning of this, Harriet?" he demanded, pulling a handkerchief from his pocket to block another sneeze. "Have you run mad in your old age? Are the servants conducting pagan rites in the small hours? Have all this damned shrubbery cleared off at once!"

"It was the duchess's doing, not mine," Lady Harriet replied evenly. "It is the custom in her mother's native Germany. You will have to bring your complaint to her, I'm afraid."

Lord Hugh grunted. "She's here, is she? Good. I will deal with her tomorrow. In the meantime, clear this rubbish away. 'Tis pagan nonsense, and 'twas confined to the nursery when her husband was alive. I'm sorry you had to see this, Nicholas."

"But I think it's charming," Nicholas protested.

Lord Hugh blinked at him. "You do?"

"Yes. It reminds me of the Christmases I had in Portsmouth when I was a child, when my parents were still alive. But, of course," Nicholas added sheepishly, "our little cottage was nothing at all compared to this place, and we only had bits of holly and mistletoe. No balsam."

"I suppose, if it does not offend you, it can stay," Lord Hugh said reluctantly. Covering his nose and mouth with his handkerchief, he hurried upstairs.

Lady Harriet smiled at Nicholas. "I am Lady Harriet Fitzroy. You must be Lord Camford," she said pleasantly, "the very fortunate young man who recently inherited the title and estates of Lady Anne's brother."

Nicholas blushed. "That is what everyone keeps telling me, ma'am," he said. "I have yet to believe it."

Lady Harriet's eyebrows went up. "Indeed? But I read all about it in the London *Times*."

Nicholas smiled. "In that case, it must be true."

"I think we must accept that it is."

Lord Hugh stopped at the top of the stairs to bellow at Lady Anne. "Madam wife! Take the girls up to their rooms at once. Octavia looks a fright, and Augusta is jumping up and down as though her bladder is fit to burst."

"Oh!" cried Lady Anne. "But Nicholas—"

"Harriet will look after my nephew," he told her. "Step lively, woman! How will you ever find husbands for these wretched girls if you let them go about looking like a pack of wet hens? What kind of mother are you?"

Lady Anne jumped. "Come, girls," she cried breathlessly, hurrying her daughters from the room.

"Now, then," said Lady Harriet, holding her candlestick up to get a better look at the young man in front of her. "Let's have a look at you. My goodness! You *are* a beauty, aren't you?"

Nicholas gaped at the old lady in astonishment.

"You must take after your mother," she stated. "As a rule, the St. Austells are small, ugly, tedious creatures. But you're like a big, bronzed Nordic god, aren't you?"

"I—I don't think so," he said, blushing. "But thank you, ma'am."

Her dark eyes twinkled at him. "Come, my lord, I will show you to your room."

"I wish you would call me Nicholas," he said. "I don't feel like a lord. Any moment now, I feel like I'm going to wake up from a dream and find myself back in the navy," he confessed.

Lady Harriet glanced back at him in surprise. "Since I am old enough to be your grandmother, I don't see why not. And you may call me Aunt Harriet, if you like. That's what the young people call me."

Nicholas followed her through a maze of corridors to a large, beautifully appointed chamber. A cheerful fire crackled in the fireplace.

"Well, Nicholas! I hope you will be comfortable here in Westphalia," Lady Harriet said. "It is not one of our best rooms, I'm sorry to say, but that is what happens when you are late. All the good rooms are taken."

The young man looked at the huge, four-poster bed in amusement. "I was put to sea, ma'am, when I was but nine years old," he told her.

"That explains it, then," said Lady Harriet.

"Explains what, ma'am?"

"Why you seem to have absolutely no idea just how attractive you are," said the old lady. "But, if you were put to sea when you were nine; if you have been in the company of men, for the most part, since that age, that would explain this strange case of modesty. Most young men with your good looks are vainglorious, insufferable peacocks."

"I hope I am not a peacock," said Nicholas. "I was going to say, ma'am, that, in the Royal Navy, we are used to sleeping in our own coffins. When one of us dies at sea, he is simply nailed inside his bed and lowered overboard into Davy Jones's Locker."

"Good God," said Lady Harriet.

"Oh, I'm sorry," he said quickly. "That is not fit conversation for delicate ladies."

"I am not so delicate as I appear," Lady Harriet said dryly. "If you would prefer to sleep in a coffin, we will, of course, have one brought in!"

"No, ma'am, I thank you. The room is more comfortable than any I have ever had the pleasure of seeing."

"Did your valet arrive earlier in the day, my lord? I will try to find him."

"Oh, we don't have such things as valets in the Royal Navy," he told her, chuckling. "I was not the captain, ma'am, merely a lowly lieutenant! And a second lieutenant at that. I can look after myself. I always have."

Lady Harriet inclined her head. "In that case, my lord, I bid you good night."

"Good night, Aunt Harriet."

*My God, they'll eat him alive,* Lady Harriet thought sadly as she left him. She had not expected him to be so nice.


Emma's French maid roused her very early the next morning. Emma sat up, rubbing her eyes as Yvette fired streams of French at her.

"What?" Emma cried, jumping out of bed. "When?"

Pulling on her dressing gown, she ran to the door. Carstairs, the dignified old butler, stood there. "When did Lord Hugh arrive?" the duchess demanded.

"Very late last night, your grace. After everyone had gone to bed. My subordinates did not make me aware of it until this morning."

"I'm sure they wanted to let you sleep, Carstairs. My sons were not with him, I understand."

"No, your grace," Carstairs answered in his funereal voice.

"You have not received any instructions regarding their arrival?" she asked hopefully.

"No, your grace. Lord Hugh has asked me to inform your grace that he will see you this afternoon at three o'clock in the Carolina Room—if he is not too busy. You are to wait for him there?"

Emma bit back a curse. "Is that so? Is there anything Lord Hugh desires?"

"No, your grace."

"I'm afraid three o'clock is not convenient," said Emma. "Where is Lord Hugh now?" she asked, forcing herself to speak calmly.

"He's been placed in the Dresden Suite, your grace."

Emma frowned. "And where the devil is that?" she wanted to know. The house was so large, and she visited it so seldom that she did not know all the rooms. "No, don't bother trying to tell me. You'll have to take me to him, Carstairs," she said decisively. "The house is full of strangers. It would never do if I went to the wrong room."

"No, your grace," he agreed.

"Wait here while I get dressed."

The duchess's toilette usually took three quarters of an hour, but this morning her maid's perfectionism had to be balanced with Emma's desire to be done quickly. In the end, it took fifteen minutes, and neither woman was satisfied. The maid ran after her mistress, putting the finishing touches to Emma's hair until she could keep up with the duchess's pace no longer.

"Is he awake, do you know?" Emma asked Carstairs. "If he's gone down to breakfast already, I shall miss him."

"I do not know, your grace. I felt it best to come to you, directly. But it is not Lord Hugh's habit to wake early."

"He brings his sad little wife with him, of course, and all their daughters," Emma murmured as she followed the butler through the house. "I'm surprised he didn't invite all his friends, too! But, perhaps, he has no friends."

"His lordship did bring one young man with him," said Carstairs.

"Only one?" Emma snapped angrily. "But why should he not invite anyone he likes to my son's house? This young man is attached to one of the girls, I suppose," she sniffed. "Do we hear wedding bells, Carstairs?"

"The night footman informs me that the young man is Lady Anne's nephew, your grace."

"*Anne's* nephew?" Emma repeated, frowning. "If Anne has got herself a nephew, why, he must be the new Earl of Camford! The one they've been looking for all these years."

"Yes, your grace."

Emma gave a short laugh. "I'd heard they were scouring the globe for some long-lost heir, but I had always assumed he was entirely fictitious. I suspect this young man is nothing more than an artful impostor. His discovery—just as the Crown was about to take possession—! well, it's too convenient for belief. Has the Crown conceded?"

"There was an announcement in the *Times* of London some weeks ago. Your grace was in Paris."

"Oh, I see," Emma said, making a face. "It must be true, then. Well! Hugh and Anne must be delighted that Camford won't be reverting to the Crown, after all."

Carstairs prudently offered no comment.

"I wonder they do not spend Christmas at Camford," Emma said after a moment. "But then again, why *shouldn't* they entertain his lordship here instead, with little trouble and no expense to themselves? The earl must be a single man."

"I believe so, your grace," Carstairs replied evenly. "At least, his lordship does not bring his wife with him."

"Of course he's single. They would not bother with him if he were married already; he would be quite safe from the

Miss Fitzroys. He will be expected to marry one of them, of course. I suppose he is to be pitied."

Emma fell silent, mentally preparing herself for the coming interview with her husband's uncle. She wondered if, in her battle with Hugh, Lord Camford could be an ally, or, at least, a useful tool.

As they passed through the long gallery that separated the east wing from the west wing, a young man suddenly stepped from behind one of the marble columns, stopping directly in Carstairs's path. Emma looked at him curiously. She was sure she had never seen him before, but, then Warwick Palace was always full of strangers at this time of year. He was too brown to be a gentleman, she decided, and his ill-fitting clothes, she noted with some amusement, were of poor quality. His coat was so tight that it all but pinned his arms to his sides. Though he was tall, much taller than she, his shoulders were pulled forward by his tight coat, giving him a round back, and causing him to stoop a little. She didn't like his long hair.

He looked distinctly out of place amid the incredible grandeur of Warwick, where even the servants were splendidly and immaculately dressed. He reminded her, oddly, of poor Cecily, who could never get it right, no matter how much she spent on clothes. Unlike Lady Harriet, Emma could not look past his flaws to see that he was actually quite good-looking. She did not see a bronzed Nordic god. She saw a scruffy-looking, badly dressed, overgrown boy.

"May I be of assistance to you, sir?" Carstairs said smoothly.

"Please! I'm completely lost, I'm afraid," the young man confessed. "One needs a compass and a map in a place like this! Would you be so kind as to direct me to the breakfast parlor? I think it's around here somewhere."

"Which breakfast parlor would that be, sir?" Carstairs asked.

The young man's eyes widened. "*Which* breakfast parlor?" he echoed in disbelief. "You have more than one, then?"

"Yes, sir," Carstairs said gravely. "There are four: the summer breakfast parlor, the spring breakfast parlor, the autumn breakfast parlor; and the winter breakfast parlor."

"Perhaps it would be simpler to ring for a footman," Emma suggested, out of patience.

At the sound of her voice, the young man's eyes flew to her face. He blushed, staring. His mouth did not hang open, but it might as well have. Emma guessed he could not be more than nineteen. She promptly dismissed him as a mooncalf.

"I beg your pardon, ma'am!" he exclaimed, stuttering and bowing. "I did not see you there."

"Do you see me now, sir?" Emma asked him tartly.

"Oh, yes, ma'am!" he answered, shy and eager at the same time. Emma did not find his lack of sophistication refreshing. She could almost imagine that he had never lain with a woman before. He behaved almost as if he had never *seen* a woman before.

"Oh, excellent. What you want to do is find a bell and ring it," Emma told him. "Do you think you can manage that, sir?"

"Yes, ma'am! Thank you, ma'am!" he said gratefully. "I don't know why I didn't think of that. I'm not used to servants, you see."

Emma caught sight of a footman at the end of the hall. She beckoned to him, and he hurried over. "Would you be good enough to take this young man to the nearest breakfast parlor, with my compliments."

"Yes, your grace. This way, my lord, if you please."

Emma started in surprise. "Did you hear that, Carstairs?" she said in amazement, when the young man was out of earshot. "Arthur milorded him. Does he know something we don't?"

Carstairs looked aggrieved. "He must be Lord Camford. Now that I think of it, he does meet the description."

"What!" Emma exclaimed in astonishment. "That—that

*cub* who gawped at me like a country bumpkin? *That* is the Earl of Camford? Where in God's name did they find him?" she went on, beginning to laugh. "In a Hertfordshire hayrick?"

Carstairs was still suffering from the mortification of having incorrectly addressed a Peer of the Realm as "sir." But he set aside his pain to answer the duchess.

"I understand his lordship was a lieutenant in the Royal Navy."

"The navy?" Emma echoed in surprise. While the younger sons of the aristocracy routinely served as officers in the army, the navy was considered quite beneath them. Naval officers typically were drawn from the gentry. Emma laughed lightly. "Well, that explains it, I suppose! What a fine thing for the Miss Fitzroys!"

A short while later, Lord Hugh was shrieking in terror as Emma threw open the door to his bathing closet. Without his corset he was fat, and without his wig he was bald. Boiled pink by the hot water, he was not a pretty sight.

"Oh, good, you're awake," said Emma, in a tone of dire boredom.

"You!" he sputtered, his round, black eyes staring from his bald head. "How dare you! I am naked!" he cried. "Have you no shame?"

"Of course not," Emma replied. "Don't you read the gossip columns? Shame is exactly what I do not have."

Lord Hugh's heavy face turned almost purple. Veins stood out in his forehead. Quickly, he snatched the corners of the bathing sheet that lined the big copper tub, wrapping himself up like a package. All the while, he screamed for his manservant.

"Don't worry, Uncle," said Emma, as Lord Hugh's valet came into the room, fluttering his hands ineffectively. "I did not come to gaze upon your crudites. You know why I'm here. I want to see my sons. Where are they?"

"Don't just stand there, you idiot!" Hugh screeched at his valet. "Get this woman out of here! Throw her *out,* you imbecile!"

"Touch me, and I'll have you killed," Emma calmly told the valet, securing his immediate withdrawal. "Now then," she said, turning back to Hugh with a wide smile. "You were just about to tell me where my children are."

Lord Hugh sank down in the tub, scowling at her. "I do not have to tell you where they are," he said petulantly. "There is nothing you can do. You are only a woman."

"I am their mother!" Emma protested.

"But I am their guardian."

"You stupid man!" said Emma, reduced by frustration to petty insults. "Where are they?"

He sniffed. She had caught him off guard, but he was back in control now. "I thought you were in Paris," he said conversationally.

"I always come home for Christmas. You know that," she said coldly.

"I could have saved you the trouble. Did you not get my letter? But I suppose," he went on contemptuously, "you were much too busy entertaining your French lovers to bother about your children."

"I received no letter," Emma snapped. "And my children were perfectly safe and content at school, along with all the other children of the nobility. You took it upon yourself to interrupt their education, take them out of Harrow, and put them God knows where! *Where* did you put them? Are they even at a school?"

"If you had read my letter, madam, you would know where they were," he told her. "You would also know that I have many debts of honor."

Emma stared at him. "And why should I be interested in your gambling debts, sir?"

"Because you must pay them, of course," he answered as if she were a simpleton.

"Indeed! Why is that?" she asked.

"Because *I* cannot pay them, and *you* are rich," Lord Hugh explained, apparently amazed by Emma's stupidity. "When he was alive, my nephew Warwick always paid my debts. I explained all this to you in my letter," he added petulantly.

Emma controlled her temper with difficulty. "Even if my husband *did* pay your debts—which I do not believe—what has it to do with *me?*" she demanded. "I am no relation to you, except by marriage. Why should *I* pay your debts?"

He sighed. "In a perfect world, madam, *your son* would pay my debts. But his grace is still a minor. If I could borrow the money from the duke's estate, I would, but these damned lawyers are very tightfisted. I can't squeeze so much as a farthing out of them! Nay, madam, it will have to come from you. My debts are very pressing. Let me be blunt. If you do not pay my debts, you will not see your children. Is that simple enough for you to understand?"

"You expect me to *pay* to see my own children?" Emma said incredulously.

"Money is nothing to you," he stated resentfully. "That German mother of yours left you millions, didn't she? Seven thousand pounds would clear me entirely."

"Then you must raise the money, sir," she said coldly.

"I am a Fitzroy. We are descended of King Henry the Eighth. A Fitzroy does not go to Jews," he said indignantly.

Emma laughed angrily. "No! He blackmails women, using their children as pawns!"

Hugh grew red in the face. "Will you pay or not, madam?" he snarled at her.

"No, I shan't!" she said.

"Then you will not see your children," he huffed, "if that matters to you."

"You are bluffing," Emma said confidently. "The war is over. Michael will be coming home any day now. He will expect to see his brother's children. How will you explain to *Lord Michael Fitzroy* that you have kidnaped his nephews and are holding them for ransom?"

"There will be nothing to explain because you will pay me, madam," he answered. "I came up with the plan myself. Therefore, it is bound to succeed."

She scoffed at his sheer stupidity. "You would not dare prevent the Duke of Warwick and his brother from returning to their own home for Christmas. You would be reviled by everyone you know. You would be blackballed from your clubs. And, if it comes to it, do you think *Lord Camford* would marry the daughter of such a man?"

Lord Hugh started up in his bath, the color draining from his face. "What do you know of Camford?" he demanded, but his voice was hollow.

Emma saw at once that she had struck a nerve. "I know you would like him to marry one of your daughters," she said, pressing her advantage. "When I expose your character, he will not be able to get away fast enough!"

"You speak to me of character?" he cried furiously. "Harlot! Jade! If my judgment is questioned, I will simply say that, as their guardian, it is my sacred duty to keep the boys away from the poisonous influence of their mother, a known wanton. Your beauty may blind others to the impurities of your own character, but I know all, madam. I know all about your little bastard, and the provisions you made for her."

Shocked, Emma trembled, her face white. "What?" she gasped.

Seeing her tremble, Hugh smiled. "It was the one thing I did not bring out in court. When my poor nephew died so suddenly, I knew it was my duty to take his private papers into safekeeping. One doesn't want such things to fall into the wrong hands, after all."

"You have my letter," Emma said dully.

He smiled. "I have your letter, madam. I always thought my nephew indulged you too much, but it is to his credit that he refused to let you pass your bastard off as one of his lawful children."

"I will kill you," Emma whispered, her nails digging deep into the palms of her hands.

He laughed harshly. "I have thought of that, madam. If anything happens to me, your letter will be made public. Your little bastard—what is her name? Althea? Athena? Attila? Unless you heed me, she will learn that her aunt is really her mother. Her little life will be ruined. As for your *legitimate* children, they will repudiate you, and despise you, too, if they don't already. I *could* make your letter public *now*, of course, if that is what you prefer?"

Blind panic seized hold of Emma. She struggled to keep her head clear. "No," she said, biting her lip. "Don't. Please."

The last word was forced from between frozen lips.

He smiled horribly. "Oh! You're prepared to be reasonable then? Good. Pay my debts, and I will be reasonable, too. There is no need for your little Agatha to ever know the truth."

Emma went rigid with contempt. Helpless hatred poured from her eyes. "You shall have a banknote for seven thousand pounds," she said icily.

His fleshy lips curved in a grotesque smile. "Could you find it in your heart to make it ten thousand?" he asked. "One is always so strapped this time of year."

# Chapter Three

Otto disliked Nicholas the moment the young man popped his golden head into the billiard room, throwing off Otto's concentration, and causing him to scratch.

"Sir, you interfered with my shot," Otto complained, retrieving the cue ball from the corner pocket. He had removed his coat for the game, but, otherwise he was impeccably overdressed in black satin breeches and a silver-embroidered waistcoat. His white silk shirt was heavily adorned with lace, and he wore his usual diamond rings.

"I beg your pardon, sir!" Nicholas stammered, lingering in the doorway. "I am just arrived at Warwick Palace. I was told I might find some of the other guests here."

"I dismissed them," Otto explained. "I do not require an audience."

To his surprise and annoyance, the younger man came deeper into the room. "You must be the Duke of Warwick," he said, extending his hand. "I'm Nicholas. Nicholas St. Austell. You have a magnificent home. Thank you for inviting me."

Otto merely looked at his hand. "I am not the Duke of Warwick," he said coldly. "The Duke of Warwick is only twelve years old. This is not my house. I did not invite you."

Nicholas withdrew his hand. "I beg your pardon."

"As I said, I don't require an audience."

"Quite," said Nicholas. "I'm sorry to disturb you, but would you mind if I rang for a servant? I keep getting lost! I've never been in a palace before."

"There's no need to state the obvious," Otto said languidly. "By all means, ring the bell."

Evidently too stupid to take offense, the young man went on doggedly, "I was in the Admiralty, in London, once, when I took my lieutenant's exam, but that was *nothing* compared to this place. It's hard to believe this is a private residence. I daresay, one could drydock a frigate in the entrance hall!"

"Yes; but to what purpose?" Otto said dryly. His exacting eye passed over the young man's ill-fitting coat with critical contempt. "*That* is not the work of a London tailor," he said.

"No, I got it in Portsmouth last year. I know it doesn't fit me anymore," Nicholas said ruefully. "My uniform fits me very well. I *did* have *that* made in London. It cost me nearly fifteen pounds! You will see it at dinner."

"I look forward to it immensely," said Otto, but it was no fun baiting a man as impervious to sarcasm as this simple, good-natured fellow.

"I should have liked to have some new clothes," Nicholas admitted, "but my uncle did not think there would be time before the blizzard."

Otto's brows went up slightly. "Blizzard?"

"Yes, apparently, there is a blizzard here every year. It makes the roads quite impassable until, oh, well after Christmas," said Nicholas. "I realize the weather is uncommonly fine at the moment," he added rather lamely, "but my uncle assures me that is usually not the case. We did not want to risk delaying our departure from Plymouth for anything as foolish as clothes."

"I see," said Otto, swallowing this pack of nonsense unblinkingly, just as, apparently, the young man had. Against his will, Otto's curiosity had been aroused. "You're not one of General Bellamy's men, are you?"

"General Bellamy? No, sir. I was in the Royal Navy."

"And, pray, who is your uncle?"

"Lord Hugh Fitzroy. Do you know him, sir?"

Otto smiled grimly. "Oh, yes. What did you say your name was?"

"Nicholas. Nicholas St. Austell. My friends call me Nick."

"Ah! You're *Anne's* nephew," Otto said, sounding slightly less bored.

"Yes. I did not mean to mislead you, sir," Nicholas said quickly. "Lord Hugh is my uncle by marriage. Lady Anne Fitzroy is my aunt. My father was her younger brother. "

Otto stared at him thoughtfully. "I read about you in the papers. The long-lost Earl of Camford."

Nicholas snapped his fingers. "Camford! Of course!" he exclaimed. "*That's* the name of the place. I keep getting it wrong."

"Do you really?" Otto said politely. "How strange."

"I keep calling it Candleford, for some reason."

"I suppose you may call it what you like," Otto said generously. "It belongs to you, after all. I am Otto. Otto Grey. My friends call me Scarlingford. Everyone else calls me *Lord* Scarlingford."

Nicholas grimaced. "Oh, no! Are you a lord, too?"

"Yes, Camford, I am," Otto said patiently. "You don't mind if I call you Camford, do you? Who knows? It may help you remember it. I am the Marquess of Scarlingford. Alas, it is only a courtesy title."

"Courtesy title?" Nicholas echoed, ignorant but eager to learn.

"My father is the Duke of Chilton," Otto explained. "I am his heir. As a courtesy, I am allowed the use of his lesser title. I should say, *one* of his lesser titles, for he has several."

Nicholas shook his head as if he would never understand.

"You were born into the nobility, then," he said glumly. "At the risk of stating the obvious again: I was not."

Otto laughed at him, a light, dry laugh. "Of course you were born to it. How else do you come by the title, if not by virtue of your birth?"

Nicholas felt foolish. "The title *is* mine by birth, of course, but I never knew it until a few months ago. I'd never even heard of Camelford."

"Camford."

"Right! The *Gorgon*—that's my ship—" He paused, a fond glint in his blue eyes. "A real beauty! A thirty-eight gunner. I wept when I left her at the dock in Plymouth."

"I'm sure you did. But you were telling me how you came to hear of your good fortune."

"My good fortune?" Nicholas said blankly.

"Inheriting the title," Otto said patiently.

"Oh, right," said Nicholas. "We had put in at the Cape for provisions, and there was this letter for me from a London attorney. I thought it was a joke, but Captain Jericho said it looked official. Turns out, it *was* official. And when we put in at Plymouth for the winter, Lord Hugh and Lady Anne Fitzroy were there on the docks waiting for me."

"Weren't they just," Otto murmured. Returning half his attention to the billiard table, he fastidiously adjusted the placement of one of the ivory balls. "All the world loves a rich nephew. And the London lawyer? Was he there on the docks too?"

"No, he was in London."

"Ask a silly question," Otto murmured.

"My uncle said it would be best not to go to London until after the first of the year—because of the weather. We set off for Warwick Palace the very next day. And here I am."

"And here you are," said Otto, chalking his cue. "But why? Strictly speaking, shouldn't you be at Camford—or Candle-ford, if you prefer? It *is* Christmas, after all. No doubt, the good people of Candleford—the Candlefordians—will expect their new lord to show an interest. Who will crack open the poor box on St. Stephen's day, if you are not at hand to do the job?"

"Uncle Hugh said it would be better—"

"To wait until after the first of the year," Otto finished, smiling.

"Well, yes," said Nicholas. "One does not want to speak ill of the dead, but, apparently, the estate was not in good form when my uncle passed away. There were debts, and liens, and whatnot against the property. My uncle tells me the house is empty, uninhabitable. The servants have all gone, and, of course, there would be no getting new ones at this time of year. My uncle was good enough to ask that I be included in the invitation to spend Christmas here. Was that not generous of him, considering we had never even met before?"

"Very generous indeed," Otto agreed pleasantly.

"We're to stay through Twelfth Night, then travel to London. I have to take my seat in the House of Lords when Parliament opens," he added, a cloud passing over his face. "Life is so much simpler in the navy!" he lamented. "One has one's orders. One knows what to do, and when to do it. Uncle Hugh says I shall have to be presented at the Court of St. James, too."

Otto bent to study his shot at eye level. "Just imagine them all naked; you'll do fine."

Nicholas laughed nervously. "You mustn't tease me, sir. This . . . *This* is a whole new world for me, and I'm not sure I'm up for it."

"It is not without its hardships, I daresay. Tell me, have you met the girls yet?"

Nicholas blushed. "My uncle has warned me that I shall be pursued relentlessly by adventuresses," he said, "but so far, I have only met my cousins. All five of them. Or is it six? It seemed rather like six at times on the journey."

"I *meant* your cousins," Otto said dryly, "of which there are only five, you'll be happy to know. Octavia, Augusta, Cornelia, Flavia, and, last, but not least, Julia."

Nicholas stared at him with admiration. "You know their names! I confess I can't seem to remember them all, try as I might."

Otto leaned on his cue stick. "Oliver's aunt cooked five jellies," he said.

"I beg your pardon?"

"Oliver's aunt cooked five jellies," Otto repeated patiently. "That is how *I* remember their names. From eldest to youngest, in order of precedence, as it were, they are: Octavia, Augusta, Cornelia, Flavia, and Julia. Oliver's aunt cooked five jellies."

"I see," said Nicholas. "That's very clever. But why not *Otto's aunt?*" he asked, smiling.

"I don't have an aunt." Dissatisfied with his cue stick, Otto went to the rack to select another. "I should probably tell you there is some talk of Octavia's being engaged," he went on. "I'll believe it when I see it. But, if so, that puts Miss Augusta on the chopping block. She's not a bad sort, really. As far as I can tell, there's nothing in her head but dogs and horses. What say you to Miss Augusta?"

Nicholas stared at him, bewildered. "I do not understand."

Otto looked slightly surprised. "Naturally, you'll be expected to marry one of your cousins. It's the usual way of things. Didn't you know?"

Nicholas gave a startled laugh. "Marry one of my cousins? You are joking me!"

"I never joke about the human tragedy. As the Earl of Camford, your first duty is to marry and produce an heir," Otto said patiently. "After all, there's no one behind you, is there?"

Nicholas actually looked over his shoulder before Otto's meaning dawned on him. "You mean there's no one to inherit Candle—Camford—if I were to die unexpectedly? No. No, I'm the last of the St. Austells. But I'm only twenty!" he added hastily. "I've plenty of time!"

"Youth is no protection against the Angel of Death," Otto told him bluntly. "Accidents happen all the time. Forgive me, but you could die at any moment. Any one of us could, after all. If you were to die without an heir, that would be the end of it. Camford would revert to the Crown."

"I had not thought of that," Nicholas said haltingly. "As a poor lieutenant, I never thought I'd have the *opportunity* to marry, let alone the *duty* to marry! I am not against the idea of marriage, of course," he added, "but I—I hardly know my cousins. I am sure they are good girls, but I only met them a few days ago. I can't even remember their names. Oliver's aunt cooked five jellies. Octavia, Augusta . . . Cornelia . . ." He grinned suddenly. "I say! It *does* work."

Otto did not smile back. "You're caught in a trap, boy. You just don't know it yet."

"I am not in a trap," Nicholas protested.

"Quiet, please," said Otto, leaning across the table.

At the exact moment he took the stroke, the door opened, causing him to scratch again.

"Damnation!" he growled as his sister ran into the room.

Emma was in tears. Sobbing, she threw herself at her brother, oblivious to everything else. "Thank God you're here!" she babbled in German. "I don't know what to do. He's here. He arrived in the night. He knows about Aleta!"

Otto had been trying to stop the flow of words, but at the mention of Aleta, he frowned.

"What?" he said sharply.

"He has my letter. He wants money. What are we going to do?"

"Emma," he said.

"I shall have to pay him, of course," she yammered on, unheedingly. "That's all there is to it. And you wanted me to be *civil!*"

"Emma!" he barked, giving her a hard shake.

She blinked up at him. "What?"

"We are not alone," he told her.

Emma turned slowly, grinding the tears from her eyes with the heel of her hand. Nicholas stood at the other end of the billiard table, looking down at his feet, his hands folded behind his back. Slowly, he raised his eyes to her. Slowly, he bowed.

Silently, Emma answered his bow with a curtsey. "I beg your pardon, sir," she said breathlessly. "I did not—I did not see you."

"Do you see me now?" he asked, with a quick smile.

Emma caught her breath. "Oh, it's you," she said, recognizing him. "That is—it *is* you, isn't it? You are Lord Camford, are you not?"

"Yes, ma'am," he said.

They stared at one another for a long moment. The germ of a diabolical idea entered Emma's mind. Hugh's nephew obviously was attracted to her. There must be some way she could turn that fact to her advantage.

Nicholas broke the silence, stuttering, "Forgive me, ma'am. You are obviously in distress. I would have left the room at once, but you are between me and the door."

Emma laughed faintly. "I am not in distress," she said merrily. "What on earth gave you that idea? I was just looking for you, as a matter of fact."

Nicholas gave a start. "Looking for me?"

"Yes! I thought—I thought you had gone to breakfast. Did you become lost again?"

"No, ma'am," he answered. "Well, that is to say, I *did* become lost, but not until after breakfast."

"You must have eaten very quickly," Emma remarked. "You must have eaten like a hungry wolf."

He blushed. "In the navy, ma'am, we are obliged to eat our meals in a hurry."

"I heard you were in the navy," said Emma. "You must tell me all about it some time."

"Emma," Otto interrupted, catching his sister's arm. "What are you doing?"

He spoke in German, under his breath.

Emma smiled widely at Nicholas. "Otto, it's very rude to speak German in front of Lord Camford," she said. "Er . . . you don't speak German, do you, my lord?"

"No, ma'am. If you would like to be alone with this gentleman," Nicholas added, "I will gladly . . . gladly go."

Emma laughed. "Oh, this is just my brother," she told him, elbowing Otto away from her. "We can practice our German any time. Otto, this is Hugh's nephew."

"I know," Otto said dryly. "We have been talking."

"Oh. Then you won't mind presenting him to me."

"I beg your pardon," Otto said, with a touch of exasperation. "I thought you knew one another already."

"We met briefly," Emma explained, "but we were not properly introduced. You may do so now, brother."

"Nothing could possibly give me greater pleasure," Otto said irritably. "May I present the Earl of Camford? My lord, this is my sister, Emma. Emma Grey."

"Emma *Fitzroy,*" Emma corrected him instantly. "And that is no introduction!"

"You are only a Fitzroy by marriage," Otto argued. "You were born a Grey, and you'll always be a Grey to me. Oh, dear! Look how sad Camford is to hear of your marriage, Emma! Don't look so woebegone, sir. My sister *is* a widow, you know."

Again, Nicholas could not help his obvious change of expression.

"Well, that's cheered him right up," Otto dryly observed. "And what's more, my good fellow, her year of mourning is nearly over. In just a few days, she will throw off her widow's weeds entirely and emerge like the butterfly from the chrysalis. She has already, as you can see, lightened her mourning considerably."

Emma's gown was of smoke-blue muslin, cut in the latest style by the finest modiste in Paris. A huge cornflower-blue sapphire on a thin ribbon of black velvet hung at her throat. She often touched the cold stone, particularly when she was nervous.

"I think your husband was a very lucky man, ma'am," Nicholas said solemnly.

"Not a very nice thing to say to a widow," Otto chided him. "It implies the lady's husband is better off dead! Though I'm sure Camford didn't mean it that way."

Nicholas was horrified. "Indeed, ma'am, I did not!"

"My lord, pay no attention to my brother," Emma said quickly. "I never do. Lord Scarlingford believes himself to be amusing, and nothing can persuade him that he is wrong. No doubt, you are as eager to get away from him as I. I have come to take you on a tour of the house. We can escape him together, if you like. If you have finished your billiards game, that is," she added, as Nicholas seemed to hesitate.

"Oh, I was not playing, ma'am," he assured her. "I should be glad to see the house. But I would not wish to inconvenience you. My uncle already has offered to show me around."

Emma forced a smile. "I've just spoken to your uncle, my lord. He has been detained by—by—" She stopped, frowning in concentration. Lord Hugh did nothing but eat and drink and play cards, so it was difficult to imagine what might be detaining him. "Oh, by something or other," she said hurriedly. "Business of some sort," she went on, improvising rapidly. "Something to do with the estate, no doubt. And, of course, your aunt and your cousins are still exhausted from the journey. They are sleeping in this morning. Uncle Hugh asked me to look after you, and, of course, I said I would. Shall we go?"

She held out her hand to him.

Nicholas had the distinct feeling that his charming new friend was lying, but he was not sure he cared. By a clear mile, her company was more agreeable to him than his uncle's or his cousins', and, if she was an adventuress, he could not wait to see how adventuresses went about their adventures.

"It would be my honor," he said, taking her hand. Breathing a sigh of relief, Emma quickly tucked her arm through his and led him from the room.

Before beginning his game, Otto had tossed his silver-embroidered coat across the leather sofa. He picked it up now and followed them. "A moment, Sister!" he called after Emma. "May I inquire if my nephews have arrived?"

Emma gave him a sharp, quick glance over her shoulder. "Not yet," she said sunnily. "We'll talk about it later, Otto," she added, gritting her teeth. "*Later.* Now, will you go back to the billiard room, please? No one wants you here."

Otto frowned. "My sister will be with you in a moment," he told Nicholas sharply. Taking his sister by the arm, he drew her to one side. "Now tell me what the devil is going on," he commanded her, speaking in German for additional privacy.

Emma answered him in German, their mother's native tongue. "Hugh is demanding ten thousand pounds," she said quickly, "or I will not see my children."

"You said he had your letter."

"Yes."

"Then, for God's sake, what do you think you're doing with this boy? Hugh obviously wants him for one of the daughters."

"That is what makes him useful," said Emma. She glanced over her shoulder at Nicholas. He stood a short distance away, his hands clasped behind his back as he pretended to study one of the paintings on the wall. "I am hoping that Lord Camford can be persuaded to assist me."

"Why?" Otto said sharply. "What does *he* know of the matter?"

"Nothing, I hope," Emma replied. "My plan is simple. I shall make him fall in love with me. Then he will do anything I ask of him. He will get my letter back for me."

"He seems half in love with you already," Otto observed. "But you cannot risk antagonizing Hugh. He may very well expose you—and Aleta. He can make your letter public at any time."

A shudder of fear went through Emma. "No," she said, shaking her head. "He will not be so quick to give up his power over me. I've agreed to give him ten thousand pounds, but you and I both know he's already thinking about the *next* ten thousand pounds. As long as he has hope of getting more money out of me, he will not do anything with my letter."

"I do not like it, Emma."

"I don't like it either," she snapped. "Do you have a better idea?"

"No," he was forced to admit.

Reluctantly, Otto let her go. With a bright smile and profuse apologies for the interruption, Emma took Nicholas's arm and led him away.

"I don't think your brother likes me," Nicholas said ruefully.

"Otto hates everyone," she shrugged, leading him down the cool, empty corridor. "*I* like you, and that is all that matters."

He turned red. "You're very kind, Mrs. Fitzroy."

Emma nearly choked. "Mrs. Fitzroy! No, my lord. I am Emma, Duchess of Warwick. I'm sorry; I thought you knew."

"You are teasing me, ma'am," Nicholas stammered. "I— I have it on very good authority that the Duke of Warwick is only twelve years old. You could not possibly be his wife!"

"I am the duke's mother," she told him bluntly. "And Harry is *thirteen*. I distinctly recall giving birth to him."

"Impossible," Nicholas declared. "Why, you're just a girl. You can't be more than eighteen or nineteen!"

Emma grimaced. If this was flattery, it was hardly original.

"Oh, forever young!" she said, with a light laugh. "I am thirty, my lord. That is to say, I *will* be thirty on the first day of the new year. But I thank you for the compliment! My late husband was the tenth Duke of Warwick. My eldest son became the eleventh last December."

"I beg your pardon, my lady," he said, flushing with embarrassment. "I meant no disrespect to you."

"Sir, I'm no lady," Emma told him smartly. "I'm a duchess, and that is not quite the same thing. You may address me as 'your grace,' or 'Duchess,' or even 'madam,' in a pinch, but, never, ever as 'my lady.'"

Not realizing that she was teasing him, Nicholas silently cursed himself for his ignorance. "Please forgive my blunder," he said. "I meant no disrespect."

"I am only joking you," she assured him gently, squeezing his arm. "Actually, I find the regulations of Society quite stifling. Shall we fly in the face of convention, you and I?"

"Ma'am?"

"What is your Christian name?"

"Oh! Nicholas."

"Nicholas," she repeated, smiling. "I hope you will call me Emma, at least when we are alone. May I call you Nicholas?"

"Of course," he said, flattered. "I prefer it."

They came to a set of tulipwood doors inlaid with mother-of-pearl. "The library," Emma announced, as two footmen silently opened the doors with gloved hands.

The room within was immense, but rather dark, with bookshelves from floor to ceiling and few windows. Nicholas stared around him in disbelief. He had never seen so many books in his life. "It's so dark," he said. "You'd ruin your eyes reading in here."

"The light is bad for the books," she explained. "One doesn't read in here, of course. We have a reading room for that, if you're interested. This is the archive. You're welcome to borrow anything you like," she added. "The secretary will fetch you any book you fancy. Are you a great reader, sir? Our secretary works very hard to keep the library thoroughly up to date."

"Apart from our technical manuals, we had nothing on board ship but the Bible and the works of Shakespeare," he told her, with an odd mixture of pride and deprecation. "When I passed my lieutenant's exam, my captain gave me Nelson's biography. I've never felt the need to read anything else."

"Oh," said Emma, quite taken aback. "I've always loved reading."

"If your grace would condescend to recommend something," he said eagerly, "I will gladly take a stab at it."

Emma thought for a moment. "I would recommend Montaigne to anyone," she said presently, "but he may be especially suitable to someone who hasn't read very much. He covers such a variety of subjects in his essays. You're almost certain to find something to interest you." ·

"What's an essay?" he asked.

Emma laughed. "You're teasing me," she accused him, wagging her finger at him playfully. "Just because you're not widely read doesn't mean I think you're completely ignorant."

"No, really," he assured her. "I *am* that ignorant. What is an essay? I assume it doesn't mean a good try?"

Emma had never been required to give a definition of an essay before, and she did not have a ready answer. "Well," she said, frowning, "I suppose it could be defined as a brief dissertation on a topic. It usually includes some personal reflection."

"Brief?" he said. "I like that. Brief is good."

Emma hid a smile. "I'm sure we have a good translation. I'll have it sent to your room, shall I?"

"Oh, I won't need a translation," he assured her. "I don't know any other languages."

Emma decided it would be useless to explain that Montaigne was a sixteenth century Frenchman. "I see. What room are you in?"

Nicholas frowned in concentration. "Ophelia, or something like that."

"Westphalia?" Emma guessed.

"That's it."

"Then I will send Montaigne to Westphalia."

Nicholas laughed. "Well, if the Westphalia won't go to the Montaigne . . ."

Emma did not like puns. Like Voltaire, she thought them the death of wit. But she managed a weak laugh. "Shall we move on?" she quickly suggested, taking his arm.

# Chapter Four

"We have so many treasures here at Warwick, I hardly know where to begin," she said smoothly as she led him back out into the brightness of the corridor. "My father-in-law, the ninth duke, was an avid collector of fine porcelain, I seem to recall. Do you like porcelain?"

"We always made do with crockery on board," he said apologetically. "The captain *did* have a you-know-what with Bonaparte's face at the bottom, now I think of it. I'm pretty sure *that* was porcelain. I shouldn't have said that," he added, catching sight of her startled face. He turned beet red. "Forgive me, ma'am! I'm afraid we sailors are a rather coarse lot."

"Not at all," she said faintly. "It was very amusing. Perhaps you would like to see some of our paintings?" she suggested as they walked. "We have a very good collection of the Flemish masters, and a rather important Raphael."

"I love paintings," he told her. "My father was an artist."

"Really?" Emma began, breaking off as she caught sight of a group of officers at the other end of the hall. "Let us go this way," she said, hurrying into another room. "As you can see, we have quite a few paintings in here," she said, closing the door behind them. "Portraits, mainly."

She looked around the room, puzzled. She could not recall seeing it before. The walls were paneled in green silk. The wainscoting was painted a dazzling white. There was no place to sit, but a big round table stood at the center of the room, supporting a tall vase of hothouse flowers. The windows faced full west. Other than showing off a few dozen overly large portraits, the room seemed to have no purpose at all.

"My father did portraits," Nicholas said, looking up at a life-sized portrait of a Restoration gentleman wearing a long curly brown wig and scarlet knee breeches. "Who's he when he's at home?" he asked her, laughing.

"That would be King Charles the Second," she told him. "Did your father ever paint anyone famous?"

"No," Nicholas said, chuckling at the very idea. "Mostly he did miniatures of people, sailors mostly, on bits of ivory. The sort of thing a man sends to his sweetheart when he goes to sea," he added, coloring faintly.

"Oh, how lovely," said Emma.

"My father was disowned when he married my mother," Nicholas told her. "She was not considered good enough, I suppose, for the younger son of an earl. My father couldn't afford to paint big canvases after that. I remember his last painting. He couldn't pay our rent. He had to give it to the landlady at the Barking Crow. She hung it in the taproom, though," he added proudly.

"It must have been a very good painting," Emma said kindly.

"Aye, it was. A ship at sea. A gentleman offered her ten shillings for it once, but she would not sell." With two fingers, he dug behind his collar, coming up with a cream-colored pendant on a long piece of brown twine. "I carved the frame myself, out of whalebone," he told her as he placed it in her palm.

It was a crude locket, made along the lines of a clamshell,

with a design of hearts carved into the lid. Emma opened it gingerly. Inside was a tiny, delicate painting of a doll-like young woman with big blue eyes and yellow curls.

"Is this your sweetheart?" she asked him.

Nicholas looked surprised. "My mother," he said.

"She was very beautiful," Emma said gently.

"She was a kind soul," said Nicholas. "She died too young. They both did. When my father died, I was put to sea. The Royal Navy is Portsmouth's orphanage, you know."

"Did you not know that your grandfather was the Earl of Camford?" Emma asked.

He shook his head. "I had no idea. My father never spoke of his family. I believe he blamed them for my mother's death."

Emma carefully closed the locket and gave it back to him. Nicholas kissed it quickly before tucking it away under his shirt. "Who's that fellow over there?" he asked.

Emma spun around, fearing that another person had come into the room.

"I like his mustaches," Nicholas went on, walking up to another painting. "Very useful for straining soup, I should think."

Emma laughed. "I don't know," she said. "I haven't the slightest idea. I'm only a Fitzroy by marriage," she reminded him. "If you're really interested, I could summon the house-keeper. The servants know everything."

"Oh, that's all right," he said quickly.

"I'm a very poor guide," she said ruefully. "To be perfectly honest, I'm not even sure I can *find* the Raphael."

"I know *I* couldn't," he said. "And I'm sleeping in it!"

Emma laughed. "You're sleeping in *Westphalia*," she told him. "*Raphael* is the Italian Renaissance painter."

Nicholas flushed with embarrassment. "Raphael," he murmured. "Of course. He painted battle scenes, I believe."

"No," she said, laughing. "He painted madonnas, saints, and angels."

"That would have been my second guess," he muttered. "You must think me so very ignorant."

Emma shrugged. "I prefer nature to art myself."

"So do I," he said eagerly. "I confess I hate to be indoors."

"Then, by all means, let us go for a ride," Emma suggested. "We keep an excellent stable here. It will take but a moment for me to change into my habit."

The grounds of Warwick Palace were extensive, and she knew a great many lonely, beautiful places where she could take him and seduce him.

Nicholas sighed. "I'm sorry, ma'am. I don't ride. I've never had the opportunity to learn," he went on, in answer to her obvious surprise. "There are not many horses at sea."

"No," she smiled. "A nice, long walk, then?"

"I would love a nice, long walk."

Emma rang the bell and sent the responding footman for her gloves, her cloak, and her walking shoes. Another footman brought her a chair. Nicholas watched in astonishment as the footman knelt at her feet to remove her high-heeled slippers. "You have servants for everything," he remarked.

"Well, he *is* a footman," said Emma, wiggling her toes. "Why do you think they're called footmen?"

"I have never thought about it."

Emma jumped up, her feet now encased in sturdy walking boots. "Shall we?" she said brightly, fastening her sable-lined cloak at her throat.

They went out onto a small terrace at the back of the house. Ornamental gardens and bright green lawns stretched out before them, and, in the far distance, shadowy woodlands crowded the horizon. The quiet enormity of it made it seem bleak. To Nicholas it lacked the dangerous energy of the constantly moving sea.

"Let us go out to the secession houses," said Emma,

deliberately leading him into an obscure, rarely traveled path screened by tall, beautiful lime trees. "We will be hungry by the time we get there. Have you ever tasted a pineapple?"

"Oh, yes," he answered immediately. "Many times."

Emma was slightly vexed. "Oh. What about a nectarine?"

"Of course."

Emma frowned as she tried to come up with something even more exotic. "Breadfruit?"

Nicholas chuckled. "I have been all over the world, ma'am," he told her. "We sailors learn very quickly to eat whatever we can get in the local markets when we put to shore. When one is subsisting on hardtack biscuits, salt pork, and watery rum, fresh fruit and vegetables are like manna from heaven. Have you ever eaten a carrot, ma'am? Raw, I mean."

Emma stared at him. "You mean . . . right out of the dirt?"

"Well, washed of course," he amended. "They're nice and crunchy."

"That doesn't sound at all healthy," Emma said disapprovingly.

Nicholas laughed.


Though her intentions had not been honest, Emma had not lied about Lady Anne and the Miss Fitzroys. The journey from Plymouth had indeed exhausted them, and, just as she had told Nicholas, they were sleeping in.

Octavia Fitzroy was the first to rise. A stately young woman of twenty-four, she was the eldest of Lord Hugh and Lady Anne's five daughters. Intelligent, cold, and pompous, she commanded more obedience from her sisters than their nervous mother ever could. While Lady Anne sat up in bed, nursing a splitting headache, Octavia herded her sisters into the room for a council of war.

Apart from herself, only Augusta was dressed.

"It was a mistake to bring *all* of us to Plymouth to meet Cousin Nicholas," Octavia declared while the younger girls were still rubbing their eyes. "By the time we got to Warwick, he was heartily sick of us all."

"Cousin Nicholas is not sick of *me*," declared Julia, preening. At fifteen, she was the youngest, and, with her lively, dark eyes, bright red hair, and flawless alabaster skin, she was the only sister with any claim to beauty.

"Yes, he is," Cornelia, the third daughter, said spitefully. "He told me so."

"Liar! You're just jealous," Julia said, quite accurately. "I can't help it if he likes me best. I am the prettiest."

"Cousin Nicholas treated you as a mere child," Octavia told her bluntly, "which is, of course, what you *are*."

"I am not a child!" shrieked Julia, causing her mother to wince in pain.

"You are not yet Out, Julia," Octavia told her firmly.

"Well, *you* cannot have him, Octopus," Julia retorted. "You are engaged already to Cousin Michael. Not that he seems eager to claim you," she added spitefully. "The war has been over for *months*. Surely he could have gotten a furlough or whatever by now, if he wanted to."

"Obviously, we are not talking of *me*, Julia," Octavia said coldly. "I am spoken for. But one of you must make a push for Cousin Nicholas. If all of you try for him at once, it is very likely that none of you shall get him."

"Cousin Nicholas will choose *me*," Julia said. "I have only to crook my little finger."

"It would be unseemly for you to marry before your elder sisters," snapped Octavia.

Augusta, aged twenty, spoke up. "May I go to the stables, Mama?" she begged. "Cousin Nicholas is not likely to choose *me*, and I don't want to be married, anyway."

Lady Anne gasped. "Miss Augusta, that is a wicked thing

to say! You know your papa and I are depending on you girls to marry well. Your papa has some very pressing debts."

"You mean he's gambled away our dowries," Octavia corrected her.

"If Augusta don't want Cousin Nicholas, then *I* should have him," said Cornelia, sitting up taller. Like her two elder sisters, she had a long, horsey face and auburn hair, but she lacked Octavia's intelligence and Augusta's positive energy. She fancied herself a musician, but she was too lazy to practice. She scratched her head, scattering curl papers to the floor.

"You! What about *me?*" demanded Flavia, the fourth daughter.

"I am the next in line," Cornelia informed her. "After Augusta, I am the eldest."

Lady Anne looked at her third and fourth daughters doubtfully. Cornelia was only tolerable looking, and poor Flavia had been cursed with horrible teeth and greasy, spotted skin. "Oh, I do hope your Aunt Susan has not brought any single ladies with her," she cried weakly. "What if Nicholas should fall in love with someone else?"

"She has not," Octavia said with authority. "I have already made certain of that. My Aunt Bellamy has only invited married ladies."

Lady Anne started up as a new, horrifying thought occurred to her. "What if Nicholas should fall in love with one of the governesses? His father had such low taste in women."

"*Both* your brothers had low taste in women," Octavia said. "At least we were never obliged to meet Cousin Nicholas's mama. The indignity of having to curtsey to my uncle Camford's wife was *quite* the outside of enough."

Lady Anne's hollow chest heaved with righteous indignation. "Haymarket ware!" she said, becoming quite animated. "When I think of that—that *woman* taking my mother's place at Camford Park—! How I endured the humiliation, I shall never know. If Nicholas should marry an unsuitable female, I do not know what I shall do!"

"I will wear my blue muslin at dinner," Julia announced. "Cousin Nicholas will want something pretty to look at while he eats. If he looks at Flavia, he will lose his appetite."

"This will not be a family dinner, Julia," Octavia told her harshly. "Aunt Bellamy has invited all the officers and their wives. You will have your dinner in the nursery with the other children."

"What!" shrieked Julia. "Mama!"

"I'm afraid your sister is right, my love," Lady Anne said, cringing. "Your father would never allow it."

"Then I will just have to make the most of luncheon and afternoon tea," Julia huffed. "I'm still allowed to have tea, ain't I?" With her nose in the air, she swept from the room.

Cornelia hopped up. "I believe I will write Cousin Nicholas a love letter. If he thinks my heart is breaking, perhaps he will marry me out of pity!"

"That is an excellent idea, my love," said Lady Anne.

"But *I* was going to write him a love letter!" cried Flavia. "You *stole* my idea!"

The two girls bolted from the room, pushing and shoving one another as they went.

Augusta stood up and quietly left the room. Lady Anne knew the impossible girl was going to sneak off to the stables, but she hadn't the energy to stop her. Alone with her eldest daughter, she wrung her hands. "Oh, what is to become of us? If only you were not engaged, Octavia! I am certain *you* would get Nicholas to come to the point. You are so clever."

"Yes," Octavia agreed. "It is a great pity that Cousin Michael was not killed in the war. Then I would be free. He is a duke's younger son—that is something, I suppose. But I should have liked to be a countess."

Lady Anne stared at her, shivering. "Octavia!" she protested weakly. "Y-y-ou cannot mean it."

Octavia looked at her scornfully. "Oh, don't be such a lily-liver, Mama," she said.

From the window of her bedroom, Lady Harriet Fitzroy watched Lord Camford disappear into the Lime Walk with the Duchess of Warwick. Emma had donned a dark cloak for the excursion, but it was unmistakably she.

"Well, well," Lady Harriet said aloud. "*That* did not take long."

Smiling faintly, the old lady sipped her tea.

It was half-past two by the time Emma and Nicholas left the greenhouses. The afternoon was as fine as the morning had been, crisp and sunny. Apart from the occasional breeze, Emma had no real need for her cloak. Their bellies were full of raw fruit and vegetables.

"Shall we go on to the lake?" Emma asked him as they reached the heights of a small hill. "Or shall we go back to the house?"

Even from two miles away, the huge house dominated the landscape, cold and white as a sepulcher.

"I suppose we'd better go back," Nicholas said reluctantly. "My aunt and uncle will be wondering about me. I'm supposed to have tea with them in the main drawing room."

They had strolled out to the secession houses in a leisurely manner, keeping up a light conversation as they went, but as they started back the way they had come, Nicholas's stride was brisk and purposeful. Emma had to struggle to keep up with him as they hurried past the old tennis courts.

"Do you know the game, Nicholas?" Emma asked, slowing

him down. "I'm told it is beneficial exercise. I prefer badminton myself."

"Badminton, ma'am?" he said, fidgeting.

Deliberately, she leaned against the stone wall of the tennis court. An expression of agony flitted across his face. "Are you late for an appointment?" she asked him coolly. "Or just eager to get away from me?"

"No, ma'am!" he said with reassuring violence. "You have been everything charming."

"Then why are we running like jackrabbits?" she wanted to know.

Nicholas's face slowly turned crimson.

"Oh," Emma murmured, as the light dawned. "You need to answer a call of nature? Why didn't you say so? You can go behind the hedge," she told him kindly. "I'll wait for you here. Go on."

"I couldn't," he stammered. "What you must think of me!"

"I think you are flesh and blood," she said, smiling. "Really, there's no need to be embarrassed. Besides, what is the alternative?"

"Thank you, ma'am," he said, running behind the hedge.

Emma lifted her face to the sun and closed her eyes. She had not slept well the night before, and she was tired. She was physically drained, too, having walked more in that one day than she had in weeks. She wondered idly if it was too early in the relationship to ask the gentleman to carry her back to the house on his back.

Presently, she heard the rustle of branches as he came back to her, but her eyelids felt too heavy to open. He took her hand and pressed it to his lips.

"Mmmm," Emma said lazily.

With both hands at her waist, he drew her close to him. He smelled pleasantly of a light scent, of tobacco, and horses. *How odd,* she thought, as his lips found hers, *that he should smell of horses when he doesn't ride.*

Her eyes popped open, looking directly into the pale green, oddly tilted eyes of Lord Ian Monteith. "Monty!" she gasped, throwing off his hands and shrinking back against the wall. "What the devil do you think you're doing?"

"I love you, Emma," Monty announced loudly. "I have come here to make love to you. I burn with desire for you. Take pity on me. I am your slave."

"What?" she snarled under her breath. "What about my brother?"

Monty blinked at her. "It was his idea," he explained, lowering his voice. "Do you see those officers over there? Don't look, for God's sake!" he cried, seizing Emma's face. "They are watching us. So we'd better put on a nice show for them."

"Go away," said Emma. "Take your hands off of me."

"Do you think I *want* to kiss you?" he said impatiently. "Is that it? Because I don't. It's only to avert suspicion."

"This is not a good time, Monty," Emma said crossly.

"What do you mean? It's the perfect time."

"I'm busy."

"No, you're not."

Lunging forward, he pinned her struggling body to the wall with his own. "Let's make love," he shouted, battering her face with loud, clumsy kisses. "Don't be shy. Give yourself to me, angel! We're completely and utterly alone."

"Not quite," said Nicholas, tapping him hard on the shoulder.

Startled, Monty whirled around, his nose connecting nicely with Nicholas's fist. The Scotsman went down, bright red blood spraying from between his fingers as he clutched his nose. A group of officers came running up. Two of them grabbed Nicholas while a third helped Monty to his feet. "You broke my nose," Monty complained.

"If you liked your nose, you should not have insulted this lady," Nicholas answered, struggling to get free. "Apologize at once, or prepare to meet me on the field of honor."

The officers scoffed. "This is Lord Ian Monteith," one of them said. "He isn't going to fight a nobody like you."

"Is that so?" said Nicholas. "Well, I am Lord . . . I am Lord . . . Damn it! I've forgotten the name of the bloody place."

"He is Lord Camford," Emma said clearly. "Now take your hands off of him before I call the servants."

"And who are you, pretty?" one of the officers demanded, but he was instantly silenced by one of his companions.

"It is the duchess," the man whispered. "I have seen her portrait in London, in the National Gallery. It is she."

Nicholas was released. "Apologize," he said, glaring at Monty.

Monty now had his handkerchief pressed over his nose. "I beg your pardon, Lord Camford," he groaned.

"Not to me, you fool! To the lady."

"I am sorry, your grace. I was run away by my feelings."

Nicholas took Emma's hand and tucked it into the crook of his arm. "He doesn't sound very sincere," he said, scowling. "I think I'd better shoot him."

"Please, my lord!" Monty cried. "I am contrite! I will never speak to the lady again. I swear it."

Emma pressed her face against Nicholas's coat. "Please don't shoot him, my lord. I abhor violence. Will you be good enough to take me back to the house? Suddenly, I am cold."

"Of course," said Nicholas. As he led her away, he glanced back at the officers. "Get that man out of here before any of the ladies see him," he snapped.

"Yes, my lord," they said. "Thank you, my lord."

Nicholas hardly heard their obsequious replies. "You're shaking," he said gently, rubbing Emma's gloved hand between his own. "Are you all right?"

"I think so," she said. "You won't leave me alone, will you?"

"Not for an instant," he assured her.

"Thank you, my lord."

"Nicholas. You're not going to start milording me now, are you?" he complained.

"I might," she said, smiling up at him. "I just might. You were very heroic."

"Heroic? No," he said. She could tell that he was pleased.

"Indeed, you were," she insisted. "I'm afraid to think what would have happened if you hadn't been there," she added mendaciously, covering her face with her hands. "That man—"

"I will not let him hurt you, Emma," he murmured, taking her in his arms. "He will never go near you again."

"I feel so safe with you, Nicholas," she said softly, lifting her face to be kissed.

"You *are* safe with me, Emma," he told her very seriously.

To her disappointment, he meant it.


Lord Hugh Fitzroy entered his wife's sitting room at precisely half-past four. Anne and her brood were already assembled there, dressed to go down to the main drawing room for tea.

"Good afternoon, Papa," the young ladies chorused.

"Well?" he said. "What progress has been made with Cousin Nicholas?"

"What progress could there be?" cried Lady Anne. "We have not seen him today."

Lord Hugh flew into a rage. "What do you mean you have not seen him today?"

"Harriet had him last," Lady Anne said, desperate to avoid his wrath. "Ask your sister where he is."

He looked amazed. "Ask my sister—! Am I to understand you have not seen your nephew since *last night?* What in God's name have you been doing with your time?"

"I have had the headache," Lady Anne whimpered.

"The headache! I will give you the headache, madam wife!"

"I wrote him a love letter, Papa," Flavia said quickly.

"Well, I am glad *someone* is thinking of the main chance," said Lord Hugh.

"It was my idea, Papa," Cornelia shrieked. "Flavia stole it from me."

"I am wearing my blue muslin," Julia pointed out. "It is very low cut, and I am not tucking lace."

"We can see that for ourselves," Cornelia sneered. "Your chest appears to have exploded."

Julia preened. "They are called bosoms," she informed them. "They are Out, even if I am not."

"Papa," Octavia said sternly, "tell your youngest daughter she cannot go to tea looking like that."

"It is not my fault that I have a chest and my sisters do not," Julia argued.

Lord Hugh took out his pocket watch and looked at it impatiently. "I need not remind you idiotic females that time is *not* on our side. One of you must be engaged to him by Twelfth Night. If he makes it to London, some scheming adventuress will be sure to trap him. And then, what will become of us? When he comes of age, we'll be nothing more to him than poor relations! He can turn us all out into the snow if he likes."

"I know, Husband," Lady Anne whispered.

"Then why have you been idle all day?" he snapped.

"I thought he was with you!" she cried.

Lord Hugh scowled at her. "With me? Why should he be with me? He is *your* nephew. I have been playing cards with General Bellamy."

"Oh, dear," Lady Anne said foolishly. "I hope you did not lose very much, Husband."

The veins bulged in Lord Hugh's forehead. "What does it

matter if I did?" he demanded. "I have ten thousand pounds coming to me."

Lady Anne clapped her hands together. "Husband! That is excellent news. Why, that is two thousand pounds for each of our girls. They shall have dowries."

"Two thousand pounds is no fitting dowry for a Fitzroy," Lord Hugh sniffed. "I should be ashamed to offer such a paltry sum to a gentleman. I would rather they find husbands who will take them for nothing."

"We shall have to, at this rate," Octavia said dryly.

Lord Hugh spun around to glare at her. Unmoved by his bullying, Octavia gazed back at him with chilly politeness. "You *did* say, Papa, that you would take Cousin Nicholas on a tour of the house," she reminded him. "We all thought he was with you."

"Indeed, we did, Husband. For no one knows the palace as well as you do."

"True," he said, somewhat mollified by his wife's flattery. "I daresay, Nicholas has made some friends among the officers. I daresay we will find him in the drawing room."

Julia jumped to her feet. "I'm so hungry I could eat the whole croquenbouche."

The door opened and Lady Susan sailed into the room. "Well, here's a to-do!" she said, her small eyes glinting. "Lord Camford and Lord Ian Monteith have been fighting—I should say *brawling*—in a most unsavory contest for the favors of a certain . . . er-hum! . . . lady."

Lady Anne jumped to her feet. "Oh, no! Was my nephew very badly injured?"

"He had to be carried back to the house," Lady Susan said ominously, freely embroidering on the truth.

Lady Anne fell back in her chair. Lord Hugh shook his fist at her. "This would not have happened, madam, if you had taken better care of him."

Julia was confused. "But I do not know Lord Ian Monteith,"

she said. "Why should he be fighting for my favors? He must have seen me in the window as I was dressing."

"It is the duchess, I mean," Lady Susan said irritably. "The Whore of Babylon herself!"

"But Nicholas doesn't even know the duchess!"

"You should have been more careful with him," Lord Hugh accused his wife. "The harlot will turn his head, and he will never think of marrying any of the girls."

Lady Anne clutched her chest. "Oh, Husband! Surely she would not marry him herself?"

"She's far too old for him," Julia sniffed.

Lord Hugh looked at his wife with contempt. "Marry him! And give up her dower portion? Not bloody likely! That's twenty thousand pounds a year she gets from the estate. Would *you* give that up? Of course you wouldn't, you imbecile."

Lady Anne crumpled before his contempt.

"In any case, the boy is still a minor. He cannot marry without my permission, not until he comes of age. I'm not likely to let him marry *her*, am I? But she may very well *distract* him."

"You mean *seduce* him!" Julia whispered eagerly.

"Oh, dear! We should not have let him out of our sight, Husband," Lady Anne wailed.

"*We*, madam?" he said coldly. "Are you suggesting that *I* follow your nephew about like a Bow Street Runner? That is *your* duty, madam, and you have failed."

Octavia's voice cut through the air. "Is Cousin Nicholas badly hurt, Aunt Bellamy? Has the surgeon seen him?"

Lady Susan took her time answering. "He will live," she said finally. "But I understand it was very near thing, very near. He was unconscious for several hours."

"But why did no one tell us?" cried Lady Anne.

"I've only just heard of it myself from Mrs. Camperdine," said Lady Susan.

"Well, don't just sit there like a bunch of wallflowers," Lord Hugh shouted, turning on his wife and daughters. "Go to him quickly before he recovers. He will be in a vulnerable state. Nurse him back to health, and he may reward one of you with his hand in marriage. Hurry! Must I think of everything?"

# Chapter Five

By established custom, the Greys always met in Emma's sitting room before going down to dinner together. Dressed in gold satin, Lady Scarlingford looked slightly less rumpled than usual as she joined her sister-in-law there that evening. "Oh, Emma!" she cried. "How perfectly splendid you look."

Seated at the pianoforte, Emma was idly playing Mozart. Her gown was of blue-violet watered silk. Wrapped around her slim neck was a strand of pearls the size of hazelnuts. Huge pearl drops hung from her ears. Her ash-brown hair was pulled back from her face, emphasizing her delicate features. She smiled at her sister-in-law. "You sound surprised, my dear Cecily."

"No!" Cecily protested. "You always look lovely, of course. But I wonder you would go to so much trouble if you are just going to eat your dinner on a tray in your room."

"But I am not going to eat my dinner on a tray in my room," Emma replied. "I've decided to break mourning a few days early."

Cecily looked troubled, but she did not dare criticize Emma. She sat down to wait for the gentlemen to arrive. "Men are always complaining about how long we women take to get ready," she said presently. "But, it seems to me, that *we* are always waiting for *them*."

Emma laughed. "That is because men live under the delusion that they can get dressed in under a minute. We women are wise enough to begin the undertaking in good time. It takes me precisely seventy-five minutes to get ready for dinner. I have it down to a science."

Of the gentlemen, Colin and Monty arrived first, Colin in correct black and white evening dress and Monty in his uniform. Apart from a slight swelling at the bridge of his nose, Monty looked none the worse for wear, thanks to the ministrations of his valet.

"You owe Monty a new pair of trousers," Colin told his twin sister. "How dare you have one of your boys rough him up! His nose is not broken, thank God. But there was so much blood, I nearly fainted."

"How dare you tell him he could *kiss* me?" Emma returned angrily. "In front of half the army, too!"

"You've done it for me before," said Colin, "on countless occasions."

"Countless!" Monty echoed indignantly.

"Well," said Colin, "I never counted, anyway."

"This time, it was not convenient," said Emma. "I was just setting up a new flirt. Your Scottish friend is fortunate that Lord Camford didn't break more than just his nose."

Colin frowned. "Who *is* this Camford brute, anyway? I thought I knew all your lovers."

"He is not my lover. He is Hugh's nephew. I'm just using him," Emma explained.

"Oh, Emma!" Cecily said in dismay.

Colin was more pragmatic. "Using him for what, may one ask?"

Quickly, Emma explained the situation to him.

"Emma! That is beastly cruel! Devious! Machiavellian! However did you think of it?"

"I asked myself, 'What would Colin do?'" she retorted.

Colin grimaced. "And *this* is what you came up with?"

"Yes."

"Then I have nothing more to teach you," he said loftily. "Now, apologize to Monty, and we'll say no more about it."

"Apologize? I explained to Monty that I was busy, but he persisted. He deserved a punch in the nose. I do not apologize."

Colin sighed. "When a gentleman has a grievance with another gentleman, he shoots him at ten paces with one of Mr. Manton's lovely little pistols. Now *that* is what I call gentlemanlike behavior! He does *not* plant him a facer, not outside of Mr. Jackson's saloon, anyway."

"I am not sorry he did so," said Emma. "The way he came roaring to my defense was most encouraging. It shows that I am on the right track."

Lord Scarlingford came into the room. "Emma," he said unpleasantly, "if you are going to lend my valet to your badly dressed friends, I would appreciate it very much if you would inform me first. I was obliged to dress myself this evening!"

"I'm sorry, Otto," said Emma. "I can't imagine what is taking so long."

"I can," he retorted. "You lent him to Camford, didn't you? Making that boy presentable could take days, if not weeks."

"He is not that bad," said Emma. "He just wants a little polishing, that's all."

"His hair is scruffy, his skin is chapped, his hands are calloused, and his clothes are execrable," said Otto.

"He was a sailor," Emma protested. "They're meant to be a bit rough around the edges."

"Well, this one is rough all over," Otto grumbled.

Colin was appalled. "This is the creature who struck my Monty? A badly dressed sailor with calluses?"

The door opened and Otto's manservant padded silently

into the room. "I give you Lord Camford," he said simply. Taking out a snowy white handkerchief, he mopped the sweat from his brow.

Nicholas stood uncertainly in the doorway, a little intimidated by the aristocrats looking back at him. His hair had been barbered and his skin looked almost like polished bronze. The dark blue uniform of the Royal Navy fit him to perfection, emphasizing his broad shoulders and long legs. His eyes looked very blue. Emma frankly was astonished by the change in him. All the potential that Lady Harriet had seen in the young man had been brought out into the open.

Cecily leaned over to whisper in her husband's ear. "I thought you said he was rough looking!"

Nicholas's eyes narrowed as he caught sight of Monty, ostentatious in his scarlet coat heavily ornamented with gold braid. "What is *he* doing here?"

Emma rose from the pianoforte and hurried over to him. "Nicholas! How handsome you do look in your uniform. You quite took my breath away."

Nicholas's eyes were fixed on the Scotsman. "That man. Why is he here?"

"Please," Emma said quickly, "let us have no more discord. Lord Ian is a close friend of my brother's. He has apologized for his mistake."

"Mistake?" cried Nicholas. "He insulted you!"

"Yes, but he didn't have his spectacles," said Emma. "He thought I was someone else."

Nicholas frowned at her. "Who?"

"I cannot say," said Monty, sounding quite affronted. "A gentleman does not bandy names, after all."

"I would like very much to avoid any hint of scandal," Emma added. "Can we please just pretend it never happened?"

Nicholas hesitated only a moment. "Of course," he said. "I would not distress you for the world, ma'am." He looked at her warmly.

Emma smiled up at him in relief. "Thank you! Before we go down to dinner, I would like to make you known to my sister-in-law, Lady Scarlingford."

Nicholas bowed over Cecily's hand. "Ma'am."

"I've heard so much about you from my husband," she said. "None of it true, I'm happy to say. He made you sound like a cross between Dick Whittington and Robinson Crusoe!"

"You did not see him *before,*" Otto said indignantly.

"I am much obliged to Lord Scarlingford," Nicholas said, laughing.

"More than you know, boy," Otto retorted, "for it was my manservant who turned you into a diamond. It was sheer genius, Croft," he called to his valet. "Bravo!"

"Thank you, my lord," the servant answered. "One does what one can."

"Shall we go?" Emma said quickly, taking Nicholas's arm and leading him from the room. "You will escort me into the dining room. You will be seated on my right. Lord Ian will sit at my left. And we will all have a lovely dinner."

"Aren't you forgetting something?" Colin said, pushing past Emma.

"No, I don't think so," said Emma.

Ignoring her, Colin addressed Nicholas, his tone belligerent. "We have not been introduced, sir. I am Lord Colin Grey. The decorative object fastened to your arm is my sister."

Emma sighed. "Colin is my twin brother, Nicholas."

"I am her *younger* twin brother," he corrected her. "I let her go first. But then I've always been selfless," he added sanctimoniously. "Unlike some. I have a bone to pick with you, Lord Camford," he said, almost in the same breath.

"Colin, please," Emma moaned.

"With *me,* Lord Colin?" Nicholas said, surprised.

"Well, with the Royal Navy anyway."

"I will answer for the navy," Nicholas said sharply.

"This embargo," Colin said slyly, "this blockade, or whatever you call it, was it really necessary, sir?"

"Yes, of course it was," said Nicholas, shocked. "We could not allow France and her subjugated territories to freely trade their goods. All their gains would be plowed back into their war machine, used to purchase weapons to be used against ourselves and our Allies."

"But the Champagne, sir! The cognac! The Beaujolais!" Colin complained. "It is very hard for a man to live without the necessities."

Belatedly realizing the joke, Nicholas laughed. "I do apologize, Lord Colin, for the inconvenience. We were obliged to enforce the embargo against the French. The Admiralty did not give us a choice in the matter."

"I shall write the Admiralty a very strongly worded letter," said Colin.

"But now the war is over, I trust we are on the same side," Nicholas said. "Shall we let bygones be bygones, in the spirit of the season?"

"Yes!" said Emma. "This beastly war is over. Let us have no more fighting."

Like a herd of cattle in a holding pen, a restless crowd had gathered in the lounge, waiting for dinner to be served. Lord Hugh pushed his way through a gaggle of officers' wives to where his wife stood with their four eldest daughters. "What are you doing here, madam wife?" he demanded. "You and the girls should be nursing Nicholas!"

Certain that he would not beat her in front of the company, Lady Anne was braver than usual. "We went to his room, Husband," she answered. "We knocked on his door, but there was no answer. He must have been resting. What could we do but go away again?"

"You imbecile," he muttered under his breath. "I will deal with you later."

Silently, Lady Anne prayed that he would be too drunk to deal with her later.

"Yes, Husband," she said meekly.

On the other side of the room, Lady Susan was pouncing on Carstairs, the butler. "We are hungry, Carstairs! What is the delay?"

"The duchess has not yet arrived, Lady Susan," he informed her.

"Why, you senile old fool," she scoffed. "The duchess does not dine in company. She is still in mourning for my poor nephew—not that she ever cared three straws for him," she added to her particular companion, Mrs. Camperdine. "But even *she* must be bound by the rules of propriety on this occasion. You may serve, Carstairs."

Carstairs merely bowed and withdrew.

"This is intolerable," Lady Susan complained, snapping open her fan. "If she *dares* to come down, she will not be granted a warm reception, I can promise you that."

"But after dinner, when we leave the gentlemen to their port, we can pick her bones clean," said Mrs. Camperdine.

Lady Susan laughed in delight.

Twenty minutes later, the duchess was announced. All conversation stopped as all eyes turned to the doorway, where the Duchess of Warwick stood flanked by Lord Camford, in the blue of the navy, and Lord Ian, in the scarlet of the army.

Burning with rage, Lord Hugh pushed his way toward her.

"Would you excuse me, Nicholas?" Emma said. "Uncle Hugh seems to be trying to get my attention. Is this about that horribly complicated piece of estate business?" she inquired of Lord Hugh with a sigh. "Very well! Let us speak about it in private."

Lord Hugh drove her before him into the alcove at one

side of the room. "You seem to forget, madam, that I hold you in the palm of my hand," he said under his breath, lest anyone in the lounge overhear.

"That is a physical impossibility," she told him. "I am not that small. But, if we are speaking metaphorically, I hold Nicholas in the palm of my hand, and *he* holds *you* in the palm of *his* hand, though he does not yet realize it, poor lamb."

"Jade! Do you forget I have your letter?"

"I am willing to pay for my letter," Emma replied. "You will have your money when you return it to me. And you will get your precious nephew back when I have my boys. Is that simple enough for you to understand?"

Without another word, she swept out of the alcove.

Lady Susan had swooped down to claim Nicholas in Emma's absence, before Lady Anne could get to him. "My dear Camford!" the aging beauty shrieked. "We were beginning to think you would never grace us with your presence! You were missed at tea. Poor Anne was beside herself."

"And . . . you are?" said Nicholas with an austerity worthy of Otto.

Her greedy black eyes blinked up at him from beneath the heavy fringe of her dyed red hair. "I am Lady Susan Bellamy, of course! Hugh's sister. My husband is General Bellamy. You see him there with my friend, Mrs. Camperdine."

"How do you do, ma'am?"

"I see you have made up your quarrel with Lord Ian," she said archly. "But, perhaps you have agreed to share the lady between you? If the *on-dit* is to be trusted—if her appetite is all they say—you might even require a third gentleman to keep her satisfied."

"I *beg* your pardon!" Nicholas said coldly.

"Oh, dear!" she exclaimed. "Did no one warn you about our naughty little Emma? My dear Camford, as lovely as she undoubtedly is, I fear the duchess is not above reproach. She is, in fact, a scandalous wanton. 'Tis well-known that her husband, my poor nephew, died of a broken heart. The poor boy was destroyed by her many, many torrid affairs. Is that not so, General?" she added, as her husband drew near with Mrs. Camperdine on his arm.

"'Tis well-known your nephew died of a broken *neck*," the general snorted. "The damn randy fool fell out of a window. Lady Bellingham's window, to be exact. Though I'm sure 'tis only wicked slander to say he was *shown* the way out by the lady's husband! Haw! Haw!"

"Nonsense, George!" Lady Susan said furiously.

The general pawed at Nicholas's dark blue coat. The aging dandy seemed to be drunk. "Lawd, is *this* what the Royal Navy are wearing these days?" he scoffed. "No lace! Scarcely any braid! I'd be ashamed, sir, ashamed!"

"I was only a lieutenant," Nicholas said stiffly, thinking to himself that Lady Susan and her husband were well matched in that they were equally revolting. "Please excuse me," he added, with a curt bow, as he saw Emma threading her way back through the crowd. Not for an instant did he give credit to any of Lady Susan's acrid assertions. Emma's delicate beauty gave him leave to think only the best of her.

"A poor excuse!" the general called after him.

Lady Anne seized Nicholas's arm as he began to move, almost involuntarily, toward the duchess. "Nicholas!" his aunt cried breathlessly. "We have been so worried about you! Where have you been all day?"

Nicholas was embarrassed by his aunt's hysteria. "I am not a child, Aunt Anne," he said sharply. "I have been most agreeably occupied."

"Agreeably occupied!" she echoed in horror. "Fighting over that—that *horrid* woman?"

Nicholas frowned at her. "I do not know who you mean," he said coldly. "If you—if you are speaking of—you should take care what you say, Aunt," he finished, pushing past her.

Almost in tears, Lady Anne made her way toward her

husband. "She has seduced him," she said, clutching at his arm. "He will not hear a word against her. You should have heard him biting my head off just now! O Husband! I fear he may *like* her."

"Of course he likes her," Lord Hugh growled. "*She* is a whore, and *he* is a sailor."

At the other end of the room, Emma had climbed the steps to stand in the doorway.

"Good evening, everyone," she said warmly, when the room had again grown quiet. "On behalf of my son, the Duke of Warwick, let me first welcome all of you to his home. I know that his grace would very much like to be here to welcome you himself, but, sadly, that is not possible tonight. Uncle Hugh? Are you still here?"

Her eyes searched the crowd, coming to rest on Lord Hugh's purple face.

"There you are! Will you be good enough to tell the company when the Duke of Warwick and Lord Grey Fitzroy will be coming home?"

Lord Hugh felt everyone's eyes on him, polite and waiting. "Soon," he said gruffly, unable to see any way out of the trap Emma had set for him. "Very soon."

"How soon?" Emma asked, smiling. "The exact date seems to have slipped my mind."

"Saturday," he said. "They will be here on Saturday. I did not want them to come home," he added defensively, "before the year of mourning was over."

"Ah, yes," said Emma, in response to this barb. "As most of you know already, I am still in mourning for my husband, who died just a little less than a year ago. But, with so many of our brave and noble military gentlemen here with us tonight, I thought it was important that I welcome you, since my son could not be here himself to do you honor. My husband, the late duke, was also a great patriot. I know that *he* would want me to be here tonight, to thank you for your service. Gentlemen, you have the thanks and the praise of a grateful nation. England, and, indeed, the whole world is better for your efforts. You have sacrificed so much for so long that the rest of us may live in comfort and security, and now, thanks to you, we are at peace. Let me assure you that your courage will never be forgotten."

"Here, here," said Otto, beginning the applause.

"I could say more," Emma went on, when the cheers and applause had died down, "but I am sure you all must be very hungry! Eat and drink, gentlemen, and don't spare the cellars! Carstairs, you may serve."

Nicholas was waiting for her at the foot of the steps, his eyes shining with pride. "I do hate making speeches," she confessed to him. "I hope I was not too nonsensical?"

"You were perfect," he said simply.

"Thank you. Will you be good enough to escort me in to the dining hall?" she prompted, as he continued staring at her. "Everyone is waiting. No one can eat, you know, until I sit down at the table."

"Of course," he said, offering his arm. He felt like the luckiest man in the world.

Two by two, the other guests followed the duchess and her partner into the dining room.

"This is not the dinner I ordered," Lady Susan complained loudly, calling down the length of the long mahogany table as the first course was brought in.

"No, madam," Emma told her sharply. "It is the dinner *I* ordered. *I* am the Duchess of Warwick, or have you forgotten?"

"The soup is far too rich for the lining of my stomach," Lady Susan pronounced, when she had finished her lobster bisque. "It will give us all indigestion. *I* had ordered a clear soup."

Lady Harriet was seated next to Lord Colin Grey. "In my

day, people did not shout down the table at one another," she informed him, speaking loudly enough for her sister to hear. "One spoke only to those persons seated immediately to one's right and to one's left." She twisted in her chair to look at Colin. "Well? What have you to say for yourself, young man?"

"Only that you're looking very pretty this evening, Aunt Harriet," he said chivalrously. "I still love your pixie cut."

"It is not a pixie cut, young man," she said indignantly. "As a young woman, I cut my hair in sympathy for the victims of the guillotine."

"How cheerful," said Colin. "It does wonderful things for your cheekbones, I must say. Why, if I were fifty years older, I'd definitely take a bite out of you, you ripe little peach, you."

"Cheeky monkey," Lady Harriet sniffed, flushing with pleasure.

Emma turned to Nicholas as the first course was brought in. Bemused, she watched him attack his soup. "I take the lobster bisque meets with *your* approval, my lord," she said. "You do not find it too rich?"

"It's delicious," he said. "I could drown in it."

"Better than a raw carrot?" she teased him.

He grinned at her. "Just. The cook is to be commended."

"Chef," Emma corrected him. "He's called Armand, and I found him in Paris."

"Paris? Paris, France?"

"Yes, of course, Paris, France," Emma laughed. "The instant the war was over—that is to say, as soon as the *navy* had got out of my way—I *flew* to Paris like one of Mr. Congreve's rockets. I was never able to go to Paris before because of the fighting. My younger son Grey was born during the Peace of Amiens, so I missed my chance there. He's an unrepentant Bonapartist, I'm sorry to say. The chef, not my son," she clarified.

"I'd like to go to Paris," Nicholas said eagerly. "I think it must have been a very fine place before the revolution."

"Now is the time to go," Emma told him seriously. "The auction houses are bursting with the spoils of war, and no one has any money but *we,* the English. I bought some rather nice Christmas presents for my boys—a rather beautiful desk that once belonged to Old Boney himself, amongst other things." She showed him her fan, taking it from her lap and spreading it open on the table. "This little fribble was the Empress Josephine's. It is ivory set with amethysts. I gave my niece Aleta a harp that once belonged to Marie Antoinette."

"No!" Nicholas said, wide-eyed.

"Yes. I plan to go back next year, for the King's auction."

"The King's auction?" Nicholas echoed. "The King of France is having an auction?"

"Poor fat Louis!" said Emma. "Imagine for a moment that you are he. You've been away from the Tuileries for many, many years. Finally, you are allowed to return home, only to find that some strange little Corsican fellow has been living in your house, putting his feet up on all the furniture, and painting bloody great Ns all over everything. Ns on all the cushions. Ns on the door handles. Imperial bees on all the carpets! A positive swarm! My God, wouldn't you throw it all out and have yourself a nice auction, too?"

"I might burn the lot," said Nicholas, laughing.

"Oh, but His Majesty needs the money. France is bankrupt. I bought my house in the Faubourg St. Honore for next to nothing." She laughed suddenly. "It just occurred to me, my lord, that your Christian name also starts with a big N, just like the Corsican's. You definitely should go to Paris and get yourself something with a big N on it. Oh, but, of course, you won't be able to go, will you? You will be in London for your presentation."

"Yes," he said. "I'm rather nervous about it. Will you be there?"

Emma shook her head, laughing. "No, indeed! I shall be in Paris."

He looked crestfallen. "I would feel better, if you were there—if I had a friend at Court. Lord Scarlingford says I should imagine everyone naked," he added, chuckling.

"Lord Camford!" she chided him. "And this is why you want me at Court so badly?"

"No, ma'am!" he cried, his face red with embarrassment. "I didn't mean *you!* I would never presume to—to imagine—" he broke off, stammering, and reached for his glass.

"You just did, didn't you?" Emma laughed. "Well? How did I look? Delightful, I hope."

Nicholas choked. "Ma'am, I beg of you!" he gasped.

"You're right," said Emma. "It is indeed most unbecoming to beg for a compliment, particularly when one is only being *imagined* naked."

"I did not mean that either," he protested, now unable to even look at her.

"I know; I'm only teasing you," she said gently. "But it's your own fault for blushing so readily. No woman can resist teasing a man who blushes so readily. I had thought, too, that it was something of a difficult task to make a sailor blush. Am I so wicked or are you so susceptible? Either way, you will change my opinion of the navy."

The strain of conversing with her seemed almost too much for the young man. He could think of no answer. To relieve his embarrassment, Emma summoned the next course.

As it was brought in, she turned to speak to Monty, who was seated at her left. Nicholas then was obliged to speak to the lady on his right, and he was as much gratified as he was piqued to spend the next twenty minutes without once blushing.

# Chapter Six

Three hours after they had sat down, Emma rose from her chair. The ladies filed out of the room, leaving the gentlemen to their port. "You have made a conquest there, dear Emma," said Lady Susan, when the ladies were settled in the main drawing room, a long, well-lit chamber with walls paneled in shimmering blue-gray silk. The floors were inlaid with black and white marble in a bold chessboard pattern.

At one end of the long room, servants were setting up the card tables in anticipation of the gentlemen. At the other end of the room, the Fitzroy sisters were preparing to entertain the company with a little musical exhibition. The majority of the ladies clustered in the middle of the room at the fireside waiting for their coffee.

Surrounded by the wives of her husband's officers, Lady Susan watched jealously as the duchess poured the coffee out into little cups emblazoned with the Duke of Warwick's coat of arms. Lady Susan felt that Emma had usurped her authority, and she was eager to put the duchess back in her place. "How pleased you must be with your latest prize!" she exclaimed.

"I can't imagine what you mean, Aunt Susan," Emma said pleasantly, as she passed out the cups. "What prize?"

"Why, Camford, of course!" shouted the general's wife, watching with satisfaction as Lady Anne, who was seated in obscurity to one side of the door, flinched. Lady Susan delighted in tormenting her sister-in-law, whom she regarded as a spineless weakling. If Emma was made uncomfortable too, then so much the better. "And Lord Ian, too—though I couldn't help but notice that you showed a marked preference for the earl—very marked. But, then, the earl is so good-looking. Much better looking than a man has the right to be. And he is head over ears for you. It was as plain as the nose on my sister's face, and that is very plain indeed."

The officers' wives laughed in appreciation of Lady Susan's wit, none laughing louder than Mrs. Camperdine, who seemed glued to Lady Susan's side.

"I thought it perfectly adorable the way he tried to follow you out of the dining room—like a lovesick little spaniel. He is completely besotted with you. It was truly pathetic to watch. I tried to warn him about you, but he would not listen."

Emma smiled. "Oh, I am sorry to hear that, Aunt Susan," she murmured. "If he is going to fall in love with me, then, perhaps it would be better if I see no more of him."

"Do you mean it, your grace?" cried Lady Anne, half rising from her chair.

Emma glanced at her. "Christmas is just around the corner," she said. "I've so much to do in preparation, and, of course, Harry and Grey will be home soon. They will keep me busy. I do so want everything to be perfect for them. From now on, Anne, I'm afraid you will have to look after your nephew yourself. I have balls and dinners to plan. I can't be bothered with training up a mooncalf."

"Are you really going to give Nicholas back to us? You're teasing me," Lady Anne accused, her voice fading into despair. "You are cruel!"

Privately, Emma marveled at the woman's lack of discretion.

"I'm sorry, Anne," she said solemnly. "I simply don't have the time for lovesick spaniels. If I were you, I'd hand him over to one of your daughters for safekeeping."

"I must say, I'm amazed you would give him up, Emma," said Lady Susan. "It's not like you to give up a handsome young man, after all. I am all astonishment!"

Her ladies tittered encouragingly.

"Lord Camford is very nicely put together, I grant you," Emma answered languidly, playing with her beautiful ivory fan. "But he is not handsome enough to tempt me. Perhaps it is only his youthful ignorance, but I find him rather a bore, I'm afraid. For a man to be *really* attractive, he must have more than good looks. He must have wit. He must be knowledgeable. The ability to make conversation is essential, do you not agree, ladies? Why, Lord Camford has never read anything but Shakespeare, the Bible, and Nelson's biography!"

Lady Susan interrupted. "You find him lacking in conversation, do you?" she snorted. "Why, the pair of you were thick as thieves down at your end of the table!"

Emma laughed lightly. "I was just explaining his dinner to him. He was a little confused by the ragout. Oh, he *is* a very pleasant young man, to be sure," she went on, "but, perhaps, a trifle gauche? Not really my sort, is he?"

Mrs. Camperdine giggled. "Perhaps your grace prefers Lord Ian?" she suggested. "He was also very attentive at dinner."

Emma waved a hand. "Oh, these overgrown boys don't really interest me."

"Look to your husbands, ladies," Lady Susan cried boisterously, smacking the ladies on either side of her with her fan. "If you lose them to this creature, you will have no one to blame but yourselves. You have been warned!"

"I shouldn't worry too much," said Mrs. Camperdine, chuckling. "Her grace did say she prefers a man of wit, after all! Such as Lord Byron, perhaps?" she added, with a knowing smile.

Emma blinked at her. "I beg your pardon?"

"I did hear that the poet was one of your grace's many lovers," Mrs. Camperdine said archly. "Is it true?"

"And the Prince Regent?" another wife asked breathlessly, curiosity overcoming propriety. "Was his highness also your lover?"

Cecily could bear no more. She started up from her chair. "How dare you!" she said, her fists clenched at her sides.

Emma only laughed. "What a sordid conversation!" she remarked. "May we at least leave the Royal Family out of it? Is nothing sacred? Let us have no more of this unseemly talk. We are not *all* married ladies, you know," she added. "There are at least five virgins in the room deserving of our protection."

"Six, if we count Harriet," Lady Susan chortled.

Lady Harriet glared at her indignantly.

"If you truly were interested in protecting my innocent nieces, Emma," Lady Susan went on, "you wouldn't be here. Your very presence is poison; they may be tainted by association."

"I'm sorry you feel that way, Aunt Susan," Emma said with mock sorrow. "It pains me that I can't seem to win your approval. But do rest assured, I have no intention of hanging about here all evening. As soon as Carstairs tells me the plate is counted and safely put away, I plan to retire— hopefully before your innocent nieces begin their little concert," she added.

"And *I* really must look in on my children in the nursery," Cecily said quickly.

Lady Susan scarcely waited until they had quit the room before congratulating herself on having chased the duchess away. "One feels so sorry for poor Lady Scarlingford, of course," she added disingenuously. "To be saddled with such a sister-in-law."

Leaning forward, she called to Lady Anne. "How fortunate

we are to have you, dear Anne. Indeed, you are as dear to me as my own sister. Are we not fortunate to have Anne, Harriet?" she called to Lady Harriet, who was pacing up and down in front of the fireplace.

Lady Harriet snorted, refusing to be drawn into Lady Susan's false picture. "I am ready to play cards," she announced. "What the devil is keeping the men?"

When the gentlemen at last rejoined the ladies, Lady Anne hurried to claim her nephew for her daughters' concert before her husband could herd him to the card tables. Augusta sat at the harp. Cornelia sat at the pianoforte. Flavia stood behind Cornelia, ready to turn the pages.

"The girls have worked so hard," their mother boasted. "I daresay, you will hear nothing better in the drawing rooms of London," she added unbelievably, inviting Nicholas to sit beside her on a small settee.

"May I join you, ma'am?" Lord Ian Monteith asked Lady Anne. "I dearly love music."

"But I was depending on you to be my partner, Lord Ian," Lady Susan protested. The general's wife was an avid card player. She took little pleasure in anything else.

To her annoyance, the Scotsman declined.

"You prefer music to cards, Monteith?" the general snorted.

"I confess I do, sir," said Monty.

The general seemed willing to accept his answer, but Lady Susan was more tenacious.

"But I'm an old friend of your father's," she told him. "Has he never mentioned me? I would have been Lady Susan Fitzroy back then."

"I beg you will excuse me, ma'am," Monty said faintly, giving her a bow.

"Well!" said Lady Susan, much offended. "I suppose when one's father is a marquis, one need not rely on the influence of friends! He will fly up the ranks without anyone's assistance, I am sure!" Tossing her head, she flounced off to play cards.

Lady Anne became flustered as Monty sat down next to her. With Nicholas on her other side, it was a tight squeeze. The little French settee really was not made to seat three. They managed to sit without touching, but it was a near thing. Lady Anne could feel the curiously strong warmth emanating from the male bodies on either side of her. It made her feel light-headed and uneasy. She was terrified they would start fighting over the duchess again at any moment, and that she would be caught in the middle of an internecine battle.

Upon entering the room, Nicholas had looked for Emma in vain. "Shouldn't we wait for the duchess to return?" he asked his aunt, as his cousins began to play.

"Oh! Her grace has excused herself for the evening," Lady Anne explained in whispers.

"She is not ill?" he asked, concerned.

"Oh, no," his aunt assured him. "The duchess has a great deal to do in preparation for Christmas, you know. There are several balls to plan. The Christmas Eve Ball. The St. Stephens' Day Ball, for the servants. There's a tenants ball at the new year, as well. And, of course, Twelfth Night. Her grace was very sorry to miss the girls' concert, but she gave us leave to enjoy ourselves without her."

Monty shushed them, and they sat, listening politely until the song was over. Nicholas thought the performance, at best, mildly pleasant. Monty, on the other hand, seemed to enjoy the performance very much. At the closing note, he jumped to his feet, applauding. Nicholas thought this was perhaps overdoing it, but, then, he did not know much about music; his preference was a sea chanty accompanied by a concertina.

Suddenly, in the midst of his applause, Monty cried out in

pain, and clutched his thigh. White faced, he collapsed onto the settee. "It is nothing," he said, through gritted teeth, as Cornelia dashed toward him. "It is just my old wound coming back to haunt me. I took a French musket ball to the leg at Talavera, you know. It likes to sting me now and again."

Nicholas stared at him in astonishment. Until this moment, there had been no sign that Monty was recovering from a war wound.

"I am better," Monty said, after a moment. "Do please continue, Miss Cornelia. Nothing soothes me as music does, and you do play so well."

Blushing with pride, Cornelia ran back to the instrument and began a new song. As she played, Monty winced and grimaced in pain. Finally, unable to bear any more, Lady Anne begged him to retire, and, though he loved music, Monty allowed himself to be persuaded that he must go to bed at once and rest.

Lady Susan observed his exit and came bustling over to Lady Anne as soon as her card game permitted. "Well, Anne, I see you have driven Lord Ian away," she observed, wedging her broad backside onto the sofa beside Nicholas.

"Shouldn't you be at the card table, Sister?" Lady Anne said, exasperated. "Your partner must be wondering where you are."

"Mrs. Camperdine has taken my place," Lady Susan said complacently. "I thought I'd better come over here before you manage to drive away poor Lord Camford, too. Eligible bachelors must be handled with some delicacy, you know. I know this, for I am something of a matchmaker."

Lady Anne could make no answer but a whimper.

"I managed to find husbands for my four daughters," Lady Susan said proudly. "Of course, my girls are so pretty and accomplished they needed but little help. *Your* girls are a very different matter, Anne. Well, Camford," she went on, jogging him in the ribs with a surprisingly sharp elbow, "do you see anything you like? Shall I help you make up your mind?"

"In what regard, ma'am?" he asked, after a short, unhappy pause.

Her eyes widened. "But which of your cousins are you going to marry? That is what I mean, of course. You're not thinking of marrying the duchess, are you?" she cried. "Dear boy! She would laugh in your face if you asked! No, you will marry one of your cousins. Of course you will. They are none of them as pretty as *my* girls—too bad for you *they* are all married! Octavia, of course, is engaged already, so you can't have *her*—more's the pity, too, for she's the most sensible of the lot."

Octavia, who was sitting quietly in the corner working a piece of embroidery while her sisters exhibited, turned pale with mortification.

Lady Susan swept on like the Juggernaut. "Your cousin Augusta plays the harp, but without much feeling for the music, as, no doubt, you've already noticed. Cornelia is actually quite competent at the pianoforte, but her conceit spoils the effect, I think. Flavia—poor little snaggle-toothed child! Flavia can do nothing more than turn the pages for her sister. She would not be so homely, Anne, if you would take her to a good dentist and have her teeth pulled."

Lady Anne was so humiliated she could scarcely breathe, let alone make any reply. Breathing hard, she fanned herself while her daughters stared in shock at the aunt who had exposed them so cruelly. The music abruptly came to a halt.

"Now, the youngest," said Lady Susan, poking Nicholas in the arm with her fan, "is not yet Out, but, I daresay, if you want to marry Julia, she can be brought Out quick enough!" She laughed coarsely. "To be sure, she is a pretty child, though not very accomplished. Unless one counts jiggling bosoms as an accomplishment."

Nicholas sat rigid with a dismay verging on horror.

"My dear boy," said Lady Susan, concerned. "You look quite shocked! Hasn't your Aunt Anne told you what's expected of you?"

Lady Anne found her voice. "I'm sure I don't know what you mean, Sister," she croaked.

Lady Susan gave a little gasp. "Oh, you haven't told him?" she cried. "Oh, Anne! Silly little Anne! That is no way to go about it. There's no need for deception. Your nephew seems to be an honest and dutiful young man. I'm sure that once he understands that it's his *duty* to marry one of your girls, he will gladly embrace his fate."

"I have no idea what you mean, Sister!" Anne repeated desperately.

"So you keep saying, my dear," Lady Susan said dryly. "Well, Camford? Are you ready to embrace your fate? Is it to be humble Augusta? Conceited Cornelia? Friday-faced Flavia? Or pretty, jiggling, little Julia?"

Unable to bear any more, Nicholas sprang to his feet.

"I beg your pardon," he stammered. "I hope my cousins will excuse me. I—I am very tired from the journey. Good night, Aunt Anne," he added.

Bowing to the ladies, he hurried from the room.

Lady Anne began to cry helplessly.

Lady Susan patted her on the back. "Poor Anne! Despite your best intentions, I'm afraid you've made a mess of it." With a grunt, she heaved herself up from the settee and went back to her card games, serene in the knowledge that *her* girls were well married, and that none of Anne's inferior brood would ever be a countess.

Nicholas strode away from the drawing room with giant steps. Lord Scarlingford had been dead right! he realized now. The abominable Lady Susan had plucked the scales from his eyes. Lady Anne's guilty expression had told him all he needed to know.

As he rounded the corner, he nearly collided with Monty, who had just stepped out into the hall in front of him.

"Your leg seems better," Nicholas observed grimly.

"Oh, it's you," Monty said, grinning. "I thought it was one of *them*. Sneaking off to spend the night with the duchess?"

"Certainly not!" Nicholas said coldly.

Monty's grin widened. "Would you like to?" he asked simply.


Emma sat on the Aubusson rug in her private sitting room, surrounded by sketches and plans, a tiny set of spectacles perched on her nose as she studied her drawings. Her brother Otto reclined on the sofa behind her, looking over her shoulder, and, from time to time, giving her the benefit of his advice. Not entirely sober, Colin sat at his sister's pianoforte, idly manipulating the keys. Cecily had gone to the nursery to check on the children. They were all drinking wine, the servants having been dismissed for the night.

"You're such a coward, Emma," Colin complained. "You should have told that bitch to her head, 'Yes, Byron was my lover. He used to eat grapes from between my toes and drink wine from my navel.'"

"Thank you, but unlike yourself, I don't care to boast of my mistakes," Emma replied tartly, pouring herself another glass of Beaujolais. "And, for your information, it was the Tsar who wanted to eat things off of me. Byron was a bit boring actually."

"Oh, how sad," said Colin. "It's true what they say, then? Poets make bad lovers? The better the poetry, the worse the lovemaking?"

Emma giggled. "If that is so, then Byron must be the greatest poet who ever lived!"

"There!" Colin complained. "Why couldn't you say something like *that* to those hags?"

"You weren't there to make me think of it," said Emma,

looking at him fondly. "You are the fountainhead of my wit. You are muse, my inspiration. My wine steward," she added hopefully, holding out her glass to be refilled.

After a moment, he obliged her.

"Then I am forgiven for Monty's interference in your romance with the sea lord?"

Emma laughed. "Thank goodness *that* is all over. Though I must tell you, no one in his right mind would ever think that *I* would take *Monteith* to bed! He's funny looking."

"He's ruggedly handsome," Colin protested.

"Ruggedly funny looking," Emma muttered.

"Well, they can't all be pretty, pretty boys like Camford."

"Why do you tax me with Camford?" she complained. "My interest in him was . . . completely disinterested. I made good use of him, but now it is over. I have won."

"What do you mean, it's over? With Camford, do you mean?"

Otto's voice startled the twins.

"Lord, Blotto, we thought you was asleep!" said Colin, his hand on his heart. "You shouldn't sneak up on a body like that!" He retreated back to the pianoforte.

Emma turned around to look at her elder brother. "Of course I am finished with Camford. You heard Hugh make the announcement," she said. "Harry and Grey will be home on Saturday. As for my letter, he will give it to me if he wants his money, which he does. I have turned the table. There's no reason to continue this farce with Camford. And you said yourself, it was a shame to drag him into this mess."

"You assume that Hugh will not break his word," said Otto.

"But how can he?" Emma wanted to know. "He has told everyone that Harry and Grey are coming home. He can't go back on his word now. I have won the battle, Otto. This is, in fact, my victory party. Can't you just congratulate me on a job well done?"

Otto did not look convinced.

"You should seduce him anyway, Emma," said Colin. "It's the only way to save him."

"Save him!" Emma scoffed. "Save him from what?"

"From the Fitzroys, of course."

"Emma, you are a heartless jade," said Otto, prodding his sister in the back with his foot. "You used Camford shamelessly, and now you cast him to the wolves, without so much as an apology."

"But that was always the plan," she protested.

"It's too cruel, Emma," Colin accused her. "You showed him a glimpse of heaven."

"I showed him a glimpse of the secession houses," Emma retorted. "I flirted with him a little. You think I should apologize?"

"That was Otto's idea. I can think of something a young man likes better than an apology. Take him to bed. You owe him that much at least."

"And what is your interest in the matter?" she demanded.

"I think you like him," Colin accused her. "You never could fool me. I saw the way your eyes lit up when you saw him in his uniform."

Emma smiled faintly. "He did look rather nice," she said, "in his blue coat."

"Nice as a Christmas present," Colin teased. "If you like him, Emma, why give him up? Why let the Fitzroys take him from you? This is not the code of the Greys, or have you turned coward? We Greys take what we want, and the world be damned."

"But I *don't* want him," Emma said firmly. "I never wanted him. And now I don't even need him. It certainly isn't necessary for me to take him to bed. The Miss Fitzroys are welcome to him. He is a good-looking young man, but that is all. We have nothing in common. We are not compatible. It's none of my business what happens to him now!"

"You're finished with him? Just like that." Colin snapped his fingers.

Emma looked at him over the rims of her spectacles. "Naturally, I wish him the very best in life, and all that sort of thing, but that's the sum of it. Now can we please talk about something else?"

Colin gaped at her. "You don't care if he marries one of the Fitzroys?"

"Not a jot. I wish them joy."

"Hmmm. I hope he's not going to get stuck with Augusta," Colin said presently, "though I *will* say she's not as bad as Octavia." He shuddered. "Is she a girl, or is she a block of ice? No one knows for sure. Flavia, of course, is quite out of the question. Poor thing! She looks like a potato with teeth stuck in. No, I hope it's Julia. She's pretty. She's . . . dramatic. She has flare. She has what the French call *c'est la vie*."

"I presume you mean *joi de vivre*," Otto said.

"I don't think so," said Colin, sniggering. "A *joi de vivre* is a streetwalker."

"No. That would be a *fille de joi*," Otto told him.

At that moment, Cecily, Lady Scarlingford, breezed into the room, her curly brown hair down around her shoulders, and her yellow satin gown a rumpled ruin. "I wish Nanny would not rub gin on the baby's gums!" she complained. "I have heard that gin is bad."

Otto yawned. "My love! What is this strange obsession you have with your children? You talk of nothing else. Come here. Look to your husband."

Without regarding his words in the least, Cecily took her place on the sofa beside her husband, who sat up to make room for her. "What did I miss?" she asked eagerly.

"Your husband was just telling us all about French streetwalkers," Colin told her. "Apparently, he's quite the expert."

"Otto!" cried the gullible Cecily.

"Actually," Emma said primly, "we were just going over my plans for the ballroom decorations."

"Actually, my love, we were just deciding which of the Fitzroy girls will get Camford for Christmas," Otto said at the same time.

Cecily seemed to find her husband's topic more interesting than Emma's. "Oh, I do hope it's not that Cornelia! She's such a nasty, spiteful, little thing. I must say, I think *he* is lovely. I don't suppose it will be possible for him to marry for love," she added, sighing.

"He will have to marry one of his cousins," said Otto. "There's nothing else for it."

Colin fluttered a hand. "But Cornelia would be better than Octavia, I say. As long as it's not Octavia, I am well satisfied."

"Why? What do you have against Octavia?" cried Cecily. "She's the stateliest of the girls. She *looks* like a countess. I wish sometimes that I had her poise and assurance."

Otto shuddered. "Never say such things, my love."

"No, indeed! She's a cold fish!" Colin protested. "We all hate her. Anyway, she's engaged already, supposedly. Julia is the obvious choice. Julia has *joi de ville.*"

"Julia's too young," Cecily objected.

"He's *obviously* going to marry Miss Augusta," Otto declared. "After Octavia, she comes next in the order of precedence. Therefore, he is hers by right of seniority. We must have Order, after all. We cannot give in to Chaos."

"I *do* prefer Augusta to that horrid Cornelia," said Cecily. "What do you think, Emma?"

"I'm sure I don't care *who* he marries!" cried Emma, getting to her feet. "Why the devil should I? I never set eyes on him before today. In the future, I hope to see him as little as possible. When he leaves here, it is very likely I will never see him again. In a month, he will be forgotten entirely. What is there to remember about him, really? He's just an ordinary boy who happened to fall backward into an earldom! I am sick of hearing his name."

In the middle of her speech, Colin suddenly ducked his head and coughed. Belatedly, Emma felt eyes on the back of her neck. Spinning around, she saw Nicholas and Monty standing in the doorway.

"Surprise," Monty said weakly, holding up two bottles of Champagne.

# Chapter Seven

Nicholas stared at Emma, a stricken look in his blue eyes.

Cecily and Otto discreetly averted their eyes from the unpleasant scene.

Emma's cheeks flamed. Ashamed of herself, she reacted irrationally by going on the attack. "You should not have brought him here," she told Monty angrily. "He should be in the drawing room with his family. What were you thinking?"

Belatedly, she snatched off her spectacles and stuffed them into her bosom.

"I'm sorry," Monty spluttered. "I thought—I thought he was your friend, Emma. I didn't see any harm in inviting him along. What's the matter?"

"What's the matter?" Emma echoed irritably. "Now you are inviting people to my private rooms? And is that Champagne from my cellar?"

"I should not have come," Nicholas said, his face stiff with embarrassment. "Lord Ian persuaded me that I would be welcome. I see that I am not. I can only beg your pardon, madam. Good night!"

"You must forgive Emma," Colin said, coming out from behind the pianoforte to prevent Nicholas from leaving.

"She's horrid. She's always been horrid. Despite our father's best efforts, daily beatings did not improve her."

Nicholas could not be drawn into the room. "If the duchess does not want me here, of course I will go," he said stiffly, avoiding looking at Emma. "Only . . . Only could someone please show me the way back to my room? I don't think I can find it on my own."

Monty set the Champagne on Emma's pianoforte. "I brought you here," he said, looking gravely at Emma. She glared back at him, unrepentant. "I'll take you back."

"No," said Nicholas. "Stay with your friends. May I ring for a servant, ma'am?"

"My servants have all retired for the night," Emma said ungraciously. "I see no reason to wake them up."

"Emma!" Cecily cried in astonishment. "That is uncivil!"

Emma rounded on her. "*He* bursts into my room, uninvited and unannounced, and you say that *I* am uncivil?"

"He hardly burst in, old girl," Monty objected. "Look, it's all my fault. By all means, be furious with *me*. Throw *me* out. Punish *me*. I deserve it. But don't take it out on poor Nick."

Walking over to the young man, he placed a sponsoring hand on his shoulder. Colin assumed a similar pose on the other side. "It's not your fault, Monty. It's *my* fault," said Colin. "I was just teasing Emma about a certain forthcoming marriage. Apparently, she's quite prickly on the subject. I think she may be jealous. As we all know, hell hath no fury like the green-eyed monster."

"Colin!" Emma said, furious and humiliated.

"But I am not getting married," Nicholas said vehemently. "Did someone tell you I was to be married?" he asked, directing the question at Emma.

"But aren't you going to marry one of your cousins?" Colin insisted.

"That's a lie!" Nicholas said hotly. "I—I beg your pardon, Lord Scarlingford. I should have taken you more seriously when you tried to warn me in the billiard room. But it all seemed so utterly fantastic!"

"But no longer?" Otto guessed, quirking a brow.

"It was that dragon, Lady Susan," said Nicholas. "Though, perhaps, I should not speak ill of her; she has done me a good turn. She made it clear that everyone thinks it is my duty to marry as soon as possible, and that my aunt and uncle expect my bride to be one of my cousins. Lady Susan as good as said I could have my pick of the litter! They will even bring Out Julia for me—a mere child of fifteen. My aunt's guilty expression confirmed all."

"Oh, you poor little lamb," said Colin. "Emma, you *can't* send him back! He's in the fire now. He doesn't want to go back to the frying pan. And, you know, you did say he looks very nice in his blue coat. She did say that."

Nicholas lifted his eyes to her. "If you want me to go . . ."

Emma threw up her hands. "Of course I don't *want* you to go," she said impatiently. "I just thought you should be with your family. Oh, all right! You can stay. But your uncle won't like it."

Nicholas smiled. "I do not answer to my uncle, ma'am," he said, "but I will gladly answer to you."

"In that case," said Emma, beginning to smile, "you must wear a tinsel hat. Otto will give you his."

"I won't," said Otto, as Monty opened one of the bottles of Champagne.

Colin ran to get glasses. "Typical, Monty!" he scolded. "Will you never learn to fetch the glasses *before* you pop the cork?"

"Not as long as I have *you* to fetch them for me," Monty said lightly.

"You're getting Champagne everywhere," said Otto, taking charge of the bottle.

Champagne in hand, Cecily sat at the pianoforte with her brother-in-law. Laughing, Monty explained to them how he had escaped from the drawing room by pretending to be in agony from an old wound.

"Don't you like music?" Cecily asked him.

"Aye, ma'am! And that is why I was so eager to escape the concert!"

Colin began to play, Monty began to sing. Cecily joined in. Otto drank his champagne. In short, everyone made a point of ignoring anything that might be taking place on the other side of the room.

Nicholas remained standing just inside the doorway. "Are you sure you want me to stay?" he asked Emma. "After all, I'm just an ordinary fellow who fell backward into an earldom. Actually, that's quite true," he admitted.

Emma knelt down to gather up her drawings. "I know I shall be sorry for this in the morning," she muttered under her breath. "Stay. I want you to."

Instantly, he was beside her, down on one knee, saying, "Let me help you."

"Thank you," she said, wishing he did not look so handsome in his uniform. "I am sorry if I was uncivil," she mumbled. Of all the things in the world, she hated apologies the most.

With a quick glance at the others, he lowered his voice. "Is that why you left the drawing room before I returned?" he asked. "Because you thought I was going to marry one of my cousins?" He seemed pleased with the idea that she might be jealous.

Emma's response was studied. "I assumed that you probably would."

"Why?" he demanded. "How could you think so?"

She shrugged.

Nicholas frowned. "Surely, you do not think it is my *duty* to marry one of them?"

Emma seated herself on the sofa, taking her plans onto her lap. "Do you not think it is your duty?" she countered. "You have inherited a great estate. Is it not fair that one of your cousins should share it with you? After all, any of them might have inherited, had she not had the misfortune to be born a female."

Nicholas was taken aback; he had never considered the matter in this light. "Naturally, if any of my cousins is in need, I will always come to her assistance. But marriage?" He shook his head. "I could never marry a girl I did not love," he said simply. "That would be a falsehood."

Emma blinked at him in surprise. "Falsehood?"

"Oh, I do not fault those who marry for other reasons," he said quickly. "But, for *me* . . . I could never wed with an empty heart."

Emma could not help but smile at such touching naivete. "Are you real, Lord Camford? You're like something from a fairy tale, you are. People wed with empty hearts every day."

"And I think it very sad," he said solemnly.

"*My* marriage was arranged," she said. "Do you pity me?"

"I beg your pardon," he said. "I didn't mean—I didn't know."

"The day I met my future husband for the first time, I was summoned from the schoolroom into the rarified atmosphere of my father's study. I was but fifteen. 'Here is your husband, girl,' my father said. Somehow, I found the courage to raise my eyes, and there he stood: the Duke of Warwick! He was horribly old, at least a hundred, or so I thought. He looked like moths had been eating him. I thought I would faint!"

"Good God," Nicholas murmured.

"He stretched out his cold, bony hand to me, and said, 'I'd like you to meet my son, Henry.'" Emma laughed, as much at Nicholas's expression as the memory of that first meeting. "And there he was! Thank God! A reasonably good-looking seventeen-year-old boy. I was so relieved, I believe I gave him my heart on the spot. And, I think, he was not too disappointed in me. We were wed three months later."

"A happy ending, then."

Emma laughed ruefully. "By no means. But we *did* have a happy beginning. That is more than some people get."

Otto's voice intruded upon their tête-à-tête. "Perhaps *Camford* can convince my sister that her mad scheme will never work," he drawled, reaching over the back of the sofa to hand them glasses of Champagne. "I have done my best to reason with her."

All at once, Nicholas realized that he was in a ridiculous position, kneeling at Emma's feet. He stood up to accept the glass of champagne. After a moment of indecision, he sat down next to Emma on the sofa. "Are you scheming, ma'am?" he asked her.

"Always," said Emma. "But my brother refers to nothing more sinister than my Christmas plans."

Nicholas looked at her drawings admiringly. "I do not think *battles* are so carefully planned," he said. "You did not tell me that you were an artist, ma'am."

"But I have not had time to tell you everything, sir!" she answered. "Here is my vision for the Great Hall," she went on, showing Nicholas her sketch. She sat looking at him as he studied it. "When the guests arrive for the ball on Christmas Eve, this is what they will see. What do you think?"

"It is what you *wish* for them to see, Emma," Otto corrected her. "You will never realize it," he declared, leaning on the back of the sofa. "My sister has never heard of gravity or Sir Isaac Newton. As you can plainly see, the tree is much too tall."

"Is that a tree?" Nicholas asked, squinting at the sketch in Emma's lap.

Emma gasped indignantly. "Yes, of course it's a tree. A remarkably well-drawn tree! A fir tree, to be exact."

"You will never get that thing through the doors," Otto predicted. "And, even if, by some miracle, you get that—that ridiculously enormous tree through the doors, into the house, how do you propose to make it stand up? Hmm?"

"That will be the servants' lookout," Emma said crossly. "I pay them handsomely enough to do my bidding."

"You *do* realize that trees only stand up outside because they've got roots stretching deep into the earth?" said her brother. "When a tree is cut away from its roots, it invariably falls over. It makes a bit of a crash, if that matters to you."

"Oh, don't be such a damper, Otto!" she snapped.

"I don't mean to discourage you, Emma," said Otto. "I'm simply pointing out that your plan will never work. You can't have a tree that reaches all the way up to the ceiling—the ceiling in the Great Hall is twenty feet high! A tree of that height would fall over and kill someone—*if* you could even get it through the doors, which you can't."

"Oh, but you don't mean to discourage me!"

"This may be a silly question," Nicholas said, "but why do you want to put a tree, of all things, in the middle of your hall?"

"Of course it makes no sense to *you;* you're English," Emma laughed. "But my mother was German. She brought her customs with her when she married my father. We always had a Christmas tree at Chilton. *Der Weihnachtsbaum,* we called it. It's usually a fir tree—*die Tannenbaum.* We always had such fun decorating it."

"We had a *small Tannenbaum* at Chilton," Otto said. "In the nursery."

Emma ignored him. "When I married into the Fitzroy family, they all thought I was mad, but my boys had a *Tannenbaum* in the nursery every year," Emma told Nicholas. "We always used to decorate it together. My boys didn't have much of a Christmas *last* year," she went on more seriously, "with their father dying so suddenly, you understand. Oh, it was dreadful. I want this year to be extra special for them, to make up for it."

"I think I can help you," Nicholas said slowly. "It can't be any more difficult than raising the mast on a ship, and I've done that a few times in my day. Not by myself, of course."

"You will have servants to assist you, of course," Emma assured him. "Anything you need. There, you see, Otto!" she said triumphantly. "It *can* be done!"

"I still think it very strange that you would want to cut down a perfectly good tree and drag it into your house," said Nicholas. "But, yes, I think it can be done."

Monty came around with the bottle to make sure their glasses were full. "A toast. To peace!"

Emma and Nicholas scrambled to their feet. "To peace!"

*"La guerre est mort!"* Colin announced in execrable French, lifting his glass in a toast no one could resist joining. *"Vive le paix!"*

Soon they were all drunk.

The party began to break up a little after midnight when Otto took his thoroughly inebriated wife to bed. Cecily, who never drank more than a glass or two with her dinner, was really suffering. Leaning heavily on her husband's arm, she left the room, white faced with nausea, yet still mumbling bravely about going to the nursery to check on the children.

Monty and Colin stood up at the same time. "I have to get up very early," said Monty, kissing Emma's hand. "I'm going out shooting with Bellamy's men. If my wound isn't troubling me, that is," he added, grinning.

Colin yawned, stretching his arms over his head. "Well, I'm off to bed, too," he said.

"No," Emma said plaintively. "Don't go! Stay! We'll get more Champagne from the cellar. We'll sing Christmas carols."

Nicholas also climbed to his feet. He was not so drunk that he didn't realize he was about to be left alone with the duchess. "I'd better go as well," he said. "Perhaps one of you gentlemen could show me the way?"

"I'm afraid we're in no condition to lead anyone anywhere," Colin apologized. "Emma will take you, won't you, Emma?"

Champagne had made Emma reckless. "I certainly will," she said. "It would be a pleasure."

"Perhaps it would be better if I went on my own," Nicholas said seriously to Emma when they were alone. "If someone should see us together . . . I would not want to make you the subject of ugly gossip," he added, remembering Lady Susan's ugly talk about Emma.

Emma climbed to her feet unsteadily. "I know this house like the back of my hand," she boasted, conveniently forgetting that earlier in the day she had needed guidance from Carstairs. "I think I can bring you safely back to your room without getting caught. And, besides, they will gossip about me no matter what I do. So I might as well live a little, *nicht wahr?* Or, as the French say, *ne c'est pas?*"

"I don't speak French."

"I'll teach you."

Swaying a little, she took his arm and led him to a door set to one side of the pianoforte, half hidden by a blue velvet curtain. The room beyond was dark, lit only by the fire in the fireplace, but, as his eyes adjusted, he could see that it was a bedroom. Emma slipped inside, while Nicholas hesitated on the threshold.

Almost to the bed, Emma turned back for him, seizing his hand. "What's the matter?" she asked, puzzled by his reluctance. Anyone would think he'd never had a casual drunken romp before.

"There must be some mistake, ma'am," he stammered. "This is not my room."

"There is no mistake, my darling," Emma replied, her

voice silky. "This is *my* room. And that is my bed," she added unnecessarily. He was perfectly aware of the bed.

"I think perhaps we have had too much to drink," he said, wide-eyed.

"I am not drunk," she said indignantly. "If I were drunk, do you think my brothers would have left me alone with you?"

"You were supposed to take me to *my* room," he reminded her gently.

"And so I shall," she said prettily. "*Afterward.*"

"Afterward!" he exclaimed, his voice breaking a little. "A-after what?"

"After you have made me happy, of course," she laughed. "Don't keep me waiting, Nicholas. I'm not at all a patient creature."

"I—I don't understand," he stammered.

She sighed impatiently. "I'm sorry," she said tartly. "Am I being too subtle? But I forget you are only twenty." Blowing out her breath again, she went to the bed and sat down on it. Holding out her arms to him, she said, clearly, "Come here, boy. I want you. Quicker," she added as he seemed rooted in the spot.

"You should not tease me like this," he said sharply. "It's very naughty."

"I am not teasing you," she said, surprised. "If anything, *you're* teasing *me.* Now get over here this instant or I'll just have to start without you. Or is that what you want?" she purred.

"Madam!" he protested weakly. "Talk like that will go straight to a man's head!"

"To his head? I think not," Emma chuckled. "It usually goes straight to his—"

"Emma!" he said, quite shocked.

She blinked at him. "What? I know you want me, Nicholas. Why are you fighting it?" She scowled at him suddenly. "You are not very gallant, sir, to leave me in hideous doubt of your desire for me! If anything, a gentleman should always show *more* passion than he feels, not less. In such cases as these, self-restraint of any kind is an insult!"

"This is a prime example of why women should not drink," he said. "It has altered you, madam, so that I hardly recognize you. I'm afraid it has robbed you of your womanly dignity."

The humiliation of rejection shocked Emma into unwelcome sobriety. "You've said quite enough, sir," she snapped angrily. "Now I shall have *my* say. You are a hypocrite! I know when a man wants me, and *you*, my lord, definitely fall into that category! I am *not* wrong about this. I am *never* wrong about *this*."

"Well, of course I *want* you," he said, almost angrily.

"That's what I said! You're just being cruel," she accused him.

"I—I don't mean to be cruel, Emma!" He was on his knees in front of her.

Emma had already decided to forgive him, but she folded her arms and turned her head away. "Yes, you do. You are punishing me. Why do you punish me?"

"I do not mean to punish you! I love you, and I want you to be happy!" he protested.

Emma's head swung back. "You *love* me?" she said. "Don't be an ass!"

"From the moment I first saw you, I have loved you," he said with absolute humility. In the near darkness, he fumbled for her hands. "Is it possible for such a thing to happen so quickly? I swear I did not believe it until today."

"No, nor did I," she said sarcastically. "But, then, Champagne has robbed me of wits as well as my womanly dignity, whatever that may be."

He pulled in a long breath. "Champagne has made me bold," he declared.

"Really? *How* bold?"

"Bold enough to tell you that I love you!"

"Talk is always bold," she sneered.

"I can't believe I have found the courage to confess," he marveled. "I did not dare hope that you could feel anything for me. Dear Emma! You are so far above me." Bending his head, he covered her hands with passionate, clumsy kisses.

Emma lifted his face. "Do you find me so *very* cold and forbidding?"

"You are wonderful! Perfect! You are an angel!"

"Is that why you do not kiss me?" she asked.

"You are a duchess," he said helplessly.

"I think you'll find," she said, tilting her face to his, "that kissing a duchess is a lot like kissing a woman."

She waited.

Nothing happened. The young man was either too inexperienced or too shy to take the lead. With a slight sigh of impatience, Emma took matters into her own hands. Holding his face firmly, she kissed him full on the mouth. "What a sweet little lamb you are," she murmured, nibbling his bottom lip. "When do you become a lion, I wonder?"

"I'll be your lamb," he agreed, whispering. "I'll be your lion. I'll be anything you want. I would do anything to please you. I believe I would *die* to please you, Emma."

She kissed him again, pulling at his shoulders. He did not take the hint. "What's the matter?" she whispered. "Come to bed, darling. Show me just how bold you are."

He obeyed, all but leaping onto her as she moved back to make room for him. He did nothing as she unbuttoned his coat and pushed it off of his shoulders, but his breathing was becoming ragged. "Help me," she instructed, and at once he began loosening his neckcloth. He removed his waistcoat, then stopped, awaiting further instructions.

"And the shirt!" she said smartly, resting against the pillows. "Hurry up."

He tugged it over his head, getting tangled in the process. She had to help him.

His skin was hot and slightly damp. She ran her hands lightly over his naked torso, pleased to find that, although he was rather thin, his muscles were firm. Gently, she tried to push him over onto his back. Instead, he collapsed on top of her, burying his face in the side of her neck.

He was pretty hopeless at taking a hint, she realized. "On your back, please," she said softly, chuckling in the back of her throat. He complied immediately, and seemed grateful for the instruction. Sitting up, Emma lifted her skirts, put one leg over him, and sat down. His affair, as she liked to call it, was of a flattering size and hardness. She could feel it through his breeches.

And yet, he did not reach for her. He did not throw her down for a quick drive to the main chance. He waited for her, his chest rising and falling rapidly, his body taut as a lute string. He puzzled her. Could he really be that shy?

"Do you love me?" she asked softly.

"Oh, yes," he answered instantly.

Her eyes closed, she tilted her head back. Reaching behind her back, she found the laces of her gown and loosened them, so that, when her young man found his courage, he would be able to undress her with perfect ease.

"Do you like it when the woman is on top?" she asked him hopefully.

She heard him lick his lips nervously. "Yes," he said. "Yes, very much."

Emma smiled. Most men were not so accommodating. Swooping down on him, she began kissing his body, her mouth moving over him hungrily. She was expert in the art of arousing a man, and the sensation was too exquisite to be endured quietly. He jumped, crying out. Holding him down, Emma trailed her tongue over his belly. Involuntarily, he began to move his hips. He bit his lip to keep from crying out again, but she took great pride in causing him to moan in spite of himself.

She lifted her head to look at him. "Do you still think I am teasing you?" she asked.

His head arched back into the pillows. "I cannot believe this is happening to me," he whispered. "A week ago, I was just an ordinary man."

Emma laughed softly. "You're still an ordinary man, I hope."

Farther and farther down she went. Her hands masterfully stroked his thighs, then skimmed up to the buttons of his trousers. In a moment, he was free. His straining member was in her hands.

"I stand corrected," she said, pleased with her prize. "You are an *extraordinary* man."

She lowered her head.

"Wait!" he cried suddenly, scrambling away from her. "Aren't you forgetting something?"

"I'm trying to forget *everything*," she purred, crawling toward him like a cat.

"But you're still in mourning," he said breathlessly.

The mood was instantly broken.

"What?" she said sharply.

"It is one thing for you to go down to dinner," he said. "That was a magnificent gesture, but *this* . . . It is wrong. Emma, we cannot do this."

"Why not?" she wanted to know.

"My love!" he said reproachfully. "I know your marriage was not happy, but the proprieties must be observed. If I led you into dishonor, how could I say I love you?"

"I don't understand," Emma said coldly. To be rejected by the same man twice in one night was not doing her temper any good. "You would use honor as an excuse to hurt and humiliate me?"

"I adore you," he said fervently, clasping her in his arms. "I love you! But I love you with honor. You cannot be truly mine until the year of mourning is over. Let us not begin like this, with a dishonorable act. I am scum, I know, but you deserve better."

His words made no sense to her. She felt only the pangs of rejection. Smarting, she left the bed, tightening the laces of her gown as she did so.

"If that is how you feel," she said coldly, "you'd better get dressed. I will take you back to your own room . . . if your *honor* allows it, that is!"

# Chapter Eight

"Don't be angry, my love," Nicholas said softly. "You know I am right."

"I am not angry," she snapped, tapping her foot. "I am waiting."

He dressed quickly. Without a word, she lit a candle, and picking it up, led the way out of the room. He followed where she led, stopping on the threshold of another bed-chamber.

"My love—" he began haltingly.

"Don't distress yourself, my angel," Emma said coolly. "I have no further designs on your precious honor." Going over to the fireplace, which was cold and dark, she pressed the carved panel of the marble mantelpiece in the spot that opened the hidden door.

"A secret passage!" he exclaimed, coming into the room.

"And you thought I was going to seduce you," Emma said lightly. "Don't you feel silly?"

Nicholas looked into the passageway, but, in the darkness, there was not much to see. "Was it used for hiding priests?"

Emma snorted. "I doubt it," she said dryly as she entered the dark passageway. "The fifth Duke of Warwick put this passageway in so he could visit his mistress without creating a scandal."

Nicholas was so tall he had to stoop to follow her. The ceiling was rather low, but otherwise the passageway was quite comfortable, and wide enough for three to walk abreast. Paintings depicting beautiful women, many of them nude, all of them posed seductively, lined the walls. Thankfully, Emma's candle did not shed enough light for him to see them clearly.

"He had several mistresses, as you see. These are not all *his*, however," Emma went on. "He merely began the tradition of hanging their portraits in this hall. Over the years, his descendants have also placed their favorites here. A sort of sportsman's trophy room, as it were, and these are their kills."

The paintings made Nicholas uncomfortable. He tried not to look at them.

Emma stopped at a painting. "*This* lady was my husband's mistress," she said matter-of-factly. "I should say *one* of his mistresses, for he had just as many as he could. My friend Thomas Lawrence painted her. He painted me at about the same time, in the same pose, I found out later. The only difference is that *I* was more formally attired."

Nicholas bit his lip. "Your husband's infidelities must have caused you a great deal of pain. I will never betray you like that, you know."

"He did cause me pain," Emma said. "I did my best to cause him pain, too, but I could never hurt him as he hurt me. Still, you insist that I mourn him properly? If I had preceded him in death, he would not have been so conscientious, I assure you!"

"It is only a few days, my love. Then we can be together, secure in the knowledge that we have done nothing wrong. I love you that much. And you love me, too, do you not?"

"Oh, yes, of course," Emma said tartly. "I forgot how much in love we are."

Holding up the candle, she turned and moved swiftly down the hall. Nicholas hurried to keep up with her.

The passage wound its way through the interstices of the palace. At last, Emma stopped and opened a doorway. Motioning for him to be silent, she looked out into the bedroom beyond, satisfying herself that it was empty. "The passageway from the duke's chamber has no direct link to your apartment," she explained, drawing him into the room. "You must go out into the hall, and cross to the other side of the gallery. Westphalia is the only apartment on that side. I will not go with you," she added, slipping back into the passageway. "If I were to be seen in this part of the house by another guest or a passing servant . . ."

"Of course," he said. Seizing her hands, he kissed them fervently. "Good night, my angel. You have made me the happiest man alive."

"What a fascinating entry in my journal this will be," she replied coolly. "I can honestly say I've never met anyone quite like you. Good night, Nicholas."

*Monday, December 12, 1814*

The next morning, Emma was still fuming. "Who does he think he is to refuse *me?*" she demanded of her twin brother as they sat in the window of her sitting room sipping chocolate from tiny cups. Otto and Monty had gone out shooting with the other gentlemen, and, although it was nearly noon, Lady Scarlingford was still sleeping off the effects of the previous night's celebration. Emma had been obliged to rise early for her daily meetings with the chef, the housekeeper, and the butler respectively. She was charmingly dressed in a morning gown of fine India muslin with a short brocaded jacket. Colin was still in his dressing gown of quilted purple satin. Bleary-eyed, he hid a yawn behind one hand.

"No one refuses me!" Emma went on, full of petulance. "If there is refusing to be done, I'll be the one doing it, thank you very much."

"Calm yourself," said Colin, wincing as her voice became a trifle high-pitched. "Really, you're like an illustration of the woman scorned. It's possible that sailors have some silly prejudice against widows," he suggested. "They *are* a superstitious lot, you know."

"If so, it is a superstition the British Army don't share," Emma said dryly. "General Bellamy's men have been sending me a constant stream of billet-doux all morning. You see them there," she added, nodding towards a little table laden with envelopes and posies set on a tray.

"It must have been that rousing welcome speech you gave last night. Naturally, they hope the thanks and praise of a grateful nation will translate into a bout of sweaty lovemaking with the Duchess of Warwick. They're only human, after all. I received a few letters of my own, as a matter of fact."

"Really?" said Emma, instantly diverted. "Who?"

"I'll never tell," Colin said piously. "Anyway, we were talking about you and Nicholas. Have you considered the possibility that he might be sincere?"

"Sincere!" Emma said incredulously. "He told me he loved me the moment he saw me, and that he knew we were destined to be together." She laughed. "Open any one of those letters from the *army,* and I daresay, you will find those exact sentiments, if not those exact words."

She turned her face away. "Is it possible that I am not as attractive as I think I am? I *am* almost thirty. What if he saw something that made him change his mind?"

"You mean like those wrinkles around your neck?"

Emma put one hand to her throat. "They are called the rings of Venus," she told him angrily.

"Yes; by liars. For heaven's sake," he went on impatiently. "He was probably just too drunk. You know some men cannot perform when they've had large amounts of drink. None of the men I know, of course, but I hear it does happen occasionally to the lesser mortals."

"It wasn't that," Emma snapped. "Everything was present and correct."

"Very mysterious," said Colin. "How will you punish him? You *are* going to punish him, of course?"

"I shall ignore him," said Emma. "If he doesn't want me, I'll find someone who does. I do not lack for admirers, you know," she added. "I'll just pick one at random." Setting down her cup, she ran over to her escritoire, where her letters had been piled. Emma snatched one up and looked at it. "General Bellamy!" she exclaimed in horror. "Ugh!"

Running over to the fire, she tossed it in.

Down in the courtyard, a few stragglers were arriving in a hired chaise. "I see Cousin Claud is here, with that frowsy little wife of his," Colin observed. "And, if that beautiful young man dancing attendance on her is her cousin, I'll eat my boots."

Emma glanced out of the window, but, before she could give her impressions of the *ménage à trois* a loud knocking at the door jerked their attention away from the window. Emma nearly jumped out of her skin.

"Good God!" Emma breathed. "Who the devil can that be?"

The servants had been trained to scratch gently at doors, and her close friends thought nothing of simply walking in on her.

"Colin, go and answer."

Colin burrowed deeper into the seat cushion. "I'm not dressed," he said. "Besides, it's your room, not mine. Perhaps it's Nicholas," he suggested. "He's come to apologize for his odiously gentlemanlike behavior. Perhaps he'll ravish you to make up for it."

Crossing the room, Emma opened the door.

A tall cavalry officer about her own age stood there, bareheaded and spattered in mud.

Without hesitation, Emma threw her arms around him. "Michael!" she cried happily, recognizing her brother-in-law, Lord Michael Fitzroy. "This is a most welcome surprise. No one told me you had arrived. When did you get here?"

"Just now," he told her, holding both her hands. "I rode across the fields from Redditch. Forgive my coming to you in all my dirt," he added with a grave smile, "but I wanted to see you, Emma, before anyone else knew I was here."

Emma stared at him. "Has something happened? Michael, you're frightening me. Is it Harry? Is it Grey?"

Colin left the window seat to be with his sister, even as Lord Michael was assuring her that her sons were perfectly well as far as he knew. His news had nothing to do with *them*.

"What is it then?" Emma asked. "Oh, do sit down. You remember my brother Colin, of course."

"Of course," Lord Michael said politely, but it was clear Colin's presence made him uneasy.

Colin sighed. "Do you wish to be private with my sister?"

Emma caught his hand. "There's nothing Michael can say to me that my brother cannot hear. What is it, Michael?"

Lord Michael walked up and down the room, his manner agitated. "I will just say it, then," he said, stopping abruptly. "Emma, I am married."

Emma almost collapsed from relief. "Is that all? I thought someone had died, Michael!"

"Someone *will* die," said Colin. "Does Octavia know about this?"

"Oh!" said Emma. "You mean you did not marry Octavia?" She stared up at her brother-in-law. *"Oh."*

"Octavia!" Lord Michael said scornfully. He sat down in a chair near the fire. Facing Emma, he leaned forward, his hands pressed together. "Emma, I don't know what they've been telling, but I was never engaged to that female, and I certainly am not inclined to honor an agreement that exists only in my uncle's fertile imagination! Warwick fully supported my decision. Did he never mention it to you?"

"Never," she said. "But, then, he wouldn't have. My husband never spoke with me about Fitzroy family matters."

"When my brother died, my uncle started up his nonsense again, claiming that I had been engaged to his eldest child. I even got a letter in Lisbon from Cousin Octavia, enthusing about our coming nuptials—and declaring her undying love for me, if you like!"

Suppressing a shudder, Colin kindly handed him a glass of brandy.

"I knew not how to answer her letter," Lord Michael went on, when he had fortified his tissues with liquor. "I was already married to Elvira by that time. I did not want to be cruel to Octavia. It is not her fault, after all. She is but an innocent pawn in her father's game."

"More like a snake in the grass, I'd say," Colin muttered.

"What is it you want me to do, Michael?" Emma asked pragmatically.

Lord Michael raked his fingers through his curly auburn hair. "I have left my wife at the inn in Redditch with my friend, Captain Charles Palafox. I did not want to bring her here until I was sure of her reception."

"Michael!" Emma said indignantly. "Of course I will receive your wife! I will welcome her as a sister. I am hurt that you would think otherwise."

"It is not *you* I doubt," he said hastily. "I merely wanted to make sure you were at home before I brought her here. I fear the other ladies will not be kind to her, for, not only is she not Octavia, she is a Portuguese. She's from a very old family, very respected."

Emma laughed. "Ye gods, man! It is enough for me that she is your wife. I do not require her pedigree."

"Others will demand it," he said darkly.

"Yes," Emma agreed sadly.

"I mean to sell out now the war is over," he went on, climbing to his feet. Emma rose with him. "I am hoping for an appointment to the Portuguese court. I wondered, Emma, if you might have any influence with Lord Castlereagh."

"Why, no," said Emma, "but Colin might."

"I'll be happy to write a letter," Colin offered.

Lord Michael looked askance. "You mean to say that Lord Castlereagh is—is—a backgammon player?"

"Not at all," Colin answered coolly. "I play backgammon with his lordship's wife."

Lady Michael arrived at Warwick within the hour. Footmen dressed in the red and gold livery of the Fitzroys lined the courtyard. The ladies of the household crowded the portico and the vestibule, eager to get a look at the Portuguese. Lady Susan Bellamy, much too important to go out to meet her nephew's wife, stayed at the window of the main drawing room, where, they had been told, Lady Michael was to be received formally.

"She seems very neat and clean, for a dago," Lady Susan reported. "I am quite surprised. Someone must have helped her. Oh, my poor Octavia," she gloated, enfolding her niece in a perfumed embrace. "To be jilted is bad enough, but to be thrown over for a swarthy, black-haired gypsy—! You are most sincerely to be pitied."

Octavia stood smiling coldly.

"Run along upstairs, darling, and I will make your excuses for you. And, to be sure, I will scold my nephew very thoroughly for treating you so ill! Will your father sue him for breach of promise, do you think?" Lady Susan wanted to know. "How very shocking it all is."

While the other ladies waited in the drawing room, Emma went down the steps to greet her new sister-in-law. Lady

Scarlingford, too, had been dragged from her bed for the occasion. Still suffering from the effects of too much Champagne, she clung to her brother-in-law's arm. Colin had dressed as if for a royal levee in velvet breeches and buckled shoes.

Going down the steps, Emma embraced the young woman. Lord Michael's wife was a black-haired beauty with caramel-colored skin and large, gentle brown eyes. She answered everything that was said to her with a lovely smile.

"I'm afraid Elvira's English is not very good," Lord Michael said, coming forward. "I am teaching her, of course, but, for now, we converse mainly in French."

Emma obligingly switched to French, and she was still speaking it when Lord Michael presented his friend to her. Captain Palafox was a handsome, self-assured gentleman with knowing gray eyes and a wide, untrustworthy, insolent smile. His dark hair looked as polished as his boots. He was clean shaven but for a thin mustache. He lingered over Emma's hand with such breathtaking impertinence that she wondered at Michael's having entrusted his wife to his care even for a short time.

They all went into the house. It was decided that Lady Michael was too exhausted to meet the ladies in the drawing room, much to Lady Susan's disappointment, and Octavia's relief. Emma escorted the bride to Lord Michael's rooms, leaving her brother-in-law to see to his friend, Captain Palafox. While Lady Michael's maid attended her mistress, Emma waited in the sitting room attached to Lord Michael's suite. Presently, Lord Michael joined her there.

"You led me to believe that you were anxious to show my wife every courtesy," he began walking up and down the room.

"What do you mean?" Emma cried, confused. "Do you not like the room? I've moved my brother farther down the hall to accommodate you."

"Room! I had hoped you would condescend to allow my nephews to meet their aunt," he said. " Am I to understand that my wife is not good enough to be presented to the Duke of Warwick? I suppose he is out shooting birds or something. You did not think it worthwhile to interrupt his grace's pleasures? Emma, you know such an oversight on your part—if indeed it *was* just an oversight—will only encourage the other ladies to behave slightingly to my wife!"

"For heaven's sake, Michael," Emma said, breaking into his tirade. "Harry wasn't *there* for the simple reason that Harry isn't *here!* Nor is Grey. Hugh is their guardian, not I. But I am assured that they will be home by Saturday."

"Hugh is their guardian? What are you talking about? *I* am their guardian, but I—I turned the responsibility over to you, at least, while I was away."

"The rest of the family did not agree with your decision. I wrote to you, but—" She shrugged helplessly.

Lord Michael was mortified. "I am sorry, Emma. I did not read your letters. I thought you were just writing to tell me that Harry had grown taller, or that Grey was still collecting bugs."

"Beetles," Emma corrected him. "Not bugs; he's very discriminating. I do not blame you, Michael. Given my history with men, your relations had little difficulty convincing the courts that I was unfit to be guardian to my own children."

"Hypocrites," he said angrily. "If *you* are guilty, then every society woman I know is equally guilty. You'd be amazed at the number of respectable ladies who pass off their lover's children as their husband's."

"No, I wouldn't."

"No, I don't suppose you would be," he agreed. "But it still shocks *me.*"

Emma smiled at him. "Which is why you married a convent girl."

Lord Michael looked sheepish. "I suppose so."

He sat down with her. "But, Emma, I am not so caught up in my own affairs that my brother's children do not concern me," he said. "I will speak to my uncle about this at the first opportunity. The term at Harrow ended some time ago. I would like to know his excuse for keeping the Duke of Warwick away from his own home."

"They are no longer at Harrow," she told him. "At present, I do not know *where* they are! While I was in Paris, Hugh went behind my back and took them out of school."

"This is monstrous. My brother thought you worthy to be their mother. He could have divorced you at any time, but he did not. That should be enough for anyone."

"Thank you, Michael."

"I will speak to my uncle," Lord Michael promised. "I will shame him into doing what he knows to be right."

"Oh, let us speak of something else," Emma said impatiently. "I hate all this doom and gloom. It's Christmas. The war is over. We should be happy! Tell me about your friend, Captain Palafox. He seems . . . charming."

"I confess I hope Cousin Octavia will find him so," Lord Michael replied sheepishly.

Emma gave a surprised laugh. "You offer him as a consolation prize?"

"Indeed I do," Lord Michael admitted. "But with his full knowledge and consent, of course. Charles has a very rich, very snobby old aunt called Mrs. Allen. Mrs. Allen is ready to make her fortune over to him on the condition that he makes a suitable match. I should think marrying into the Duke of Warwick's family would qualify!"

"Yes, indeed. But I fear Octavia will be more interested in a certain Lord Camford now that you have jilted her."

"I did not jilt her!" he protested. "Still, I am glad she has a suitor. A lord, no less! She will not be mourning the loss of me. I am but a younger son, after all."

"I feel sure she has already forgiven you," Emma said.

Between them, they decided that Lady Michael should rest for the remainder of the afternoon. Tea with the ladies would not be attempted. Lady Michael could meet everyone before dinner. There Lady Michael could meet her new family with every possible advantage.

A servant came in with a jewel box, which Emma presented to Michael. "For the bride."

Opening the box, Lord Michael saw a magnificent set of diamonds and emeralds, a necklace, drop earrings, and two matching bracelets.

Lord Michael protested that she was too generous.

"Don't you recognize them?" said Emma. "They were your mother's. Warwick gave them to me years ago, but they are not entailed upon the estate. We had no daughter; they really should go to your wife, don't you think? I never wear emeralds myself, so don't you dare accuse me of generosity."

Brushing aside his thanks, she left him.


The news that Lord Michael had returned to Warwick with a Portuguese bride made its way across the duke's fields to the gentlemen, who were industriously bagging pheasant half a mile away. Lord Hugh's face turned brick red with anger. He immediately broke down his gun and made for the house, threatening to sue his brother's son for breach of promise.

"It is very sad for Cousin Octavia," Nicholas remarked to Monty. "I understand they had been engaged for a very long time."

"It is always sad when a man marries," Monty replied. "Don't you think?"

"No," said Nicholas. "I hope to be married very soon."

"Well, it's your funeral," Monty replied.

The gentlemen resumed shooting.

As the day drew to a close, they walked back across the

fields to the great house. Monty went his own way. Nicholas was able to find his way back to his own apartment without assistance, delayed by only a few wrong turns. The door to Westphalia stood ajar, and, as he approached it, he heard voices, a man's and a girl's. As he pushed the door open, he saw a young girl with bright red hair seated in the window seat. A cavalry officer easily twice her age stood over her, one booted foot on the seat. They both seemed to be discussing the view from the window.

Nicholas was shocked.

"Cousin Jellies!" he exclaimed in disbelief. "I mean: Julia!"

The gentleman gave a guilty start, but Julia Fitzroy simply jumped up and ran to Nicholas, wrapping her arms tightly around him. "Cousin Nicholas! I've missed you so much! Did you have good hunting? I bet you're an excellent shot!"

"You should not be here, Cousin Julia," he told her sternly. "Where is your governess?"

As he held her at arm's length, Julia tossed her head prettily, her long hair rippling down her back. "I am too old to have a governess!" she pouted. "It is insupportable!"

"And you, sir," said Nicholas, addressing the gentleman. "What are you doing in my room?"

The officer had lost his guilty expression, and in its place was a look of superiority. His uniform was impeccable: a scarlet coat with black facings, edged in gold braid; white leather breeches; and tall, black top boots. He had gray eyes and a little mustache. Nicholas disliked him more and more with every passing second.

"*Your* room, sir?" he smiled. "I am just arrived with Lord Michael Fitzroy. He said this was to be *my* room, and I believed him."

"I told him this was *your* room, Cousin Nicholas," Julia put in. "Gentlemen, allow me to make you known to one another. Cousin Nicholas, this is Captain Palafox. Captain Palafox, this is my cousin, the Earl of Camford."

Captain Palafox blinked. Then he bowed.

"I beg your pardon, my lord," he said contritely, his smile slipping. "Obviously there has been some mistake. Oh, dear, and my man's just finished unpacking my things," he added apologetically.

"Surely your man noticed that *my* things are already in the closet!" said Nicholas.

"No. Just a few old rags in the wardrobe."

"Those would be *my* old rags, sir," said Nicholas.

Palafox looked him over curiously. "I see. I suppose I *could* have my man pack me up again and move me, but that could take as much as an hour. Is it really worth it to your lordship? Potentially, it could make us late for tea."

Nicholas shrugged. "I wouldn't bother," he muttered. "Just—just tell me what your man did with my old rags, and I'll be on my way."

Palafox was already ushering Nicholas to the door. "Thank you, my lord. I do believe he put them in the room on the other side of the stairs—the small, dark one—very cozy."

"Not the one on the left?" Nicholas exclaimed, a slight smile touching his lips. Inside that room, he knew, was an entrance to the secret passage that connected this part of the house to Emma's.

"Indeed, my lord. The very one," Palafox assured him.

"Come, Cousin Julia," Nicholas said firmly, leading his fifteen-year-old cousin from the room. "You should not be here; these are bachelor's quarters. If someone else had found you alone with that gentleman, your reputation would have been in shreds."

"But I was only looking for *you,* Cousin Nicholas," Julia said, snuggling up against him. "I have not seen you in ages!"

"Don't be silly. We saw each other only yesterday," he corrected her.

"Not at all!" she complained. "You were not at tea. And I wore my blue muslin for you. And I am not allowed to dine in company, for I am not yet Out, so I could not see you at dinner either. I have been hoping to see you all day today. If you do not make an effort, I shall never see you at all!"

"Yesterday I lost track of time," he apologized. "Today I have been out in the fields with the other gentlemen."

"There is a conspiracy to keep us apart," Julia whined. "Mama and Papa are being perfectly beastly about the whole thing. It's not my fault I'm the youngest. *I* think a man should be allowed to choose his own wife."

"So do I," he said gravely.

"You should hear how they talk about you, Cousin Nicholas," she went on slyly. "As if you were a head of beef! First, they wanted you to marry Augusta, when everyone knows she only cares about the four-leggeds! That was bad enough, but, now—! Oh, Cousin Nicholas! *Now* they expect you to marry Octavia! Just because she's been jilted by Cousin Michael."

Julia barely stifled a giggle. "But you mustn't let them force her down your throat, Cousin Nicholas," she said earnestly. "That is what I came to tell you. Octavia is worse than Augusta ever could be. Augusta is really quite harmless. But Octavia is perfectly cold-blooded. And she is twenty-four! Positively ancient. I shall be sixteen in seven months."

"You should not laugh at the misfortunes of others," he said sternly. "Your eldest sister is to be pitied. The marriage of her betrothed to another must have come as a great shock to her."

Julia stared at him. "Of course it is all very sad for *her,*" she agreed. "But wouldn't *you* rather marry *me?*"

"I am not going to marry any of you, Cousin Julia," Nicholas said firmly. Glancing over the marble balustrade of the gallery, he spied a footman crossing the hall below.

"You there! Miss Julia has become lost. Would you be so good as to take her back to her mama?"

"Oh, Cousin Nicholas!" Julia howled, stamping her foot.

Ignoring her completely, Nicholas shut himself up in his new room.

# Chapter Nine

When Colin went down to dinner that evening, he found Lady Harriet sitting in a corner of the lounge like a neglected old ruin. "How is poor, pitiful Octavia taking the news?" he asked, slipping into a chair close to her.

Across the room, Monty stood with a group of young officers, swapping stories. Monty was always careful never to be seen in public with Colin.

Lady Harriet watched Colin watch Monty for a moment before answering. "You know Octavia. She wears the mask. But I'd be terrified to see what lies beneath. Being jilted is never a pleasant thing, of course, but when a woman is twenty-four—"

"Is she as old as that?" Colin laughed. "If *I* were that old, I'd kill myself."

She glared at him. "I happen to know, sir, that you are nearly *thirty*."

"Thirty!" he squawked indignantly. "I am only twenty-nine. I meant *if I were a woman,* I'd kill myself, of course. Especially if I were still a spinster like the egregious Octavia."

"There are worse things than being a spinster, dear boy," the sixty-year-old spinster informed him severely. "You needn't feel sorry for Octavia. Naturally, she will claim Lord Camford as her consolation prize. The poor girl's just been jilted, after all, and she *does* have seniority."

"She's too old for him," Colin protested. "*I* want him to marry Julia."

"Pshaw!" said the old lady. "She has beauty, I grant you, but Octavia has brains."

"Brains didn't do you much good when you and Aunt Susan were vying for George Bellamy," he reminded her.

"I would choose brains over beauty any day of the week," she said coldly.

"Yes; but would Camford? That is the question. Shall we have a wager?"

"I am an old lady on a fixed income," Lady Harriet said crossly.

"A week's allowance then," Colin said amiably. "I clear about seven hundred pounds. And you?"

"Ten shillings," said she. "You're on, dear boy! Mind you," she added, placing a clawlike hand on his arm, "he will not marry *anyone* as long as he is dangling after your sister."

"I'll take care of Emma," Colin said. "She's half over him already. I'll finish her off."

The duchess was standing in the receiving line with Lady Michael as the guests filed past into the lounge. Colin sidled up to her and whispered in her ear. "I know why a certain gentleman rejected your advances."

Emma half turned her head. "Why?" she asked, smiling at a young officer and his wife.

"He has the pox."

Emma was so overcome by a sudden choking cough that she had to excuse herself from the line and go sit down. "You can't just say that to a person," she hissed, as Colin brought her a glass of cool, clear liquid. "You must prepare her first! How do you know he has the pox?"

"Croft said it was the worst case he'd ever seen."

"Dear God," Emma murmured. Seizing the glass from his hand, she drained it, exploding into another round of coughing. "What *was* that?" she demanded, her eyes full of tears.

"Pure gin," he replied.

"I thought it was water," she said, glaring at him.

"Don't get tetchy with me, baggage. It's not *my* fault your latest toy has the pox. You should have expected it, really. I mean, he *is* a sailor. Don't shoot the messenger," he called after her as she pushed past him to take her place in the receiving line.

Julia was not yet Out, of course, which gave Lady Harriet the first advantage. Octavia did not disappoint her. The moment Nicholas entered the room, she glued herself to his side, much to his dismay. He was too polite, however, to shake her off. Besides, he did feel rather sorry for her. Doubtless, she wanted someone with her when she faced Lord Michael and his beautiful bride for the first time. "This must be very unpleasant for you, Cousin Octavia," he said civilly, offering her his arm as they stood in line.

"I do not know which is worse," she replied, "my Aunt Bellamy's gloating, or everyone else's pity. There is nothing I can do, it seems, to convince people that I was never in love with Cousin Michael." She shrugged helplessly.

Nicholas blinked at her in surprise. "Oh? You were not in love with him? I am glad, for your sake. I was afraid of finding you heartbroken this evening."

Octavia smiled faintly. "No, indeed. Why, Lord Michael and I practically were brought up as brother and sister. He has not injured me. I am truly happy for him and his bride."

"That is a relief to me," said Nicholas. "But, all the same, I think it infamous for a man to marry one lady when he is engaged to another."

"Oh, but Lord Michael and I were never engaged," she assured him quickly. "That was merely a fantasy of my parents. My father may have spoken to *his* father on the subject, but there was never anything in writing, and there was no understanding whatsoever between Lord Michael and me. None at all," she added, smiling. "I am completely unattached, just as I've always been."

"I am glad to hear it," Nicholas said, and he really was. "I don't like to think a gentleman would behave so dishonorably."

"Why, Cousin Nicholas!" she said. "I think you believe me."

"Of course I believe you," he said, puzzled. "Why wouldn't I believe you?"

She smiled ruefully. "No one else does, I'm afraid. They are all certain I am nursing a broken heart, and they are all determined to pity me and console me. Except for Aunt Bellamy, of course. *She* seeks to rub salt into a wound that does not exist, but I will never convince her of *that*. Even Mama thinks I was in love with Cousin Michael. I cannot convince her otherwise."

"Well, I believe you," he said warmly. "If your heart were broken, could you be standing here talking to me with such equanimity? You would be in your bedroom crying your eyes out."

"Exactly so! How nice it is to have someone who believes me. I fear the rest of the holiday will be a very trying time for me. I should like to be out of the house as much as possible, but I can't think of any excuse. Can you, Cousin Nicholas?"

The line moved up, distracting him. He could now catch glimpses of Emma standing between Lord Michael and his bride. The bride wore a blazing set of diamonds and emeralds with a gown of white satin, but Nicholas had eyes only for Emma. In her simple gown of silver-gray silk, she looked quiet and dignified. He loved her for not outshining the bride, which she could easily have done, he thought.

"Er, what?" he said to his companion.

"I was wondering if you could think of some excuse I

could make in order to escape from the house in the days ahead," Octavia said. "I cannot bear the pity of my relations."

"Oh, yes, of course," he murmured.

Emma was surprised to see him with Octavia, but she quickly concealed it. Miss Fitzroy was efficient, if not profuse, in her congratulations to the bride and groom, which she delivered in the stilted, anglicized French of the schoolroom.

"Thank you, Cousin Octavia," Lord Michael said, surprised and grateful for her performance, which he had been dreading for months.

Octavia shook hands with him very cordially. "I am truly happy for you, Cousin Michael," she said, looking him in the eye. Her face might have been carved from bone.

When his turn came, Nicholas bowed to the bride. *"Muito prazer,"* he said in rudimentary Portuguese. *"Parabens,"* he added.

Lady Michael's eyes lit up. *"Voce fala portugues?"* she asked shyly.

Nicholas answered slowly. *"Falo um pouquinho."*

"You did not tell me Lord Camford spoke Portuguese," Lord Michael murmured to Emma.

"I wonder where he caught it," said Emma. "That is, I wonder where he *learned* it."

"We had some Portuguese men in our crew," Nicholas explained. "England and Portugal are allies, after all. Their ship got broken up near Madagascar, poor chaps, and we were in need of crew. We were always in need of crew. I am by no means fluent," he added modestly.

Octavia shook her head in wonder. "You're so clever, Cousin Nicholas."

Emma had already turned away to speak to Captain Palafox.

"I'm glad somebody speaks Portuguese," said Lord Michael. "I'd be grateful, my lord, if you would escort my wife to dinner. She has no friends here, and it would do her good to be able to converse with someone in her native tongue."

"Of course," said Nicholas. "If the duchess will give me leave."

"I do, my lord," Emma answered, "with all my heart."


Throughout the first course, Nicholas entertained Lady Michael, quickly exhausting his scant Portuguese, but, when the course changed, he was obliged to devote himself to Octavia, who had managed somehow to be seated to his immediate right.

"You must tell me all about the navy, Cousin Nicholas," she encouraged him. "I think there can be no braver men in all the world than our sailors."

Nicholas had never had a more attentive listener. Octavia smiled and nodded continually as he spoke, occasionally shaking her head in wide-eyed wonder.

At the next course, he was obliged again to attempt conversation with the Portuguese lady. By the end of the course, they were reduced to pointing at things. Lady Michael would pick up her fork and give him the Portuguese word for that utensil. He would respond in kind, pointing at his crystal goblet and giving her the English word for *glass*.

Lord Scarlingford, who was seated to Lady Michael's left, sensed the crisis and intervened, keeping the guest of honor supplied with a steady stream of French.

With Nicholas all to herself, Octavia said, "I have thought of a way to escape from the pity of my family."

"Oh?"

Glancing down the table, Nicholas saw Emma deep in conversation with Captain Palafox. The sight made him frown.

"I shall go riding every day," Octavia went on bravely. "Only . . . I shall need someone to go with me. Mama would never permit me to go out with just the groom."

Nicholas realized that his attention to Emma was making him behave rudely to Octavia. Turning, he gave Octavia his full attention. "One of your sisters, perhaps, might go with you."

"My sisters do not ride," Octavia said quickly. "None of them. Do you ride, Cousin Nicholas? It would only be two or three hours a day. I would not ask more of you."

"Sadly, I do not ride," he answered. "I mean to learn, of course."

"Oh, you must learn, Cousin Nicholas," Octavia said immediately. "I could teach you. Now that *would* be a good excuse, would it not?" She gave a little, tinkling laugh.

"Thank you," Nicholas replied uneasily, "but the duchess has offered to teach me."

Octavia's eyes went to Emma's end of the table. "The duchess is an excellent horsewoman, to be sure, but I'm afraid her grace will be far too busy in the coming days to give you riding lessons. Now, of course, her first priority must be to make Lady Michael feel welcome. And, then, of course, there are all the entertainments, the balls, the dinners. These things do not plan themselves. Would you really want to add to her burdens, Cousin Nicholas?"

Nicholas risked another look at the duchess. Emma was listening to Captain Palafox with a faint smile on her lips. He longed to rescue her from the man's fatuous attentions.

Octavia leaned closer to Nicholas. "She is very beautiful, Cousin Nicholas," she whispered. "I don't wonder at your being infatuated with her."

He flushed. "I am not infatuated with the duchess," he stammered.

Octavia smiled understandingly.

"She is still in mourning for her husband," he protested weakly.

"And while she is so, it would be very strange for her to ride about the country with a young man," said Octavia. "You must think of her reputation. And why not let me teach you? At least, let me show you the basics. Then, when her grace has time for you, you will be able to impress her with your skills as an equestrian. You would not be her pupil. You could ride together as equals. It would be more pleasant for her, I should think, to have an equal partner."

Nicholas hesitated.

"Captain Palafox no doubt, is an excellent rider," Octavia went on. "He is in a cavalry regiment, you know."

"What has that to say to anything?" Nicholas said crossly.

"Oh, nothing," Octavia said innocently.

"Forgive me," Nicholas said. "I did not mean to be uncivil. If . . . if the duchess has no commission for me tomorrow, I should be glad to accept your offer."

"Commission, Cousin Nicholas?" Octavia echoed curiously.

"I am helping her with her Christmas arrangements. She wants to put a very large tree up in the Great Hall, and I am going to raise it for her."

"A tree in the Great Hall? How . . . how quaint."

The meal dragged on. Finally, Emma rose and the ladies withdrew. The port was passed. Across the table from Nicholas, Lord Michael argued with his uncle.

"Be reasonable, sir! We were not engaged, and nothing would come of a lawsuit but a great deal of unpleasantness for my wife and your daughter. Whatever my father may have said to you on his deathbed, *I* never promised Octavia anything!"

"You lie, sir!"

"No, Uncle!" The words fell from Nicholas's lips before he had time to consider that the two parties might not welcome his interference. Having taken the plunge, he muddled on. "Forgive me, Lord Michael. I could not help overhearing. Uncle, I have it from Octavia's own lips that she was never engaged to Lord Michael. She told me there was never any understanding between them! There has been no breach of promise. Your daughter has not been injured."

Lord Michael looked at him gratefully, but Lord Hugh frowned. "Octavia told you this?"

"Yes. I have been with her all evening. I assure you, sir, her heart is not broken. Lord Michael has neither imposed on her nor injured her. Surely, there is no need to talk of lawsuits, gentlemen, with Christmas practically upon us!"

"No, I suppose not," Lord Hugh said grudgingly. "If you are quite certain, my lord, that Octavia is not injured. She is, of course, my only concern in the matter."

"I was at her side when she wished them happy," Nicholas replied. "There was no bitterness, no jealousy, no hurt feelings. She would have married Lord Michael to please her parents, of course, but her feelings, sir, are the feelings of a sister for a brother, not those of a wife or sweetheart. I hope I have put your fears to rest, Uncle."

"You have, dear boy," Lord Hugh said, brightening up. "You have indeed. I am glad you were at her side in this trying time. I am glad that someone cares for her."

He seemed restored to the best of spirits as he took the port.

"I understand my brother's children are not expected at home until Saturday," Lord Michael said presently. "Why is that, Uncle?"

Lord Hugh looked uncomfortable. "There were . . . difficulties with the travel arrangements. But the boys will be here very soon."

"What sort of difficulties?" Lord Michael wanted to know. "I wish I'd known. I've just come from London. I could have collected my nephews on the way. They're still at Harrow, of course?" he added sharply. "I can't imagine them anywhere else. The Fitzroys have always sent their sons to Harrow."

General Bellamy overheard this and snorted. "If you can't get a pair of boys from Harrow to Warwick in good order, Brother, I'd say it's a good thing you never went into the Army!"

"I had to remove them from Harrow," Lord Hugh admitted sullenly.

"It's true then," Lord Michael said grimly. "Why?"

"To keep them from my sister, of course," said Otto. "It's sheer mindless cruelty."

The accusation shocked Nicholas. "Is this true, Uncle?"

"Of course not," Lord Hugh said coldly. "It's nothing to do with the duchess. The Latin master was caught in a compromising position in a back room of a London tavern. He's to be charged with sodomitical acts and thrown in prison, I shouldn't wonder. I judged it best to remove the boys until the scandal-broth cooled."

"That's the state of civilian justice," General Bellamy said contemptuously. "In the Army, we *hang* a man for buggery."

"Aye! That's the way to go about it, General," said Lord Ian Monteith. "After all, it's not fair to thieves and murderers to have to share quarters with these—these shirtlifters."

"You mean share *hind*quarters," said the general, roaring with laughter. "The navy, of course, is full of buggers," he went on amid the hilarity of his officers. "Rear admirals and vice admirals. Ain't that so, Camford?"

The room fell silent.

"I believe you're drunk, General," Nicholas said coldly. "You should ask one of your men to carry you up to bed."

The general glared at him, his face reddening with rage. "Ask one of my—! What are you implying?" He started up from his chair, but quickly, his aides closed around him, exerting a calming influence on his temper. They began to speak of other things.

"Bloody old fool," Otto muttered under his breath, and Lord Michael resumed his conversation with Lord Hugh.

"If they are not at Harrow, sir, then where are they? You haven't put them at Eton?"

General Bellamy's leonine head swivelled around. "Eton! Don't get me started on Eton! There's more buggery at Eton than there is in the Royal Navy!"

Nicholas jumped to his feet. "That's it!"

"We're taking him to bed now, my lord," one of the general's men said hastily. "He is in his cups, as you can see. He will remember none of this in the morning. Do please give our apologies to the ladies."

A brief struggle ensued, but the general, overwhelmed by the combined strength of his officers, was soon forced out of the room.

"Ye gods!" Nicholas said, when they had gone. "Can you imagine being on his staff?"

Colin tried but did not quite succeed in keeping his countenance.

"If we could get back to the matter in hand," Lord Michael said sternly. "Uncle, I believe I have a right to know where my nephews are!"

"They're at Westminster," said Lord Hugh. "It's a perfectly good school," he said defensively, as Lord Michael recoiled in horror.

"Lord, yes," Otto drawled. "'Tis an excellent school for the sons of bankers and barristers! However, I can't possibly think it a proper setting for my nephews."

"No! Nor can I," said Lord Michael, roused to anger. "Westminster! What *can* you be thinking, sir?"

"They will be here in a few days, and you will see that no harm has come to them," Lord Hugh said belligerently.

"I just hope the roads will still be passable," said Otto.

"What are you talking about?" Lord Michael said curiously. "There's nothing wrong with our roads. I was just on them."

"Uncle Hugh seems to be expecting some heavy weather," said Otto. "Blizzards, in fact."

"Nonsense! It never snows at Warwick until after the first

of the year," Lord Michael said flatly. "We're known for our fine weather."

Nicholas frowned. "Uncle? You said we could not risk going to London because, if we delayed even a few days, the road to Warwick would be impassable."

"I was speaking of Camford, Nephew," Lord Hugh quickly explained. "I was not speaking of Warwick. The road to Camford is dreadful, I'm sorry to say. I said we could not risk going to *Camford* this time of year. You must have misunderstood me."

"No, I don't think I did," Nicholas argued.

"Remember, your head would have been in the clouds," Hugh insisted, smiling. "You'd just been told you were the Earl of Camford. Anyone in your place would have been confused."

"I was not confused!" Nicholas said angrily.

Otto stood up. "Shall we rejoin the ladies?" he said pleasantly. "Emma has arranged for some music, and, I daresay, Lord Michael is eager to see his bride again."

Lord Michael flushed with embarrassment, but did not protest. "I just hope the ladies have left my poor girl in one piece," he said wearily, climbing to his feet.

"No fear of that," Otto replied. "My wife and my sister will be taking excellent care of her, I assure you. They'd wrap her up in swaddling clothes, if they could. Besides, your charming wife has the advantage of not being able to understand the other ladies."

"She understands a little English," Lord Michael said.

Otto smiled. "Ah! But *they* will be attempting to speak to her in *French!*"

# Chapter Ten

*Tuesday, December 13, 1814*

The following morning, Nicholas met Octavia downstairs. The stately, auburn haired young woman wore a brilliant emerald-green habit trimmed with heavy black ball fringe. "You certainly look the part of an equestrian," she told him, smiling. She was always careful to smile with her mouth closed because her teeth were not her best feature.

Lord Hugh's manservant had supplied Nicholas with a riding coat, buckskins, and a pair of very good boots. "Your father's valet is taking care of me," he said modestly.

"I do hope you tipped him well," she said, meaning it as a compliment.

"Oh, no," Nicholas sighed. "I didn't tip him at all. I didn't think of it. I'll do it now."

But Octavia was not about to let him go. "Never mind! You can do it later."

They walked out to the stables together, arriving just as Lord Colin Grey came strolling out of the building. He was looking at his watch, but as he caught sight of them, he hastily put it away.

"Oh, hullo!" he said, flexing a riding crop between his

gloved hands. "Going for a gallop, are we? You don't mind if I go with, do you?"

Colin was the last person Octavia would ever have expected to meet at the stables before noon. "Lord Colin," she exclaimed. "I'm afraid you would be bored! My cousin is a beginner."

"Oh, but I love beginners," said Colin. "And so does Julia."

Octavia stiffened. "Julia?"

"Yes," Colin told her, smiling. "She should be here any minute. Camford will have *three* very accomplished teachers this morning."

Nicholas frowned. "Didn't you tell me that none of your sisters ride?" he asked Octavia.

"Nonsense; Julia rides like a centaur," Colin answered before Octavia could. "Or is it a centauress? Is there such a thing as a female centaur?" he wondered.

"Possibly not," Octavia said coldly. "After all, there's no such thing as a centaur, period, is there?"

"You've obviously never been to Venice at Carnevale," Colin retorted.

"I meant none of my sisters who are Out," Octavia told Nicholas. "Julia is not Out. In any case, she is not here. There's no reason to wait for her, just because she has an appointment with Lord Colin."

"She's a tiny bit late, that's all," said Colin. "Be a dear little girl and go ask the stableboy to saddle Charmer for her. Go on, fair little maid! Obey your elders."

"Yes, Lord Colin," Octavia said angrily.

When she had gone, Colin put an arm across Nicholas's shoulders. "Nicholas, Nicholas," he said, shaking his head. "I'm surprised at you! Why, you're playing right into the she-wolf's hands. Or paws, as it were."

"What do you mean?" said Nicholas. "Who is a she-wolf?"

"Octavia! Honestly, sometimes I think you were born without a suspicious bone in your body. You'll end up married to that harpy, if you're not careful. You *must* know the moment Lord Michael jilted her, she set her cap for you."

"You are mistaken," Nicholas told him. "Lord Michael did not jilt her. There was never an engagement. And she hasn't set her cap for me," he added. "She's aware of my feelings for—for your sister."

Colin frowned. "Emma? But you must have noticed that *she* has gone cold on you. You didn't meet with her alone last night, did you? Did you?"

"Of course not," said Nicholas.

"I am sorry for you, Nicholas. But Emma's obviously tired of you. Not to worry, though. There are plenty more fish in the sea. Take Julia, for instance—"

Nicholas was laughing. "You've got it all wrong! Emma is not tired of me. Why, we're like two halves of one being."

"Indeed?" said Colin, a little startled. "Which half are you?"

"You jest, sir. Emma is still in mourning. We are determined to be discreet. I do my best not to even look at her, lest anyone suspect our true feelings."

"And what might those be?" Colin asked politely.

Nicholas blinked at him. "Why, that we are in love, of course. As soon as her period of mourning is up, we intend to be married."

"Married?" Colin echoed in blank astonishment. "To whom?"

"To each other, of course," said Nicholas.

"You and Emma?"

"Yes."

"But you can't marry Emma," Colin scoffed. "You have the pox."

Nicholas gaped at him. "What? No, I don't."

"Yes, you do," Colin insisted. "You're a sailor. All sailors have the pox."

"That is not true," Nicholas protested. "I believe in clean living."

Colin snorted. "A girl in every port, and any port in a storm. That's your motto. That's a sailor's idea of clean living."

"I resent that," said Nicholas.

"Well, I resent you aspiring to marry my sister when you have the pox!" said Colin.

"I do *not* have the pox," Nicholas said angrily.

"How do you know?"

Nicholas blinked at him. "What do you mean, how do I know? I *know*."

"You could have an exotic strain, a strain that is nothing like the pox you people usually get," said Colin. "Perhaps you got it from that girl in that tavern in Singapore."

"I've never been to Singapore."

"You're completely missing the point! The point is, you have the pox. Not that there's anything wrong with that," Colin added quickly. "Lots of people do. When one has congress with strange women, these things are bound to happen."

"But I don't have congress with strange women," Nicholas said flatly. "As an officer of the Royal Navy, it is my duty to set a good example for the crew. I am . . . untouched by a woman. It simply isn't possible that I could be infected."

"Good Lord," breathed Colin. "You mean you're a virgin?"

"Yes," Nicholas said simply.

"And you don't have the pox?"

"I do not. Now, I don't need your approval to marry Emma," Nicholas went on, "but you are her brother. I should like to have your approval."

"Well," said Colin. "If you don't have the pox, what objection could there be?"

"Thank you, sir," Nicholas said, as Octavia returned with a groom leading two mounts.

"Julia not yet arrived?" she said coolly. "Pity. Charmer wasn't available anyway. It looks as though we'll have to go without you, Lord Colin."

"Not at all," said Colin. "Julia's obviously forgotten the appointment. I'll ride with you. Fetch Bumblebee," he commanded the groom.

"Sorry, Lord Colin," the man replied. "Miss Augusta's taken Bumblebee."

"Miss Augusta?" Nicholas repeated in astonishment.

At that very moment, Augusta Fitzroy, mounted on a beautiful bay mare, came cantering at them from across the meadow. Woman and horse seemed melded into a single creature as they sailed easily over a boxwood hedge. Colin gave her a friendly wave with his hat, and Augusta obligingly guided her mount over to them.

Nicholas stared at Octavia in disbelief. "You lied!"

Although she would never be as pretty as her youngest sister, Augusta looked as well as she could on the back of her horse. Her dark eyes had been brightened by the exercise, and her color was high.

"Are you going riding, Cousin Nicholas?" she cried gaily. "I've just come from the meadow! You'll want to watch out for the rabbits!" Her mount turned in circles, eager to be off again, but Augusta seemed quite used to her antics. "Quiet, you brute!" she told the mare curtly, bringing her firmly under control. "A beautiful day, is it not? The air is so crisp!"

White with rage, Octavia clenched her fists. "Augusta, how dare you! I *told* you I was taking Cousin Nicholas for a ride. How dare you intrude on our appointment!"

Augusta stared at her blankly. "Intrude on your appointment? Don't be daft! *I* don't want to marry him. No offense, Cousin Nicholas," she quickly added, "but I don't want to marry anyone. I realized it quite forcibly when I met you."

"I'm glad I helped you realize it, Cousin Augusta," said Nicholas.

"Well, you did!" said Augusta. "You're so good-looking, you see. All my sisters were in such a state about you, but I felt nothing. Absolutely nothing, and *I* was the one who was supposed to marry you! I was ever so glad when Cousin Michael jilted Octavia, because it meant that I was reprieved. You see," she said earnestly, "*I* want to be like my Aunt Harriet."

Colin was fascinated. "Do you really, Miss Augusta? Why?"

Augusta leaned forward to pat the mare's neck. "Oh, I know she is poor, but she has her freedom. She is no one's property. And she gets to live here, at Warwick, all year round!"

"Only because no one wants her!" Colin protested.

"Lord Michael did not jilt me," Octavia spat.

"If you say so, Octopus!" Augusta said cheerfully. "Well, I'd better get Bumblebee back to the stables for her rubdown! She won't admit it, of course, but she's completely exhausted! Remember what I said about the meadow, Cousin Nicholas! Rabbit warrens everywhere! Best avoid it altogether, I say! Your horse could break a leg."

With that, she was off.

Octavia composed herself. "I will not be treated in this manner by anyone!" she said. "I must beg to return to the house."

Without a backward glance, she swept off toward the house.

"We are well rid of her, I think," said Colin.

"I cannot bear to think of a young woman telling lies!" said Nicholas. "I beg your pardon, Lord Colin, but I do not think I care to ride today. I must speak to my poor aunt about my cousin's behavior. I must speak to her at once."

With murmured apologies, he strode off.

"Take that, Aunt Harriet," Colin murmured to himself with a smile.

Earlier that morning, Lady Harriet had spied Julia leaving the house. Thinking quickly, she had grabbed a basket and run after the girl.

"Julia?" she had called after her. "Julia! Where do you think you're going?"

Julia stopped short of the shrubbery at the edge of the lawn. She was wearing a riding ensemble of royal blue. "Where does it look like I'm going, Aunt Harriet?" she said saucily, holding out both arms. "I'm going for a ride with Lord Colin."

"Nonsense," said Lady Harriet, hurrying across the lawn to claim her niece. "I need you to come with me to the kitchen garden. We're snipping herbs this morning. There was a shocking lack of fennel in the pantry this morning."

"You're hurting me, Aunt Harriet," Julia complained as her aunt twisted her arm.

Before Julia knew what was happening, she was in the little walled garden behind the kitchen with her aunt's basket over one arm and a set of shears in the other. "I'll be right back," said Lady Harriet, closing the iron gate behind her. "I'm just going to fetch my shawl. Get to work. You young girls today are so idle."

Julia waited but three or four minutes after her aunt's departure, listlessly decapitating a few stalks of mint and sage, before deciding to make a run for it.

To her annoyance, the gate proved to be locked. Vexed, Julia fetched the kitchen shears and attacked the lock. Attracted by the noise, a handsome young cavalry officer came around the corner and found her there, on her knees. Julia looked up as his shadow fell across the lock.

"Captain Palafox," she exclaimed happily. "My aunt has accidentally locked me in. I cannot get out."

Palafox chuckled. "Miss Julia! Perhaps I can help," he said, kneeling down. "I'm quite good with small openings, as it happens."

Julia had every hope of his success, and, in just a few moments, she was free.

"I was going for a ride," she told him, "before my aunt accidentally locked me in."

"I will walk with you, if I may," he said gallantly.

"I suppose that would be all right," she said, giving him a sly, sidelong look. "As long as Cousin Nicholas doesn't find out. He's fearfully jealous, you know."

"I am not surprised," said Palafox. "You must make conquests wherever you go."

Julia stared up at him, thrilled. "Why? Have I made a conquest of you?"

"Oh, yes, Miss Julia," he said huskily.

"My goodness!" said Julia. "I wasn't even *trying* to make a conquest of you! It's as if I have some strange, hypnotic power over the opposite sex, but I have not yet learned how to wield it properly."

Palafox looked around sharply for witnesses. Finding none, he led the young girl behind a hedge. Julia sat down on a small garden bench, trembling with anticipation.

"Are you very eager to learn, Miss Julia?" he asked her.

She looked up at him provocatively. "It would not be proper for me to learn," she answered, "until I am safely married."

"Oh? You mean to have lovers, then?"

"Sir!" she protested, fluttering her lashes at him. "My husband will be my teacher, of course."

"Oh, but husbands never teach their wives anything worthwhile. If you want to learn, Miss Julia—if you *really* want to learn—you're going to need a lover."

"Then I shall have one," she said, bright-eyed. "Why shouldn't I? Many married ladies do have lovers, after all. Look at the duchess! She is notorious for her affairs. They say she bore Lord Byron an illegitimate child, and they keep it hidden away somewhere in Italy."

"I had not heard that," he laughed. "I have only heard that

she is more skilled than any courtesan in the art of giving a man pleasure."

Julia squirmed in delight. "Who told you that?" she demanded breathlessly.

Smiling, he laid a finger across her lips. "That would be telling."

"Tell me!" she demanded, taking his hand. "Tell me, or I shall break your little finger!"

He laughed. "Shall I whisper in your ear?"

When she nodded eagerly, he put one boot on the bench next to her. Her pretty lips parted in anticipation, as his sleek head bent low.

Julia sighed happily. "I should like to be as skilled as a courtesan in the art of giving a man pleasure," she murmured.

"Julia!" cried a shocked voice.

Nicholas was the shocked man who went with the voice.

Julia jumped. "Cousin Nicholas!" she cried, guilty color spreading across her face. "Captain Palafox was just telling me the most delicious piece of gossip about the duchess!"

This revelation only made her cousin look angrier. "Where is your governess?" he demanded. "I'm beginning to think you don't have one! Never mind! Go back to the house at once! I am shocked, Julia! Shocked and grieved."

Julia stamped her foot. "At least *he* does not treat me like a child," she declared, her chin quivering as she fought back tears. "He treats me like a woman!"

Nicholas raised his hand threateningly. "By God, if you do not go back to the house this instant, I will put you over my knee and spank you!"

Her face dissolving in tears, she ran away.

"As for you, sir—" Nicholas began, turning to Captain Palafox. "This is the second time I have found you importuning my little cousin."

Palafox looked bored. "Importuning! I protest, my lord. I found the child locked in the kitchen garden. I rescued her from captivity. She told me she had an appointment at the stables. I was simply escorting her to her friends."

"You were almost kissing her!"

"It may have appeared that way, my lord," Palafox admitted. "She had something in her eye, and I was getting it out. Your lordship will excuse me."

Bowing, he left Nicholas. His excuses seemed so plausible that Nicholas almost wondered if they might be true. His first inclination was to trust the word of an officer, albeit an army officer. But he still did not trust the man.

"You're up very early," Emma remarked as Colin slipped into her room. Seated at her escritoire, she was writing letters. She looked at him over the tops of her spectacles. "Monty's been looking for you. What have you been up to?"

"You mustn't question me," he replied, sprawling on the sofa. "Ring for more chocolate, will you?" he said, after looking into the pot on the tray. "This stuff is curdled."

Impatiently, Emma set down her pen and rang the bell.

"Have you ever thought of marrying again?" Colin asked her.

"Lord, no," Emma replied with an astonished laugh. "Why should I?"

"No, reason," he said, moving his feet so the servant could take away the old tray. Since parting company with Nicholas at the stables, Colin's conscience had been troubling him. The poor man actually seemed to be in love with Emma, and he seemed to believe that his feelings were returned. This made Colin feel slightly guilty for having told Emma that Nicholas had the pox. "I was only wondering," he went on presently. "You wouldn't, say, want to marry young Camford, would you?"

Emma looked at him incredulously. "He has the pox."

"Yes, I know he has the pox," Colin said. "I'm the one

who told you he has the pox. What I'm asking is: if he didn't have the pox, would you marry him?"

"No, of course not. Colin, what is this about?" she demanded, her hands on her hips.

"Oh, nothing. Just a little wager I have going with Aunt Harriet."

Emma laughed. "She thinks I'm going to marry Nicholas? You should feel guilty, Colin, for taking an old lady's money."

"It's only ten shillings. And you're definitely not interested in Camford?"

"Not even if he weren't infected with the pox," said Emma, going back to her correspondence. "Aunt Harriet might as well pay you her ten shillings now. I think I can safely promise you that I shall never marry Lord Camford!"

Colin heaved a sigh of relief, and his conscience was clear.


"Whatever happened to fair play?" Lady Harriet lamented at tea that afternoon as Colin brought her cup.

"This from a woman who locked her own niece in the kitchen garden," Colin retorted.

"What about you?" she snapped back. "You did everything you could to spoil Octavia's chances. How dare you expose her lies? You are shameless, sir."

"I just happened to be going for a ride myself," Colin said loftily. "I just happened to meet Nicholas and Octavia at the stables."

"At eight o'clock?" she scoffed. "You never got up so early before, and you know it."

"All right," he said. "But you *locked* poor Julia in the garden! There is no comparison. You'll be drowning her in the lake next, I shouldn't wonder. That's one way to make sure he don't marry her!"

"I wouldn't actually *harm* the child," Lady Harriet said

indignantly. "I wouldn't have interfered at all, if you hadn't interfered first."

"Well, then, let us have a pact," Colin said reasonably. "No more interference. Shall we let nature take its course? There's an idea."

"Oh, yes?" she said angrily. "Now that you have completely spoiled Octavia's chances? Say what you will of *my* methods, but Julia may still get him if she applies herself. Thanks to you, Camford is now convinced that Octavia is a liar."

"She *is* a liar," Colin pointed out. "Oh, I don't want to quarrel with you, old woman," he added quickly. "We've always been friends, sort of." Reaching into his pocket, he brought out a gold coin. "Here's a guinea. Shall we call it even?"

Lady Harriet snatched it from him. "Considering I might have had seven hundred pounds . . ." she grumbled, tucking the coin into the decollete of her purple lace gown.

"What would *you* do with seven hundred pounds anyway?" he jabbed back, but his heart wasn't really in it. His steel-blue eyes were searching the room. "Now, where the devil is Monty?" he murmured. "I've not seen him all day. Do you see him?"

"These officers all look alike to me," sniffed Lady Harriet. "Their red coats and their fat necks. Perhaps your Scotsman has made a new friend," she suggested. "Perhaps you should have paid more attention to him instead of chasing after poor Octavia."

"It's not like him to miss his tea," Colin fretted. "He gets a sick headache if he misses his tea. I'd better go and see if he's all right."

Absently, he handed Lady Harriet his cup, and made his way out of the room.

He found Monty in his room, writing letters.

"Monty? Aren't you coming down for tea?" he called

curiously from the door. "We have those little cakes you like. Shall we risk going down together?" he added waggishly.

Monty would not look at him. "Something has happened. I have to go."

The door to his dressing room stood open and Colin could see Monty's man within, packing his master's trunks.

"You're leaving?" Colin said incredulously. "Why? What has happened?"

Monty set down his pen and sprinkled sand over the letter he was writing to absorb any excess ink. "My father's ill. I am called home."

Colin sat down on the chest at the foot of the bed. "I can always tell when you're lying, Monty," he said. "What aren't you telling me?"

Monty sprang up from the desk. "Very well," he said. "When I woke up this morning, *this* had been pushed under the door." He threw a screwed-up piece of paper at Colin.

Colin calmly smoothed it out and read it. "An anonymous warning," he observed contemptuously, "sent by some well-meaning soul, no doubt."

"No doubt!"

"'Lord Colin is a backgammon player. You have been warned,'" Colin read out loud before tossing the scrap of paper aside in disgust. "Oh, how tiresome! It's Eton all over again. I do hope you're not too shocked, dear boy," he added dryly.

"I certainly intend to make it look that way!" Monty replied grimly. "If this gets back to my regiment, I'm done for."

"They couldn't bring it to a trial," Colin scoffed. "There's no proof of anything."

"The chaps in my regiment won't bother themselves about proof," said Monty. "They'll just kill me in my sleep to preserve the honor of the regiment."

"Sell out, then, you goose! The war's over, anyway."

"You'd like me to sell out, wouldn't you?" Monty said bitterly.

"Look, don't panic. This is about *me*," said Colin. "I stand accused, not *you*. This charming letter says absolutely nothing about *you*. If you were suspected, would your well-wisher have sent you this friendly warning? No!"

"Lots of people got them, not just me. Oh, God! If my father hears of this, he'll cut me off without a penny."

Colin shrugged impatiently. "So what if he does? We'll go abroad. We'll go to Paris. The French are not such prudes. We wouldn't be treated like criminals there."

Monty set his jaw. "Go to Paris? With no money?"

"Don't be ridiculous, Monty," said Colin. "I've got plenty of money."

Monty shook his head angrily. "Oh, no. You're not going to pay my way."

"Why on earth not?"

"Because I am not one your boys," Monty said coldly.

He was gone within the hour.

# Chapter Eleven

"Who could have done such a cruel, cowardly thing?" Emma murmured, passing the note back to Otto that evening in her sitting room. "They are all over the house. Captain Palafox brought this one to me, but he said most of the officers got something similar. Will Colin be arrested, do you think?"

"On the basis of an anonymous note? I shouldn't think so," said Otto. "There's no proof of anything criminal. Is there?" he asked sharply, looking at his younger brother.

Colin walked about Emma's sitting room restlessly. "No, of course not. I'm always very careful. There's no proof of anything. We don't write letters, and I trust my servants completely."

"The servants are of no consequence," said Otto. "Their testimony would be meaningless in court."

"Maybe I should just leave," Colin pouted, looking at his siblings. "You don't really want me around. You don't accept me. Not really. You just pretend to. I know you're all really ashamed of me. You'll be glad when I'm gone."

Emma found his self-pity infuriating. "That's right, Colin," she snapped. "*We* wrote the letters! Otto and I were up all night, scribbling them out, left-handed to disguise our handwriting. Then we scurried all over the house, shoving them under doors like demented postmen! We have *always* stood by you. When one of us is attacked, we are all attacked. It's just a pity that your *friend* doesn't have more courage," she added scathingly.

"You don't know anything about Monty!" Colin shouted at her. "You don't know anything about anything! I'm leaving. I will go to Paris and spend Christmas gambling and drinking in the Palais Royal. In Paris, I can be *myself.*"

"Oh, spare me your self-pity," Emma called after him angrily as he made for the door. "Do you think you're the only person who's ever been forced to live a lie?"

Otto's calm voice stopped their brother at the door. "Colin, you cannot run away. If you leave now, it's as good as an admission of guilt, and it may be assumed you are going to meet Monteith. There will be consequences for *him,* if not for you."

"Oh, who cares about *him?*" cried Emma. "*He* ran away at the first sign of trouble. From this moment, I have no opinion of Lord Ian Monteith!"

"I believe our brother cares about him," Otto told her gently.

Colin flung himself down in a chair. "Perfect!" he said bitterly. "Just perfect. Happy Christmas to me. Stuck here with you lot!"

"Yes, we're fairly excited about it, too," Emma said dryly.

"I am going to find out who did this," Colin fumed, "and I am going to get him."

"Count me in," Emma said immediately. "Otto?"

"Revenge is a dish best served cold," said Otto.

"In that case, can we count on *you* to supply the ice?" said Emma.

"You don't think I'd let you two fools go about it on your own, do you?" he answered dryly. Parting his coat tails, he sat down and crossed his legs. "Get out your notebook, Emma, and let us convene this council of war."

Emma obediently opened her journal to a clean page.

"First, we identify the enemy," Otto began. "Then we formulate a plan to destroy him. Then we execute said plan."

"It was obviously General Bellamy," Colin said presently. "He became positively incensed on the subject of buggery last night."

Emma made a face. "But I know his ugly black scrawl," she said. "He wrote me a cheeky letter. I don't think he's clever enough to disguise his handwriting."

"And he was far too drunk to have accomplished anything last night," Otto pointed out. "It's obviously a woman."

Emma frowned at him. "Why do you say that?"

"Men are forthright. They favor the direct attack, preferably physical. A man would simply find Colin on his own and beat him to a pulp."

"That's how they did it at school, anyway," said Colin. "I don't remember anybody passing notes under doors at Eton."

"Quite," said Otto. "But women are deplorably sneaky. And it looks like a woman's handwriting to me."

Emma frowned, but she was unable to argue the point. "It would have to be someone who knows the house," she said. "None of these officers' wives have ever been here before."

"That leaves Aunt Susan, Aunt Harriet, and Aunt Anne," said Otto.

"It could have been Octavia," said Colin. "We quarreled this morning at the stables."

"Did you?" said Emma. "But the letters would have been delivered sometime last night. She could not have predicted that you would quarrel with her the following morning."

"True," he said. "Well, it must be Aunt Susan, then. Aunt Harriet is a friend of mine, and poor Anne wouldn't say boo to a goose." Colin's steel-blue eyes glinted. "Now, then," he said. "What are we going to do about it?"

* * *

The duchess was very late in arriving for dinner that evening, and the company went in to the banquet hall like a pack of hungry wolves. Colin sat between Lady Harriet and his sister-in-law, Lady Scarlingford. Cecily's nervous laughter drifted down the room. To Emma's left, Captain Palafox kept up a stream of easy banter, while farther down the table, Otto conversed in his careful, perfect French with Lady Michael. Nicholas divided his attention between Lady Susan and Mrs. Camperdine, the wife of General Bellamy's quartermaster. Nothing unpleasant took place until the ladies withdrew.

"Shouldn't you retire with the other ladies, Lord Colin?" General Bellamy began at once. "Lord Colin Buggerbum, that's what you are, from what I hear!"

He sniggered, vastly pleased with his witticism. Hardly anyone laughed, and more gentlemen than usual left the room for the privy.

"Just ignore him," Otto quietly advised his brother. "Whatever the provocation."

"I am looking forward to my first riding lesson, Lord Colin," Nicholas said. "Her grace assures me that I cannot get along in the country unless I learn all about horses. Would tomorrow morning be convenient for you?"

Colin shrugged. "I seem to have plenty of free time," he said dryly. "If you're sure you still want me for a teacher," he added. "Or didn't you get a letter?"

"I did," said Nicholas, "and a number of these officers were good enough to share theirs with me as well."

Lord Hugh cleared his throat delicately. "Perhaps, Nephew, it would be better if one of your cousins were to give you lessons. All my girls are excellent riders."

"But what does your nephew want with a girl, Hugh?" snorted the general. "He's a bloody navy man."

Lord Hugh glared at his brother-in-law. "You go too far, Bellamy," he complained.

"You don't care if the boy's a shirt-lifter, as long as he marries one of your ugly daughters," the general retorted.

"Let's just finish our port and rejoin the ladies, shall we?" Lord Michael interrupted.

"But there *is* a lady among us!" cried General Bellamy. "That's what I've been trying to tell you! She wants a good bumming, too, unless I miss my guess."

"Uncle Bellamy, you're drunk," Lord Michael snapped. "As loathe as I would be to aggrieve my Aunt Susan, if you cannot keep a civil tongue in your head, I shall have to ask you to leave Warwick."

"But don't you care that there is a pederast among us?" the general bawled. "You arouse my suspicions, Lord Michael. Indeed, you do! What possible reason could you have for wanting someone like that around? Hmmm? You do not answer me, sir!"

"You remind me of a mate we had on board when I was a midshipman on the *Redoubtable*," Nicholas said suddenly. "He had buggery on the brain, I think. He went about accusing everyone of having indecent relations with everybody else."

"He was probably right," snarled the general. "That's the Royal Navy for you."

"As it happens, he was only trying to deflect suspicion from himself," Nicholas answered calmly. "One night, we caught him trying to rape the cabin boy. Turns out, *he* was the only danger we had on board. We hanged him off the yardarm and buried him at sea. Now, whenever I hear someone going on and on about buggery, I can't help but think of him, and wonder."

The general glared at him helplessly. "What are you implying, sir?"

"Shall we rejoin the ladies?" Lord Michael said quickly.

* * *

"What happened?" Emma demanded of Colin, when the gentlemen joined the ladies in the drawing room a little later. She was sitting a little apart from the others with Cecily. The general went immediately to the card tables set up at the back of the room, and surrounded himself with his officers. "The general looks as though he's about to have an apoplexy!"

"He is rather puce," Colin said smugly. "But your young man put him in his place."

"Captain Palafox?" Emma said incredulously. "I would have thought Charles much too politic to antagonize a superior officer!"

"O faithless one," Colin chided her. "I refer to lovesick young Camford, of course. *He* defended my honor most admirably. Though I can't help but think that, if you were not my sister, he'd like to see me and all my kind hanged off the yard-axe or whatever it is."

Quickly, he told her about the unpleasant exchange that had taken place over port.

"That was very good of Nicholas," Emma admitted. "It's a pity he has the pox."

"I suppose I ought to tell you," Colin said slowly. "He doesn't actually have the pox."

Emma opened her fan and spoke behind the Italian scene painted on its silk-covered silver blades. "You mean he's cured?"

"No. He never had it."

"But you *told* me he had the pox," Emma reminded him.

"Ixnay on the oxpay," said Colin. "Croft was mistaken."

Emma frowned. "How do we know he isn't mistaken now when he says Nicholas doesn't have the pox."

"When I say that Croft was mistaken, what I mean is that I lied."

"You *lied?*" Emma echoed in disbelief.

"I made the whole thing up," he clarified.

"Colin, how could you lie about something like that?"

"I had a bet going with Aunt Harriet," he explained. "But that's all over now. He's clean as the proverbial whistle. In fact, he's a virgin."

Emma stared at him. "A what?"

"Are you so far gone that you don't even *remember* what a virgin is?" Colin teased her.

"This is ridiculous," said Emma, fanning herself rapidly. "He's been all over the world."

"But not to Singapore."

"What does *that* mean?" Emma demanded.

"It *means* that *you* could be the lucky lady who *takes* him to Singapore," Colin said. "Metaphorically speaking, of course."

Emma sighed. "Oh, I don't know. I've moved on, Colin. There's Charles to think of now. From the moment he arrived, he has devoted himself to me. It wouldn't be fair to throw him over. It'd break his heart."

Colin gave a loud snort. "Let me tell you about your friend Palafox! He's been caught twice in as many days making love to little Julia Fitzroy. If Nicholas hadn't caught them this morning, Palafox would probably have ravished her in the shrubbery!"

Emma laughed incredulously. "Oh, yes! And, I suppose, he has the pox as well?"

"Ask Nicholas if you don't believe me."

Emma snapped her fan closed. "Perhaps I will ask him now," she threatened.

"I dare you," Colin responded with a shrug.

Nicholas was sitting in a quiet corner of the room playing chess with Otto. "Cecily wants you," Emma told her elder brother, walking up to them. When Otto had gone, she sat down in his place. "Is it my turn?" she asked Nicholas.

"Are you sure it's safe for us to be together like this?" he whispered. "People are looking."

"I'm sure it's very dangerous," she answered. "But I feel reckless this evening."

Taking up the white knight, she moved it diagonally across the board until it collided with the white bishop on the other side of the board.

Nicholas smiled. "That is not how a knight moves, ma'am," he told her. "And you cannot take your own man. Not if you want to win."

"Is that so? Otto has taught you well."

"But I already knew how to play," he told her. "I often played with my captain."

She smiled faintly. "At sea? But don't the pieces slide all over the place?"

"Not at all. I carved the pieces with little pegs on the bottom, and drilled little holes in the chessboard."

"And the little pegs fit in the little holes, do they? How ingenious. But I didn't come here to talk to you about chess," she went on. "I have been hearing the cruelest gossip about poor Captain Palafox."

Nicholas's eyes lit up with anger. "Poor Captain Palafox, indeed!" he said angrily.

"Lower your voice. Go on!" she urged him, as he obeyed her with complete silence.

"Emma, that man is not to be trusted," he whispered. "Yesterday, I caught him in my room with Julia. I told her she was not yet sixteen, but his interest in her was undiminished. This afternoon, I found them together again in the shrubbery. They appeared to be very . . . intimate. He gave me some story about her having something in her eye, but I—I do not like to accuse an officer of lying, of course . . ."

"I see," Emma said, tight-lipped with anger. "Something in her eye."

"If he were not a friend of Lord Michael's, I think I would be obliged to challenge him."

"I will speak to my brother-in-law about his friend's behavior," said Emma.

"I did want to warn you about him," said Nicholas. "He seemed to be flattering you at dinner. I should have known you would see right through him."

"Of course," said Emma. With a wave of her hand, she dismissed the subject of Palafox completely. "Where's your queen?" she asked Nicholas curiously, looking at the board. "Or don't you have one?"

"Your brother has taken it," he answered. "But I am not at all worried. I will get her back when my pawn crosses the board. Then I shall checkmate him in two moves. There's really nothing he can do about it. But he thinks he can still win."

Emma picked up the white queen from where it stood beside the chessboard, on Otto's side. "If you want her back," she said, tucking the piece between her breasts, "you may come to my room tomorrow, at the stroke of midnight."

"Emma!" he protested, blushing.

"People are staring," she said, rising from her brother's chair. "I'd better go before they start *talking*."

"But I cannot win the game without my queen!"

"Just as well you will have to forfeit," she answered. "Otto is a very poor loser. Beat him at chess, and you'll never be his friend."

She had scarcely returned to her place at Colin's side when Lady Susan was upon them.

"I sincerely hope you are not pining for the loss of Lord Ian Monteith," she began, smiling archly.

Colin glared up at her. "I am enduring it the best I can, Aunt Susan."

"But I was talking to your sister, of course," Lady Susan tittered. "At least, we all *supposed* it was dear Emma to whom he was so devoted! Such a fine young man," she went on. "He seemed so reliable, too! I *had* hoped to get him for one of my poor little nieces, but I fear they are not as attractive as my girls. I wonder, *what* could have made him go away so suddenly? Trouble at home, was it? I trust his father is well?"

"I'm afraid we don't know anything more about it than you do, Aunt Susan," Emma answered firmly, placing a restraining hand on her brother's arm.

"I'm sure it had *nothing* to do with those dreadful letters going around," Lady Susan said smugly. "Who could have done such a thing?"

This was too much for Colin. "You know perfectly well who did it, you nasty old cow," he told her. "But don't worry. You'll get yours. We Greys do not take these things lying down, you know."

Lady Susan blinked at him. "You don't think that *I* had anything to do with it, do you? Anonymous letters? I prefer to be recognized for all my hard work."

She laughed heartily. "Besides, why should I care if you're a poof or whatever it is you call it. Some of them are very talented people—not *you*, of course, Lord Colin—but the man who makes my corsets is an absolute genius. And, then there's Mr. Grigg, in London, who makes the most wonderful hats. And, of course, the theaters would all be empty if it weren't for you people, and I do love the theater. If you *really* want to know who's behind these nasty letters, just ask Harriet."

Lady Harriet was at the back of the room playing cards.

"I don't believe you," said Colin. "Why would Aunt Harriet do such a thing? We've always been good friends."

"It's a case of the green-eyed monster, I'm afraid," said Lady Susan. "Ridiculous, I know, but how else do you explain it? Spinsterhood can do strange things to a woman. She had to get rid of your Scotsman because she wants you all to herself."

Colin was staring at Lady Susan, almost paralyzed by horror. "Are you saying that Aunt Harriet is in love with me?" he yelped.

"You are the wayward child she never had, and never will have."

"So you're saying it's a maternal sort of thing?" To Colin, this seemed even less likely than the alternative. Lady Harriet seemed not to have a maternal bone in her body.

"Take her pulse on the subject, if you don't believe me. Invite her to take a turn about the room with you. I'll take her place at the card table."

"Go on," said Emma. "I *dare* you."

Lady Harriet was delighted to take a turn about the room with Lord Colin. "You've rescued me just in time, dear boy," she told him happily, giving his arm a squeeze. Colin could have dispensed with the familiarity, but he was nowhere near to giving credit to Lady Susan's assertions. "Now Susan will have to cover my losses," she added gleefully.

"Who will cover my loss, I wonder," Colin murmured as they began their promenade down one side of the room.

"Why, have you suffered a loss?" she inquired solicitously.

"Surely, you noticed that my friend, Lord Ian, is no longer with us."

"Really? I hadn't noticed," said Lady Harriet, shrugging. "But I daresay we can do very well without the likes of him. He wasn't worthy of you, dear boy." Her skinny hand patted Colin's arm fondly. "There was a littleness to him. I trust you see it now."

Colin stopped in his tracks. "Aunt Susan was telling the truth, then," he whispered.

Lady Harriet's ginger-brown eyes narrowed. "Susan? What has *she* been telling you?"

"That you hated Monty," he hissed at her. "That you'd do anything to get rid of him. That it was *you* who wrote those beastly letters! Do you deny it?"

"Why should I deny it?" she answered coolly. "Monty, Monty, Monty! I am sick to death of Monty! Yes, I hate him. You were always so attentive to your Aunt Harriet, before he came along. But then you changed! You'd speak to me, but always, *always,* your eyes would be searching the crowd— for *him,* the loathsome beast. I could tell at once he wasn't worthy of you, Colin. He proved as much by walking out on you. We're well rid of him, my darling," she added, patting his arm with her skinny hand. "Now that it's just the two of us again, everything is going to be just perfect."

She sighed contentedly.

"I will never forgive you for this, old woman," he said coldly, breaking free of her.

"Oh, my poor little lamb," she said soothingly. "In time you'll see that I was right. You cannot stay angry with your Aunt Harriet forever."

"Shall we wager on it?" he said coldly, going back to his sister. "Aunt Susan was right," he told her. "Aunt Harriet is guilty."

"Then we know what to do," Emma said grimly.

It was not until the following evening, at dinner, that Charles Palafox realized he had been banished. No longer was he seated at the duchess's elbow. Instead, he had been pushed almost to the opposite end of the table, sandwiched between Octavia and Augusta Fitzroy. It was not difficult to guess that someone had told Emma of his dealings with Julia Fitzroy.

Thwarted, Captain Palafox felt himself to be the victim. Never had he sought out Julia's company, after all. On the first occasion, he had found her in his room. On the second, he had discovered her, quite by accident, locked in the kitchen garden. He wrote letters to Emma, pleading his case, but they were all sent back to him unopened.

\* \* \*

To Emma's annoyance, Nicholas was late to the rendezvous, but he burst into her bedchamber in such a desperate hurry that she instantly forgave him. She greeted him from her bed, dressed to please him in a beautiful negligee of pale blue silk trimmed with silver ribbons, her ash-brown hair arranged in long, loose ringlets. He went straight to her, kneeling by the bed and seizing her hand. "My love, what is the matter? Are you ill?"

Emma laughed at his panic. "Don't be silly," she murmured languidly, caressing his cheek with the back of her hand. "I am not ill. Why would you think so?"

"You are in bed," he pointed out. "Did you not ask me to meet you here?"

"I am not ill," she told him firmly. "I am free. My year of mourning is over. It ended at the stroke of midnight. I am yours . . . if you still want me, of course," she added provocatively.

She heard him swallow hard. "Would—would you not rather wait?" he said nervously.

"I *have* waited," she reminded him. "If you ask me, I've been awfully good about it. I am not known for my patience. But I've suffered enough for you, I think. Now I must have satisfaction."

"You shall have it then," he promised. He kissed her clumsily in the near dark, his hands falling heavily on her shoulders, rather like a pair of leaden weights. He was shaking like a lamb suddenly confronted by the wolf.

Emma resigned herself to having to perform the lion's share of the work. "Shall I undress you?" she whispered, reaching for him. "Shall I be your valet tonight as well as your lover?"

He seemed to take this as some form of rebuke. Instantly,

he sprang to his feet. "Not at all, my love. I can do it. You need not trouble yourself."

He danced around the room on one leg as he pulled off first one boot, then the other. Realizing she was missing the entertainment, Emma sat up and lit a candle. Half out of his shirt, he froze. "W-what are you doing?"

"I want to see you," she explained. "I want to see my beautiful young man. And doesn't *he* want to see *me?* Don't you want to look deep into my adoring eyes as we give one another the supreme pleasure?"

"Good God, no!" He looked quite shocked. His round eyes glowed in the candlelight like a frightened animal's.

"You have some other idea?" Emma asked curiously.

"My love," he said earnestly. "I would never ask you to do anything so degrading, so unworthy of your—your elegant womanhood."

"N-no?" Emma was quite surprised. "My God! Is it true that you are a virgin?"

"Of course," he said indignantly. "I would not be worthy of your love if I had defiled myself with other women."

"In that case, I'd say it's high time you were defiled," she purred, sliding toward him. "Let me show you how."

"Absolutely not, my love," he said sternly. "Now, Emma, I know that your husband was a depraved man. I know he hurt you. The last time we were alone together—when you started to do those shameful things to me—I realized that *he* must have forced you to service him in that disgusting, intimate manner, as if you were some back-alley creature. Oh, Emma, my queen, my angel! *I* will never make such demands of you. You need not do anything at all. I take full responsibility. You are blameless in the act. The sin is all mine."

To complete her astonishment, he blew out the candle.

"When it is over, you will think it was a dream," he promised.

\* \* \*

"And was it?" Colin asked her the next morning over cups of chocolate. "Was it like a dream?"

Emma sat curled up on her sofa, grumpy and unspeakably sore.

"Come on, Emma," he coaxed. "Let me live vicariously through you. I'm all alone now, you know."

"It *was* like a dream," Emma said. "A bloody awful dream! A nightmare!"

He winced. "As bad as that? As bad as Byron?"

"Worse than Byron," she said emphatically. "At least with Byron, it was over and done in the blink of an eye, and his little tiny affair hardly even made an impression. *This* was a massacre and a marathon."

"If it were done when 'tis done, then 'twere well it were done quickly," Colin quoted.

"He was plenty quick," she retorted. "He just kept doing it over and over again. I was killed repeatedly by this fool. It was abundantly clear he hadn't a clue what he was doing."

"So he *was* a virgin?"

"Lord, yes! But that is no excuse for what he put me through," said Emma. "I hung on, just to see how long he could go, and how much I could endure, but, after about the eighth crises, I confess I gave up. I simply closed my eyes and placed my thoughts in a better place while he hammered away at me like a battering ram. I almost felt sorry for him."

"My dear girl! If you had eight crises, what the devil are you complaining about?"

"*He* had eight," she explained bitterly. "Or thereabouts. *I* had none. I can barely walk, I'm so sore. Just because the damn thing *looks* like a truncheon doesn't mean it ought to be *used* as a truncheon!"

"That's always been my motto. But why didn't you speak up for yourself?"

Emma shrugged. "He was so proud of himself, I didn't have the heart to tell him what a disaster he was. He really *did* try his best, you know, and he was so grateful to me afterward. I can't remember the last time a man actually *thanked* me for my 'sacrifice.' Then again, I've never actually *felt* like a sacrifice before."

"Are you going to let him try again?" Colin asked, laughing.

"Not bloody likely! My poor elegant womanhood has suffered enough, I think."

"You could teach him, Emma."

"Not interested," she said firmly. "Anyway, I'm not sure he *can* be taught. He has some very strange ideas about women. Apparently, we are angels, and angels do not take matters into their own hands, so to speak. We are to lie there, silent and immaculate, while the man knocks about in search of the correct opening."

Colin winced. "How dreadful for you. But, perhaps, Captain Palafox can console you."

Emma made a face. "Do you know," she said dully, "I think I've lost my appetite for men. *All* men."

"Oh, no. It's finally happened."

"What?"

"You are officially a matron," he teased.

He meant to rile her up, but, to his surprise, she sighed. "Do you know, I think you could be right," she said sadly.

"You know some people say there's more to life than sex," Colin remarked.

"Well," Emma sighed, "let us hope they are right."

For his part, Nicholas had never been so happy. That evening at dinner, as the consomme was being removed, he scraped back his chair and got to his feet.

"To the duchess," he said, raising his glass, "for she has

made me the happiest of men. In fact, she has agreed to be my wife. We are to be married!"

Blushing with pride and joy, he looked into the faces of the other guests. They stared back at him in blank astonishment. No one was more astonished than Colin Grey, except possibly his sister. All the color had drained from Emma's face.

Lord Michael Fitzroy found his voice first. "May I be the first to congratulate you, my lord. Your grace," he said, looking question marks at his sister-in-law.

"No!" said Emma.

Nicholas laughed. "My dearest love, if he wants to congratulate us, we should hear him out, I think."

"How dare you!" she breathed. Two spots of harsh, bright color appeared in her cheeks, spreading rapidly over her entire face. "Sit down."

"I forbid it!" cried Lord Hugh Fitzroy, starting up from his chair. "My nephew is not yet of age, madam. He cannot wed without my permission, and I certainly do not give it!"

"I shall be twenty-one in a few months!" said Nicholas, ironically sounding far, far younger than his actual age as he protested.

"There will not be the least need for you to exercise your authority as this young man's guardian," Emma coldly told Lord Hugh. "We are *not* engaged. I have *not* agreed to be his wife. I have not the *slightest* idea of what he is talking!"

"Emma!" cried Nicholas, both horrified and bewildered by her strange reaction.

"Sit down, Lord Camford," Emma said sharply. "I do not like your joke."

"Joke? What do you mean?" Nicholas's face was ashen.

Emma was furious. "What do *I* mean, sir? What do *you* mean by announcing an engagement between ourselves? You know perfectly well there is no such thing in existence."

"Emma! H-how can you say that, after—after—well, you

know, *after*. After all we have meant to each other," he finished lamely, inadvertently choosing a euphemism well known to everyone present. "We are in love."

"Sir!" Emma interrupted him coldly. "Are you drunk?"

His mouth worked helplessly. "Why are you doing this to me?" he whispered.

Emma glared at him. "Uncle Hugh!" she said sharply. "Your nephew obviously is drunk! Kindly remove him from my table, or I will have him carried out by my footmen."

Lord Hugh went around the table and took Nicholas by the arm.

"Come, Nephew," he said gruffly.

Almost in shock, Nicholas allowed himself to be led from the room.

When they had gone, Emma took a deep, cleansing breath. Reaching for the golden bell that rested next to her plate, she shook it violently to summon the next course.

# Chapter Twelve

With a wave of his hand, Lord Hugh sent the servants from the smoking room. Nicholas scarcely noticed them, he was so upset. "How could she do this to me?" he demanded, anger quickly replacing his surprise and humiliation. "She told me we would be together. I thought . . . We only waited to make the announcement until her year of mourning was over."

Lord Hugh snorted. "Mourning! Emma Grey doesn't know the meaning of the word. When her husband died, there was scarcely a pause in her . . . activities. I *am* sorry for you, Nicholas, but, considering her reputation, you cannot have expected any better!"

"What reputation?" Nicholas wanted to know.

Lord Hugh stared at him. "Dear boy, you must have heard about Emma Grey! She is the most notorious jade in England! The country, and, indeed, all of Europe, is littered with her former lovers. We are obliged to tolerate her presence *here,* for my nephews' sake, but, I assure you, when we are in London, we do not know her. No respectable lady will receive her, apart from her sister-in-law, Lady Scarlingford."

Nicholas drove his fingers through his hair. "Lady Susan

tried to warn me, but I refused to listen. Why didn't *you* tell me, Uncle?"

Lord Hugh blinked at him. "But I assumed you knew. You must have heard the stories about the Duchess of Warwick. She has been steeped in scandal all her life."

"Uncle, I have been at sea for most of my life," Nicholas reminded him. "How could I have heard anything? I know only that she told me she loved me."

"That harlot loves only herself," Lord Hugh said scathingly. "Men are playthings to her. I am sorry to cause you more pain, Nicholas, but . . . are you not well rid of her? Now that you know what she is, she can do you no more harm."

"I can't believe she feels nothing for me," Nicholas said stubbornly. "I must speak to her. There must be some explanation for this . . . this horrible change in her. I must know why . . . in what way I have offended her. I . . . I shall go mad if I do not speak to her."

Lord Hugh stared at him in alarm. "Her hold over you is strong, indeed! Let me break it for all time. Emma Grey is a modern-day Messalina! I know for a fact she has at least one bastard secreted amongst her brother's brood."

Nicholas's face was white. "*That* I cannot believe."

"I have a letter that proves it," Lord Hugh told him. "I will show it to you, and the scales will fall from your eyes! She is an immoral and unscrupulous woman. She never cared for you, Nicholas. She was only using you. That is what she does: she uses men to get what she wants. Why, she only took up with you in the first place to blackmail *me!*"

Nicholas swung around to look at his uncle. "Blackmail you? What do you mean?"

"She threatened to seduce you. Then she offered to 'give you back' if I let her see her sons. Of course, she wants her letter back, too. She actually had the gall to offer me money," Lord Hugh went on, assuming an air of injury. "Naturally,

I refused. As if *I* could be bribed or bullied by this common strumpet!"

"If you *let* her see her sons?" Nicholas repeated, shocked. "Are you—Uncle, are you keeping her children from her? Please tell me I am wrong!"

Lord Hugh frowned. "It sounds heartless, I know," he said quickly. "But I am their guardian, Nicholas. It is my duty to protect my great-nephews from unwholesome influences. Though it is hard, I take my duty very seriously," he added virtuously.

Nicholas was deeply shaken. "She must have wanted to see her children very badly," he murmured, the words dripping with bitterness, "to take up with *me*. I hope it was not too unpleasant for her."

Lord Hugh shook his head sadly. "I did my best to protect you, Nicholas. The harlot agreed to leave you alone if I let her have her children for Christmas, but I see she has reneged on our agreement. Her lascivious nature has overruled the maternal instinct."

He would have touched Nicholas, but Nicholas shook him off, his lip curled in contempt. "I think you have it backwards, Uncle. I think it was *you* who was blackmailing the duchess! As for protecting *me,* you did not want her to interfere in your plans for me, that is all."

Lord Hugh gave a display of bewilderment. "Plans? What plans? Nephew, I do not know what this wicked woman has told you, but, I can assure you—"

"You cannot assure me, sir," Nicholas interrupted him. "Since the moment you heard of my existence, you have been plotting to trap me into marrying one of your daughters! Admit it!"

"Trap you? My dear boy, nothing could be further from the truth. However, if you have fallen in *love* with one of the girls—"

"Oh, God! I must leave here at once," said Nicholas,

moving swiftly to the door. "She must be wishing me gone—gone to the devil!"

Lord Hugh ran after him. "Nicholas! You must not let Emma Grey drive you away from your family. It's the holidays! Families should be together."

Nicholas turned on him. "Oh? Does that not include a mother and her children?"

"Dear boy!"

Nicholas had almost torn the door from its hinges in his eagerness to leave the room, but the endearment stopped him in his tracks. "I am not your dear boy," he said coldly. "And I am sick of listening to your self-serving lies! Understand me, sir, there is not the least chance that I will *ever* marry any of your daughters! I am leaving this place, and I hope never to see *any* of you again."

Lord Hugh's expression hardened. "You cannot leave, Nicholas. I will not permit you to take any of the duke's vehicles or horses or servants. You have no transportation of your own! Unless you propose to *steal* from his grace, the Duke of Warwick—"

"I have my feet, sir," Nicholas told him. "I will walk to the nearest village and take the stagecoach. Where I go and how I get there is really none of your concern."

Lord Hugh tried a more conciliatory tone. "None of my concern? Nicholas, how can you say so? I am your uncle and your guardian and—I hope—your true friend. You are upset, dear . . . er . . . nephew. You are not thinking clearly. At least wait until morning."

Nicholas laughed dryly. "It was not my idea to stumble around in the dark, sir. I will leave at first light." He left the room with a quick stride.

Lord Hugh ran after him. "I am persuaded that, upon a period of reflection, you will change your mind," he called desperately. "Of course, if you still wish to leave in the morning, we will go with you. You should not be alone at a time like this!"

"Are you not afraid the roads will be unpassable?" Nicholas said sarcastically. "Your blizzard is long overdue, sir."

"Nephew, I forbid you to go!" Lord Hugh's voice was shrill.

Nicholas's eyes narrowed as he turned slowly to face his uncle. "You *forbid* me?" he said quietly. "Are you my master? Am I your servant?"

Lord Hugh cowered in fear as the young man advanced on him, but, after a moment, Nicholas only glared at him with contempt, turned on his heel, and continued down the hall alone.

After dinner, the most uncomfortable dinner of her life, Emma retreated to her sitting room with her brothers and her sister-in-law. "Good God!" she ejaculated, throwing herself down on the damask sofa.

Colin brought her a large brandy. "I told you this would happen," he said. "I told you Nicholas would fall madly in love with you, and you wouldn't be able to get rid of him."

Emma looked at him incredulously. "No, you didn't!"

"That was remiss of me," Colin apologized. "I should have said something. It was fairly obvious where this thing was going. Your plan was flawed from the beginning, Emma."

"Obvious! Was it obvious that he was going to tell to the world we're engaged?"

"Was it a *secret* engagement?" Cecily asked curiously.

"There was no engagement!" cried Emma.

"You really ought to have told *him* that," said Colin.

"We never even discussed marriage," Emma said resentfully.

Seating himself on the sofa, Otto brought out his snuff-box. "The sensible thing would have been to accept the engagement, at least until Harry and Grey were returned to you, Emma. You could have broken it off later."

"I am not that cruel," Emma said indignantly.

"Then perhaps you should not have taken him to bed," Otto suggested harshly.

Emma glared at Colin. "What makes you think I took him to bed, Otto?"

"No, Colin didn't tell me," said Otto. "He didn't have to. It was perfectly apparent that the two of you were on terms of intimacy. You took him to bed, and, fool that he is, he thought it meant something."

"Well, he's obviously a lunatic," Emma said angrily. "I never said I would marry him. This is not my fault, Otto."

"Blame is beside the point," Otto said impatiently. "Emma, this will complicate things with Hugh Fitzroy. You promised to leave Camford alone in exchange for your children and your letter. Instead, you seduced the boy."

"I did *not* seduce him," Emma argued.

"Again, you miss the point," Otto snapped. "You have placed your children at risk—all three of them. For what? A tumble with some young idiot you don't even want to marry? Have you no self-control?"

"Otto!" Cecily cried in dismay.

Emma sprang to her feet, trembling with rage. "I did not place my children at risk!" she shouted at him. "Why should I not take a lover if that is my wish? How dare you! It is Hugh! Hugh is using them as pawns against me. You should be angry at *him*."

"And you were using *my nephew* as a pawn!" said Lord Hugh, bursting into the room. "But you have made a false move, my dear."

Emma spun around. It seemed useless to complain that he was invading her privacy. "You cannot possibly believe that I would agree to marry Nicholas!" she protested.

"I don't know what promises you made him," Lord Hugh replied bitterly. "But you have ruined my plans, Emma Grey. I warned you what would happen if you crossed swords with me. You will leave this house in the morning, and never return. And you can take your unnatural brother with you. He is no more a fit companion for two impressionable young boys than you are."

"If you are implying," Colin said coldly, "that I am a danger to my own nephews—"

Emma held up her hand. "You cannot make me leave Warwick, Hugh. I have dower rights. And I have the right to invite anyone I choose. This is my son's house, not yours."

"No, I cannot make you leave," he agreed. "But I have the power to keep Harry and Grey away. As long as you are under this roof, madam, I will. The choice is yours. Either you quit Warwick on the morrow, or your sons will spend Christmas alone, locked in a room somewhere, under guard like criminals."

"Now, look here!" Otto began irritably.

"You would not dare!" said Emma. "You have already announced that they are coming home. You cannot go back on your word."

"People will now understand why I am so determined to keep them away from you."

"I will tell Nicholas that you have been stealing from the estate!"

"It matters not," said Lord Hugh. "He will find out soon enough, and, since he won't be marrying any of my daughters, thanks to you, my ruin is certain. Very likely, he will throw me into prison. But if I am headed for a fall, then you, my dear, are in for a plummet."

"Why, you—you horrid old man!" cried Cecily. "Otto! Can't you do something?"

"What do you suggest?" Otto said coldly.

"But, Hugh, I am not engaged to Nicholas," Emma protested. "He is free to marry anyone he chooses!"

"You made him fall in love with you," Lord Hugh accused her. "He is too brokenhearted to even think of marrying anyone else. You have ruined my life, madam, and I intend to return the favor."

"You forget one thing," said Otto. "Once your crime is exposed, you will be removed as guardian to my nephews. Then you will not be able to keep my sister from her children."

"I don't care about the future," Lord Hugh said recklessly. "Harry and Grey are in my power now. And so is your little bastard, my dear," he told Emma. "I want you to hurt."

"I will pay you," Emma said suddenly. She was already walking to her writing desk. "What was the sum you wanted? Ten thousand pounds? You could leave the country. With ten thousand pounds, you could live like a king in America. You need not fear prison."

"I don't want your money," said Lord Hugh. "I want you to suffer. If you do not leave here in the morning, I will expose your daughter. If your brother does not go with you, I will expose your daughter. Oh, and, if anything unpleasant should happen to me in the night—if I should die unexpectedly, say—my attorney will know what to do!"

They could only watch helplessly as he strutted from the room.

"He's bluffing," Emma said. "When did Hugh Fitzroy ever say no to money?"

"It seems you have underestimated his anger," said Otto.

Cecily rushed to Emma's side. "Don't worry, Emma! Otto will think of something."

"With any luck, he'll fall down the stairs and break his neck," said Colin.

Otto shook his head. "As long as he has Emma's letter, we must pray for his safety. Cecily, my dear," he went on, "I think you should go to bed. I must speak to my sister. You should not hear what I have to say."

Cecily protested, but Otto's was the stronger personality. When she had gone, Emma faced her eldest brother defiantly.

"Well, Otto? You were right. I was wrong, as usual. Feel free to triumph over me, now that I am beaten and helpless."

"This is no time to feel sorry for yourself, Emma," Otto said curtly. "If this is to be our last night at Warwick, then it is our last chance to take revenge. We have a lot of work to do."

Colin's eyes lit up. "Aunt Harriet?"

Otto nodded. "It will have to be tonight, I'm afraid. You remember the plan?"

"It's seared into my memory like the sacred flame," Colin replied. "The large sack is in my room."

"Good."

"But have we decided on that plan absolutely?" Emma protested. "She is an old woman, you know. What if she should die of fright?"

"Nonsense!" said Colin. "She's made of old boots and rusty saw blades. She's tough as a rat."

"I think we should go with *my* idea," Emma said stubbornly. "Not as brutal, perhaps, but quite seriously nasty."

"Colin will take Aunt Harriet," Otto said firmly. "Emma, you will be dealing with Hugh this night. Short of murder, you may use whatever method you think best."

"And what will *you* be doing in the meantime?" Emma demanded.

Otto smiled. "We mustn't overlook General Bellamy. The servants tell me he leaves Mrs. Camperdine's room every morning between two and half-past. I've never approved of adultery."

"I'm so glad you're not angry with *me*," Emma said gratefully.

"Oh, I'm angry with you," Otto replied. "If you weren't my sister, I'd rip you limb from limb. Then again, if you weren't my sister, I don't suppose I'd care what sort of mess you made of your life."

"Thank you, Otto," Emma said faintly. "I think."

*Saturday, December 17, 1814*

After leaving his uncle in the smoking room, Nicholas went directly to his room and packed his few belongings. He no longer felt like a guest at Warwick. Leaving the bed untouched, he sat in a chair at the fireside, with his coat over him. For a long time he stared into the flames, unable to sleep. From time to time, he heard the faint faraway chimes of a clock striking the hours. He thought he would never find sleep.

He must have drifted off sometime after midnight, however, because the slight creaking of the door handle woke him just as his friend the clock was striking two o'clock. The fire guttered from the sudden draft of cold air as the door swung open. Nicholas jumped to his feet as a shadowy figure entered the room backward, dragging a large burlap sack. Something inside the sack squirmed, mewling pitifully.

"Who's there?" Nicholas demanded, reaching for the fireplace poker.

Colin nearly jumped out of his skin. He was dressed head to toe in black with a black kerchief covering the lower half of his face. He looked like a highwayman. Whirling around, he saw Nicholas and relaxed somewhat. "Oh, it's you," he panted. "You shouldn't sneak up on a body like that."

"Lord Colin! What are you doing here?" Nicholas asked. "Why are you dressed like that? What's in the sack? What is going on?"

Colin looked at him blankly. "What's going on? Just an old German holiday tradition. Nothing for you to worry about. What are you doing in here, anyway? This isn't your room."

"Yes, it is," said Nicholas.

"Oh? I thought it was empty."

"No," Nicholas said, frowning.

"Well, this *is* awkward."

"Not at all. I assume you want to use the passageway

leading from the fireplace to the duke's chamber?" said Nicholas. "Allow me," he added, pressing the panel that triggered the mechanism.

"Thank you." Colin resumed dragging the sack across the carpet. Whatever was inside kicked and howled like a half dozen cats.

"Wait!" said Nicholas, as Colin disappeared into the narrow opening. "What's in the sack?"

"Rabbits," Colin replied cheerfully. "Rabbits for the Christmas hassenpfeffer. I'm just going to take them up to the roof and throw them off—you know, to tenderize them."

Muffled screams came from the sack.

"It doesn't sound like rabbits," said Nicholas, frowning. "Anyway, they're still alive! Isn't that somewhat cruel?"

Colin laughed. "Of course it's cruel. We're German! Look, just forget you ever saw me. I was never here."

He was gone, closing the door behind him.

Nicholas stared at the door for a long moment. When closed, it looked like part of the elaborately carved marble fireplace. It had taken him quite some time to discover how to open it. It had made him late for his assignation with Emma the night before.

The night before . . .

He did not want to think about Emma. He would leave in the morning and never see her again. He certainly was not going to open the secret door and make his way to her room via the passageway. If she had anything to say for herself, she could come to him. The passageway ran both ways, after all.

He was now too restless to sleep. He walked up and down in front of the fireplace for a while, then forced himself to sit down. Taking up his coat, he covered himself with it. From this angle, he could see that the secret doorway was standing slightly ajar. Colin had not closed it properly. Muttering under his breath, Nicholas threw off his coat and went to the door, intending to close it. Instead, he found himself opening the door wider. He could hear faint thuds and stifled shrieks ahead of him in the darkness. Someone cursed, probably Colin. Then, clear as a crystal bell, Nicholas heard Emma's voice:

*"All ist klar?"*

*"All ist klar,"* Colin's voice answered.

"No, all is not *klar,*" Nicholas said, stepping into the passageway and making his way to them. "I strongly suspect those are not rabbits," he added, pointing at the burlap sack.

"What is *he* doing here?" Emma demanded. Like her brother, she was dressed in black, with a black scarf covering her nose and moth. Black velvet breeches and tall leather boots encased her legs. She was carrying a large, cloth-covered bucket in her gloved hands. In spite of the cloth covering, a strong odor emanated from the bucket.

"He must have followed me," Colin complained. "I told him it was just one of our cruel, German holiday traditions, but, I suppose he had to see for himself."

Emma glared at Nicholas. "Go on, Colin. I'll take care of Lord Camford."

Colin trudged on into the darkness, dragging his burden behind him. Nicholas and Emma squared off. She would not permit him to go any deeper into the passageway, and he would not permit her to leave.

"My lord, you are in my way," Emma said.

"What's in the bucket?" he asked. "Another German holiday tradition?"

"Yes, that's right. It's a bucket full of fruit and nuts and candy."

"It doesn't smell like candy."

"That's because it's horse shit," she snapped.

"Intended for *me,* I suppose!"

"Not you," she answered. "*Hugh.* I'm going to put it over his door, and tie a bit of string from the handle to the doorknob, so when he leaves his room in the morning, he'll get a nice, lovely bath. Do you have a problem with that?"

"Not really, no."

"Then kindly get out of my way."

He would not move. "Not until I hear your explanation."

"It's very simple," said Emma. "I don't like him! I thought, before I leave, I might as well give him a little Christmas present, a little token of my esteem."

Nicholas had wanted to hear her explain her cruelty to him at dinner, but he was too distracted by her answer to correct the misunderstanding. "What do you mean *before you leave?*" he demanded. "Are you leaving? But your children arrive tomorrow."

"I am not to be allowed to see them," she explained bitterly. "I have been a naughty girl, and I have to be punished."

Nicholas's mouth went dry. "Because of me?" he whispered.

"Yes, of course, because of you!" Setting down her bucket, she struck him in the chest. "What in God's name did you think you were doing, proclaiming to the world that *I* had consented to be your wife! I, the Duchess of Warwick! You know perfectly well I never promised you any such thing!"

He stared at her. Of her face, he could only see her eyes, glittering coldly in the torchlight. "Emma, how can you say that? After—after what happened between us last night, it was understood that we would marry. Indeed, we *must* marry."

Emma laughed at him. "Are you simple, boy? Or simply out of your wits?"

"You said you loved me," he accused.

"That was in bed, you fool! Everyone says I love you in bed. It's considered polite. It doesn't *mean* anything, you know."

He stared at her as if he had never seen her before. "But you gave yourself to me. You said we would be together when you were out of mourning."

"And we *were* together," she reminded him. "For heaven's

sake! Did you think I meant *marriage?* I knew you were green; I didn't think you were *grass!* Nicholas! If I married every man I gave myself to—well, I'd be the female version of Solomon, wouldn't I?"

"Would you?" he said quietly. "You do not love me, then?"

"No," said Emma. "Of course not."

"Then my uncle was telling the truth. You only used me—used me to get your children back. I understand, madam."

Emma blinked at him in total surprise. "He told you that, did he? I should have thought he'd be too ashamed!"

"My uncle has no shame."

"Yes, Nicholas, I used you. I am not proud of it. But it has backfired against me royally, so you needn't think my misdeeds will go unpunished."

"I would have helped you, if you had only confided in me," he said sadly. "It was not necessary for you to—to prostitute yourself."

"Oh, but I like prostituting myself," she said angrily. "Didn't your precious uncle tell you?"

"I did not want to believe the things he said about you."

Emma laughed recklessly. "I can imagine! I was no more faithful to my husband than he was to me. What was I supposed to do? Be a good little wife and turn a blind eye to his affairs? Cry myself to sleep at night in my lonely bed? I am not a martyr, Nicholas. Anyway, who are you to judge me?" she went on angrily. "You know nothing of my life. You know nothing of life, period! You have spent your whole life at sea. You may as well have been living on a ship in a bottle, for all you know of real temptation! But you will learn, Nicholas."

Her voice was low and ominous.

"When you get to London, women will throw themselves at you. Let us see how well you resist their advances! Men, too, will pretend to befriend you because you have power and money and influence. Let us see how you get on. When you have been tested in fire, Sir Galahad, *then* you may pass judgment on me."

"I don't judge you, Emma," he said quietly. "I pity you. I pity you with all my heart."

"Oh! Just get out of my way," she snarled.

"Give me the bucket," he said. "You should not be walking the corridors with a bucket of horse manure."

"Why ever not? 'Tis an old German tradition!"

"I'm sorry. I can't let you do it. I will stand guard at my uncle's door all night, if I have to," he snapped.

Emma kicked over the bucket. "Take it! Damn you! I wish I'd never set eyes on you!"

When she had gone, Nicholas carefully cleaned up the mess. It did not disgust him. In his career at sea, he'd cleaned up much worse.

Lord Hugh could not sleep. Even snug in his bed, with the coverlet pulled up to his chin, he did not feel entirely safe from the wrath of the Greys. He sat up in bed, a loaded pistol in his hand, his eyes glued to the door. Beside him, Lady Anne snored gently.

The knock on the door made him jump. Lady Anne continued to snore. Lord Hugh elbowed her until she woke up, sputtering.

"Go and see who it is," he commanded her.

While she padded to the door in her bare feet, he carefully cocked the pistol.

"Who is it?" Lady Anne called through the door.

"It is I, Nicholas," said her nephew from the other side of the door.

Lord Hugh flung away his pistol. Running to the door, he pushed his wife aside. "Come in, dear boy," he cried, throwing the door open. "Come in! Dare I hope you have changed your mind?"

Nicholas would not come into the room.

"I would make a bargain with you, Uncle," he said grimly. "I will marry one of your daughters. In exchange, you will stop tormenting Emma! You will stop coming between her and her children. And you will return her letter to her."

"Of course," said Lord Hugh, smiling. "Your happiness, Nicholas, is all I have ever cared about."

Nicholas recoiled from him in disgust. "On second thought," he said. "You will give *me* her letter. I don't trust you to keep your word."

"There's no need to insult me," said Lord Hugh, but he was too happy to even pretend to be indignant. "The letter is in London with my attorney. I will send for it tomorrow."

"See that you do. And you will send word to the duchess," Nicholas went on. "It will not be necessary for her to leave. It ends tonight, Uncle. This vendetta you have against her. No more. If you so much as cast a wry look in her direction, you will answer to me."

"Now you are safe from her, I have no quarrel with the woman," said Lord Hugh. "I have no reason to cast a wry look."

"Which of the girls has caught your fancy, Nicholas?" Lady Anne asked him, smiling as if she had not heard anything unpleasant passing between her husband and her nephew.

Nicholas looked at her incredulously. "None," he said curtly.

Lady Anne stared back blankly. "But which of them do you mean to marry?"

Nicholas shrugged impatiently. "I don't really care. The eldest, I suppose. She seems eager enough," he added contemptuously.

"Octavia will be delighted!" cried Lady Anne, clapping her hands together. "We will make the announcement tomorrow."

"No!" Nicholas said sharply. "Are you insane? Just this evening I announced that I was going to marry the duchess!

In any case, no announcement will be made until I have the letter."

"Of course," said Lord Hugh. "When you have her letter, she will be entirely in your power. You may take whatever revenge you like for her having humiliated you."

"I seek no revenge," Nicholas said coldly.

"But, surely, Nicholas, you will be staying at Warwick, after all?" Lady Anne said eagerly. "You would not leave us now?"

Nicholas looked at his uncle with revulsion. "I must stay to be in receipt of the duchess's letter. Do we have a bargain, sir?"

"We do, my lord," Lord Hugh answered, rubbing his hands together.

"You will write to the duchess immediately, informing her of your change of heart," Nicholas commanded. He waited until the note was completed, then he tucked it into his pocket. "I will see that she gets it."

Lady Anne ran to her nephew and kissed him. "You will not be sorry, Nicholas! Octavia will make you the best of wives. I have always thought she was born to be a countess."

Nicholas looked down into her watery blue eyes. "Right," he said grimly.

"May I tell her now?" Lady Anne begged. "She will not mind my waking her. She will be overjoyed! Of course, I will explain that it's to be kept a secret for now."

"I will walk you out," said Nicholas, as she whipped a heavy shawl around her shoulders. "You will want to stay with your daughter tonight, Aunt Anne," he told her when they were out in the hall.

Lady Anne wrinkled her nose. "Heavens! What is that smell?"

"It's a bucket of excrement, I'm afraid," he explained. "I am going to put it over the door, and, if all goes to plan, it will fall on your husband when he gets up in the morning. You don't have a problem with that, do you?"

Lady Anne thought of all the times Lord Hugh had mistreated her. "Not really, no," she answered.

Nicholas kissed her papery cheek. "Good night, Aunt."

Early the next morning, Colin found his sister in her sitting room. He was dressed for travel, but Emma was still in her dressing gown, sipping chocolate. "Why aren't you dressed?" he demanded crossly. "If we're going, we might as well get an early start."

"We're not going," Emma told him, with a brief smile. "I've had a note from dear Uncle Hugh. Apparently, he's had a change of heart."

"Vipers don't have hearts," Colin retorted.

"No, but they do have pockets," said Emma. "He's decided to take the money after all. I daresay, he meant to take the money all along. He just wanted to torture me a bit."

"Bastard."

"Quite. Anyway, I've sent him a banknote. Harry and Grey will arrive this afternoon, as planned, and we will be here to greet them. I suppose I should be glad that Nicholas stopped me from carrying out my revenge."

Colin scowled. "What do you mean?"

With a shrug, Emma explained how Nicholas had thwarted her.

"Well, someone rigged a bucket above his door," said Colin. "The servants are all atwitter this morning."

"Why, it must have been Otto," Emma said, baffled. "He never said a word."

"You've seen him this morning?"

She nodded. "I sent him back to bed; he's quite worn out, poor lamb. Cecily fears he may be coming down with a cold. You know how susceptible he is to infections of the lung."

Emma's eyes danced with malicious glee. "As for Bellamy, they found him early this morning, cowering in one corner of the pigsty. The pigs had just finished eating his nightshirt. He was calling for his mama!"

"That's because she'd just eaten his nightshirt," said Colin.

# Chapter Thirteen

Later that morning, the news that a vehicle had passed through the front gates brought the family out onto the steps. Manservants in livery scrambled to line the drive.

An unassuming black gig came into view. It stopped at the foot of the stairs.

The door opened and a clergyman stepped out.

The family was confused. "What on earth—?" Emma murmured to her twin brother. "Isn't that the vicar?"

Scorning to take the hand that was offered to her, Lady Harriet Fitzroy stepped out of the vehicle under her own power. Wearing only a burlap sack, she walked up the steps with her head high. Her cropped white hair was wet, plastered to her skull. Pausing on the threshold, she gave Colin a look that could have melted iron.

"You're dead to me," she said in a low voice.

Colin pretended not to hear.

Lady Susan, meanwhile, had ripped the tale from the vicar's throat. Arriving at the church that morning, his curate had discovered a burlap sack at the lych-gate. When he unlocked the church doors, he had found Lady Harriet, innocent of all clothing and shivering from the cold. To cover her shame, she had jumped into the baptismal font. The vicar could only suppose it had been an episode of madness. Lady Harriet had refused the clothes offered to her by the vicar's wife, preferring to wear her burlap. To preserve what remained of the lady's modesty, the vicar had left his spectacles at home.

Having taken all the fruit, Lady Susan was eager to be rid of the rind. "I'd invite you in, Vicar," she said in a syrupy voice, "but we are expecting his grace the duke this afternoon."

She made no mention of Lord Grey Fitzroy, the duke's younger brother.

"Oh?" said the vicar. "I thought his grace must be home already. Isn't that the ducal standard flying from the ramparts?"

In order to see what he was talking about, it was necessary for Lady Susan to climb down the steps and stand in the courtyard. "That? That is not the ducal standard," she trilled. "Unless I miss my guess, those are poor Harriet's drawers!"

The vicar was sent away with scarcely a word of thanks. Lady Harriet's drawers were restored to her in short order, and the company returned to the house.

That afternoon, the family gathered again on the front steps, and, as the duke's carriage approached the house, manservants in livery lined the drive as far as the eye could see.

Nicholas stood with Lady Anne and her daughters, eager to see the two boys reunited with their mother. Emma need never know that he was responsible for her happiness. Indeed, it was better for everyone concerned if Nicholas's interference remained a secret.

The carriage came to a stop. Amid cheers and applause from the servants, the two boys jumped out. Lord Grey Fitzroy, the younger of the two, ran at once up the steps of polished stone and threw his arms around his mother's waist. Tall for his age, he was sturdily built with a wing of dark red hair falling over one eye. Emma's eyes filled with tears as she embraced him. All fear and anxiety seemed to leave her. She looked radiant.

Though he was only thirteen, the duke had more self-awareness. He climbed the steps at a more dignified pace than his younger brother, stopping frequently to return the servants' salutes with a solemn wave.

At the top of the steps, he kissed his mother formally. Emma knew he considered himself too old for hugs and kisses from his mama, and she controlled the impulse to throw her arms around him. He was nearly as tall as his mother, and, with his steel-blue eyes and curly, ash-brown hair, he looked thoroughly a Grey. "How tall you have become, Harry," she said. "And Grey, too! You're practically grown men now! I would hardly have known you. But, then I have not seen you since—since—"

"Steady on, Mama," said Harry, embarrassed by his mother's tears. "And I'm to be called Warwick, now, not Harry."

Emma frowned at him. "Not by me, young man," she said. "Warwick is what I called your father! I'm still your mother."

Though this challenge to his authority rankled the young man, Harry was not sufficiently confident to argue with his parent. "All right," he said reluctantly. "You may call me Harry. But everyone else must call me Warwick."

"Of course, my love," Emma said. "Shall we go into the house?"

"I certainly don't intend to stand outside all day," he answered her sullenly, "for it looks like rain."

"So it does," Emma said pleasantly. "Why don't you go up to your room for a bit? It will give the servants a chance to get themselves back in order. They did so want to come out to greet you. Then we will have tea in the main drawing room, if that is agreeable."

"I should be glad of a proper tea," Harry said eagerly. "The teas at Westminster School were not very generous, were they, Grey?"

"No," Grey answered shortly.

Harry looked around, setting off a round of curtseying, first from Lady Susan and her daughters and then from Lady Anne and her daughters. "Where *is* my great-uncle?" Harry demanded, descending on poor Lady Anne. "I would thank him for sending my brother and me to Westminster School. It has been a remarkable experience."

Lady Anne cowered before him. Not even Octavia had the courage to answer.

Nicholas spoke up. "My uncle is indisposed, I'm afraid. Your grace," he added, sketching a bow.

Cold blue eyes flicked over him. "And who are you, sir?" Harry asked, sounding rather like his uncle, Lord Scarlingford.

Emma hurried over. "This is Lord Camford, Harry," she said quickly. "He is Lady Anne's nephew."

"Oh, I see," Harry said coldly. "And this means he can *talk* to me, I suppose! Is Uncle Hugh now inviting his wife's relations to my home? How presumptuous of him."

Emma felt her face growing hot with embarrassment. "But Lord Camford is very welcome, Harry," she protested. "He has promised to help me with my decorations this year." Quickly, she told her son about her plans to erect an enormous *tannenbaum* in the great hall. "I do not think we will be able to manage it without Lord Camford's expertise."

"It is superstitious German nonsense," Lady Susan remarked to her eldest daughter, her loud voice carrying like a bugle. "If the duchess wants to celebrate Walpurgis Night or whatever, perhaps she should go back to her mother's land. I see no reason for our Christian holiday to be defiled by these pagan rites."

Forgetting Nicholas, Harry turned on her, demanding angrily, "*What* did you say, Aunt Susan?"

Lady Susan had never realized just how loud she was. She blinked at Harry in surprise. "It's—it's nothing the bishop hasn't said," she stammered out.

"Well, this is *my* house, not the bishop's," he told her. "And I think it sounds charming! A *tannenbaum* will be a very nice treat for the children," he went on, clearly separating himself from that category. "Lord Camford, you may carry on," he added as an afterthought, giving Nicholas a vague wave.

"Thank you, your grace," Nicholas answered correctly, without emotion.

Emma looked at him sharply, but she could detect no mockery.

Harry moved on toward the house, stopping as Julia Fitzroy caught his eye. "Why, Cousin Julia!" he exclaimed, staring at her. "How—how grown-up you look!"

Julia bobbed a saucy little curtsey, delighted but not at all surprised that she had been singled out from amongst her four elder sisters; men were doing that more and more these days. She was wearing a low-cut gown of sea-green muslin. It was far too cold an afternoon for such a flimsy confection, and her rosy nipples stood out stiffly, clearly visible through the thin fabric. "Hello, Cousin Harry! You look very grown-up, too," she added, looking at him through her lashes.

As alarmed by Julia as Harry was intrigued, Emma hurried both her sons into the house. While the rest of the family waited for the boys in the drawing room, Harry and Grey went upstairs to wash. Hardly aware of anyone else, Emma made sure that all their favorite cakes and confections were among the arrangements. When Colin tried to snatch a petit four from the table, he received a sharp blow across the knuckles from his sister.

"You're turning into a household angel," Colin accused her, nursing his injured hand.

"I just want everything to be perfect," said Emma, pointing out a subpar cake to a servant, who whisked it away.

"Speaking of perfect," Colin went on as his sister fussed

needlessly. "Did you see that little exchange between Harry and Julia?"

"No," Emma said sharply. "I didn't. Harry is only thirteen," she added, almost in the same breath. "He's far too young for that sort of thing."

"Oh, I don't know," said Colin. "By the time *I* was thirteen—"

"Pray, spare me the details!" she pleaded.

"Don't I always spare you the details?" Colin drawled. "I'm just saying that Harry's growing up."

"You're wrong," she answered. "Harry is just tall. It doesn't make him a man."

"Well, here comes the infantry now," Colin remarked, as Harry and Grey came into the room. Accustomed to being a part of the background, eleven-year-old Grey sat down near his mother, but Harry remained standing.

"There used to be a painting of my mother in this room," he said, looking around the room. He did not look pleased. "You remember it, Mama. It was your wedding portrait. Where is that painting?"

"I don't know, Harry," said Emma, bringing him his cup. "I suppose it was put away."

"Put away? Put away! By whom, may I ask?" He looked around angrily.

Lady Susan, still smarting from his rebuke earlier, looked down at her hands. Emma quietly sat down next to Grey.

"Who would dare do such a thing? Carstairs!" Harry shouted, catching sight of the old butler at the other end of the room. "Do you know the picture I mean? It was one of my father's favorites."

"Yes, your grace," Carstairs answered placidly.

"By whose authority was it taken away?" Harry demanded.

"Lord Hugh's, your grace," Carstairs replied.

A quick glance around the room told Harry that his father's uncle still had not put in an appearance. "Where is he? Go and fetch him at once."

"Yes, your grace."

"And have that painting restored to its proper place."

"Yes, your grace."

"And, Carstairs? In the future, you may disregard anything Lord Hugh says to you. Just disregard it. That goes for all the servants."

"Oh, *very* good, your grace," said Carstairs.

As he withdrew, Julia sidled up to the duke. "What are you going to *do* to Papa, Cousin Harry?" she asked curiously.

He glanced at her. "Well, if he weren't your father, I suppose I'd throw him out."

From her chair a few feet away, Emma noticed that Harry did not insist that his pretty cousin call him Warwick. She hurried to interrupt the tête-à-tête. "You have not yet met your uncle's wife," she said, leading him up to Lady Michael.

Harry's French was of the worst English schoolboy variety, perfectly incomprehensible. "I see they do not teach French at Westminster School," Lord Michael joked.

Harry's face reddened. "I remember nothing of my time at Westminster," he said. "Nothing but the birch!"

Emma gasped. "You were not *beaten*, Harry!"

"Grey got the worst of it," Harry answered grimly.

Seeing Emma's white face, Lord Michael said quickly. "Of course you were birched at Harrow, too. I know I was, and so was your father, Harry."

Harry sniffed. "One doesn't mind being beaten in front of one's own class," he answered. "But, at Westminster, we were surrounded by the sons of bankers and lawyers—*Cits*," he added, summing up middle-class London with one scathing syllable. "I will not be beaten in front of Cits. No doubt the loathsome creatures have all gone home to their families, gloating of how they saw the Duke of Warwick and Lord Grey Fitzroy birched."

"Don't worry, my love," said Emma. "You will not be going back there."

"Quite," Harry said, rather coldly.

"Pity it's going to rain," said Emma, after a moment. "I had hoped we could all ride out together to the forest to select the *Wienachtsbaum*."

"I couldn't go in any case," Harry answered carelessly. "Rain or not, I'm going to have a look at my stag this afternoon."

"Your stag?" Emma echoed.

Harry's eyes widened. "You haven't *forgotten*, Mama!" he exclaimed. "It's only the most important moment of my whole life!"

"Your first stag hunt," Emma whispered. "Of course I haven't forgotten," she lied.

"Not my first *hunt*," he said impatiently. "My first stag. My first *kill*. I'm afraid I won't have time for anything else. I selected a beast last year, and I'm eager to get another look at him. He will have grown."

"He has," Lord Michael assured him. "The most splendid red hart! I vow, he's as big as a Cumberland!"

"I trust he has nice horns," said Emma, a little sourly, because she felt left out.

They both laughed at her. "By that, I think she means antlers!" said Lord Michael. "Yes, Emma! The beast has very nice antlers—eighteen points. And while you have been planning your ball, I have been meeting secretly with the harbourer. We've been observing Harry's stag. He's magnificent, Harry."

Harry was staring at his uncle. "Did you say *eighteen* points?" he said breathlessly. "It was *sixteen* points last year!"

"That's impossible," said Lord Michael. "It must be another buck, new to the herd."

"I have to see him," Harry exclaimed. "An eighteen-pointer! I don't think I can wait another minute! Who cares if it rains? I don't regard it in the least."

"You will when you catch cold and your nose swells up," Emma protested.

Harry frowned at her. "You mustn't fuss over me, Mama," he said irritably. "Go and fuss over Grey, if you must fuss. What do you say, Uncle Michael?"

"All right," said Lord Michael. "I confess I'm eager for you to see him. I remember my first stag like it was yesterday."

"Grey and I will go with you," Emma said quickly.

"You don't like hunting, Mama," Harry reminded her. "You don't even ride to hounds."

"Since your father is not here, it's my duty to take an interest," said Emma. "And it will be Grey's turn in two years. I must prepare myself for that. *And,*" she added a little tartly, "it is apparent to me that I shall never see you unless I *do* take an interest. Come, Grey," she called. "We're going out to see your brother's stag. I want you warmly dressed."

Lord Hugh came blustering into the room just as Emma was leaving with her younger son. "You stink!" Grey cried, recoiling with his hand over his mouth. "You smell like horse shit!"

Lord Hugh had no time for Lord Grey. He hurried over to the duke to pay his respects.

Harry stood looking at him, with one fist on his hip. "Why were you not here to greet me, Uncle Hugh?" he asked coldly.

Grey paused in the doorway, eagerly watching his brother. "Come, Grey," Emma said quietly and firmly.

Lord Hugh babbled his excuses.

"Cousin Harry wishes to be called Warwick now," Julia told her father helpfully.

"But you may address me as 'your grace,'" Harry told Lord Hugh coldly. "We will talk later, sir. What I have to say to you should not be heard by the delicate ears of females, anyway. Ah, here is the painting!" he added, as a servant came in, bearing Emma's portrait. Another servant cleared a space for it on the wall by removing another painting.

"I am going out," Harry announced, watching the operation

with satisfaction. "While I am gone, Uncle, do you think you can refrain from redecorating my house?"

Julia tittered appreciatively.

"Of course, your grace," Lord Hugh said, the picture of humility.

Harry smirked, enjoying the effect he was having on Julia. "And take a bath," he ordered his father's uncle. "You smell like horse shit."


Emma spent a miserable, cold, wet afternoon in the woods, sometimes on horseback, and sometimes on her belly, spying on the splendid animal that had been marked for death. She hated stag hunting. In her view, it was even more brutal than fox hunting, but there was no getting away from the Fitzroy family tradition, not without completely alienating her children.

First, the stag would be selected. Then it would be separated from the herd. The night before the hunt, the harbourer would watch over it all night, keeping it in a tightly defined area. On the day of the hunt, the beast would be chased through the woods for hours, until it literally was too exhausted to take another step. Then it would be shot at point blank range.

This year, Harry would take the shot.

Within a few hours, Emma had had more than enough of the sport, but the males of the party showed no signs of tiring of the spectacle of deer munching grass. Despite the rain, they fully intended to watch the herd until nightfall. Before long, Harry was talking of spending the night with the harbourer in his rude hut; that way, he would be able to see his stag at first light. Nor would Grey be denied the pleasure of sleeping on a dirt floor. With both boys clamoring for the privilege, and Lord Michael aligned with them against her, Emma could not refuse.

Lord Michael accompanied her back to the house. "If you were not a married man, I believe you would spend the night with them," she accused him.

"I cannot deny it," he answered, laughing.

## Sunday, December 18, 1814

The following morning, Emma rode out to the harbourer's hut, expecting to find two exhausted boys eager to return to the comforts of the house. Instead, she found them with bright eyes and rosy cheeks, cheerfully eating porridge from wooden bowls. They had no intention of leaving until after the hunt. Or so Harry told his mother.

The hunt was to take place on the twenty-first of December, at the Winter Solstice.

"That's three days!" Emma protested.

"You can come to see us every day," Harry told her. "Bring me my portable writing desk when you come tomorrow, will you?" he added. "I want to write down all of my thoughts and observations. And Grey wants his bug collection."

"Beetle collection," Grey corrected him indignantly. "I want to show Hawkins."

Emma looked at the harbourer and sighed. "I'm not going to win this argument, am I, Hawkins?" she said with mock sorrow. "All right! I'll see you tomorrow."

Grey hugged her. "Thank you, Mama!"

Harry only gave his mother a curt nod. "Don't forget my writing materials."

Emma rode back to the stables feeling cross and slightly depressed. Dismounting, she led her mount into the stables, walking in on a loud argument between the head groom and Miss Octavia Fitzroy.

Emma handed her mare's reins to one of the stableboys.

"Miss Fitzroy!" she said sharply, just as Octavia struck the groom across the face with her riding crop.

Emma sprang forward and removed the crop from Octavia's grasp. "How dare you strike my servant!" she gasped.

The young lady and the head groom began to speak at once.

"One at a time, please!" Emma said holding up a hand.

Instantly, they again spoke at once.

"Miss Fitzroy," Emma interrupted. "Please explain yourself."

Octavia was slightly out of breath. "I am trying to teach my cousin, Lord Camford, to ride," she said coldly, "but this *idiot* will not give his lordship another horse."

"His lordship's already ruined one of my mares," the head groom said belligerently. "I'll not give him the chance to ruin another."

"One of *your* mares?" Octavia cried furiously. "Why, you ought to be beaten for your insolence, and then turned off without a character!"

"Where is Lord Camford?" Emma asked. "And since when are *you* giving him lessons?"

"His lordship was so insulted by this cretin that he has gone back to the house," Octavia answered. "I gave him his first lesson yesterday. We have become good friends."

"Is that so?" Emma said coolly.

"Does your grace think it impossible?"

Emma was spared the trouble of a reply, as the head groom demanded her attention. "Your grace, I arsk you to have a look at our Parley. His lordship brought her in yesterday arternoon. Cut to bits, she were, and frightened harf to death. And today he comes and arsks me for another! As if our Parley were one of his fancy silk neckties and not a living creature like you and me. Begging your grace's pardon," he went on fiercely, "but I won't do it. I don't care what anybody says."

"What are you going to do about this?" Octavia demanded of Emma. "The man is insubordinate."

"Benjamin, I'm sure Lord Camford didn't mean to harm Parley," Emma began gently.

"Of course it wasn't his fault," Octavia snapped. "It was completely the mare's fault. She refused the wall."

Emma fired up. "What the devil was he doing *jumping*, Miss Fitzroy? Lord Camford is an absolute beginner! Was Parley badly hurt?"

"She's an old mare," said Octavia. "His lordship wanted to try jumping. What does it matter? She's obviously not been very well trained."

"Good God," Emma said faintly. "You're banned! Lord Camford, too, if he has no more sense than that! You will never come into these stables again, Miss Fitzroy. Is that clear?"

"You can't do that!" Octavia protested.

"I just did! Now, you'd better go, or I shall have the stableboys drag you out!"

Trembling with impotent rage, Octavia flounced away.

The head groom led Emma to the injured mare's stall. A boy was dressing the mare's cuts and scrapes. As they approached, the old brown mare shied away nervously, her eyes rolling back in her head, but the boy calmed her with a few soft words.

"Your grace can see her mouth is swollen to hell, and that's a serious cut on her leg," the head groom complained.

"Will she be all right?" Emma asked anxiously.

"With proper care," the head groom assured her.

"I'll take over," said Emma. "I have nothing better to do, after all, now that my sons have decided to become woodsmen."

Clucking her tongue softly to the mare, she entered the stall.


*Tuesday, December 20, 1814*

The morning before the stag hunt, Emma rode out to the harbourer's hut as usual. Upon her return to the stables, she was surprised and more than a little vexed to see that Nicholas was there, apparently waiting for her.

"What are you doing here?" she demanded as she dismounted. "I've banned you from the stables," she went on, as a groom came to take her mare. "Didn't your friend Miss Fitzroy tell you?"

"She did," he answered, and Emma felt even more irritated because he had not denied that Octavia was his friend. "I have not gone in the stables. Nor do I intend to. Indeed, ma'am, I will never go near another horse as long as I live. Is the little horse all right?"

"Mare," she corrected him. "She is recovering."

"I am glad," he said. "I would not have hurt her for the world. I feel horrible. I would like to send her flowers or something."

Emma frowned impatiently. "Don't be nonsensical. No one thinks you did it on purpose. I will have one of the stableboys keep you apprised of her recovery, if you like."

"Thank you," he said gratefully. "I really am sorry."

She nodded. "Now, if you will excuse me, I must see to my own horse."

"Please," he said, stepping toward her. "I must speak to you."

Emma shook her head in disgust. "Here I thought you were really concerned about the mare!" she said caustically.

"I am," he insisted. "But I must speak to you, all the same, in private, if you please."

"For heaven's sake, Nicholas!" she snapped. "Will you stop making a cake of yourself? It should be obvious by now that I want nothing more to do with you. Leave me alone!"

"I have your letter," he said sharply, as she turned away.

Emma's head whipped around. Her face was white.

"My uncle was good enough to send a special messenger to London for it," Nicholas went on, not looking at her. "It arrived last night. This is the first opportunity I have had to see you."

"You have my letter?" she repeated stupidly.

"Yes," he said simply. "I have it here," he added, patting the pocket of his coat.

"Let us walk," she said, taking him by the arm.

Nicholas almost had to run to keep up as she led him down the paths into the Lime Walk. Bitterly cold, it was a good place to be private.

"You brought me here the day we met," he said sadly.

"My letter, sir, if you please," Emma said coldly.

Opening his coat, he took out the envelope, smoothing it between his hands before holding it out to her.

Emma looked at it, certain that if she reached for it, he would snatch it from her grasp.

"I wanted to return it to you myself," he said. "I dare not entrust it to a servant."

Emma smiled incredulously. "I see. You mean to return it to me?"

He looked surprised. "Of course. Take it."

He held it out to her, but she merely looked at it, still not trusting him.

"What must I give you in return?" she asked. "You must know I would do anything to get it back. If you think this will change my mind about marrying you—"

He caught his breath. "No, ma'am," he said. "You have silenced me on that subject forever. But you say I know nothing of temptation!" he added with an ill-conceived attempt at levity. "Take the letter, Emma. Let it trouble you no more."

Emma snatched it from his hand.

"You are safe," he said. "And the child is safe. Aleta, is that her name?"

Emma did not know whether he meant to threaten her or assure her. She stared up at him, confused.

"I must ask you to look at the letter, if it is not too painful.

We must be sure it is *the* letter, after all," he added in answer to her unspoken question.

"You've read it, of course," she said. "Why pretend otherwise?"

The accusation angered him. "No, actually. I don't read letters addressed to other people. Is this your grace's letter?" he asked coldly.

Emma opened it and glanced over the page.

"It is, my lord."

Nicholas bit his lip. "I wonder," he said. "I wonder you do not marry the man!"

"What man?" she asked, puzzled.

"The child's father, of course. You are free now. Do you intend to marry him?"

Emma stared at him. If Nicholas thought there was the least chance of ever marrying Aleta's father, then he really had not read her letter. "He is dead."

His eyes flew to hers. "You must have loved him very much," he said, looking away again.

Emma laughed. "Oh, yes," she said. "I adored him—right up until the day he began blackmailing me! I had no choice but to throw myself on my husband's mercy. Warwick killed him in a duel. Of course, it was all kept secret. It was passed off as a hunting accident. It was never spoken of again. I don't know why Warwick kept that letter. Hugh found it amongst his effects after he died."

Nicholas was appalled by the casual way in which she spoke of death and blackmail.

"Your husband killed your lover," he said slowly, "but he would not let you keep the child."

"No," she said. "He would not. But he had no objection to my brother raising her as his own. He probably *would* have let me keep her if her father had been a man he respected. Let's just say, my husband did not admire my taste in men."

Nicholas looked down at the ground. Her way of life was

so very different from his own. He felt sorry for her, but also disgusted. "Well, you have your letter now," he said quietly. "It cannot be used against you ever again."

Bowing, he took his leave.

"Wait, sir!" she said suddenly. "You must allow me to thank you."

He flushed. "I do not want your gratitude," he said.

To Emma, it sounded like an insult, but she bore it without rancor. "You have it all the same," she insisted.

He bowed quickly. "Good-bye, your grace."

Turning on his heel, he left her before she could speak again.

It was just as well. She had no idea what to say to him.

# Chapter Fourteen

Four days before Christmas, the Duke of Warwick killed his first stag. After a chase of nearly ten hours, the beast was brought to bay in a stream. Harry took his shot, killing the red hart instantly, and, the ladies were assured, painlessly.

Emma watched from her horse, shuddering as Harry's cheeks were blooded after the kill. Harry himself glowed with the triumph of a successful hunter. There would be venison for the Christmas dinner, venison provided by himself, and the animal's head would be mounted and hung in the trophy room with all the rest of them. He felt like a man. But, of course, his mother still saw him as a child.

To please her, Harry rode out the next morning before dawn to select the *tannenbaum,* leaving it to the woodsman to cut it down on the morning of Christmas Eve. It took an hour to fell the enormous tree. Twelve men were required to carry it out of the woods, and four carriage horses dragged it up to the house, where it arrived safely just before noon. Even though its branches had been tightly bound with rope, the front doors had to be taken off to allow it to fit inside the great house.

As he had promised, Nicholas oversaw the installation of the tree, which took longer than anyone had anticipated.

It was not until well after three o'clock in the afternoon that the bindings could be cut and the branches fluffed out, leaving just a few scant hours for Emma and her staff to decorate the tree before the guests began arriving for the Christmas Eve Ball. Each shiny ornament of mouth-blown glass had to be tied onto a branch by hand, and the duchess was very particular about where each one went. In addition to the glass ornaments, there were clusters of nuts tied up in bags of netting with gaily colored bows. Emma had made these herself, with the help of the children, Harry excepted, of course.

Somehow, the Herculean task was completed, but it was a very near thing. Glass and tinsel glittered like jewels on all the branches, reflected endlessly in the immense mirrors lining the walls. With her spectacles on her nose, Emma climbed onto the ladder to place the last ornament on the tree with her own hands. Nicholas instinctively went to hold the ladder steady. "Is that a *pickle?*" he asked her curiously.

"The child who finds the pickle first gets an extra present," Emma explained, trying to sound pleasant and normal. Since he had returned her letter to her, her feelings toward him had been confused by overwhelming gratitude. She felt nervous around him, and avoided him as much as possible. "The others will have to wait until tomorrow."

The duke came into the room and hurried over to them.

"Harry!" Emma scolded him. "You know you're not supposed to see the tree until after you've had your supper!"

He scowled at her. "That only applies to the children, Mama," he told her loftily. "I certainly won't be looking for the *pickle* this year!"

"You never found it anyway," she retorted. "You were always rooting about in the presents like a pig looking for truffles."

"Shouldn't you be getting ready for the ball?" he said

coldly, his cheeks reddening. "Though you are my mother, I shan't lead you out for the first dance looking like *that*."

Flustered, Emma hurried down the ladder.

When she had left them, Harry stood looking up at the tree. "The children will be delighted with it, I think," he said, once again deliberately separating himself from the ranks of the infantry. He never seemed to miss an opportunity to speak of "the children."

"I have never seen anything like it," said Nicholas.

Harry glanced at Nicholas. "You should know, my lord, that my mother has no desire ever to marry again."

"I beg your pardon?" said Nicholas.

"It has come to my attention that you have been aspiring to my mother's hand," said Harry, using a courtly, almost pompous turn of phrase. "I have nothing against you, mind, but Mama is a wealthy woman in her own right. She has no need to marry. Besides, you will need an heir, and Mama is much too *old* to be thinking of having any more children. You would do well to look elsewhere for a bride."

Nicholas was red in the face. "Indeed, your grace," he murmured. "I have already chosen a bride. My cousin Octavia has agreed to do me the honor."

Harry blinked in surprise. "Oh, I see. Aunt Susan's got it wrong as usual!" he laughed cheerfully. "My, but you *do* like older women!" he added merrily. "Octavia must be twenty-five if she's a day!"

"Your grace will excuse me," said Nicholas, with a curt bow.

"Of course," said Harry. "You need to get changed yourself. I will see you at the ball."

As Nicholas hurried to his room, guests were already arriving for the ball, exclaiming in awe over the duchess's strange and extravagant decorations. The duke received them with a mixture of warmth and condescension, accepting their flattering attentions as his due.

At nine o'clock, the duke opened the festivities by dancing

with his mother. Emma looked exquisite in a low-cut gown of raspberry silk. Diamonds glittered at her throat and in her hair. Harry directed her attention to Lord Camford, who was leading Octavia Fitzroy onto the dance floor. "Theirs will be a great match," he told her, laughing.

"What do you mean?" said Emma.

"Why, Camford and Cousin Octavia," he said. "They are to be married."

"Nonsense!" said Emma.

"I have it from the horse's mouth," Harry insisted.

"Octavia?"

"No; Camford himself. So you needn't worry about him mooning after you anymore."

Emma did not know what to think. "That is a relief," she murmured.

After the first dance, the children were allowed to come down from the nursery to see the Christmas tree. Some of the adults left the ballroom to watch the spectacle as the candles on the tree were lit. The duke, of course, could not be bothered with such a trifle, but, instead seized the chance to dance with his pretty cousin Julia, who had been allowed out of the nursery with the rest of the children.

Lady Aleta Grey found the pickle. As her special present Emma gave her the gilded ivory fan that had once belonged to the Empress Josephine. "And I have another present for you," she told the child, hugging her close. "Next month, when the boys go back to school, and your mama and papa go back to London, you and I shall sneak off to Paris together. Just the two of us."

"Ahem!" said Colin. "I'm coming for a visit!"

"A short visit," said Emma.

As he watched Emma teaching the child how to make different signals with her new fan, Nicholas began to see a resemblance between them, although it was clear that the black-haired, black-eyed child took after her father. She certainly looked nothing like Otto or his wife.

"There is something in the ballroom you must see," Colin said in Emma's ear. Taking her hand, he dragged her from the room. "They make a lovely couple, don't they?" he said, directing her attention to the dancers. In the center of the throng, Julia Fitzroy was dancing with her second cousin, the Duke of Warwick. Emma was dismayed, to say the least.

"That hussy!" she muttered. "I could just about strangle her!"

"Now we know why Julia is not yet Out," said Colin. "They're saving her for Harry. Julia, Duchess of Warwick. How do you like the sound of that, Emma?"

"Over my dead body!" Emma said violently. "She's too old for him."

He laughed. "She's only two years older than he. 'Twas not so long ago that *you* were practically engaged to a man nearly ten years your junior."

"I was no such thing!" Emma snapped.

Colin could not resist teasing her. "Harry is thirteen now, you know. That's old enough to marry—with his guardian's consent, of course."

"That will never happen," Emma said grimly.

"I'm sure you're right," he said dryly. "Uncle Hugh would *never* allow his precious daughter to become Duchess of Warwick."

Across the room, Lord Hugh and Lady Anne were watching their youngest daughter with the utmost complacency.

"That one will not go quietly back to the nursery," Colin warned Emma. "You'll have better luck putting a genie back in the bottle. Pity Nicholas could not be persuaded to take her."

Emma flinched, remembering what Harry had told her about Nicholas's marriage plans.

But, before she could speak, Lady Harriet was upon them, wearing a decades-old ball gown of emerald-green watered silk. "You owe me seven hundred pounds, you loathsome, mangy little squirrel," she told Colin without preamble.

"Look who's talking to me," Colin said lightly. "A super-annuated virgin! I thought I was dead to you, madam."

"You *are* dead to me, scum," she answered. "But that doesn't mean I won't collect on a bet. Lord Camford is to marry Octavia Fitzroy. You owe me seven hundred pounds."

Colin laughed. "They are only dancing, you toothless old baggage. Besides, we called off our bet. I paid you for your trouble. Now move along, why don't you. For a dead person, I'm awfully busy."

"They are engaged," Lady Harriet insisted. "Octavia and Lord Camford are to be married. Ask your sister, if you don't believe me."

"It's true," said Emma. "Harry just told me. I can't imagine how it happened."

"Oh, can't you?" said Lady Harriet. "Well, I can tell you how it happened. Camford agreed to marry Octavia in exchange for your letter, Emma. It's as simple as that."

Emma's face was ashen. "I don't know what you mean, Aunt Harriet," she stammered.

"Pish!" said Harriet. "You know exactly what I mean. I want my seven hundred pounds in gold, if you please," she went on, turning to Colin. "I don't trust these banks and their paper money."

"They are not married yet, old woman," Colin said darkly, but Emma silenced him, placing an unsteady hand on his arm.

"Aunt Harriet, are you saying that Camford offered himself up like some sort of human sacrifice?" she said breath-lessly. "For my sake? For my letter?"

"Of course," Lady Harriet said impatiently, "and his offer was immediately accepted. How did you think he got your letter back for you?"

"I did not think," said Emma, with growing distress. "I supposed he must have stolen it."

Lady Harriet snorted. "Camford? Steal? He'd consider it a disgrace to the Royal Navy, I'm sure. He'd sooner cut off his right arm."

"How do you know all this?" Emma demanded.

"I heard it from Cornelia," Lady Harriet said proudly. "She's beastly jealous, so it was not very hard to get her to talk. Camford is to marry Octavia. They mean to announce it tomorrow, on Christmas Day."

"Oh, no," Emma murmured.

"Why Octavia?" Colin wanted to know. "Why not Julia? What did you do, old woman? You must have cheated! We agreed to let nature take its course!"

"To be perfectly honest," said Lady Harriet, "I don't think the young man cared which one of them he married. He chose Octavia because she is the eldest."

"Would you be good enough to excuse us, Aunt Harriet?" said Emma. "I need Colin to make the punch."

"Don't forget my money, boy," Lady Harriet called after Colin.

Taking a firm hold of her brother's arm, Emma led him into the refreshment room, where a splendid German-style Christmas banquet had been laid out. In the German states, Christmas Eve was known as Dickbauch, meaning, simply, "pot belly," and the long table groaned under the weight of numerous tiered silver dishes piled high with rich meats, fruits, and pastries.

"Emma, this is no time for punch," said Colin. "I can feel my seven hundred pounds slipping away. I'll be damned if I let that scabby old hag beat me."

"I thought your bet was only ten shillings," said Emma. "No! Never mind your stupid bet!" she went on, shaking her head. "Nicholas is about to make the worst mistake of his life! I should have guessed as much. Oh, he can't be that great of a fool, can he?"

"I'd say yes, he can, but, then again, you know him better than I do."

"You're right," Emma said sadly. "If he's promised to marry Octavia, then marry her he will, come hell or high water! He's that sort of man. Honorable, dependable, chivalrous."

"Idiotish," Colin added helpfully.

"Yes, a damn fool!" she agreed angrily. "He must really have loved me," she added sadly. "Well, I can't let him do it. I can't let him throw his life away. What do we do, Colin? How do we save him from himself? Oh, God! If only Otto were not still suffering from that trifling cold! He would know what to do."

"We do not need Otto," said Colin, annoyed. "I know exactly what to do."

"What?"

"Nothing so easy! You get Nicholas to go to his bedroom at the stroke of midnight. If anyone can do it, I know you can."

"Do you think Octavia will release him if she thinks I'm his mistress?" Emma shook her head. "Frankly, I don't think she'd bat an eye if she found him in bed with *you*. She is determined to be Lady Camford."

"You leave Octavia to me," Colin said airily. "Just get the damn fool to his bedroom at midnight."

"What if he won't go? I'm sure he hates me. The last thing he will want is a rendezvous with me!"

Colin took out his watch and checked it. "Don't be a self-pitying ass," he told his sister bluntly. "He's obviously in love with you. Why else would he agree to marry the gruesome Octavia? He'll jump at the chance to meet you in private. Tell him not to light the candle. Just have him take off all his clothes and get into bed. I'll take care of the rest."

"What are you going to do?" she asked, wincing. "I'm not going to like it, am I?"

"Do you want to save him from the proverbial fate worse than death?"

"Yes, of course I do!" Emma exclaimed. "But—"

"But me no buts!" he said. "Obviously, if my plan doesn't work, we can always try *your* plan."

"I don't have a plan!" she wailed.

"Then you had better hope that *my* plan works," he told her, before slipping back into the crowded ballroom.

Nicholas had finished dancing with Octavia. Emma nearly collided with him as he made his way to the refreshments.

Nicholas frowned down at her. "Good evening, your grace. You are not dancing?"

Emma stared mutely into his blue eyes, her heart pounding. Even if she suggested an assignation now, she was not at all certain he would accept. She did not care to be rejected face to face. Her courage deserted her. She felt like a clumsy schoolgirl at her first dance.

"Are you looking for Mr. Palafox?" he suggested woodenly. "I know he has been looking for you."

"Yes," she said, seizing on the suggestion with absurd gratitude. "I was indeed looking for Mr. Palafox. Have you seen him?"

Nicholas knew perfectly well that Captain Palafox was currently performing the Boulangere with Miss Cornelia Fitzroy as his partner. "No," he said stonily. "I haven't seen him. But, then, these army officers all look alike to me."

"Oh," said Emma. "Thank you, my lord. He must be in the card room."

"Very likely," Nicholas said, moving on.

Feeling quite like an idiot, Emma ran to her room to find pen and paper. She wrote quickly, before her courage deserted her again, hardly knowing what she wrote.

*Dear C—*
  *I beg you will do me the honor of meeting with me
privately in your room at midnight. I implore you.*

*Yours,*

*E—*

Folding the page over, she sealed it with a wafer, gave it to Carstairs, the butler, the only servant in whom she had perfect trust, and instructed him to place it in Lord Camford's hand personally.

Nicholas was all astonishment when he read it. Why, he wondered, would she send him a *note* when they had been face-to-face not five minutes before? She had been looking for that scoundrel Palafox, with a rather desperate look in her eyes. This must be a mistake, he thought grimly. And the rascal's first name was Charles—with a C.

Of course, he thought grimly. The invitation was for Charles Palafox.

Did Emma have so many lovers that even the servants could not keep them straight?

"Are you quite sure this note is for me?" Nicholas asked, detaining the butler.

"Certainly, my lord. Would your lordship care to reply?"

Nicholas opened his mouth to argue the point, but then thought better of it. It would not be such a bad thing, after all, if Charles Palafox never got the duchess's note.

"No," Nicholas said. "No reply. Thank you, Carstairs."

"Very good, my lord."

But before Carstairs could withdraw, Nicholas had changed his mind. It would be uncivil to keep Emma waiting for a man who would never come. Worse yet, what if Palafox decided to go back to his room for some other reason?

"Wait! No! There *is* a reply, Carstairs. Please tell the lady that the gentleman cannot do as she requests."

Carstairs bowed. "Very good, my lord."

"No, wait," Nicholas said, detaining him again. "If you're quite sure this is for *me,* perhaps I *should* go." He could always tell the surprised Emma that Carstairs had given him her note by mistake. After all, it was the truth.

Before Carstairs could speak, Nicholas reversed himself again. "No, I can't. Tell her I'm sorry, but I can't. Tell her that. On the other hand," he went on, almost in the same breath, "it *is* my room, and I have every right to go there if I want. She can't keep me out of my own room."

There is a limit to everything, including Carstairs's patience. "My lord, if you please!"

"Cousin Nicholas?"

Octavia's voice preceded her into the hallway.

Nicholas jumped. "No reply, Carstairs," he said quickly. "No reply at all."

"Is that your final answer, my lord?" Carstairs drawled.

"Yes, of course," said Nicholas.

He hurried to meet Octavia. "I'm so sorry, Cousin Octavia. This is our dance, is it?"

"Yes, Cousin Nicholas, the supper dance. What did Carstairs want?"

"Nothing," Nicholas lied. "A slight wobble in the Christmas tree, that's all. Nothing to worry about."

"It would serve her right," Octavia sniffed, "if the whole ridiculous thing fell over."

"But I put it up," Nicholas reminded her as they returned to the ballroom.

She looked at him blankly. "Yes? And?"

Nicholas had a sudden, repellent vision of his future: a lifetime of Octavia's blank stares, her cold voice, her handsome but masklike face. There would be children, too, little children with blank stares and cold voices. He wanted to run away to the nearest port and take the first ship bound for anywhere. Instead, he was going to have to keep his word and marry Octavia.

"Nothing, Cousin Octavia," he said quickly, and they went to rejoin the dancers.

It was just then a little after eleven o'clock. As Nicholas danced with his cousin, it became crystal clear what he must do. Or, rather, what he must *not* do. Emma Fitzroy was the first woman, the only woman, with whom he had ever been intimate. She still excited him physically, and the desire to see her again was very strong. But, sadly, she was a loose-moraled woman, and, besides, he was spoken for, engaged to Octavia. It would be wrong to meet in secret with another woman. He would not go.

And, up until the very moment the clock began to strike twelve, he was perfectly at peace with his virtuous decision. He had just escorted Octavia down the steps into the dining room, and was on his way to the banquet hall to prepare a plate for her, when he saw Charles Palafox, with a look of urgency on his face, leaving the ballroom. And the handsome officer was not going in the direction of the dining room.

Emma was nowhere in sight. All thoughts of right and wrong vanished from Nicholas's mind. So! He had been right, after all. Carstairs had gotten it wrong; Emma's letter obviously had been meant for Palafox. The assignation Emma had been attempting to make in her note must have been made by some other method, probably face-to-face.

*It should be me,* Nicholas thought furiously. *If she's going to rendezvous with anyone, it should be me. I saved her. I got her letter back. And this is how she thanks me?*

He could have used that letter to make her his mistress. Now he regretted letting that power out of his hands. *She should be mine,* he thought, almost blind with rage.

Suddenly, he forgot that he was engaged to Octavia, and that, at this very moment, she was waiting patiently for him to return to her with a plate of lobster patties and caviar. Forgetting everything but his own fury, he started after

Palafox, moving across the ballroom, going against the flow of traffic.

Naked as the day she was born, Emma lay shivering in Nicholas's bed, thinking over and over: *this isn't going to work, this isn't going to work.* Octavia could discover Nicholas in bed with a dozen women, and she would still not release her fiancé from the engagement, Emma was sure. She did not have much faith in Colin's plan, whatever it was, but she clung to hope.

She heard the clock strike midnight. Nicholas was late, and she began to fear that he was not coming. *He does not want me, after all,* she thought, wounded, but not really surprised. She felt ridiculous lying there naked, waiting for a man who obviously did not want her. Not even the memory of his egregious attempt at lovemaking could soothe her injured pride.

She dreaded having to get out of bed and get dressed, but she was on the verge of doing just that when the door opened, flinging a rectangle of light across the bedroom of Westphalia. The light disappeared as the door closed. Swiftly, Nicholas crossed the room and went into his dressing closet. After a moment, she heard the unmistakable sound of a man answering the call of nature.

"That wasn't very nice," she said as he emerged from the closet.

"Who's there?" His voice was sharp with surprise.

"Who do you think?" she whispered, sitting up. "It is I, Emma. Hurry! Take off all your clothes and get into bed."

Charles Palafox held up the candle and grinned at her. "Duchess! Does this mean you have forgiven me?"

Shocked, Emma pulled the eiderdown quilt up to her chin so hard that her feet were exposed. "You!" she shrieked. "What are *you* doing in Lord Camford's room?"

Palafox was taken aback. "Camford? No, this is *my* room."

"I don't think so, Captain Palafox," Emma said coldly. Now she had her knees tucked under her chin, her body completely covered by the quilt. "I'm quite sure this is his lordship's room. It's Westphalia, isn't it?" She looked around desperately. It was a long way to the door, and Charles was between her and her clothes.

Palafox was enjoying himself. "If you're looking for Camford's room, my dear duchess, it's across the hall," he said. "We switched."

"Switched?"

"We exchanged rooms," he clarified. "I preferred the view from this chamber, and his lordship didn't care, so . . . we switched. I must say, the view keeps getting better!"

"I see," Emma said primly. "It would seem that I have made a mistake. I apologize for intruding on your privacy, sir."

"Madam, I forgive you," he said warmly.

"Thank you," she said tartly. "Now, if you wouldn't mind leaving me," she went on, with all the dignity she could conjure. "I seem to have . . . Oh, hell! I need to get dressed."

He chuckled. "I can help you with that. I'm good with my hands."

"No, thank you!" she snapped.

"Really, I'm very good at dressing ladies. That is, I'm very good at *un*dressing them. I'll just do what I usually do, except in reverse, shall I?"

"Mr. Palafox!" she said sharply.

"You're wasting your time with Camford, you know," he told her irritably. "The *on-dit* is that he's going to marry the eldest Miss Fitzroy. Personally, I'd sooner marry an eel, but there's no accounting for taste, is there? You and I could have such fun together," he went on. "I know I can please you, if you would just give me the chance."

"Captain Palafox, I must ask you to recall that you are an English gentleman!"

"At least let me watch you get dressed," he pleaded.

"Certainly not!"

"Fair enough," he said. "Just let me see your breasts."

"No," she answered.

"Let me see your breasts, and I'll go away directly and forget I ever saw you."

"Oh, all right," Emma said crossly, throwing off the quilt. "Anything to be rid of you!"

Staring at her naked torso, he gave a deep, contented sigh. "Glorious," he murmured appreciatively. "But then I knew they would be. Are you *quite* sure you wouldn't care for a tumble? I've got something very nice for you in my breeches. You will not be disappointed."

"Get out!" she said, snatching up the book from the bedside table and throwing it at him. He knew better than to duck and Montaigne's essays whizzed harmlessly past his head, hitting the floor with a thud.

Chuckling, Palafox went to the door. As he opened it, Nicholas, Lord Camford, fell into the room. The earl caught himself, regained his feet, and stood red faced with anger and embarrassment. "If I'd known we had an audience, I'd have projected more," Palafox drawled. "Perhaps you've forgotten, my lord, but this is *my* room. Yours is across the hall."

"I haven't forgotten," Nicholas said stiffly. He glanced at Emma, who was sitting up in Palafox's bed, half hidden by the quilt. "I beg your pardon, ma'am," he said contemptuously. "Your note was delivered to me by mistake. I daresay Carstairs cannot keep up with all your lovers!"

He flung her crumpled note in her direction.

"Nicholas!" she cried, struggling to get out of bed with the quilt wrapped around her. "This is not what it looks like. Please, you must believe me!" She followed him into the hall.

"I may be an idiot," said Nicholas, "but I am not an idiot!"

"I don't think you are an idiot!" she said quickly. "Please, just listen to me! Charles and I are not lovers."

"What are you, then? A pair of rutting beasts?" he shouted. "It's bloody obvious what you've been about, madam! Do not imagine that I care," he added unconvincingly. "If your note had not been delivered to me by mistake, I would not be here."

"But it was *not* delivered to you by mistake," she protested.

Nicholas recoiled as if she had struck. "You *meant* for me to find you like this? With this—this paltry excuse for a Casanova? If you were any sort of gentleman, sir," he went on, eyeing Palafox with contempt, "you would at least propose marriage to this . . . this *lady*. And if *you* were any sort of a *lady,* you would accept," he added scathingly, glaring at Emma. "But I fear you are no more a lady than he is a gentleman."

"How dare you!" Emma gasped.

"Allow me to point out to you, sir," Palafox said coldly, "that this is really none of your business. You are not her husband, after all."

Nicholas laughed bitterly. "I am thankful for that, at least."

Palafox laughed back at him. "Sour grapes, Camford?"

"Hardly!" Nicholas spat. "You are welcome to this—this *strumpet!* In fact, I'd say you were perfect for each other! You, madam, are a brazen hussy!"

Emma bristled at the insult. "How dare you speak to me like that? I wash my hands of you. If you're foolish enough to marry Octavia, then you deserve every ounce of misery that's coming your way!" She took a deep breath. "Come, Charles," she said, taking a firm hold of Palafox's arm. "Are we going to make love or not? We mustn't let this ridiculous *boy* spoil our fun."

"No, indeed," Palafox answered warmly.

Emma paused in the doorway to deliver one last blow to her one-time lover. "My lord? If you're going to eavesdrop while Charles and I make love, I recommend you press a glass to the door. I'm not sure how it works, but I'm told it amplifies the sound beautifully."

Palafox chuckled. "Unless the poor sap is completely deaf, he will have no difficulty hearing your sweet cries of ecstasy," he said, pulling her back into his room, and closed the door in Nicholas's face.

Alone with Palafox, Emma snatched up her clothes and ran into the dressing closet.

"Does this mean we're *not* going to be making love?" Palafox pouted in the bedroom.

"Don't be ridiculous, Charles," she shouted through the door.

Nicholas went back to his room to lick his wounds. He thought guiltily of Octavia. No doubt she was still waiting for her lobster patties. He should return to her, he knew. But the last thing he wanted at the moment was to be among other people. In the state he was in, he was either going to break his hand punching a wall or burst into tears like a bereft child. Either way, he could only disgrace himself. He needed time alone to cleanse himself of all thoughts of the cruel and faithless Emma.

In the darkness, he threw himself down on the bed, striking it with his fists.

"Ouch!" howled Julia Fitzroy. At Colin's insistence, she had been waiting in his bed, stark naked for nearly a quarter of an hour, and this was not quite the greeting she had expected.

Nicholas scrambled to his feet. With shaking hands, he lit a candle. "Julia!" he gasped, as his fifteen-year-old cousin sat up in his bed, the coverlet slipping from her small, firm breasts, and her rich red hair cascading about her shoulders. "What are you doing?"

Barely holding a sheet around her body, Julia walked to

the end of the bed on her knees. "Isn't it obvious?" she pouted. "I'm saving you from Octavia. You can't marry *her*. She's too, too awful! Tell the truth," she went on coquettishly. "Wouldn't you rather marry *me?*" She looked up at him with wide, dark eyes.

Nicholas scowled at her. "Dress yourself, child," he said harshly. "I will wait for you outside."

He strode to the door and opened it. Lady Anne Fitzroy stood there, poised to knock. "Nicholas!" she cried. "Have you seen Julia?"

"I'm here, Mama!" Julia cried cheerfully.


"How do I look?" Emma asked, coming out of Charles's dressing room with her clothes back on.

"Like you've had a good rogering," he said approvingly. "May at least I escort you back to the ballroom?"

Emma took his arm. "You may."

They went out into the hall together just in time to see Julia Fitzroy come dancing out of Nicholas's bedroom wearing nothing but a bed sheet. "*She* looks like she's had a good rogering, too," Palafox remarked, sounding a little envious.

Emma could only stare.

"Oh, hullo, Duchess, Mr. Palafox!" Julia called to them. "Would you happen to have a little hartshorn or lavender water? Mama found me naked in bed with Cousin Nicholas, and I'm afraid she's fainted dead away."

"I say!" Palafox murmured.

Emma stalked into Nicholas's room. Lady Anne had collapsed into her nephew's arms. Nicholas had lowered her to the rug and was fanning her ineffectively with his hands.

Nicholas looked up at her, panic in his eyes. "She just sort of fell over," he said weakly.

"I'm not a bit surprised," Emma said dryly. Sinking down to the floor, she began chafing Lady Anne's wrists together.

Julia appeared over Emma's shoulder with smelling salts. Her loose hair brushed against Emma's cheek. "Charles had these in his room."

"Dress yourself, child," Emma told her in an awful voice. "Let not your shame be the first thing your poor mother sees when she returns to us."

"Yes, your grace," Julia said, scampering off to Nicholas's closet.

"I can assure you, madam, this is not what it looks like!" Nicholas protested as Emma opened the bottle.

"Really?" Emma said coldly. "Because it looks a bit like the pot has called the kettle black."

"No!" he cried. "I just came back to my room, and there she was. Nothing happened. I never touched her. You do believe me, don't you? Emma?"

"It doesn't matter what I believe," said Emma, helping Lady Anne sit up. Lady Anne gasped for breath, but she was conscious.

"Aunt Anne? You believe me, don't you?" Nicholas said anxiously. "Julia just appeared in my room. I—I did not invite her here."

"Come now, my lord," Palafox said coldly. "It's damned obvious what you've been up to with your pretty little cousin! And if you were any sort of a gentleman, you would make that poor child an offer of marriage. After all, if you do not marry her, she's ruined."

"Ruined!" Lady Anne sobbed. "My youngest child!"

"What do you mean, ruined?" cried Nicholas. "I never touched her!"

"Julia is not a widow with a certain reputation," Emma told Nicholas coolly. "In other words, she ain't me! She will be ruined unless you marry her."

"Can we not . . . Can we not keep it quiet?" Nicholas pleaded with them.

"*I'm* not keeping it quiet," said Palafox. "Are you, Duchess?"

"I shall be silent as the grave," said Emma. "But will Julia? Will her mother?"

"My youngest daughter is ruined," Lady Anne wailed. "Nicholas must marry her. There's nothing else to be done."

"But—but I am promised to marry Octavia," Nicholas protested weakly.

"Oh, my God!" Lady Anne gasped. "Who is going to tell Octavia?"

She fainted dead away, collapsing into Emma's arm.

"I'll tell her," said Julia, shrugging.

# Chapter Fifteen

*December 1815*

Julia, Lady Camford, pushed her head out of the window of her husband's carriage as it rumbled up the avenue to Warwick Palace. Dark clouds filled the wintry sky, casting a heavy, gray-violet pall over the great house, which looked forbidding and deserted in its brilliant emerald-green setting. A light, cold drizzle had been falling, but, as the carriage drew near the front steps, thunder broke overhead, and the heavens opened up, sending rain down in hard sheets. Quickly, Julia pulled her head in, losing a feather from her wide-brimmed bonnet in the process. "It's too bad!" she complained to her husband, who was seated opposite her in the carriage.

Nicholas was no longer the cheerful, good-natured young man he had been the year before. He looked older now, closer to thirty than twenty, and, though he was still handsome, there were grim lines around his mouth, and a hard, cynical glint in his blue eyes. His hair was finely barbered, and, after a year in the wan English sun, it had darkened from blond almost to chestnut brown. He sat reading a book, paying no attention whatsoever to his sixteen-year-old wife.

Julia tried again. "Nicky! I said it's too bad."

She knew perfectly well that her husband loathed being called Nicky, at least by her, but it usually elicited some response from him. This time, however, the Earl of Camford merely turned the page of his book, a very dry, dull treatise on estate management.

Julia sighed, exasperated by her husband's indifference. Julia was the most interesting person that Julia had ever known. Why anyone would willingly deny himself her companionship was completely beyond her power to comprehend. "Nicky, are you listening to me?" she demanded. "Cousin Harry is not yet arrived."

Nicholas glanced at her, frowning. He had been married to Julia nearly a year, and, for nearly a year, he had been frowning at her, unwilling to forgive her for tricking him into marriage. At first, Julia had tried to make him love her, but her efforts had only served to make him resent her all the more. Nor could he be seduced, she had discovered. He had never visited her bed, and she knew by now that he had no intention of ever doing so. One night, he had told her frankly that he would sooner mate with a cat.

After that, Julia had stopped trying to make him love her. Instead, she had begun to hate him, and the triumph of having made herself Countess of Camford turned to ashes in her mouth.

"How could you possibly know the duke is not at home?" Nicholas asked her sharply. "We have not yet arrived ourselves."

"If he were here, the ducal standard would be flying from the ramparts," she explained.

Nicholas stuck his finger in his book. "You told me his grace invited us," he said. "I don't like showing up at a house when the owner is not home."

"His grace *did* invite us," said Julia. "That is to say, I

wrote to him, and asked him to invite us, which amounts to the same thing."

"You did what?" Nicholas said angrily.

"Harry wouldn't say no to me," she said smugly. "I'm his favorite cousin."

"He might say no to you, out of deference to his mother. Her grace, certainly, will not want to see us. You assured me—"

Julia waved a careless hand encased in fine yellow kid leather. "Oh, the duchess won't care," she scoffed. "She sees her old lovers everywhere she goes, without any awkwardness at all. Indeed, from what I hear, she's quite friendly with her former flames. Why should *you* be any different?"

Her wide, dark eyes looked at him very frankly. She knew perfectly well that Emma had been Nicholas's first and only lover, and that any mention of the woman still caused him pain.

Nicholas was sorry he had brought up the subject of Emma. He had not seen her since January 6, 1815, Twelfth Night. She had left Warwick before first light on the following day. After returning her sons to Harrow, she had gone to Paris, taking the child, Aleta, with her.

Nicholas, meanwhile, had been obliged to go to London, to make his presentation at Court, to formally take his seat in the House of Lords, and, of course, to marry Julia. But hardly a day passed that he was not reminded of Emma. His brief affair with her at Warwick had become public knowledge, and he was taxed with it on every possible occasion. All of London gossiped of wicked Emma and her escapades in Paris, real or imagined, and all of London felt obliged to keep Lord Camford abreast of her affair with Chateaubriand, the great man of letters, or her intrigue with the Duc de Bourbon. Every report stung Nicholas like a fresh betrayal.

Then, as February gave way to March, the situation in Europe changed. Napoleon Bonaparte escaped from Elba at the end of February 1815, landing on the French coast on March 1. Within three weeks, he had seized control of France from the weak Bourbon king, who fled with his court to Belgium. Abandoned by her French friends, Emma had been trapped in Paris. The Congress of Vienna had lost no time declaring war on France, making Emma's position even more precarious.

For several weeks, there was no word of Emma's situation, and speculating about the fate of the unfortunate Duchess of Warwick briefly became a favorite pastime in London society. The duchess had been thrown to an angry mob, and subjected to every form of degradation before being ripped to pieces. Or she had been tried as a spy, found guilty, and sent to the guillotine. Or she had been thrown into the Bastille—a structure that had been torn down before the turn of the century, but why bother with facts?

The truth, when it came out, was rather less sinister. In the early days of his return, Napoleon had hoped to treat with Great Britain in a separate peace. According to the newspapers, the Duchess of Warwick had been offered parole, on the condition that she carry back to England a letter for the Prince Regent from Napoleon himself. Emma had politely declined, reportedly saying that she was neither a messenger nor an agent of France. Irate, Napoleon had placed her under house arrest.

Even if, as Lady Jersey slyly observed, it was the first time the Duchess of Warwick ever said no to a man, that simple refusal was enough to restore Emma to the good graces of society. In absentia, she became the toast of London.

While the rest of London celebrated Emma's small act of defiance, Nicholas had a very different reaction. He had wanted to strangle Emma for her recklessness. She should have had more sense than to antagonize the most powerful man in France. She should have taken the tyrant's letter and returned to the safety of England. That spring, as war gathered like an inevitable storm on the horizon, Nicholas had nearly driven himself mad with worry over Emma.

But by June of that year, Napoleon had been defeated at Waterloo, and by July, Louis XVIII once again sat on the throne of France. Emma came through her ordeal not only unscathed, but more popular in her own country than she had been before. Her vouchers to Almack's were restored; the old Queen welcomed the duchess at the royal levees; and the Prince Regent gave a dinner in her honor at Carlton House, where he presented her with a little gold medal.

To avoid seeing her, Nicholas had retreated to the countryside, to Camford, returning to London only when he was certain she had gone away again.

"Nicky? Did you hear me?" Julia's voice pierced the air. "I said—"

"I heard you, madam," he said sharply. "You forget, Julia, that our marriage was a scandal. We cannot assume that we are welcome everywhere."

"Silly!" said Julia. "We got married to *avoid* the scandal, remember?"

"I do not like going to a house when the owner is away from it," he repeated stubbornly.

"Nonsense, my love. We arrived at Warwick last year when the duke was not at home."

The endearment made Nicholas shudder. "That was your father's doing," he said darkly. "I shall never forget my embarrassment when I met the duke for the first time, and he said, 'Who the devil are you?' Not in so many words," he amended. "But that was his grace's meaning."

Julia shrugged. "Papa didn't want you going to London to meet with the attorney," she said simply. "The attorney would have told you about Cousin Catherine."

Before meeting with the attorney in London, Nicholas had had no idea of Lady Catherine St. Austell's existence. She was his cousin, the daughter and only child of the last

Earl of Camford, from whom Nicholas had inherited the title. Hugh Fitzroy had been her legal guardian, as he had been Nicholas's before Nicholas came of age.

Fearful that Nicholas would marry this other cousin, rather than one of their daughters, the Fitzroys had kept Lady Catherine a secret until after Nicholas was safely engaged to Julia.

Julia, too, had kept the secret; it was another thing for which Nicholas could not forgive her. Not that she seemed to require forgiveness. She certainly felt no remorse.

"We simply couldn't let you find out about Catherine," she explained. "You *had* to marry one of *us*. It was the only way."

"It was the only way to keep your father out of prison," Nicholas agreed coldly. "Yes, madam, I do understand. He'd been stealing from the Camford estate for years."

Julia sighed impatiently. "I wish you would not glare at *me*," she complained. "What did *I* do? If you keep blaming me for all the dreadful things my father has done, we will never get on. We will never be husband and wife."

"You were complicit," he told her stubbornly. "You could have told me that the last Earl of Camford had left behind a daughter."

"But then you might have married *her* instead of me," said Julia, a puzzled frown on her pretty face. "I would not be Countess of Camford."

"That is a distinct possibility."

"Well, then!" she said, laughing. "Only an idiot would have told you. Besides, Catherine seems very happy married to her young man."

"That is the silver lining," Nicholas agreed. In April, when Nicholas had come of age, he had replaced Julia's father as Catherine's guardian. At that time, he had provided Catherine with a generous dowry, making it possible for her to marry the young man of her choice. Lord Hugh Fitzroy previously had refused to allow the match because the young man was only a poor curate.

"Mama and Papa forbade us to tell you about Catherine," Julia went on. "I was only trying to be an obedient daughter. I didn't even *know* Papa was stealing from the estate. He always said it was borrowing. It was very wrong of him to steal, of course, when he should only have borrowed, and I think you were right to turf him out of the house when you came of age. But am I to be punished forever for the sins of my father?"

The day he had sent his in-laws packing had been one of the most satisfying of Nicholas's life, but even the memory of that happy occasion was not enough to bring a smile to his face as he looked at his wife. After all, he had not been able to send *her* packing. "You are not blameless. It was not your *father* who climbed naked into my bed," he reminded her.

Julia giggled provocatively. "Lucky for you!"

Nicholas shook his head in disgust.

Julia scowled, hating him for his complete immunity to her charms. "I wonder what my mother will say when I tell her you have not yet consummated our marriage," she said threateningly.

"I neither know nor care," Nicholas said as the carriage rolled to a stop.

"But aren't you afraid of looking ridiculous? Everyone will think you are impotent!" she protested, quite bewildered by his nonchalance.

"When it comes to you, madam, I am," he answered rudely.

Servants dressed in black livery trotted out to meet the carriage, and huge black wreaths hung on the double doors of the great house. At the sight, Nicholas was forcibly reminded that Lord Michael Fitzroy had died less than six months before, fully ten days after the Battle of Waterloo, from wounds he had sustained in the action. Warwick was in the depths of mourning.

Nicholas suddenly felt ashamed of himself. Despite Lord Hugh's pilfering, Camford was still a rich estate, throwing off a staggering income of ten thousand a year. And, as unappealing as he found the idea of making love to his sixteen-year-old cousin, Nicholas knew that few men in his place would be so particular. Sometimes he envied those other men for their ability to use women without regret or remorse.

The footmen were already removing Julia's trunk from the boot. There could be no turning back from Warwick now. Barring some calamity, Nicholas and Julia would be obliged to stay until Twelfth Night. Darting through the icy rain, Julia hurried into the house, lifting her skirts to show off expensive stockings of purple silk. The more soberly dressed Nicholas followed her slowly. He did not mind the cold rain. It reminded him of his days at sea when exposure to the elements was an everyday occurrence.

"Where is everyone?" Julia called to the butler.

Carstairs, looking about a hundred years old in a suit of funereal black, was moving slowing across the Great Hall to them. Gone were the garlands and wreaths of balsam fir that had filled the room with their scent the year before. In their place were drapes of black bunting.

"I have the distinct impression that you were not expecting us, Carstairs," Nicholas said, when the butler had greeted them. He glared at Julia, who merely tossed her head.

Carstairs looked frailer than he had the year before. "Lady Anne did give us to understand that your lordship and your ladyship would be spending Christmas at Camford," he apologized. "I shall have a suite readied for you at once, my lord, if you would be good enough to wait."

"I am sorry for the misunderstanding," said Nicholas. "If

it's not too much trouble, Lady Camford and I would prefer separate rooms."

Julia shot him a hurt, angry look.

"Very good, my lord," Carstairs replied without a change of expression. "We have several rooms at the ready now. I had assumed your lordship required an apartment. If you will follow me . . ."

"Was that really necessary?" Julia hissed at her husband as they followed the butler. "Must the whole world know that you hate me? What will people think?"

Nicholas shrugged. "Tell them that I snore. Tell them I am impotent. I don't really care. I will not share a room with you. Indeed, I can hardly bear to share a house with you."

Julia forgot to keep her voice down. "Oh, you take delight in humiliating me!" she complained. "I should have let Octavia have you. *Then* you would be sorry!"

"I'm quite sorry enough as it is, thank you," he returned, drawing from her an inarticulate burst of rage. "Compose yourself, madam," he said severely. "You wanted to be my wife. You have no right to complain of your treatment."

Julia flounced into her room and banged the door shut. Nicholas moved on to his. When he had washed and changed his clothes, he headed for the stairs. Julia caught up to him on the landing. Insisting that they go down together, she seized his arm.

The yellow drawing room was about half the length of the main, or blue drawing room. It was used by the family for smaller, intimate gatherings. As Carstairs opened the doors to announce the arrival of Lord and Lady Camford, three ladies dressed in black looked back at them, startled.

Julia snickered at the sight. "Double, double, toil and trouble," she murmured under her breath before surging forward to kiss her mother and her two aunts.

"Mama! Aunt Harriet! Aunt Susan!"

Lady Harriet and Lady Susan were playing piquet. With

her severe white crop of hair, Lady Harriet looked much the same—tough and thin as a whip—but Lady Susan had grown so fat that her newest chin almost rested on the broad shelf of her bosom. She seemed to have abandoned her corset entirely, and her bright red hair had been allowed to go gray. Like an actress without cosmetics, she was almost unrecognizable.

"My dear Julia," Lady Anne said faintly, as her daughter embraced her. She had been working at her embroidery frame, and the sudden arrival of her daughter had caused her to prick her finger. Next to her mother, Julia looked like an exotic bird with her vivid red hair and her bright blue and green costume. Lady Anne's black gown emphasized her thinness and made her faded blue eyes look almost colorless. These eyes widened as she caught sight of her son-in-law, who had followed Julia into the room. Nicholas looked every bit as angry as he had when Lady Anne had seen him last, but she gave him a hopeful smile. For added protection, she touched the gold cross that hung around her neck on a fine chain.

"Nicholas! I did not expect to see you here. Oh, but you should be at Camford, both of you! Who will give the Christmas Ball at Camford if you are not there?"

Nicholas bowed to his aunt. "The same person who gave it last year, I should imagine."

"But there *was* no ball last year," Lady Anne said, puzzled. "Catherine could not give a ball on her own, and you were here with us."

"You need not remind me of that, Aunt!" he said sharply.

Lady Anne was bewildered. "But you said—you said the same person—I asked you who would give the ball this year, and you said the same person who gave it last year."

Julia rolled her eyes. "Honestly, Mama! You seem to grow stupider every year."

Nicholas sighed. "My cousin, Lady Catherine, and her husband will be giving the ball this year at Camford."

"But *you* are the Earl of Camford, not he," Lady Anne protested mulishly. "*He* is nothing more than the son of my late brother's steward! A mere country curate!"

Julia snorted. "With the dowry my husband gave poor Catherine, Mr. Prescott can well afford to play the country gentleman."

"It is the least I could do after the way my uncle treated her when she was his ward," Nicholas argued.

The jet ornaments on Lady Susan's gown rattled like beetles as she bristled with anger. "You accuse my brother of being a poor guardian? Why, he doted on the chit!"

Nicholas snorted. "How? By stealing her allowance and gambling it away? Locking her in her room? Intercepting her letters? These are signs of affection, indeed! Why, he was like a villain in a novel, preying upon the weak, defenseless girl. His own niece, too!"

Lady Anne's fingers felt at her throat for her gold cross. "Let us not speak of my husband," she pleaded with Nicholas. "God has punished him for his misdeeds," she added with a certain relish. "He can do no more harm to anyone."

In July, Lord Hugh had suffered a severe apoplectic attack that had left him partially paralyzed. He had a nurse now, a brawny woman who pushed him around in a Bath chair. Every evening, Lady Anne sat with her husband for one hour, reading to him from the Bible. Otherwise, she had nothing to do with him. She had never known such contentment.

Julia flung herself down in a chair. "Is God punishing me, too?" she wanted to know. "Practically speaking, Nicky has *given* Camford to Catherine," she told the other ladies with the air of one reporting a terrible crime. "After he turfed out my mother, my father, and all my sisters, *we* did not stay long ourselves. I have been living in London all these months, while *Catherine* plays the great lady at Camford. Anyone would think that *she* was the countess."

"London?" Lady Anne echoed in disbelief. In her usual way, she missed the crux of Julia's complaint. "London in the summer? But it is so very hot. How can you bear it?"

"I'm sure I don't know," Julia said resentfully. "But my husband is determined that Catherine should be mistress of Camford, and that *I,* his wife, should be a vagabond."

"Lady Catherine was born in that house," Nicholas told her sharply. "It is the only home she has ever known. I will not take it from her and give it to you. Besides, she is very popular with the local people. Her goodness will repair some of the harm my father-in-law caused."

"I'm sure my brother only did what he thought was best," Lady Susan snapped.

"Now it is *my* turn to do what *I* think best," Nicholas replied shortly.

Lady Harriet looked at him shrewdly. "Have you come here for revenge, sir? What can you do to my brother? He can't even walk. He can barely talk. He can't even feed himself."

Nicholas blinked at her in surprise. "Revenge? Not at all, ma'am. It would be cruel to pursue a vendetta against a man in a Bath chair."

"Then why are you here?" Lady Harriet asked bluntly. "Anne is right—and I do not say this often. You should be at Camford."

"I did not want to come to Warwick," Nicholas admitted, "but Julia has not seen her family since April. She has not seen her father since his unfortunate . . . decline. She wanted to be with her family at Christmas. I am prepared to be civil to everyone," he added.

"Does that include me, Nicky?" Julia drawled. "Are you going to be civil to me?"

A servant entered the room with refreshments. Lady Anne hurried to make the tea.

"Aren't you glad to see me, Mama?" Julia demanded, watching her mother with narrowed eyes. "You look nervous. What are you hiding?"

"Of course I am glad to see you," Lady Anne protested. "And Nicholas, too, of course. I am just surprised, that's all. You might have written to me, Julia."

"I'm a married woman," Julia said loftily. "I'm far too busy to write letters. Where are my sisters?" she asked, her suspicions now thoroughly aroused. "They should be here to pay their respects to me. Has Cornelia brought her new husband? I long to see him. He must be a great fool to have taken her. Or, perhaps his spectacles were broken the day he proposed."

Lady Anne flushed faintly. "Regrettably, Mr. Farnsworth has obligations to his family, and Cornelia, of course, will not want to be parted from her husband. She is with child, you know."

Julia laughed unpleasantly. "How nice for Cornelia! And my other sisters? *They* are here, surely. *They* have no husbands to take them anywhere."

Lady Anne made a silent appeal to Lady Harriet.

Lady Harriet grimaced. "Your sisters went out for a ride with Mr. Palafox, but they were caught in the rain. I am sure they will join us presently, when they have dried off."

Nicholas frowned at the mention of Palafox. He had thought that he had seen the last of that gentleman. "Charles Palafox?" he said stiffly. "He is here?"

Julia sat forward in her chair. "*Charles?*" she shrieked. "What is *he* doing here?"

Lady Anne now looked quite frightened. Again, it was left to Lady Harriet to explain. "Charles Palafox is engaged to your sister, Octavia," she said bluntly.

"Octavia! I am all astonishment," Julia said coolly. "Poor Mr. Palafox!"

Lady Harriet snorted. "Not he! When the marriage takes place, Mr. Palafox will be a very rich man, from what I understand. His rich old aunt, Mrs. Allen, approves the match."

"How nice for Octavia," Julia said sourly. "I am glad she finally has found someone. I *do* feel rather guilty at times for having stolen Nicky from her. That is why I have never allowed him to buy me that enormous pink diamond he is always raving about! Why, how merry we shall be this Christmas!" she went on gaily. "Who knows? Perhaps we will find husbands for poor Flavia and Augusta!"

"I doubt it," Lady Harriet said dryly. "In case you hadn't noticed, Julia, we are all in mourning for Lord Michael."

"We mourn General Bellamy, too, Sister!" Lady Susan said angrily.

Nicholas was startled. "I beg your pardon, ma'am! I—I did not know that your husband had died. I thought—"

"Killed at Waterloo," Lady Susan interrupted. "Just like poor Michael."

"I am sorry," Nicholas stammered. "I could have sworn I read in the papers that General Bellamy had been sent to India to put down the latest mutiny."

Lady Harriet sighed. "He was, Camford. He was. George Bellamy is not dead, Sister," she told Lady Susan firmly. "I don't doubt you *wish* he were dead, but wishing don't make it so. He has gone to India with his mistress, that Camperdine creature, but he is not dead."

"Slander!" snarled Lady Susan. "I tell you, my husband was killed leading a cavalry charge at Waterloo. That was *my* George, brave and faithful to the end. He died with my name on his lips!" she shouted, glaring at them defiantly. "This other Bellamy, that one reads of in the newspapers, is nothing more than an imposter."

Lady Harriet rolled her eyes. "There is no arguing with

her," she told Nicholas. "Bellamy's desertion has driven her out of her wits, I'm sorry to say."

"You must forgive my sister's stupidity," Lady Susan interrupted coldly. "She has been in love with George these many years, and his death has unhinged her mind. She cannot accept that he is dead. She cannot accept that he died loving me," she added. "But, then, ever since the curate found her naked in the baptismal font, she's been a little bit off."

"I . . . I see," said Nicholas, wondering if it were not too soon to make some excuse and run back to his room, or perhaps even back to London. If the sisters' irrational bickering was any indication, it was going to be a most tedious Christmas.

"Will you not sit down, Nicholas?" Lady Anne said pleasantly.

Nicholas declined. "I have been sitting in the carriage all day. I prefer to be on my feet."

Julia, in a burst of wifely duty, brought Nicholas a cup of tea. "Where is everyone?" she demanded, returning to her seat. "The duke isn't here."

"His grace has been delayed," Lady Anne told her. "We expect him tomorrow."

"Very well, but where are the other guests? Nicky and I expected the house to be full of people and gaiety. Instead, it's quiet and dull."

"Julia, we are in mourning," Lady Harriet reminded her. "I'm afraid that means you can expect a very quiet, dull Christmas. There's to be no Christmas Eve Ball this year."

"Why not?" cried Julia. "I have brought the most beautiful ball gown from London. I had it made specially! It cost me a fortune."

"You mean it cost *me* a fortune," Nicholas corrected her.

"It has not been six months since I lost my poor Bellamy!" Lady Susan bawled. "Not to mention poor Michael. Would you dance on their graves, young woman?"

"I don't think they're buried under the ballroom floor, Aunt Susan," said Julia.

"My George is interred in the Fitzroy crypt, of course," said Lady Susan. "There is a place beside him waiting for me. I will join him soon, I daresay. But poor Michael was buried in godless Belgium. It was the most terrific scandal! But I suppose that dago wife of his couldn't be bothered to bring him home," she sniffed. "Well, she has gone back to her own dusky people now, I understand. I still say she should *not* have been allowed to keep Michael's fortune—or the little boy, for that matter. Though, personally, I doubt the child is my nephew's."

"Based on what, you old fool?" Lady Harriet demanded.

"These dago women are all the same," Lady Susan informed her curtly. "Fast! Very fast indeed! I am sure she was deceiving poor Michael. She tried to seduce my poor Bellamy, you know. But George could never stop loving me. He died with my name on his lips."

"And Mrs. Camperdine on his whatsit," Lady Harriet muttered under her breath.

Nicholas could endure no more. Hastily, he made his excuses and returned to his room, where he spent the rest of the afternoon writing letters.

# Chapter Sixteen

That evening, before dinner, Nicholas was the first to arrive at the lounge. His attention was immediately caught by the painting hung prominently beside the fireplace. It showed Emma, Duchess of Warwick, seated beneath a beautiful spreading oak tree, flanked by her two sons, the younger being encircled in his mother's arms. The 11$^{th}$ Duke of Warwick looked straight at the viewer with an expression of arrogant condescension as he placed a crown of leaves on his mother's head.

The triple portrait had not hung there last Christmas, but Nicholas recognized it all the same. Earlier in the year, it had been on display in London in the atelier of the famed society portrait painter, Sir Thomas Lawrence, who had been knighted only that January. Engravings had been available for purchase all over London, but crowds flocked to Russell Square to see the original, especially after Napoleon Bonaparte's return to France, when the duchess's fate was still in doubt.

"Quite a good likeness, don't you think?" said a voice at Nicholas's elbow.

Lady Susan had sailed into the room

"Ma'am," he muttered, embarrassed to have been caught staring at Emma's portrait like a lovesick schoolboy.

"But then no one knows her better than Lawrence," Lady Susan went on. "They were lovers, of course. They are still good friends. Such a philanderer! Why, he even tried his charm on *me,* if you can believe that!"

Jealousy writhed in Nicholas's breast. He could not contain it. "Is there anyone who was not her lover?" he muttered bitterly.

Lady Susan looked at him with pity. "Oh, you poor man," she said.

Mr. Charles Palafox escorted Octavia Fitzroy into the room. Or, perhaps, it was the other way around. To Nicholas's annoyance, Octavia brought her fiancé directly to him. Pale and slim, Octavia looked like a scarecrow in her black gown. "Good evening, Cousin Nicholas," she said evenly. "You remember Mr. Palafox, of course."

"Vaguely," Nicholas said, yielding to childish pique as Palafox smiled at him.

The man had not changed at all. He was as handsome and false as ever. He had sold out of the army just in time to be spared any danger of having to fight at Waterloo.

"My lord," he said, offering Nicholas an ironic bow. "You have heard our good news?"

"Yes. My congratulations," Nicholas answered shortly.

"Thank you, Cousin Nicholas," Octavia answered evenly, her handsome face as masklike as ever. "Is Julia not with you? She will want to congratulate us, I am sure."

"Yes, indeed," said Palafox, his gray eyes sweeping the room. "Where is the vivacious Lady Camford this evening?"

"If she is true to form," Nicholas answered, "she will be the last to arrive."

Octavia suddenly stiffened, looking over Nicholas's shoulder. "Lord, what are *they* doing here?" she murmured resentfully.

Turning, Nicholas saw two gentlemen in evening dress standing on the threshold. One was Lord Colin Grey. The other Nicholas recognized belatedly as Lord Ian Monteith. Monty had been badly wounded at Waterloo, and he was still recovering.

As Colin helped his friend down the steps, Nicholas made his excuses to Octavia.

"Hullo," he greeted the two men cheerfully. "Am I glad to see you! I thought I was going to have to pass the port with Palafox."

"Fetch that footstool for me, will you?" Colin said, hardly acknowledging Nicholas's greeting as Monty lowered himself onto a sofa, his rugged face pale from exertion.

"I am *using* this footstool," Lady Harriet snarled at Colin.

"Hand it over, you old witch, or I shall make you eat it," he threatened.

"Please don't fight," Monty said wearily.

Muttering a curse, Lady Harriet pushed the footstool away from her with her foot. Thanking her, Nicholas carried it over to the sofa. "Compliments of Lady Harriet," he said, as Colin eased Monty's foot up onto the stool.

A horrifying scar cut across the Scotsman's cheek, slicing him right across the lips. At Waterloo, he had been slashed across the face by a French cuirassier, and thrown from his horse. Left with a broken leg, he somehow had dragged himself into the relative safety of a farmyard, where he had lain overnight before being found the next morning, one of the few to have survived the night. He had been thrown on a cart and taken to a cottage.

"The most unsanitary little hovel you ever saw," Colin elaborated, shuddering delicately, as he related this part of the tale. Colin looked incredibly unchanged, as slim and young and beautiful as ever, and no less flamboyant. "I nearly fainted when I saw it. What a nightmare! I couldn't sleep a wink, I was so terrified of the rats. I still wake up in a cold sweat. But *this* is not the work of a Portsmouth tailor!" he suddenly exclaimed, eyeing Nicholas's attire with warm approval. "Why, Camford, I do believe you have acquired the London stamp!"

Nicholas hardly heard the compliment. "You were there? In Belgium?"

"My dear, everyone was there," Colin replied. "Except you, of course, and poor Emma, who was stuck in Paris missing all the fun."

"Fun!" Nicholas protested.

"Oh, yes; it was great fun while it lasted," Colin replied. "When the London Season ended, we just picked up and moved the party to Brussels. It was nothing but balls and parties until that horrid little man invaded with his nasty little army. Why, the night before the invasion, Monty was doing his sword dance at the Duchess of Richmond's ball, weren't you Monty?"

Without waiting for a reply from his friend, Colin ran on. "Of course, *I* knew all along that Bonaparte would move to strike before the Allies had consolidated their forces. But no one ever listens to me." He sighed. "I spent three days looking for Monty, first in all the makeshift hospitals. Then I screwed my courage to the sticking place, and rode out to the battlefield. I found Lord Michael first, just clinging to life. His wife was with him already. He'd been knocked off his horse by a cannonball. They'd taken him to some dreadful farmhouse, too. I didn't find Monty in his hovel until the twenty-first of June! He'd not seen a surgeon; indeed, there were scarcely any surgeons to be had. By this time, the army was in pursuit of the French, and they naturally had taken their surgeons with them. I ended up having to nurse him myself. What a bore! I really thought that Michael would live, and Monty would die, but mysterious are the ways of God and man."

He made no mention of his sister, and Nicholas did not ask.

Colin shook his head as if to clear it of all gloomy thoughts. "But enough of that! *Damme,* I'm hungry. Who are we waiting for?" he asked brightly. "Julia, of course."

Julia arrived at last, looking ravishing in a satin gown of royal blue. "Sorry, I don't have anything black to wear," she said carelessly, enjoying the effect her entrance had on her drab unmarried sisters, especially Octavia, who looked positively green with envy.

"Oh, dear!" she said, looking at the gentlemen in the room. "Only four men! And seven ladies? I'm afraid my sisters will have to console each other. Now then! Which of you handsome gentlemen will be taking *me?* To dinner, I mean," she added with a laugh. "Let's see . . . Nicky should take Mama. Lord Colin, of course will take Aunt Harriet. That leaves Lord Ian for Aunt Susan, and Mr. Palafox for me.

"You'll have to give him up, I'm afraid," she said, marching up to her eldest sister with breathtaking arrogance.

"I'm not taking that moldy old nanny goat anywhere!" Colin declared. "'Tis enough to make a man lose his appetite. Come, Julia, I'll take you."

Lady Harriet glared back at Colin with venomous hostility. "Whoreson! As though I should go anywhere with a tedious, puking, milk-livered, mincing fop like you."

"*What* did you call me?"

"Oh, you're not still fighting, are you?" said Julia, taking Mr. Palafox's arm, even though Octavia had not relinquished him. "I thought for sure you would have mended fences by now. So he kidnaped you, Aunt Harriet. He stripped you naked and locked you in the church. It's Christmas! Can't you just forgive him?"

"She?" Colin shouted. "She—forgive *me?* She's the one who started it! I'm the victim here! I should be forgiving her for writing her poison letters."

"Oh, but it was not Aunt Harriet who wrote those letters," Julia said gaily, her beautiful, dark eyes dancing with amusement.

"Of course it was," said Colin. "She admitted it!"

"No, I didn't," said Lady Harriet, her lip curled back over her teeth like an angry dog's. "I refused to deny it, that's all. I refused to answer your impertinent questions."

"That's because you did it," Colin growled at her. "You were jealous of Monty, so you got rid of him."

"It wasn't her," Julia insisted. "*I* did it. If you could see your faces right now!" she went on, giggling as they all stared at her in disbelief. "Oh, I could just die laughing! Did you really never suspect me?"

"Julia!" Nicholas rebuked her.

"I must say, I never saw what all the fuss was about," Julia babbled on. "So *what* if Lord Colin is a backgammon player? Lots of people play backgammon. *I* play backgammon. When I am in a mood, I can even prefer it to cards. Charles, do you play backgammon?"

"Never mind all that," Nicholas said impatiently. "Why would you do such a thing, Julia?"

His tone was that of an autocratic husband, but nearly a year of marriage had taught Julia that his bark was worse than his bite. She had no fear of him.

"I'll never tell," she said coyly.

"I put her up to it," Monty quietly announced. Pushing aside the footstool, he struggled to his feet. "I'm responsible."

"Ha!" said Lady Harriet. "I guessed as much. You never fooled me for an instant!"

Colin was stunned. "What? Monty!" he said, fumbling his words.

"He told me it was a joke," said Julia, eager to reclaim everyone's attention. "He told me he'd do it himself, but that Colin would recognize his handwriting."

"After Emma rejected my advances, I really had no

excuse to stay," Monty explained. "I had to leave. So . . . I asked Julia to write the letters."

"But why, Monty? I don't understand."

"Isn't it obvious?" Lady Harriet sneered. "He wanted to poison the well. He was afraid you'd find someone else to take his place, Lord Colin. Those letters were meant to scare everybody else away. If *he* couldn't have you, no one else would."

"Oh, Monty!" Colin said sadly. "Is it true what the ugly old hag is saying?"

"Can you ever forgive me?" Monty asked contritely.

"Of course he'll never forgive you," Lady Harriet snapped. "You've cost him the only true friend he's ever had—me! He wouldn't piss on you if you were on fire!"

"Don't be an ass, Monty," Colin said impatiently. "Of course I forgive you. There's nothing to forgive. I just wish you'd told me, that's all."

"What!" howled Lady Harriet. "What do you mean you forgive him? How can you even possibly *think* of forgiving him? What he did was *un*forgivable!"

"So is what I did to you," Colin pointed out. "But you've already forgiven me for that, haven't you?"

"No," she said darkly. "No, I haven't!"

"But it's Christmas," he protested.

"Not yet, it isn't."

"Well!" he said indignantly. "May I at least escort you to dinner?"

"No, you may not," she sniffed. "And I don't want your Scotsman either. Lord Camford, would you be good enough to lend me your arm?"

"Of course, ma'am," said Nicholas.

They went in to dinner. The food was plain English cookery, nothing like the sumptuous feasts they had enjoyed the year before. At the close of the meal, Lady Harriet rose to lead the ladies out, but Julia jumped up, insisting that she, the Countess of Camford, take precedence over her aunt, her mother, and her three elder sisters.

"I have a terrible feeling," said Palafox, when the gentlemen were alone, "that we shall all be very dull until the duchess arrives. She brings her French chef with her, I hope, when she comes tomorrow?"

It vexed Nicholas that Palafox seemed to know when Emma planned to arrive. "If the food is not to your liking, Palafox," he said irritably, "then perhaps you should go elsewhere."

"I didn't say I didn't like the food," Palafox answered coolly. "I expect it will be better when the duchess arrives, that is all. Your lordship needn't bite my head off. Will you be good enough to pass the port, my lord?"

"You wouldn't like it," Nicholas assured him, helping himself to more port. "It's not very good. How is your brother?" he asked, turning to Colin. "I've not seen Lord Scarlingford since the parliamentary recess. Will he be here for Christmas?"

"Heavens, no. My brother is now the Duke of Chilton," Colin said. "Far too busy and important to visit his relations at Christmastime."

"I'm sorry," said Nicholas. "I had not heard that your father was dead. My condolences. Perhaps your sister is at Chilton now?"

"Emma at Chilton? Our father died months ago. I believe Emma was in Germany when he died. She took the boys there for the summer, to visit our mother's people, the Brandenburgs. At present, my sister is purchasing an estate for Grey; she stayed at Wingate an extra day to close with the attorneys. She will be here tomorrow, unless something delays her."

"What a charming Christmas present!" Mr. Palafox remarked. "I wish someone would buy *me* an estate. Is it a very large estate?"

"Not at all," said Colin. "Only about twenty thousand acres or so. Nothing to Warwick, of course, but what is? I would not have bought it myself. The attics are drafty, and the breakfast parlor has the most hideous green wallpaper you ever saw."

"Paper can be changed," said Palafox, "and I never look into attics."

"I believe my sister means to refurbish the place, but nothing can change the fact that it is too close to the village church."

"What is so terrible about that?" asked Nicholas.

"The bells, man, the bells!" said Colin. "One needs one's beauty sleep."

"Is Wingate convenient to Warwick?" Palafox asked. "I shall need a place in the country when Octavia and I wed. I've no intention of taking her with me everywhere I go, after all! Perhaps Wingate will suit, if the duchess is looking for a tenant."

"Wingate is not thirty miles away," Colin answered. "We could drive there in less than three hours in my curricle. I daresay Emma would be glad of a tenant at Wingate," he added. "Grey isn't likely to live there for quite some time. You will have to speak to her about it, however."

"I shall," said Palafox. "Now, may I please have the port?"

The rain cleared away in the night, and the next day dawned brightly. The weather remained fine all day, but there was no sign of the duke, his mother, or Lord Grey. By evening, Nicholas was worried that they might have met with some accident. He urged Colin to send riders, but Emma's brother was not in the least concerned. He continued to play cards with Mr. Palafox, Octavia, and Julia. Julia was Colin's partner.

"My sister often changes her plans without notice," Colin

explained. "If they had met with an accident, I'm sure we would have been informed." Seeing that Nicholas was far from satisfied, he added, "If they are not here by noon tomorrow, Monty and I will drive over to Wingate in my curricle. If we meet them on the way, so much the better. The fresh air will do him good, I think."

Charles Palafox looked up from his cards. "Oh? Perhaps the Miss Fitzroys and I could follow in the barouche," he suggested. "I should like to show the place to my betrothed."

"I have seen Wingate," Octavia said, rather severely. "It will not suit."

"I think Wingate is charming," said Julia.

Lady Anne set aside her embroidery. "Are you thinking of taking Wingate, Mr. Palafox?" she asked her future son-in-law. "As you know, we have been living in Bath since Lord Hugh's unfortunate reversal. If you take Wingate, sir, we will never see Octavia. Cornelia, at least, is settled very close to us."

"Nothing has been decided, Mama," said Octavia.

"But you would all be most welcome at Wingate, Lady Anne," said Mr. Palafox. "I daresay the place will have rooms enough for all my relations."

Lady Anne stared at him. "Do you mean . . . ? Mr. Palafox, do not tease me! Are you offering us a home with you?"

"Of course, Lady Anne," he replied. "I shall be obliged to travel a great deal—for business, you understand."

"What sort of business?" Colin asked suspiciously. "Surely not the kind that puts dirt under a man's nails?"

"Charles is going to stand for Parliament," Octavia said proudly.

Colin nodded.

"While I am away . . . er . . . campaigning, Octavia will be glad to have her family around her," said Palafox. "What sort of a son-in-law would I be if I did not embrace my wife's relations as my own? Eh, Lord Camford?"

Nicholas gazed past the other man stonily, while Octavia sought in vain to catch her betrothed's eye.

Lady Anne was already going into raptures. "Oh, my dear Mr. Palafox! That is generosity! I never knew such generosity, I'm sure. Mr. Farnsworth has a generous heart, but I fear he lacks resources. And, of course, Nicholas—" She broke off in embarrassment. "Of course I do not mean to criticize my nephew," she added, "for making us leave Camford."

"May I go to Wingate tomorrow?" Flavia asked. "If we are to live there, Mama, I should like to see it."

"Oh, yes!" said Lady Anne. "We shall all go."

Octavia cleared her throat. "I think, perhaps, what Mr. Palafox means, Mama, is that you and Papa and my unmarried sisters will be very welcome to *visit* us."

"No, no," Palafox contradicted her immediately. "I invite them to live with us, Miss Fitzroy. What sort of husband would I be if I left you with only my quarrelsome aunt for a companion?"

For a moment, Octavia's mask slipped, revealing an expression of profound dismay. "Your aunt?" she echoed rather shrilly. "You do not mean *Mrs. Allen?* Mrs. Allen is to live with us? Mr. Palafox, I protest! Mrs. Allen is common and vulgar. Her husband was in Trade! I will not have it."

"When Mrs. Allen makes her fortune over to me, she will have nowhere else to go," Palafox said curtly. "It is the only condition she places on me—apart from her demand that I marry *you,* of course, my dear."

Octavia closed her lips tightly.

"Poor Charles!" Julia cried softly. "That is *two* conditions! How I detest conditions! I would never allow anyone to put conditions on me."

"No, nor I," Colin agreed. "But, then again, I am rich."

The next morning at breakfast, Julia announced her intention of going to Wingate with the rest of the party. When Octavia told her sourly that there was no room in the barouche,

Mr. Palafox retaliated by offering Julia his seat. He would rather ride, anyway.

"So would I," Miss Augusta said immediately.

"It was never my intention to sit in the barouche," Julia told them, tossing her head.

It was decided that Octavia would share the barouche with her mother and Flavia. Monty and Colin would ride out in the latter's curricle. Mr. Palafox, Lady Camford, and Miss Augusta would go on horseback. Lord Camford did not intend to go at all, even though his anxiety had been the impetus for the scheme.

They had no sooner settled on this plan, when a servant brought them the news that baggage carts had begun to arrive. Within the hour, the Duke of Warwick was seen riding up the avenue on a fine black charger. With him were his younger brother, Lord Grey, and a stout, silver-haired man of soldierly bearing with a black patch over one eye. The family assembled in the yellow drawing room to greet them.

"Harry!" Julia cried exuberantly, running down the length of the room to embrace her second cousin. "How grown-up and handsome you look!"

The duke flushed. "I hope I look grown up," he said, a bit sullenly. "I'm fourteen, after all. Who are you?"

Julia threw back her head and laughed. "Have I changed so much? Oh, Harry, you're joking me! 'Tis I, Cousin Julia!"

"Of course I'm joking you! You do look a bit different with your hair up like that," he added, his eyes involuntarily resting on the high round breasts that threatened to spill from her pink muslin gown. "I have not seen you since your wedding," he added.

"Well, I hope you're happy to see me now," she said, with the pretty little pout she tried so often, and without success, on her husband. "Even though I'm married, I am still your favorite cousin, I hope."

Harry was more susceptible than Nicholas. "Y-yes, of

course!" he exclaimed as she latched on to his arm. "You remember Grey, of course. Say hello to your cousin Julia, Grey. And, may I present my tutor, Major von Schroeder, late of the King's German Legion. Fritz, this is my cousin Julia—er, Lady Camford."

The soldierly man with the eyepatch bowed correctly to Julia. He spoke with a heavy German accent. Julia immediately dismissed him as an old man, a servant. "Your tutor?" she teased Harry, taking his arm. "I hope you don't mean to spend *all* your time in the schoolroom, Harry."

"No, indeed," the duke hastened to assure her. "I've promised Fritz a proper holiday, with lots of hunting and shooting. Anyway, he's much more than a tutor, you know. He's a great friend. I don't really need a tutor anymore, you know. Mainly, he's Grey's tutor. Mama found him when we were in Germany. It was splendid having him for a guide when we visited the battlefield at Waterloo."

"Sacred ground!" exclaimed Lady Susan, clasping her hands together and raising her eyes to heaven.

"It's quite an interesting place," said Harry. "The curious terrain, I believe, had a great deal to do with how the battle was fought and won."

"It must have been terrible for you," Julia murmured. "Was there very much blood?"

"All that sort of thing had been cleared away by the time we saw it," Harry said, evidently disappointed. "But we dined at the inn at La Belle Alliance, where Napoleon had his headquarters. And Grey found an eagle from a French cap. Even Mama said the experience had improved her understanding of the battle. And, of course, we paid our respects at my uncle's grave, which was our principle object in going there."

"I wanted to go to Brussels," said Julia, "but Nicky wouldn't hear of it."

Harry frowned. "Nicky?"

"Of course you remember my husband," Julia interrupted, still holding her cousin's arm. "The Earl of Camford."

"Yes, of course," the duke murmured. "The fellow who raised the tannenbaum for us. How do you do, sir?"

"Harry!" twelve-year-old Grey interrupted. "Are we going to see the harbourer now, or what? I want a look at the herd before dark. You promised!"

Lady Harriet reminded her grandnephew that he had yet to pay his respects to the rest of his family, and Grey reluctantly gave her two fingers to shake.

"Your grace may remember Mr. Palafox from last year," Lady Anne said quickly as Harry looked curiously at the fellow. "Mr. Palafox is now engaged to my eldest daughter."

"Your grace."

"I am glad to see you, Harry," said Colin, shaking the duke's hand after having greeted Grey more informally, by mussing his red hair. "When you didn't come yesterday some of us were worried. Not I, of course, but some others. Where is my sister, by the way?"

Harry sighed impatiently. "Oh, that woman! She travels at her own pace in that enormous carriage of hers," he said. "With any luck, she'll be here before nightfall! Perhaps! But you are all dressed to go out!" he said suddenly. "Have I interrupted your plans?"

"Yes, but it don't signify," said Colin. "We were just going over to Wingate to see what had happened to you."

"Mr. Palafox is thinking of taking it," said Julia, "if your mama is looking for a tenant."

"I'm afraid my mother has plans to improve the place," Harry replied. "That's why we stayed an extra day—so that Mama could meet with the architect. It will be six months or more before the place is done."

"Six months would do very well, your grace," said Mr. Palafox. "Miss Fitzroy and I mean to wed in June. I should like to see the place, of course."

"I don't see why we couldn't all go the day after St. Stephen's Day," said the duke. "If the weather holds, we could ride. Mama bought me some rather good bloodstock for Christmas, and I'm eager to see them in action in my home county."

"*After* Christmas?" Julia pouted.

Harry laughed. "Before Christmas, I shall be very busy with the hunt, Julia."

"Yes! The hunt!" Grey said impatiently. "May we go to the harbourer now? I want to show the major the herd."

"First, I must just check to see that my charger is settling in all right," his elder brother told him. "He's quite temperamental, you know."

"Oh, yes, the charger," Augusta Fitzroy exclaimed. "He looks a real goer, Cousin Warwick. May I go and have a look at him with you?"

Harry grinned at her. "I knew you'd like him, Gussie! He cost me nearly a thousand guineas. That is to say, he cost *Mama* nearly a thousand guineas."

Julia clung to Harry's arm. "I would like to go, too," she declared jealously. "I love horses as much as Augusta does, though I confess I've not had a proper mount since I married. Lord Camford does not care for horses. He does not ride, and he does not keep a stable."

Harry stared at Nicholas, as though almost unable to comprehend such a sad state of affairs. "Indeed!"

"I would like to see the charger that cost nearly a thousand guineas," said Mr. Palafox.

One by one, the young people succumbed to the lure of the stables. Lady Harriet offered to show Major von Schroeder to his room. Rather than remain with his aunt, Nicholas wandered off to the billiard room to amuse himself. In the past year, he had taken up the game with a vengeance, spending hours at it.

As he was playing, a pair of footmen came into the room

to remove one of the paintings from the wall, a portrait of an old man in a long white wig. Nicholas watched them curiously, but did not inquire. Nor did they offer any explanation, but, in a few moments, an explanation offered itself as two more footmen carried in another painting, obviously meant to replace the one that had been taken away. The new picture was a portrait of Henry Fitzroy, 11th Duke of Warwick. Life-sized, it showed the adolescent in an outdoor scene with a gun broken over one arm, a beautiful setter at his side. Dead at his feet lay a huge stag with magnificent antlers. While not completely realistic, it commemorated the occasion of the duke's first hunt admirably.

As the servants hung the new portrait, the Duchess of Warwick came into the room to supervise their work. She must have slipped quietly into the house after everyone else had gone to the stables. Concentrating on the painting, she did not see Nicholas, for which he was grateful. The delay of just a few moments was enough for him to compose himself.

He had thought that he was prepared to see her again, but now he realized that he was not. He had told himself that all feeling for her had died with the old year, but he now knew he had been lying to himself. He could feel the forces of attraction at work, as powerful as they had been the first time he had set eyes on her.

"It's *crooked*," Emma complained, with her back to Nicholas. "A little to the left, if you please, John. Your *other* left," she added tartly. "Hurry! It's meant to be a surprise."

"Hello, Emma," Nicholas said quietly.

As she spun around to look at him, he was startled all over again by her delicate beauty. She did not seem to have changed at all physically.

"Nicholas!" she exclaimed, almost stunned. "Good heavens! What are you doing here?"

"I have been practicing my bank shot."

"I meant at Warwick. I was not expecting to see you this year."

"My—my wife dragged me here," he answered, drawing his brows together in a frown. "She has not seen her family in some time. But, of course, if you wish me to leave—"

"Oh, don't be silly," she said quickly, her cheeks pink with embarrassment. "You surprised me, that's all. I should have thought you'd be at Camford, but, of course, you and Julia are very welcome here. You are looking very well," she went on quite pleasantly. "I can see that marriage agrees with you."

"And you as well," he answered.

Emma tilted her head. "Oh?"

Nicholas flushed. "I meant, of course, that you are looking well. Not that marriage agrees with you. I remember that marriage does *not* agree with you."

She laughed graciously. "But it *does* agree with you!" she repeated. "You are happy?"

Nicholas stared at her. She could not possibly think *he* could be happy with a vain, silly girl like Julia, could she? he thought angrily. "Yes, we're very happy," he heard his own voice say. "Very happy indeed! I never dreamed I could be so happy."

"I am glad to hear it," Emma said warmly. "Julia is a such a spirited, affectionate girl. I was sure you would be happier with her than you would have been with—with Octavia. Indeed, if you cannot be happy with Julia, I do not think you can be happy with anyone," she laughed.

"Octavia is to marry Mr. Palafox," he told her abruptly.

Emma showed only slight surprise. "Charles Palafox? How interesting!"

"You do not regret losing Mr. Palafox?" Nicholas said sharply.

Her steel-blue eyes widened. "Losing him? But Charles and I were never anything to each other. We were not lovers, if that is what you think."

Nicholas snorted. "You forget, madam, that I found you together on Christmas Eve last year. You were in his bed."

"Oh, *that*," Emma laughed. "I'd almost forgotten. But that was nothing, you know."

"Nothing!" he echoed in disbelief.

"I don't suppose there's any harm in telling you now!" she said, laughing harder. "I went to the wrong room. I didn't know I was in *Charles's* bed. I *thought* I was in *your* bed! Your room. Westphalia. We can laugh about it now, can't we?"

"What?" he said faintly.

"I didn't realize at the time that you'd changed rooms with Mr. Palafox," Emma explained, controlling her hilarity. "It was my intention to meet *you,* Nicholas. That's why I sent you that note, the one you crumpled up and threw at me."

"I *did* change rooms with Palafox," he murmured.

"Yes, I know. I realized it when he returned to Westphalia for a call of nature."

"You meant to rendezvous with *me?*" he said slowly, staring at her. "Not Palafox?"

"Well, yes. But it isn't what you think," she quickly added. "I mean, it was not to be that sort of rendezvous. I had heard that you were going to marry Octavia. I knew instantly—*instantly*—that *that* was how you'd . . ." She paused, drawing in a deep breath. "How you'd gotten my letter back. I'm so sorry, Nicholas. I should have guessed sooner. I don't even think I thanked you properly! Did I?"

"Of course you did," he said.

"Did I? You're very kind," she murmured, "but I'm sure I didn't. I was in such a state, I'm sure I was nasty to you. But when Harry told me at the ball that you were going to marry Octavia—! I knew I couldn't let you ruin your life. I knew you'd never go back on your word, Nicholas, but we thought, Colin and I, that if Octavia found you with me in a compromising position, *she* might jilt *you.* Then you would have been free."

Emma laughed. "It probably would not have worked. In any case, it doesn't matter now, does it? Octavia is to marry Mr. Palafox, and you and Julia are happy together. I got my letter back. Aleta is safe. All's well that ends well."

Nicholas felt that his world had been turned upside down. Outwardly, he remained calm, however. "Yes," he said faintly, his voice tinny and hollow. "All's well that ends well."

# Chapter Seventeen

At Emma's insistence, Nicholas went back to his billiards while she fussed over the painting. "Do you think the picture is straight, my lord?" she asked him as the servants stood ready to leave the room. "Harry hasn't seen it yet," she added. "I want it to look perfect."

Nicholas gave his approval, and Emma dismissed the servants.

"Do you think he will like it?" Emma asked doubtfully. "Oh, sorry! I've made you scratch," she murmured, fishing the ivory ball from the pocket and rolling it to him gently.

"It don't signify," he assured her. "I'm only practicing. You bought him some horses, too, I understand. He is pleased with *them*, so, even if he doesn't like the painting . . ."

Emma laughed briefly. "That is comforting! I begin to think you do not approve of my picture, Lord Camford! But, then, I had forgotten that you are an artist's son. Obviously, that qualifies you to be an art critic!"

"If I have any criticism to offer," said Nicholas, "it is not of the picture, but, rather of the motive behind the gift."

"My motive, sir?" she said, less playfully.

He shrugged. "You obviously feel guilty for having bought your younger son an estate for Christmas. You are trying to make up for it by presenting your eldest son with a number of expensive gifts like this painting. You mean to flatter him with this romantic depiction of his first hunt."

"Indeed, sir! Am I so transparent?" Emma said sarcastically.

"To me," he answered.

"And what, pray, is your motive for beginning an argument with me?"

"That was not my intention."

"You think it romantic, do you?" she said, after a moment, looking up at the picture. "I'll be sure to ask Sir Thomas to slather a little blood on the canvas the next time I see him! If my motives are in doubt, I wonder what you will make of my Christmas present to *you?*" she added, attempting a lighter tone.

"You got me a Christmas present?" he said, surprised.

"You, and Julia, of course. I wish I could give it to you now. I daresay you will think it quite sinister when you do see it, but it's all part of my elaborate plan! I didn't know you were coming to Warwick, so I'm afraid I sent it to your London house," she added seriously.

"I'm sorry," he stammered. "I didn't get you anything."

"But of course you did," she said, smiling. "You sent me a lovely paperweight made of the famous black Camford-shire marble. Thank you! Thank you for your thoughtfulness. One can never have too many paperweights, after all."

"That must have been Julia," Nicholas said, embarrassed. "I would not have sent you a paperweight."

"No," she agreed pleasantly. "You sent me nothing! To which I can ascribe no motive at all. But I have taken too much of your time, my lord," she said, moving swiftly to the door. "I will leave you to break your balls in peace."


Nicholas visited Julia's room as she was dressing for dinner.

"Did you send the duchess a paperweight for Christmas?" he demanded, slamming the door and sending Julia's maid from the room with a look.

Attired in a scarlet evening gown, Julia held up two different earrings. "Rubies or pearls, Nicky?" she asked him. "Rubies or pearls?"

"Did you or did you not send the duchess a paperweight for Christmas?"

"Pearls," Julia said stubbornly, "or rubies?"

"I don't care! Pearls," Nicholas said impatiently. "Now answer my question!"

"Let me think," said Julia. "Yes, I did. I did send her a paperweight. But it was a very nice paperweight, made of our very own Camfordshire marble. Why?"

"Was it your *intention* to insult her grace?" he demanded, furious.

"You didn't see what *she* sent *us*," Julia said coldly.

"No, I didn't, madam! But—but *you* did, I take it?"

"The most dreadful little picture," Julia answered, fastening the ruby earrings to her earlobes. "Just because you were once a sailor does not mean we want some wretched little painting of a wretched little sailboat!"

Nicholas frowned at her. "Sailboat!"

"I took it to an art dealer, but he said it was not an important artist," Julia said indignantly. "It was not worth the canvas it was painted on, he said. Insult her grace, you say? She's fortunate I didn't *throw* that paperweight at her! As much money as she has! What does she mean sending us a stupid, worthless picture!"

"I suppose," said Nicholas, "it was her idea of a joke. As I recall, she found my taste in art to be rather crude. All because I didn't go into raptures over her Rubens and Raphaels!"

"There! You see? She insulted us first," said Julia.

* * *

"How gloomy you look, Mama," the Duke of Warwick complained as Emma walked into her sitting room that evening.

"I'll allow I do not look my best in black," Emma said, glancing at the mirror. "But gloomy? Perhaps a little pale."

"I wish we were not in mourning," he said, as she fiddled with his snow-white cravat. "There can be no Christmas Eve Ball this year, of course," he went on, "but, Mama, could we not have a small do at New Year's Eve?"

"Oh, yes, please, Mama," Colin chimed in. "Just a small do. What could it hurt?"

Emma sighed. "Where is your brother?" she asked Harry, avoiding the subject of New Year's Eve completely.

"He's going to spend the night with the harbourer. We've chosen the Christmas stag for this year already. Fritz is going to take the shot. But Grey has his eye on a handsome buck for next year."

Emma frowned. "Do you mean to go back tonight after dinner?"

"No, Mama. I have to play the host, you know. Grey's all right," Harry added. "Anyway, Fritz is with him."

"Oh, no!" Emma exclaimed softly. "With gentleman so scarce, we can ill afford to lose the major."

"I'm afraid you have lost Monty as well," Colin said apologetically. "His leg is bothering him, poor lamb."

"Four men and eight women," Emma complained. "What a nightmare! Each of you will have to escort two women. There's nothing else to be done."

"I'll take Julia," Harry offered, "and the other one, the one that's getting married. I mean, if it helps *you,* Mama," he added piously.

When they reached the lounge, everyone except Nicholas and Julia had arrived already. Emma found their tardiness very annoying. "Oh, stop tapping your fan," Colin told her. "They've only been married ten months."

"What has that to do with being late for dinner?" Emma demanded.

"You know," he muttered under his breath. "Perhaps they got caught up in the moment. They're both young, good-looking people. It's been known to happen."

Pressing her lips together, Emma snapped open her fan and whipped it back and forth to cool her face. Her temper did not improve when, as Lord and Lady Camford finally appeared, her eldest son made an involuntary sound that sounded suspiciously like "Woof!"

Emma dug her nails into Colin's arm. "Did he just say woof?" she hissed.

"No, of course not," Colin assured her, carefully taking his arm from her grasp. "He said 'oof!' as if the air had all been knocked out of him."

Emma watched with a jaundiced eye as the duke led Julia and her eldest sister in to dinner. Lady Harriet refused the offer of Lord Colin's arm, but Lady Anne and Lady Susan accepted. Mr. Palafox offered one arm to Augusta, and Emma quickly seized the other, leaving Nicholas to attend to Lady Harriet and Flavia.

With half her attention she conversed with Mr. Palafox on the subject of Wingate. With the other half, she watched her son with his cousin Julia as they laughed and chatted together at the other end of the table.

"Mama!" Harry called down the table to her suddenly. "Mama, did you give Julia some sad little picture of a boat?"

"I beg your pardon?" said Emma.

Harry shook his finger at her. "Just because Lord Camford used to be a sailor, doesn't mean he likes pictures of leaky old boats! Really, Mama!"

"Oh, I see," Emma said coolly. Looking at Nicholas, she braided her fingers together and rested her chin on her knuckles. "His lordship does not like the picture?"

"Why should I?" Nicholas replied, shrugging. "It's not an

important artist. I am no longer a sailor. I am the Earl of Camford. If I am going to collect art, it will be first-rate stuff."

"You could put it in your nursery, Nicholas," Lady Anne suggested helpfully. "Indeed, if I recall correctly, we had one very sweet picture of a boat in the nursery at Camford when I was a child. No," she corrected herself, biting her lower lip. "No, it was Noah's ark. I remember now."

"Oh, just send the damn thing back to Mama," Harry said impatiently. "Mama will get you something better, won't you, Mama? Something you'll like."

"Yes, of course," Emma said sweetly. "What would you like, Julia?"

"Well," said Julia. "Since you ask . . . I would like to have my portrait painted by Sir Thomas Lawrence. But since he's been knighted, he's become *so* exclusive. I tried all season to get a sitting with him, but no luck. He's a friend of yours, isn't he, Duchess?"

"You can get Julia a sitting, can't you, Mama?" Harry put in. "Lord knows, we've kept the man in business all these years. He's painted my mother twenty-seven times if he's painted her once."

"I'm afraid Sir Thomas has gone to Vienna," Emma replied. "The Congress has reconvened, and he has commissions from simply everyone, from the Tsar to Monsieur Talleyrand. But, as soon as he returns to England, I'm sure I can persuade him to paint Lady Camford."

"He'll be heartily sick of painting men by then," Harry predicted. "He'll be glad of a pretty face."

"It will give me time to decide what I am going to wear," said Julia. "Will Sir Thomas mind sketching me several different ways?" she inquired. "With different hairstyles, I mean?"

"Lord, no," Emma said dryly. "It's what he lives for."

"That's settled then," Harry said happily.

"Not quite," said Emma. "Was the *wedding* present satisfactory, at least? Did I do all right there, Julia?" she asked solicitously.

"Oh, yes, ma'am," Julia replied. "The Worcestershire tea service emblazoned with the St. Austell coat of arms. We like it very much, don't we, Nicky? We haven't broken a single piece, have we? But, then, I haven't actually got around to unpacking it," she laughed. "You know how it is, when one is newly married."

As soon as dinner was over, Colin went upstairs to look in on Monty, and Emma went with him while the other ladies gathered in the drawing room for coffee.

In Emma's absence, Julia imagined herself the queen of Warwick Palace. "No, Aunt Susan," she preened. "I take the duchess's place, for I am top lady."

Lady Susan presided at the coffee table, undeterred. Her black-clad bulk had already settled into the duchess's place, and she had no intention of moving.

"I am the Countess of Camford!" Julia said, stamping her foot.

"My dear," her mother pleaded. "No one doubts that you take precedence over us, but it is not very becoming to insist."

"Besides which you are not breeding, Miss Julia," said Lady Susan in her far-reaching voice. "You are no one until you breed. Until you give Camford an heir, you take no precedence over me, I can assure you."

"How dare you!" said Julia, her face turning almost as red as her hair.

"What's the matter with you, anyway?" Lady Susan demanded. "Your sister Cornelia married three months after you, and she's already breeding. How often do you copulate with your husband? I trust his lordship is adequately equipped for the task?"

"My dear Susan!" Lady Anne protested weakly, clapping her hands over her ears. "You shouldn't say such things. It is not very nice."

"I'm just getting started," Lady Susan replied. "Come, now, Anne! Let us not be squeamish. You want Julia to breed an heir, don't you?"

"Of course, but—"

"Octavia is soon to be married. She can hear this," Lady Susan declared. "It is useful information for a bride. Flavia and Augusta can go play some music while we chat."

Since they could be assured of hearing every loud word their Aunt Susan uttered, Flavia and Augusta readily assented.

"Now, then," said Lady Susan, studying Julia through her big quizzing glass. "How often do you copulate? Is Camford vigorous or lackadaisical? Does he spend copiously?"

"Of course he does," Julia said, glaring at her. "He's violently in love with me."

"What has that to do with anything?" said Lady Susan. "One of my sons-in-law—I can't remember which one it was now—he had some sort of impediment at the tip of his affair. Two snips with the nail scissors, and he was right as rain. But, you say, he spends like a champion, so that can't be it. Perhaps his spunk is of poor quality."

"I wouldn't know, I'm sure!" Julia snapped. "I never looked!"

"Well, you had better start looking!" said Lady Susan. "Do you at least stand on your head after he has his way with you?"

"Of course," Julia said. "Do you take me for a fool?"

"Oh? Well, you seem to be doing *your* part," Lady Susan observed. "And Camford is doing his. I confess I'm mystified. By all accounts, you should be breeding."

"Perhaps I *am* breeding," said Julia. "Perhaps I'm just not very far along. Have you thought of that, Aunt Susan?"

"She is not breeding," Octavia said flatly. "When we were at the stables, the duke invited us to ride with him tomorrow. Naturally, I suggested that Julia might be in no condition to ride. But she only tossed her head and said quite happily,

'Lord, I ain't breeding! I told Camford I ain't spoiling my figure for him or anyone until I'm at least twenty-five!'"

Octavia sat on the sofa, her back very straight, one ankle wedged behind the other. "Everyone was offended by the indelicacy of her remark," she added, meaning that she herself had been offended. "But Julia gets away with everything!"

"Julia would never say anything so wicked," Lady Anne exclaimed, twisting her hands together. "She knows it is her duty to give Camford an heir. Julia?"

"I need hardly remind you that our cousin Catherine is now married," Octavia went on. "What if she bears her Mr. Prescott a son? A Prescott could then inherit Camford."

Harsh red color stained Lady Anne's cheeks. "That marriage should never have taken place!" she burst out. "When your father was her guardian, he forbade the match! How Nicholas *could*—! Why, Mr. Prescott is nothing more than my late brother's steward! His son shall never be Earl of Camford!"

"If *I* had been Nicholas's wife, I would never have permitted the marriage," said Octavia. "I should be breeding by now, too."

"Perhaps Julia is barren," Lady Susan suggested.

Lady Anne bristled. "Barren! By no means! The women in my family have always been the most conscientious breeders!"

"Until now," said Octavia.

"I was only joking at the stables," said Julia fiercely. "I *am* breeding. I know I am. I'm certain of it. So there!"

"No, you're not!" From across the room, Flavia taunted her younger, prettier sister. Julia had never been kind to her, and now she seized her chance for revenge. "You're bleeding. My maid told me, and your maid told her. What's more: Camford asked for separate rooms! They don't even share a bed!"

"We do not share a bed," Julia screeched, "because I no

longer permit it! The man is a brute. All he ever wants to do is copulate. He loves me *too* much. That is the only problem. He never leaves me alone. Never! He is too vigorous! He hurts me, Mama! My womanhood is in tatters! But he does not dare attack me here. I am safe from him here."

"Attack you?" cried Lady Anne. "Nicholas?"

"It is beyond horrible!" said Julia.

"Of course it's beyond horrible," Lady Susan scoffed. "He is a man. But he is also your husband, and you must submit to his odious caresses or suffer the consequences."

"I won't submit to his odious caresses," said Julia. "I shall get a divorce!"

The ladies gasped as one.

Satisfied with their reaction, Julia turned on her heel and left the room, her red dress trailing behind her like the fiery tail of a dragon.

"Divorce! It's worse than I thought," said Octavia, when Julia had gone. "What do you mean to do, Mama?"

Lady Anne looked startled. "Do?" she echoed, puzzled. "We must hope she does not mean it, of course. There would be such a scandal! She cannot mean it."

"But we cannot depend on Julia to come to her senses, Mama," Octavia said brusquely. "The situation calls for decisive action. Someone must make Julia understand that breeding is her only purpose in life. Someone must talk to her."

"Talk to Julia? Talk to Julia about . . . about . . . Oh, no!" Lady Anne shook her head frantically. "I'm sure that talking about it will only make things worse."

"Someone must speak to her," Octavia insisted. "It should be someone who understands men and their disgusting inner workings."

"But I've already talked to the girl," Lady Susan scoffed.

"Someone who understands *Nicholas*," said Octavia. "Someone who knows him intimately."

Lady Anne frowned in concentration. "He's always spoken fondly of his captain from his days in the Royal Navy."

"For God's sake," Lady Harriet said impatiently. "She means someone who has had sexual relations with the man! *Emma*, you fool. If anyone can help Julia deal with the brute, it is she. Let Emma speak to Julia."

"Yes," Lady Anne said eagerly. "Anything is better than divorce. But . . . who will ask the duchess to speak to Julia?"

"You're her mother," said Lady Harriet. "You do it."

"If it were my daughter, I would not hesitate," said Lady Susan.

"You must do it, Mama," said Octavia. "Everything depends on you."

Lady Anne's pale eyes goggled. "I? Talk to the duchess?"

Lady Anne had scarcely recovered from her surprise when Emma returned to the room with Colin. "My dear Emma!" Lady Susan brayed. "Anne would speak to you."

"Oh?" Emma said politely.

"Invite her grace to take a turn around the room with you," Octavia hissed, giving her mother a push.

Lady Anne obediently climbed to her feet. "Would your grace be good enough to take a turn around the room with me?" she quavered.

"What's that all about?" Colin demanded of Lady Harriet as his sister strolled away with Lady Anne. "What could Anne have to say to my sister that the rest of the room cannot hear?"

"I don't know," Lady Harriet answered with a cruel smile. "I haven't the slightest idea. And, even if I *did* know, I wouldn't tell *you*."

"You're killing me, witch," he complained.

Lady Anne and the duchess had not taken twenty steps together when the rest of the gentlemen returned to the room. Already nervous, Lady Anne discovered that it was quite impossible to take up the sensitive subject with men in the

room. The attempt had to be given up. Emma kindly led
Lady Anne back to the sofa and left her with a cup of coffee.

"What was *that* about?" Colin demanded. "Aunt Harriet
would not say."

"I haven't the slightest idea," Emma answered with a
shrug. "Poor Anne! She opens her mouth, and the words just
sort of fall out in no particular order. I could make no sense
of it. But she's promised to come see me tomorrow morning, and try again."

"I say, Mama!" Harry called loudly. "Where's Julia gone?"

"She was tired, your grace; she's gone to bed," said Lady
Susan. "Perhaps Lord Camford should go and check on her."

"No! No!" Lady Anne protested, starting up in alarm.
"Julia *really* is very tired, Nicholas. You should let her rest."

"Fine," Nicholas said agreeably. "Would anyone care to
give me a game of chess?"

"I will, if you like, my lord," said Palafox.

Palafox was not the antagonist Nicholas had hoped for,
but he bowed graciously and went to set up the chess board.

Harry sat down with his mother, fidgeting as Flavia sat
down at the pianoforte to play. "I suppose I might go out to
the harbourer's, after all," he said presently. "I mean, I know
how you worry about Grey, Mama."

At the moment, Emma was more worried about Harry's
unhealthy fascination with his cousin Julia, but she did not
tell him that.

"Thank you, my love," she said. "I shall rest easier knowing that you are with him. He is at an age, you know, when
he needs his elder brother."

Harry listened to this speech impatiently, and got away as
quickly as he could.

The following morning, Lady Anne was a little better
prepared for her discussion with the duchess. "I hope you

know I would not come to you unless the situation was quite desperate," she began. Reassured by the privacy of the duchess's sitting room, she hardly stammered.

"No, I don't suppose you would," Emma agreed, her eyebrows raised in a question.

"I-I never liked you, you know," Lady Anne said, with such an earnest expression that Emma was hard-pressed not to laugh. "I always thought you were a scarlet woman."

"I never liked you either," Emma answered. "I always thought you were a spineless weakling."

"Oh!" Lady Anne flinched as though she had been slapped across the face.

"Is that all you wanted to tell me?" Emma asked impatiently.

"No, your grace. Julia wants a divorce," Lady Anne whined. "She cannot bear copulating with her husband, and she intends to leave him. If you do not help me, I—I don't know what I'll do! There has never been a divorce in the family before!" she wailed, sinking to her knees on the duchess's Aubusson rug. "Never!"

"Compose yourself, Anne," Emma commanded her. "You're not making any sense. Julia can't possibly want a divorce, and Lord Camford told me himself that they are happy."

"*He* may be happy," Lady Anne said, glowering, "but my daughter is not! It pains me to say it, because he is my nephew, but Nicholas is a horrid beast."

"In what way is he horrid?" Emma scoffed. "Does he beat her? Shout at her?"

"Of course not," said Lady Anne. "Her complaint is more serious. Her womanhood is in tatters. Yes, tatters!" she insisted as Emma looked skeptical. "I have explained to Julia that she cannot deny him his rights as a husband, but she will not listen to me. She says she cannot bear any more—any more—*copulation*."

Modesty compelled Lady Anne to whisper.

Emma jumped to her feet and walked to the window. "But, really, Anne, this is none of my business. I am sorry Julia is unhappy, but what am *I* to do about it? And do get up from the floor," she added impatiently, motioning for Lady Anne to take a seat. "You look ridiculous."

Lady Anne meekly settled into a chair. "Your grace must not offer Julia sanctuary. If she has no place else to go, she must stay with Camford. Will you promise not to let her stay here?"

"I will promise nothing of the kind," Emma said sharply. "If I were Julia's mother, I'd be more worried of making her feel desperate. Whatever happens with Camford, she should be able to depend on her mother's support."

"Oh, I knew you would not help me," Lady Anne said bitterly. "You delight in watching me grovel. Everyone does."

"Oh, for heaven's sake," Emma said impatiently. "If Julia has quarreled with her husband, I daresay it will blow over in a day or two. You are worrying for nothing, Anne. Julia may *feel* that Camford is a horrid beast, but I rather doubt it."

"All men are horrid beasts in the bedchamber," said Lady Anne. "I was brought up to submit to my duty no matter how unpleasant, but Julia . . . She seems to think she deserves better. She is headstrong. She vows never to let him touch her again. I don't expect a woman like *you* to understand, but respectable young ladies do not find that sort of thing at all pleasant."

"I beg your pardon," Emma said coldly.

"Oh, I mean no offense, your grace!" Lady Anne said hastily. "It is well-known that you have had many, many affairs. You would not have done so, if you did not find it enjoyable. Therefore, I must conclude that you *do* like the act which to all respectable females must be highly repugnant. I don't judge," she went on kindly. "It's not your fault; your mama was a foreign lady. Foreigners are so . . . so *earthy,* aren't they? We see it all the time in the Royal Family. It would be easier, I know, if Julia had not inherited my delicate English sensibility, my ladylike horror of men. If she were more like *you*, she would not be disgusted by her husband's appalling habits. She would not be shocked by anything he could want! You did not find Nicholas so odious when he was *your* lover, I daresay."

Emma controlled her temper with difficulty. "Anne, what is it you want from me?"

"Is there not some trick you could teach Julia? Some . . . technique . . . some method for getting through the ordeal with a minimum of discomfort?"

"You want me to teach Julia a trick?"

Lady Anne immediately heaved a sigh of relief. "Oh, I knew you would help me," she happily declared. "I knew you were not completely heartless. You will teach Julia the secret of painless copulation, and she will submit to her husband like a good wife, and Camford will have an heir. There will be no more talk of divorce."

"Madam, I said no such thing," Emma said sharply. "If Camford is truly as bad as your daughter says, then I think she *should* leave him."

As the words left her mouth, she had a sudden, fleeting vision of Julia cozying up to Harry. Such a scenario could not be ruled out, if the Camfords were to divorce.

"What?" Lady Anne was crying. "How can you say so?"

Emma held up a hand. "However, I doubt he's all that bad. Nicholas is young and inexperienced, perhaps—they both are! There's bound to be a period of adjustment. I'm sure if Camford knew his wife was unhappy, he'd be aggrieved, mortified."

"You're not going to *tell* him!" Lady Anne gasped. "If he knew she was even thinking of divorce, he'd be sure to divorce *her*. You must teach her your—your bedroom tricks. With this one little favor to me, one good act, you might atone a little for a lifetime of sin," she went on wildly. "I am giving you the chance to put your wicked stores of carnal knowledge to some good purpose. Wouldn't that be nice for you, dear?"

"Oh, *very* nice," Emma replied. "But I'm afraid it would be useless to talk to Julia. The problem, as I see it, is Nicholas."

"Nicholas?" Lady Anne breathed. "Really? I thought it was always the woman's fault. You see, *this* is why it was proper to consult an expert. So the fault lies with Nicholas. Can anything be done about it? Is it hopeless?"

"Not at all. If Nicholas were a better lover, Julia would not find her duty so unpleasant."

"Oh, I see," said Lady Anne. "You're going to have to give him lessons, is that it?"

"Yes," Emma replied, struggling to keep a straight face. "I'll have to give him lessons. Lots of lessons," she added. "I'm fairly certain he's a slow learner, but I'll do my best."

"You said *what?*" cried Colin, when this was related to him a few minutes later. He usually enjoyed a cup of chocolate and a bit of gossip with his sister in the mornings before reporting to his valet. This morning, he had come into the room just as Lady Anne was leaving.

Emma calmly took a sip of her chocolate. "I said I'd give him lessons. My good deed for the year. I did not in a hundred years think the notion would find favor with the old girl! Guess my surprise when she offered to keep Julia out of the way tomorrow."

Emma laughed until tears streamed down her cheeks.

"I should have thought a respectable lady would have been driven, screaming, from the room, by such a wicked idea! But she really seemed to think it would answer!"

Colin inspected the sleeve of his silk dressing gown. "It is rather sad, though, to think of him, rutting away like an animal, while poor Julia suffers in silence."

"At least she's not bored," said Emma.

"Oh? You found him boring, did you?"

"No; clumsy. Well-meaning, and deadly earnest, but clumsy. He *was* very passionate, however. If his skill were to equal his passion, no woman would complain, I think. He could only benefit from instruction."

"You're actually considering it," he accused her.

"No," said Emma.

"Yes, you are," he insisted. "I can see it in your eyes."

"I was thinking I might just give him just a few, small, helpful hints. There's no harm in that, is there?"

"I see," Colin said, tapping the side of his nose. "You'll teach him the *theory,* not the practice."

"Exactly," Emma said, as a servant came into the room.

"Begging your grace's pardon, but there is a lady waiting downstairs to see Lord Colin."

Colin snorted. "She'll be waiting a long time," he said. "I'm not even dressed. I haven't even finished my chocolate."

"Who is the lady?" Emma asked.

"The lady gave her name as Lady Colin Grey," replied the footman impassively.

"Elke!" Emma exclaimed in astonishment. "Here?"

"Who?" Colin said sullenly.

"Princess Elke von Hindenburg," Emma told him impatiently. "Your wife."

"Oh, is that her name?" Colin sniffed. "What's she *doing* here? I didn't send for her."

Emma bit her lip. "Oh, dear! I may have invited her," she said slowly.

Colin slammed down his cup. "What do you mean, you may have invited her? I was not aware you even knew the creature."

"Oh, I met her—briefly—this summer when the boys and I were touring the continent. Didn't I mention it?"

"No, you didn't," he said coldly.

"No? How silly of me. Anyway, we did happen to meet her over the summer, and the subject of you may have come up. And I may have just mentioned that you would be here for Christmas. It's possible I asked her to come for a visit."

Colin scowled at her.

"I never thought she'd actually show up," said Emma. "What do you think she wants?"

"I neither know nor care," said Colin. "Get rid of her!"

# Chapter Eighteen

Emma received her sister-in-law in her private sitting room. Princess Elke von Hindenburg was a very tall, Amazonian young woman, aged twenty-five, more handsome than pretty, with honey-blond hair and a long, thin nose. Her rich black carriage dress was cut in the military style and trimmed liberally with gold braid and gilded buttons. Her manner was rather grand and aloof. In spite of herself, Emma was a little intimidated by the other woman. Princess Elke's English was not very good, so they spoke German.

"Won't you sit down, your Highness?"

The princess looked around the room curiously. "This is a very small, crowded room," she observed. "At Hindenburg we have only very large rooms. What is the meaning of all these little tables and chairs?"

"This *is* a bit of a hodgepodge, I suppose," Emma apologized. "It's my private little room. It must answer to anything I want at the time. As you can see, it's a bit of a sitting room, a bit of a music room, a bit of an office, a bit of a breakfast parlor . . ."

"You do not have these things?" Princess Elke asked curiously. "You have no music room? No breakfast parlor? At Hindenburg—"

"Of course we have a music room and a breakfast parlor," Emma said, with a touch of annoyance. "In fact, we have several. I'm just too lazy to walk half a mile for my morning cup."

"Oh, but walking is such beneficial exercise," Princess Elke informed her. "Where is my husband? Where is my apartment?"

"Your apartment? Does your highness mean to stay with us, then?"

"Of course. You invited me, did you not?"

"Yes," Emma admitted. "Would your highness care for some chocolate?" she offered, brandishing the pot.

Princess Elke tilted her golden head to one side. Coming across the room, she accepted the cup of chocolate, towering over Emma, who was obliged to lean back in her chair to look the other woman in the eye. *"Ich verstehe nicht,"* said the princess. "I do not understand. My rooms, they are not ready?"

"If I'd known your highness was arriving today, everything would have been in readiness," Emma assured her.

"But I am to share my husband's apartment, of course," said Princess Elke, with a slight frown. "There is no need to prepare a separate apartment for me. We are man and wife, after all. We have been married since I was nine years old. Then I was too young to be a wife. Now I am prepared. Now is the time to consummate the marriage."

"Oh," Emma said blankly. "I see. You're here to—to—you mean to share your husband's apartment. I had not anticipated that."

Princess Elke glared down at her sister-in-law. "Is it not the custom in England for husbands and wives to share the bedchamber?"

"No! Oh, no," said Emma, becoming rather flustered. "It's—it's quite unheard of, actually. Colin would never dream of—of invading your highness's privacy, I'm sure."

"Then where do English babies come from?" Princess Elke demanded.

"No one really knows," Emma said, after a long, uncomfortable pause.

Princess Elke clucked impatiently. "It is time for me to have a baby, you understand."

"I-is it?" Emma said faintly. "Is it really?"

"Hindenburg must have an heir," Princess Elke announced. "My brothers, my uncles, my father . . . All were killed in the war with the cursed French."

For emphasis, Princess Elke spat on the Aubusson rug. Emma stared at her in disbelief.

"I am the last of my family," Princess Elke continued, taking a seat. "It is my duty to breed an heir, you understand. I do not have time for this English prudery. Where is my husband?" she demanded. "We will begin at once. There is no more time to lose. Hindenburg must have an heir. You will fetch him. I will wait."

"I'm afraid my brother is not fetchable." Emma snapped. "The men go out very early in the morning, riding and shooting, and all that sort of thing. I don't expect to see Colin for hours and hours. It's even possible that he has left Warwick entirely."

The words had hardly left her mouth when the door opened and Emma's brother walked in. Monty shuffled into the room behind him, favoring one leg. Princess Elke sat up straight and looked at the new arrivals with scientific curiosity.

"Ah, Colin!" Emma said, her voice bright with relief. "I thought you'd gone out shooting with the other men. I was just making your excuses to Princess Elke."

"You didn't tell me she was a princess," Monty complained staring at Elke indignantly. "You said she was a pig! You said she had a Hapsburg jaw and a Bourbon nose! She's beautiful!"

"She's not beautiful," Colin argued. "She's a giantess.

Look at those great big shoulders of hers. She's built like a prizefighter."

"In Scotland, she would be considered a prize," Monty informed him angrily.

"Then by all means, take her to Scotland!" Colin retorted.

"I think I will take *myself* to Scotland," Monty shot back. "I'm leaving!"

And, with a curt bow to Emma, he did just that, shutting the door with a loud crash that rattled the cups on Emma's tray.

Colin threw himself down into a chair. "Are you happy now?"

"She *spit* on my rug," Emma hissed at him.

"My God! Where?" he said, lifting his feet.

"Was *that* my husband?" Princess Elke cried in English, jumping up. "He is big and strong, like warrior. I will go after him!"

"With any luck, she'll follow him all the way to Scotland," Colin said, when his wife had gone.

"Aren't *you* going to go after Monty?" Emma asked him.

"I am Lord Colin Grey. I do not run after people."

"But did you explain to him that the marriage was arranged when you were only seventeen?" Emma pressed him. "Our father was going to cut off your allowance."

"I was young," he agreed eagerly. "I needed the money."

"Did you tell Monty? I'm sure if you explained—"

"No. Monty should trust me no matter what I do," Colin said angrily. "I shouldn't have to *explain* anything. I am married to a German princess. If he can't accept that, then to hell with him, I say."

Princess Elke came back into the room and closed the door with a sharp bang. "Strong warrior says he is *not* Princess Elke's husband."

"Er . . . no, your highness," Emma told her. "I knew it would be useless to run after you, because you're—you're so athletic. *This* is your husband, my brother, Lord Colin Grey."

Princess Elke wrinkled her nose. *"Er ist ein Schwachling!"*

Colin glared at her. "Who is she calling a weakling?" he asked Emma in English. "Why's she looking me over like that? Like I'm a head of cattle or something? And tell her I'm no weakling; I'm delightfully slender. Tell her she is a *Puddingbrumsel!*"

Emma set down her cup. "Tell her yourself. You speak perfect German."

Colin ignored her. "Tell her she can have her annulment on one condition: she goes back to Hassenpfeffer *today,* and I never have to see her again."

"I don't think she wants an annulment," Emma said slowly, looking down at her hands.

Colin scowled. "Well, if she thinks she's getting her dowry back, she can guess again!"

"She hasn't mentioned her dowry," Emma told him. "But, apparently, Hassenpfeffer needs an heir. She seems to expect *you* to give her one."

Colin sat bolt upright in his chair. "*Moi?*" he cried, horrified.

"*Toi.* You *are* her husband, after all," Emma reminded him.

"I'd rather eat my own liver," said Colin. "I'd rather eat my own tongue! Scratch that; I shall never eat again."

Princess Elke stood up, her delft-blue eyes blazing. "You insult Princess Elke," she announced in her heavily accented German. Slowly, she poured the contents of her cup onto Emma's Aubusson rug. Then she dropped the cup and crushed it under the heel of her shiny black leather boot. Then she strode from the room.

"Serves you right," Colin snapped as his sister contemplated her ruined rug. "This is going to be the worst Christmas ever!" he shouted at her.

He left the room at top speed, slamming the door.

Emma rang the bell for the servant. "Don't bother trying to clean it," she instructed him wearily, showing him the spilled chocolate. "Just roll it up and take it away. Burn it."

* * *

With heavy steps, Colin dragged himself to the door of
Lady Harriet's sitting room. "Come in," she said pleasantly,
in response to his timid knock. "I've been expecting you,"
she added sweetly, setting aside her racy French novel as
Colin crept over to the mantelpiece and began rearranging
her collection of china shepherdesses.

"I understand your wife is here," Lady Harriet said
presently.

"Good news travels fast," he muttered glumly.

"She wants to have sex with you, doesn't she?" Lady Harriet said gleefully.

"All she wants is a baby, an heir for Hoggle-poggleburg.
I am nothing more to her than a stud boy."

"Oh, dear. And your Scotsman has left you . . . again?"

"Yes," he admitted. "Monty is gone."

"Too bad. Well, you have your sister, anyway."

"Emma's the one who invited the Hindenburg," Colin
complained.

"Treachery! Why, you must feel like you haven't a friend
in the world."

"I still have you, don't I?" he said piteously. "Don't I?"

Lady Harriet laughed harshly.

Colin's hand twitched involuntarily, sending a shepherdess crashing to the floor.

"You did that on purpose!" she accused him.

"No, I didn't," he said, smashing another one. "I may have
done *that* on purpose, but the other one—the first one—that
was a complete accident."

Lady Harriet was on her feet. "How dare you!"

Colin grabbed a shepherdess and ran to the window.
Jumping up on the seat, he opened the casement. "Forgive
me," he said, dangling the china ornament. "I need you, after

all, Aunt Harriet. You're the mean old governess I never had, and I need that."

"You had governesses," she said.

"Yes, but they were all young and pretty."

Lady Harriet snorted. "That's because they were all your father's mistresses!"

"What?" Colin was so surprised that he dropped Lady Harriet's shepherdess. It plummeted to the terrace below, bouncing just once before it shivered to pieces.

Colin was horrified. "Oh, Aunt Harriet!" he gasped. "I'm sorry. I didn't mean it."

Lady Harriet calmly rang the bell. "That's all right," she said, taking her seat. "I never liked the bloody things. Susan gives me one every Christmas."

"Does this mean you forgive me?"

Lady Harriet sighed. "I suppose," she said grudgingly.


Major von Schroeder returned to the house for dinner, but nothing, it seemed, could pry Emma's two sons away from the herd they were stalking. Not even the possibility of seeing Julia was now enough to drag Harry away from the harbourer's hut.

Princess Elke arrived late, even later than Julia. Looking very stern and grand in a gown heavily embroidered in gold and a heavy diadem of wrought gold studded with fat pearls, she marched right up to the tallest, best-looking man in the room.

"This one is not puny," she announced in her native language, walking directly to him. "This one you may present to me," she added, beckoning to Emma.

Emma hurried over to make the introductions. "This is Lord Camford, your highness."

The princess was incredulous. "He is Englishman?

Impossible. Such a tall, beautiful man must be German. He is fertile?"

"What did you say?" Julia demanded, taking a firm hold of Nicholas's arm.

Emma quickly intervened. "Lord Camford, Lady Camford, allow me to make you known to my sister-in-law, her highness, the Princess Elke von Hindenburg. Her English is not—not very good, I'm afraid."

The princess never took her eyes off of Nicholas. "The female is of no consequence," she said in German. "This one looks strong. He will give me a strong, fat baby, yes?"

Reaching out, she gave Nicholas's upper arm a squeeze, much to his surprise.

*"Nein!"* cried Emma. "This one is married," she said, forcibly removing the princess's hand from the gentleman's anatomy.

Princess Elke shrugged. "So? There will be no complications when I take the child back to Hindenburg."

"Don't be absurd," Emma said irritably. "What would you talk about? He doesn't speak a word of German."

Princess Elka snorted. "I do not want him for his ability to make conversation, you know," she said.

"I'm afraid Lord Camford has the pox," Emma told her sharply.

Princess Elke recoiled in horror. *"Halt die Klappe!"*

"I'm sorry," said Emma, leading the princess away. "But do please allow me to introduce you to someone—someone more deserving of your highness's . . . ahem . . . favor. May I present my dear friend, Major Friedrich von Schroeder. Major von Schroeder is one of our great heroes from the battle of Waterloo."

As Emma had hoped, the princess was intrigued by the major's soldierly bearing and black eyepatch. "Ah! He is Prussian, yes?"

"Hanoverian," Emma replied. "He fought with our King's German Legion."

She presented the major to the princess. They immediately began to converse amiably in German. When Carstairs announced that dinner was served, the major escorted the princess to her seat at the head of the table.

"She doesn't look so bad," Lady Harriet observed as Colin brought her to the table.

"Then why don't *you* have sex with her?"

"Don't be rude," said Lady Harriet. "Haven't you ever thought of it? Having a child, I mean? Someone to carry on your name when you die?"

"I am immortal."

"I'm quite serious. You could be a father. Personally, I think it would be a terrible shame if you were to leave nothing behind when you go," she told him.

"When I go where?" he demanded. "I told you I'm immortal."

"If all the attractive people stop having children, we'll soon find ourselves living in a world full of nothing but ugly people," Lady Harriet pointed out.

"It's happening already," Colin said gloomily.

Outranked by her sister-in-law, Emma took her place at the foot of the table. To her annoyance, Lady Anne had contrived to place Nicholas between herself and the duchess. Emma avoided speaking to him as long as she possibly could, but it was inevitable that they should have some conversation. When she could not avoid it any longer, she turned to him with the idea of not letting him get a word in edgewise.

"I'm so sorry you didn't like the painting I sent you," she said, when she had exhausted all other topics. "Do please allow me to apologize again. I did not anticipate that you would have changed so much in less than year!"

"I have changed," he interrupted. "You still think me the

crude, unsophisticated sailor you met last year. You think me a man of no taste, no refinement. You look down your nose at me. But I am different now. I have spent some time educating myself. I am the Earl of Camford. I sit in the House of Lords. And I know the difference, madam, between a good painting and a bad joke."

"It wasn't a joke," she said irritably. "I thought you would appreciate it. That's all. I never dreamed you would become so pompous so quickly. And to think I went all the way to Plymouth for that picture, and *this* is the thanks I get."

"Plymouth," he repeated doubtfully. "Why should you go to Plymouth?"

Emma stared at him. "Oh, Nicholas," she said softly, after a moment. "You haven't seen it at all, have you? I should have known."

"No, I haven't seen it," he admitted, "but Julia has told me about it."

"It is a rather gloomy picture," said Emma. "I can see how your wife wouldn't like it. But, then, I suppose it's rather gloomy to be left behind on shore while someone you love sails away into the unknown in a leaky little boat. I got it at the Barking Crow, in Plymouth," she told him gently. "It's one of your father's, the one you told me about, the one he gave to the landlady when he fell behind on his rent."

Nicholas's face was ashen. "My father? Please excuse me," he choked, leaving the table in a hurry.

"Too much pepper in the chausseur," Emma said quickly, as all eyes turned to her for an explanation.

"For heaven's sake, don't anyone tell the chef," Colin said lightly. "He's French. He might commit suicide."

"Now we're down to three men," Lady Susan observed critically, sandwiched between Julia and Flavia. "Three men and nine women. It's insupportable!"

"Hadn't you better go and check on your husband, Julia?" Octavia said sharply. She was seated on the opposite side of the table from her fiancé and her sister, between Major von Schroeder and Colin. With the major devoted to the princess, and Colin equally devoted to Lady Harriet, Octavia had nothing to do besides watch Julia flirt with Mr. Palafox.

"Oh, Nicky's always complaining about something," Julia answered carelessly.

"I—I will check on him," said Lady Anne.

She found Nicholas composing himself in the lounge. "Are you all right, nephew?"

"Yes, I think so, aunt," he answered, red faced. "I choked on a small bone, I think, but I'm all right now. Just a little embarrassed."

"Oh, you mustn't be *embarrassed,* Nicholas," she told him gently. "When someone is as ignorant as you are, it's a blessing to be able to receive instruction from one of the world's foremost authorities. It was very kind of the duchess to offer to give you lessons."

"I don't understand," said Nicholas. "The duchess offered to give me lessons?"

"I think she would like to make amends for all the terrible things she did to you last year," said Lady Anne. "Were you not speaking of this before you left the table? I thought it was why you choked."

"No, I told you it was a bone. We were speaking of something else."

"Oh," Lady Anne said faintly. "How silly of me. Well, when she does make you the offer, I hope you will not be too embarrassed to accept."

"No," he said. "I would not be too embarrassed."

Satisfied, she brought him back to the table, and they resumed their seats. "Forgive me," Nicholas said quietly to Emma, when he next had the opportunity to speak to her. "I was overwhelmed by my feelings. I should have guessed that it was my father's painting. But that you should have gone to Plymouth—! I could not have imagined such a thing. You—"

"Oh, but I didn't go to Plymouth," she said quickly. "Not on purpose, I mean. At least, not for the sole purpose of finding the painting. You mustn't think that! I just happened to be near Plymouth."

"Oh, I see," he said incredulously. "You just happened to be *near* Plymouth."

"Yes," Emma said, becoming rather flustered. "I was looking at some houses in Devonshire—for my son Grey, you understand. Plymouth was not very far out of my way. I was curious to see this place of yours, the Barking Crow."

"And you bought the picture," he prompted, "for me."

"Now, you mustn't make too much of it," Emma told him firmly. "I meant it as a kind gesture, that's all. I know we did not part on very good terms last year, but I was—am—truly grateful for the help you gave me. The picture was just a token of thanks."

"I shall treasure it," he said. "I don't know why I never thought of going to Plymouth myself and getting it back. I thought it was out of my hands forever, I suppose, rather like—"

He broke off, and took a long drink from his glass.

"Like what?" she asked curiously. "Remember, you are the Earl of Camford now. You sit in the House of Lords. You dine with princesses. Nothing should be out of your reach."

"Now you are teasing me," he complained lightly.

"Yes, for we cannot always be so serious."

Signaling for the course to be removed, Emma would have turned to converse with Augusta, who sat to the right of her, but Nicholas said quickly, "My aunt tells me you have offered to give me lessons."

Emma swung back to stare at him, wide-eyed. "What?" she managed to ask.

"I accept," he said. "Thank you."

Emma began to cough uncontrollably. Reaching for her glass, she hastily took a sip of wine. "Y-you accept?" she stuttered, still coughing. "What about Julia?" she croaked.

"Julia?" Nicholas sighed. "Well, she's always complaining about my inadequacies. This should make her happy."

"Excuse me," Emma gasped, fleeing the room.

Colin brought her a glass of water in the lounge. "What the devil is going on with you and Camford?" he demanded. "Are you taking turns making disgusting noises?"

"Water!" she complained when she had drained the glass. "You bring me gin when I need water, and water when I need gin!"

"Why should you need gin?" he demanded.

"Because Anne has told Nicholas that I offered to give him lessons."

Colin snickered. "Joke's on you, is it?"

"Colin, he accepted! He *wants* me to give him lessons. He thinks it will make *Julia* happy!" she added sourly.

"Don't *you* want Julia to be happy?"

"Not particularly. Are you suggesting that I give Nicholas lessons—in lovemaking?"

"Well, I don't think he wants lessons in flower arranging," said Colin. "Anyway, you're not that good at flower arranging. Shall we go back to dinner? Only four more courses."

"Fishbone," Emma said, patting the hollow of her throat as she returned to the table.

"Fishbones in the pheasant," Lady Harriet remarked to Colin. "Perhaps Armand should commit suicide, after all."

"Are you all right?" Nicholas asked Emma.

"Oh, yes, perfectly," she assured him. "You just surprised me, that's all. I didn't think you'd be open to the idea."

"No, I want to learn," he told her earnestly. "I just haven't had the right teacher."

The skin at the back of Emma's neck began to tingle. "And you think that I'm the right teacher?" she asked slowly.

"If I can't learn from the best, I don't think I care to learn at all," he replied. "And you're the best, aren't you? From what I hear."

"Well, you mustn't believe *everything* you hear," Emma told him modestly.

"I'm sure you'll be firm with me when I need it," he said. "And forgiving and patient when I need it. Emma, I can think of no one I'd rather have for a teacher. Honestly."

Emma's face felt hot. "That's very flattering, Nicholas," she said faintly. "I'm sure I must be blushing."

He laughed. "Shall we start tomorrow, then? I can meet you at the stables at, say, eight o'clock? Or is that too early?"

"Stables?" Emma repeated blankly.

"I shall have to find some riding clothes, too," he said, "but I daresay it won't be a problem. The servants are so efficient."

Abruptly, Emma's vanity came crashing down to earth. "Riding clothes," she said in a very small voice. "Yes, you will definitely need riding clothes for the riding lessons I'm going to be giving you starting tomorrow at eight o'clock at the stables."

Nicholas looked at her curiously. "Are you all right? I haven't offended you, have I? Is this . . . Oh, God! You're not still upset about the paperweight, are you?"

"What paperweight?" Emma asked blankly.

"The one Julia sent you for Christmas," he answered.

Emma smiled at him. Why, he had not changed at all, she realized. He was just as simple and sweet as he had been the day she met him.

"No, Nicholas," she told him warmly. "I'm not at all upset about the paperweight."

# Chapter Nineteen

The next morning, Emma's maid woke her at seven o'clock. As a young girl, the duchess had been accustomed to rising early to go riding, even in winter, but, over the years she had gotten out of the habit. In fact, she was downright lazy. Nowadays, she usually did not get out of bed until at least ten o'clock, and seven o'clock was, to her, almost an ungodly hour. Her maid brought her a bowl of ice-cold water, into which Emma plunged her face, but, even so, by the time she was dressed, the invigorating effect had worn off. Like a sleepwalker, she trudged downstairs to the breakfast parlor for a steaming cup of strong black coffee.

"Good morning, your grace," Lady Anne greeted her from the table.

"Good morning, Anne," Emma replied, stifling a yawn.

A gentleman in very tight riding breeches was filling his plate at the sideboard. At the sound of their voices, he turned around, and Emma saw that it was Nicholas, looking exceptionally well-groomed. Belatedly, she thought of her own toilette, which she had slept through for the most part. Her maid had put her in a beautifully tailored habit of brilliant peacock-blue superfine. She would just have to trust that her hair was in good order.

"Good morning, my lord," she greeted him, adding with approval, "I must say, you certainly look the part of an equestrian! That is an important first step, I have always thought."

He flushed slightly. "I have a valet now," he explained. "He puts me together, ties my neckcloth, and all that sort of thing. He found these clothes for me. I fear the breeches are too tight."

Emma privately thought his riding clothes fit him very well indeed. The dark blue coat made his eyes look very blue, and the buckskin breeches molded the hard lines of his buttocks and thighs. "I shouldn't worry about it too much," she said. "The buckskin will move with you."

She sat down and poured herself a cup of coffee.

"Nicholas has been fattening up," said Lady Anne. "No more hardtack biscuits!"

"No," Nicholas agreed ruefully, joining the ladies at the table. His plate was piled high with eggs and bacon. "Too many English breakfasts, I'm afraid. Too many rich dinners at the Admiralty Club."

"And fewer raw vegetables, I should think," said Emma.

"Oh, I still like my raw carrots," he assured her. "Much to my cook's dismay."

"I still recall how you prevailed on me last year to try it! I nearly broke a tooth."

Nicholas laughed. "Spoken like a true, namby-pamby, milk-and-water aristocrat."

As it was far too early in the morning to come up with a clever answer, Emma could only scowl at him.

"Well, I think Nicholas looks very handsome," Lady Anne said quickly. "I believe that is what we were talking about. I say it though I am his aunt. Last year, he was quite thin—like a scarecrow. The Royal Navy really had ought to feed its officers better! But Nicholas is much improved this year. Does your grace not agree?"

"It is obvious he enjoys the attentions of a very good valet," said Emma. "Perhaps all the credit should go to his servant. Your nephew could be a padded man for all we know."

"A padded man!" Nicholas said indignantly.

Lady Anne quickly changed the subject. "Nicholas tells me that your grace is giving him a riding lesson this morning," she said brightly, giving the words "riding lesson" undue emphasis. "How nice! What a wonderful surprise for Julia. And you need not worry," she added, in the tone of a conspirator. "I'll make sure she doesn't suspect a thing. They have all ridden out very early this morning to meet with the duke. They will not be back for hours and hours."

"All?" Emma echoed, frowning.

"Yes, your grace. Princess Elke was interested in the hunt, so the Major offered to escort her to see the herd. Augusta would not be denied her share of sport, and Julia, of course, wanted to go, too. Mr. Palafox then persuaded Octavia. Even Flavia could not resist when she learned they were to bring a picnic lunch. So you need not fear that anyone will find out about your—your *lesson*," she added, almost in a whisper. "Is that not fortuitous? It will be so much easier for Nicholas to learn the proper technique if the lesson is not interrupted."

Nicholas looked up from his food. "You're behaving very strangely, Aunt."

"I am just happy, my lord," Lady Anne answered. "With two daughters married, and a third engaged, I cannot help twittering! Only two left."

"Is it to be a London wedding?" Emma asked politely.

"Mr. Palafox would have it so," said Lady Anne. "Or, I should say, Mrs. Allen would have it so. It is to take place in March, at the height of the Season. Your grace will attend, of course?"

"Of course," said Emma. "We must give Mrs. Allen the full treatment! She should get her money's worth, after all."

"They are to honeymoon in Italy," said Lady Anne. "If the war does not start up again."

"It won't, Aunt," Nicholas assured her. "Napoleon is now the permanent guest of the Royal Navy at St. Helena. Elba was quite a different matter. If the Royal Navy had been in charge of him at Elba—"

"And now we know what you talk about at the Admiralty Club," Emma said.

Nicholas pushed his empty plate away. "I suppose we *are* a rather predictable breed," he said. "I should follow your grace's example, and speak only when I have something amazing to say. But then people might mistake me for a wit."

"Oh! As they do me, I suppose!"

His mouth twitched. "I have never heard you described as a wit, ma'am."

Again, Emma could think of no reply. Angrily, she took a bite of toast.

Lady Anne again tried to rescue the conversation. "I do hope Mr. Palafox takes Wingate! Would it not be a wonderful thing for us to live so close to Warwick? Would your grace say the house is large enough for us all to live in harmony? We would not want to be too crowded."

"I would not care to spend even one night under that man's roof," Nicholas declared.

"Poor Mr. Palafox! It is true that his aunt, Mrs. Allen, is a very coarse, vulgar woman," Lady Anne replied, apparently misunderstanding the thrust of her nephew's comment. "Perhaps we can persuade her to remain hidden in the attic, at least when anyone of quality visits us. She is a perfectly dreadful little woman," she went on. "Why, she insisted on looking in Octavia's mouth—as if she were a horse!"

Nicholas blew out his breath. "Speaking of horses," he said, rising from the table. "I believe I'll make my way to the stables now. Please, madam, stay and finish your breakfast," he added quickly as Emma set down her cup.

"I am finished," Emma said, leaving the table. "We may as well walk together."

"There is not the least need for you to worry if you are seen together," Lady Anne assured them. "It's not as though you're doing anything wrong, after all. It's just a lesson."

Emma took Nicholas's arm. "Exactly so. It's not as though we're having an affair," she said mischievously. "Nicholas is my pupil, and I am his teacher. That's all."

"Good luck, Nicholas!" said Lady Anne. "Remember, the duchess is an expert in these matters. Be guided by her."

"I shall," said Nicholas. "After all, we don't want a repeat of last year."

"No, indeed," said Emma, trying to keep a straight face.

"I sometimes think my aunt has lost her wits," Nicholas remarked when he and Emma were free of the house.

The day was clear but rather cold, even in the sun. Emma shivered.

"She was behaving even more dithery and nonsensical than usual," Nicholas went on. "The way she was talking just now . . . it was almost as if she thought . . ."

He stopped, biting his lip.

"As if she thought what?" Emma prompted him.

He glanced down at her. "As if she thought something really *was* going on between us."

Emma laughed. "Your aunt is a funny little creature."

"My aunt is a birdwit," he grumbled. "Even so, I cannot imagine what she must have been thinking, saying 'riding lesson' in that suggestive tone! I was quite embarrassed. I do not have your ability to laugh off these things."

"Then perhaps I shouldn't tell you just how much we have to laugh off," Emma said.

"What do you mean?" he demanded.

"Your aunt doesn't think I'm going to teach you how to ride. She thinks I'm going to teach you how to make love properly."

Nicholas came to a standstill. *"What?"*

"To be fair, I did make the offer—all in jest, of course! But your poor aunt has no sense of humor, as you've probably noticed already. She took me quite seriously, I'm afraid."

"Oh, I see," he said, relaxing. "You're joking me. Naturally, I did not take you seriously," he went on. "Unlike my aunt, I *do* have a sense of humor. Small and ill defined, I admit, but it is there. It just needs exercise." He laughed weakly.

"Oh, but I wasn't joking *you,* Nicholas," Emma answered. "I was joking *your aunt,* but she took me seriously, so the joke is on *me,* I suppose. When you came back to the table last night, and told me you wanted to accept my offer of lessons—! I'll admit I was quite flattered. However, you soon took me down a peg or two. You know, I can't help but feel I've been *cozened* into giving you riding lessons."

"My aunt must be insane," Nicholas said, beginning to stammer. "Emma, I apologize, of course. But what a thing to say, even if you were only joking!"

"As you say, I am not known for my wit," she said tartly. "Your aunt came to me. She's very worried about you and Julia. I know that your marriage is in trouble," she told him gently. "Nicholas, I did not seek the information, but now that I have it . . . Well, perhaps I *can* help you. I would like to help you, if I can."

He glanced back at the house. "She dared speak to *you* about my marriage?" he said angrily. "Then she is as brazen as she is bird-witted! She should mind her own bloody business! And so should you," he added furiously.

"You're right, of course," said Emma. "If I were you, I would be just as angry. Shall we walk on? Or would you rather go back to the house, and have nothing more to do with me?"

"My aunt's stupidity is not your fault," he said, after a moment, and they began walking again. "I have always felt that I could talk to you, Emma," he added awkwardly. "The very first day we met, I told you everything about me. How bored you must have been! I realize that now. But, at the time, I felt you were listening to me."

"Of course I listened to you," she said. "And you were not so very boring," she added lightly, hoping to raise a smile.

Nicholas remained serious. "I never had such a friend, a woman friend. One doesn't talk about one's feelings with other men, you know. Not at sea. Not at the Admiralty Club. But I cannot burden you now. After all, what do you care of me and my life?"

"I am still your friend, Nicholas," she said quietly. "It's true, I was not a very good friend to you last year. I was selfish, unkind, ungrateful, but let me make up for it now. Let me be your friend."

"This is not how I imagined our reunion," he murmured. "I could strangle my aunt!"

"Your aunt is worried about you, Nicholas. So am I. You have been married nearly a year, and Julia has not conceived."

"Of course," he said grimly. "That is all they care about. Camford must have an heir! I am nothing but livestock to them."

"Yes; poor you," Emma said sharply. "You have been given a title and a great fortune, scads of land, and the means to attain everything you could possibly want, and all you must do in return is father a child—with a very beautiful girl! Is it really so much to ask? It is our first duty as namby-pamby, milk-and-water aristocrats, you know," she went on in a gentler tone. "We are very privileged people, Nicholas, but let us not forget the duties that go with the privileges. Right now, your duty is to make love to your wife . . . *properly.*"

"What are you implying? I know how to make love properly. I don't need any help in that area, thank you very much, madam!"

"Could it be possible that you're not as good as you think you are?"

"What?" he said sharply.

"Forgive me, Nicholas," she said, "but I know your marriage is not as happy as you would have me believe. I know, for example, that Julia has banished you from her bed. I know you sleep in separate rooms."

He scowled. "Did *Julia* tell you that? That *she* has banished me from *her* bed?"

"I have not spoken to Julia," Emma said quickly. "Please don't be angry with your wife. I've spoken only with her mother. I don't want to pain you, Nicholas, but, apparently Julia is so unhappy that she is actually thinking of leaving you."

"My aunt told you that?"

"Yes."

"Was this before or after you offered to teach me how to make love *properly?* Whatever the hell that means," he added under his breath.

"Well, there's your problem. You don't know what it means."

"Oh, but you're going to teach me!"

Emma sighed. "Nicholas, I know you're angry—"

"No, I'm not. I'm looking forward to it. Shall we strip naked here, or would you prefer we go into the bushes?"

Emma frowned at him. "Sir, I have just told you that your wife of less than a year is contemplating desertion, if not divorce, and all you can do is make jokes? Julia literally cannot bear your touch. She described your lovemaking as if it were some sort of brutal attack. Based on my own experience of your—your technique, for lack of a better word, I can see how an inexperienced young girl might very easily find you appalling, even frightening!"

To her astonishment and dismay, he laughed.

"Thank you for your assessment, ma'am," he said, still laughing. "If you think lessons will improve my technique, by all means, give me the benefit of your vast experience! I am willing to learn, nay, eager."

"I am going to teach you how to ride a horse, Nicholas," Emma said sternly. "What goes on between you and your wife is entirely up to you."

"Precisely," he said, quickening his step. "I'm glad we understand each other! Mind you," he went on as she hurried to keep up with him, "I suppose there's a lot of overlap between riding a horse and making love to a woman."

"Only a brute would think so! They are two *very* different things, I assure you."

"But I *am* a brute," he said. "We've established that already. I can only hope the techniques I learn from you in the stables may answer very well in the bedchamber with my wife. Mounting is to be the first lesson, is it not?"

"I liked you better last year! I did not think you were a brute last year."

"I'd rather be thought a brute than a fool," he said curtly.

As they drew near to the stables, the head groom came hurrying out to meet them. "Your grace!" he cried, ignoring Nicholas. "I was not informed that your grace meant to ride this morning. Will I have Storm saddled for you, your grace?"

"I don't mean to ride this morning," Emma assured him, going past him into the warm building. "I've just brought Lord Camford to see Parley. She's not been taken out, has she?"

The groom had not forgotten Nicholas. He glared at him with open dislike. "Tom's just brought her back from her exercise," he said, glowering.

"Perfect," said Emma. "Lord Camford can give her a good rubbing down. It's quite all right; I'll be with him the whole time," she added quickly, as the man opened his mouth to protest.

"You remember Parley, of course," Emma went on, leading

Nicholas down the length of the stables to the stall of a brown mare.

"Polly?" he echoed, looking at the animal.

At the sound of his voice, the mare skittered sideways, backing up until her haunches touched the back of the stall. Her nostrils flared and her eyes rolled back.

"Par-ley," she enunciated. "Short for Parliament. In her youth, she had the bad habit of stealing oats from her neighbors, hence the name. You rode her last year. Don't you remember? She certainly remembers *you*. I'd say apologies are in order."

"Of course! I'm very sorry she was hurt."

"There's no need to apologize to *me*," Emma told him. "*I* wasn't the one you hurt."

He blinked at her. "You expect me to apologize . . . to a horse?"

"Of course. If you are ever going to ride her again, you will have to win her forgiveness and earn back her trust. Tell her you're sorry you hurt her," she instructed him. "Tell her you were a clumsy fool. Tell her you won't do it again. And beg her to take you back."

"This is ridiculous," he complained.

"You're right," she said. "You should get down on your knees, too. You'll seem less threatening to her, smaller, if you are on your knees."

"Oh, well! As long as there is a good reason for it," he muttered, lowering himself to one knee. "Hear me, O horse," he declaimed. "I, Lord Camford, am sorry I hurt you. I was a clumsy fool. It won't happen again. Please, oh, please, let me ride thee again."

"Hmmm," said Emma, studying the horse. "You've got her attention, but not in a good way. There was a strong note of anger in your voice. I fear she doubts your sincerity. Pretend you are apologizing to your wife."

"I was. Hence the strong note of anger in my voice."

"Try talking to her in a gentle, soothing voice. It's no use barking at her—or at Julia, for that matter. If you're really sorry, that is."

"As far as the horse goes, I really am."

"That's a start anyway," said Emma. "You'll find some apples in that barrel over there. See if you can't get her to eat from your hand. But be patient. Let her come to you in her own time. When you've managed that, we'll see about putting you in the stall with her. I'll be right over here if you need me. The key is patience."

Settling down on a bale of hay, she watched as he tried to coax the mare to take the apple from his hand. Within a few moments, lulled by the sound of his voice, she had fallen asleep, her shoulder against the stall opposite Parley's, her head propped up on one hand.

Some time later, she jerked awake, striking her head on the side of the stall against which she had been leaning. The stable clock had begun to chime. Nicholas stood looking down at her, his fists on his hips.

"What time is it?" she murmured, stretching her arms.

"Ten o'clock, I should think," he replied, looking at her intently.

"Oh, dear," she said, dismayed. "Well, how many apples did you feed her?"

"Just the one," he said grimly. "And *that* she snatched from my hand after two hours of sweet talk. I haven't heard from her since. I think I should start over with another horse. This one obviously hates me."

Emma frowned at him. "I'm afraid it doesn't work that way, my lord. I'm not about to let you ruin all my horses. You will ride Parley, or you'll not ride at all!"

"Another emblem of marriage!" he said bitterly.

"Yes, if you like. Your wife may hate you at present, but you cannot simply cast her aside and get another one."

"I could get a mistress," he retorted. "If Julia finds me

so unappealing, then perhaps it would be better if I never go near her. That should bring her great peace of mind," he added bitterly. "Poor girl! Her suffering is at an end. I will get a mistress."

"You'll do no such thing!" Emma said angrily.

He met her eyes defiantly. "I might have one already, for all you know."

"No."

"No," he admitted, "but only because it was so difficult to choose! There were so many elegant ladies in London, and they all liked me. Lady Bellingham. Lady Melbourne. Lady Caroline Arbuthnot."

"Why not have them all?" Emma said pleasantly. "I know those ladies. They will not mind sharing you."

"Of course! I can have them all, can't I? That's how it works, is it not? In Society? All the gentlemen keep mistresses, and all the ladies have lovers, and, every so often, they change partners, for the sake of variety?"

"No, Nicholas, that is not how it works," she told him sharply.

He smiled. "I beg your pardon, ma'am, but I have seen enough of Society this past year to know that that is *exactly* how it works!"

"Not for you," she said quietly.

"Why not me? Am I so special?"

"I had thought you were," she said, looking down at her hands. "When I met you last year, I thought you quite . . ."

"Stupid? Gauche? Naive? Oh, what's that word—I hear it all the time! Farouche?"

"Unspoiled. I did not think Society could corrupt you."

"You are rewriting history, ma'am," he said coldly. "Let me correct you. When you met me last year, you thought me a mere boy, and a fool."

"I did at first," she admitted. "You were so different from the men I know. Now, it seems, you are to be just like them!

That, I think, makes you a fool, and you will be an unhappy fool, too. I can promise you that. You once told me that, if you were my husband, you would not betray me."

He stared at her for a moment. "If I were your husband, I wouldn't," he said. "But I am *not* your husband. I am Julia's husband. I never wanted to marry Julia. She tricked me."

"That doesn't mean you can treat her badly for the rest of her life," Emma argued. "However it came to be, you *are* married to her. You're stuck with each other, whether you like it or not, so you might as well make the best of it. It will take time to earn back her trust and affection, but it can be done."

"What about *my* trust and affection?" he demanded. "When is *she* going to earn *that?*"

Emma threw up her hands. "Very well! She tricked you! Can you not understand why she did it? You should be flattered!"

"Flattered!"

"She has been taught all her life that marrying well is her only reason for existing. You were the Holy Grail to her, Nicholas. You can hardly blame her for wanting to marry you. Can you not forgive her for being . . . human? I did not think you were so hard-hearted!"

"Well, I am. I cannot forgive her."

"Poor Julia!" Emma murmured. "Her wedding night must have been a nightmare. She must have felt how much you hated her. If this is how you feel, you should never have touched her! How could you do it? How could you use your wedding night to *punish* that poor foolish girl? Because that is what you did, is it not? Instead of making love to her, you— you *punished* her! Small wonder she wants to leave you!"

He stared at her, white-faced. "That is what you think of me?"

"What am I supposed to think?" cried Emma. "Julia was so happy to be your wife. If you had showed her the smallest bit of kindness, I know she would have loved you. Instead, you chose to be cruel. I did not want to believe it of you! I had convinced myself that Julia must be exaggerating, or that your mistakes were due to your own inexperience in love, but you are cruel. You are heartless and cruel. You are not the man I thought you were. I do not know you at all."

"Why?" he said coldly. "Who did you think I was?"

She laughed bitterly. "You were Galahad to me. But I was mistaken. I don't know how a human being with a conscience could do what you have done to Julia. You should beg her forgiveness. You should do whatever it takes to win her back. You should try to make her happy."

"Thank you for the lesson, ma'am."

Emma jumped to her feet as he turned to go. "If you are angry, Nicholas, your anger should be directed toward me," she told him sharply. "Promise me you will not seek revenge against Julia. She knows nothing of my interference. Indeed, I am the last person from whom she would accept help."

"Julia has nothing to fear from me," he answered coldly. "I shan't go near her. If she wants a divorce, she may have it."

"You should never have married her!"

"Madam," he said, "I couldn't possibly agree with you more."

Giving her a stiff bow, Nicholas turned on his heel and left her.

Deeply shaken, Emma remained where she was until Parley's restless movements drew her out of her unhappy thoughts. "My poor darling," she murmured, stroking the mare's nose. "He is gone. The bad man is gone. He will never touch you again."

Emma stayed twenty minutes, comforting the nervous horse, then went back to the house feeling gloomy and depressed and slightly sick. As she entered her private sitting room, Colin dove behind the sofa. Emma was in no mood for his antics.

"I know you're here," she said wearily. "You might as well come out."

Colin peeked at her over the back of the sofa. Mustering his dignity, he came out of hiding. "I thought you were my wife," he gruffly explained.

Emma sat down at the pianoforte and mechanically began to play finger exercises. "You were not *hiding* from Elke," she said impatiently.

"Of course not," he agreed. "I am Lord Colin Grey. I do not hide from amazons. But I do skillfully avoid them."

"There is no need to hide from Elke. She has gone out with the others to see the herd. They will not be back for hours. They are to have a picnic."

"Good to know," he said, taking a seat. "Play a song, can't you?" he said presently, as she continued her exercises. "Nobody wants to hear all that noise."

"My fingers are in need of exercise," Emma replied. "If you don't like it, you can go somewhere else, you know. You've made up with Aunt Harriet, haven't you? Why don't you go and hide in *her* rooms?"

"Maybe I will," he said indignantly.

"Please do!"

"Well!" he said. "What's got your drawers in a knot? Where have you been anyway? Riding?" he guessed, after looking over her habit. "It's not like you to go riding so early."

"It's not all that early," she pointed out. "If you must know, I was giving Lord Camford a lesson. Trying to, anyway. Oh, the whole thing just makes me want to cry!"

Instead of crying, however, she brought both hands crashing down on the pianoforte.

"You're not giving up on him after just one lesson?" Colin said incredulously. "I'm sure, with a few more of your expert tutorials, he'll be an excellent lover."

Emma groaned. "I was trying to teach him about *horses,* Colin. *Horses.* It seems we had a misunderstanding," she explained. "He thought I was talking about horses all along, and I thought he was talking about sex."

"Oh, I hate when that happens," Colin said sympathetically. "And you got up so early, too! You would not have minded getting up early for sex."

Emma shuddered. "After what I've learned, I don't think he's fit to go near a mare, let alone a woman. If Julia is brave enough to seek a divorce, she has my full support. I did not want to believe it, but the man is a thorough brute. Julia will be better off without him."

"Divorce?" Colin murmured. "My dear, this is serious talk."

Emma left the pianoforte and walked up and down the room. The carpet had been removed, revealing the parquet floor, and her riding boots echoed loudly. "It *is* serious, Colin," she told her brother. "He resents her for tricking him into marriage, and he showed her all his resentment on their wedding night. On that night of all nights, he should have been kind and gentle. At the very least, he ought to have left her alone entirely. Instead, he was a brute."

"A brute? To my little Julia?" Colin frowned.

"Yes, poor girl! As much as I dislike her, my pity for her is sincere. She would have been expecting the ending to a fairy tale. Instead, she got a monster with a heart full of revenge. He says he will give her a divorce if she wants one."

"But he cannot be allowed to divorce her," Colin objected. "That would ruin her life. He must allow *her* to divorce *him*. You could be correspondent, Emma."

"Thank you, no," Emma said dryly. "I don't care to have my name blackened in the House of Lords! Harry would never forgive me. And I certainly don't want my name linked to Camford's."

"My dear girl, it already is," he told her. "It was all over London that you had an affair with him last Christmas before he married Julia. Naturally, people will think the affair is ongoing. It will be assumed that you are the cause of their divorce."

"Colin, there is a great deal of difference between idle talk and legal testimony in a divorce case," Emma said firmly. "Julia will have to bring charges of cruelty against him."

"He's not likely to put up with *that*," Colin pointed out. "I have it!" he exclaimed suddenly. "We'll kill two birds with one stone. Elke can be his correspondent. They can have all the criminal conversations they want. We'll get lots of proof. Then I will divorce *her,* and Julia can divorce *him*."

"I think we had better stay out of it altogether, Colin."

"Stay out of it?" he said incredulously.

"Yes, Colin; stay out of it," Emma commanded. "*Well* out of it."

"If that's how you feel," he said sulkily. "Of course, I'll stay out of it."

"I'm going to have a bath," Emma announced crossly. "And then I'm going back to bed!"

"Pleasant dreams," he called after her.

# Chapter Twenty

Octavia Fitzroy had no interest whatsoever in stag hunting. She was not a keen rider like her sister Augusta. Nor was she mad for a picnic, like Flavia. Her sole reason for riding out with the others that morning was to keep an eye on Mr. Palafox.

In general, Octavia did not care if Charles ran after other women, but his flirtation with Julia cut her to the quick. If not for Julia, she, Octavia, would almost certainly be Countess of Camford! Under no circumstances would Octavia lose a second husband to Julia's machinations. In her anxiety to keep Charles in line, Octavia had threatened to break their engagement, reminding him that, if she did so, his aunt undoubtedly would cut him off without a penny.

Her threat had brought her no peace of mind, however. In fact, Charles seemed to resent it. His flirtation with Julia continued unabated. It was as though he were daring Octavia to jilt him. This she could not do, of course, having been jilted twice already. Therefore, it was imperative that she not let Charles and Julia out of her sight.

Octavia was the last of the party to mount, and the only lady to insist on using the mounting block. The other ladies, even Princess Elke, had been content to be tossed into the saddle by a gentleman or a groom. In Princess Elke's case, Major von Schroeder was given the honor. Kneeling down, he made a stirrup of his hands. The princess stepped into them, and, though she was a big woman, he tossed her easily up into the saddle.

"You are very strong, Major," she complimented him, and when he was mounted they spoke to one another exclusively in German.

Mr. Palafox was annoyed by Octavia's insistence on the mounting block. "For heaven's sake, Miss Fitzroy!" he said sharply. "If the Princess von Hindenburg can do without it; if Lady Camford can do without it, so can you. Let the man give you a leg up, or *I* will give you a leg up," he threatened.

"It is not correct, Mr. Palafox," Octavia said firmly. "I will not put my foot in a man's hands, unless they be my husband's."

Julia groaned. "What a nonsensical little prude you are! Get on the horse, spinster!"

"What is this?" Princess Elke demanded. "Princess Elke is not correct? But Princess Elke, she is always correct!" She continued to argue loudly, unopposed, while the mounting block was brought to Octavia.

While Octavia was engaged, Palafox guided his mount alongside Julia's. He had only to murmur a few words in her ear, and the assignation was made.

Julia flashed him a look of surprise, then gave him a coy little smile.

Later that afternoon, when the party had returned to the house, and Octavia had been obliged to go to her maid for repairs, Julia went to meet Palafox, her heart pounding with excitement. As instructed, she had not washed or changed her clothes. She felt quite dirty and unsafe and completely grown-up. That her first lover should be her eldest sister's betrothed could only add to the fun.

For his first rendezvous with Lady Camford, Palafox had

chosen the Porcelain Room. To gawking summer tourists, this room was always a place of great interest, and the housekeeper took great pride in showing off some of Warwick's most priceless treasures, but no one else ever visited the place as far as Palafox could tell. Meant to be a gallery, it offered few places to sit; just a few backless sofas covered in sheets of thick, brown holland. Even the chandelier had been wrapped for the winter, and all the candles had been removed from the sconces. A rose window of stained glass offered the only light.

He pounced on Julia the moment she entered the long, narrow room. "Alone at last," he murmured.

Julia coyly eluded his grasp. "Did you want to be alone with me, Charles?" she asked innocently. Casting him a sidelong glance, she let her carefully darkened lashes sweep across her cheekbones. The effect was almost lost in the shadowy room.

"Yes, very much," he answered softly. "For one thing, we need not tell such shocking lies to each other when we are alone." Reaching about her person, he found her hand and guided her to one of the backless sofas. Seating himself beside her, he leaned over her and began an exhaustive search for her other hand.

Excited and confused by his attentions, Julia did not resist, even when she felt his hand skim over her breast. "Lies, Charles?" she said, in what she hoped was the tone of a sophisticated woman of the world. "What can you mean?"

"You know very well, minx," he answered, almost in a growl. "I need not pretend to be happy about my fate, and you . . . you can tell me how you really feel about that dunderheaded husband of yours."

Julia choked on a sob. "Oh, Charles!" she said wretchedly. "It's just as you warned me it would be! I shall need a lover, after all."

"My poor Julia!" he murmured, gathering her into his arms. "So soon?"

As he spoke, his nimble fingers searched along her back for the fastenings of her gown. After a moment, he recalled that she was still wearing her riding habit, and that the fastenings were in the front.

"I hate him!" she sobbed brokenly, burying her face in his shirt.

"He doesn't deserve you," Palafox murmured, easing her away from him until she was half reclining on the length of the sofa. "Remember, my love, he's been a sailor his whole life. The only women he's ever known have been dockside whores."

"And the duchess, of course," Julia said, with an angry laugh. "He never thinks of anything but *her!* You should have seen him when he found out she was trapped in Paris at Bonaparte's return. He scoured the newspapers for any mention of her. He hired people to go and smuggle her out, but they just took his money and laughed behind his back. If it had been *me,* he wouldn't have cared three straws, but he is obsessed with *her.*"

Palafox made all the appropriate sympathetic sounds, all the while hunting for buttons.

"He spent all morning with her," Julia whined. "I'm not supposed to know anything about it, of course. Why is everyone so in love with her? She is old! And I never saw anything so extraordinary in her looks. Her eyes are rather pretty, I suppose, but her hair is plain brown!"

He lifted her chin with one finger. "Well, *I* am not in love with her," he murmured. With his other hand, he loosened the lace jabot at her neck. "I could have had her a hundred times, but she is not to my taste. I prefer lamb to mutton."

"Oh, Charles!" Julia cried happily. "Do you really like me better?"

"My darling girl, I was up all night thinking of you," he told her. As she lay unresisting, he slowly opened her jacket.

"Poor Charles," she purred. "If your horrid old aunt would just give you your money *now,* you wouldn't have to marry Octavia at all!"

"Poor Julia," he answered smoothly, opening the front of her white lawn shirt. In the reclining position, her breasts mounded over the tops of her stays. "To be married to such a simpleton. If I were rich, I could take you away from Nicky."

Her eyes sparkled with delight. "Elope? Oh, Charles! Octavia would simply *die!*"

He sighed, one finger trailing down to the tiny square buckle at her waist. "Alas, I am not rich—not yet. But there's no reason we can't console each other. Hmmm?" Bending his head, he kissed her breasts, first one, then the other, very lightly.

"Mmmm," Julia breathed. "I should like to see the look on Octavia's face!" she giggled. "If she could only see us now. I *stole* Nicky from her, you know, and now I'm stealing you! What a fine joke!"

Charles frowned slightly as he tried to free her breasts from her corset. "Well, it is a fine joke," he said. "But, for now, I'm afraid it must remain a *private* joke. If Octavia were to call off the wedding, I'd be well and truly in the suds."

She gasped as he pinched one of her nipples between his index finger and thumb. "Do you understand me, Julia?"

She pouted. "I daresay Camford will make me a nice settlement in the divorce."

Palafox drew away from her abruptly. "Divorce!"

"Of course, silly," she told him, puzzled. "If you and I are to be married, I must first get a divorce. Since it is all *his* fault, *he* will have to pay." Sitting up, she shrugged out of her jacket and twined her arms around him. "How much do you mean to get from your aunt?" she asked, nibbling his ear.

"Fifty thousand, I should think."

Julia's face fell. "Nicky will never give me as much as that!" she said bitterly. "He is the worse pinchpenny miser that ever lived. I should be lucky to get *ten* thousand pounds from him! No, you will just have to marry Octavia, my love." Lying back, she held out her arms to him.

Charles relaxed visibly. "I fear so," he sadly agreed, returning to the business of undressing her. "We shall have to keep our love a great secret until after I have secured my fortune. Then there will be nothing Octavia can do."

Julia gurgled with laughter. "How I shall laugh! But we must be very careful, you know. She spies on me and reports to Mama! She's interviewed all the servants. I wouldn't put it past her to examine my sheets in the morning."

Palafox was startled. "Good God! Why? Does she suspect me?"

"Oh, no," Julia assured him. "She and Mama are hounding me to give Camford an heir. They made it their business to find out that Nicky and I sleep in separate rooms. I have been looking for a way to punish them for their meddling. This is perfect."

Palafox snickered. "Camford does not sleep with you?"

"I will tell you a secret, Charles," Julia said earnestly, clasping his hand to her breast. "I am still a virgin. And when I give myself to you, it will be my first time. You *will* be gentle with me, won't you?"

Palafox laughed softly.

"To be sure I will," he said. He began kissing her mouth, one hand roaming over her upper body, while the other hand found its way beneath the hem of her skirt. Tugging at her stays, he succeeded in freeing her breasts, attacking them immediately with his mouth. In the grip of sensations she had never before experienced, Julia hardly knew what he was doing until she felt his hand at the opening of her drawers.

To his annoyance, she squirmed out of reach. "What are you doing?" she cried, covering her breasts with her arms.

"What do you think I'm doing?" he snapped. Then, softening his voice, he said, "Let me make you happy, darling."

"Not *here*," she protested.

"Yes, here," he murmured huskily, his hand traveling up her skirts again. "*Now.* I cannot wait to taste you."

"Really?" she said, faltering.

Leaning forward, he looked her in the eyes as he forced his hand between her tightly closed legs. She did not resist much.

"Do you—do you love me, Charles?" she asked tremulously.

"I adore you," he said extravagantly. "Now open your legs like a good girl."

Enthralled by his male power, Julia obeyed. With just the tip of his finger, Palafox gave her pleasure beyond anything she could imagine. She actually swooned, coming to just in time to feel him drive the length of his member into her body. Julia screamed in pain.

"Bloody hell!" Palafox growled, withdrawing. "You really are a virgin."

Julia blinked back tears. She felt betrayed, betrayed by the deep pain, and betrayed by the fact that he had not believed her. "I told you I was," she whimpered. "I told you to be gentle."

For the next few moments, Palafox was truly remorseful. He comforted Julia as best he could, holding her in his arms and murmuring endearments. "I'm so sorry, my love. I should not have doubted you. But it is almost incredible that any man could resist you."

Clinging to him, Julia began to sob. The pain in her loins was virtually gone, but the pain of her husband's indifference to her never seemed to go away. "He does not want me. The only woman he cares about is *her.* The duchess."

"Lord, your husband is a fool!" Charles said angrily. "Only a fool would neglect a little beauty like you. He has neglected you shamefully."

"He *has* neglected me," Julia moaned. "He never loved me. He never even gave me a chance. Oh, Charles! If only *you* were the Earl of Camford! How happy I would be!"

Pushing her face against his, she kissed him wildly, tears streaming down her face.

The needs of the moment overruled any guilt Palafox may have felt in taking advantage of the neglected wife. Julia offered her body and he took it. Afterward, he gave her his handkerchief. "You must go to your maid now," he told her as he put his own clothing to rights. "She will be waiting to dress you for dinner. Tidy yourself up," he added as he left the room. "You can't go walking the halls looking like *that*."

He did not mean to be unkind, but Julia felt his words were cold and curt. It stung to be left alone so abruptly. He hadn't even kissed her good-bye properly. With stiff, trembling fingers she dressed herself. He had given her pleasure, to be sure, but the pleasure had not lingered. She had imagined herself wrapped in the mantle of Charles's love, but that comfort had been ripped away at his departure. There was not even the satisfaction of revenge; Octavia did not know she was betrayed. As for Camford, he would not care, even if he did know.

All that remained of the encounter was cold shame. She was now an adulteress.

Julia finished dressing and fled the room as if it were the scene of a horrible crime. She ran to the safety of her room, hoping for consolation from her maid.

Instead, the Duchess of Warwick was there, waiting for her.

Already dressed for dinner in a black silk gown, Emma was seated in the window seat leafing through one of Julia's magazines. The sight of her sent Julia into a rage. Defiance replaced all feelings of guilt.

Crossing the room, she tore the magazine from Emma's

hands and threw it to the floor. "What are you doing in my room? Am I to have no privacy whatsoever?"

Emma was taken aback by Julia's violence, but she said calmly, "Forgive me, Julia. I have been looking for you everywhere. I knew you must return to your room to dress for dinner. I wanted to speak with you privately."

Julia regained control of herself. She knew that her hair and dress were disheveled, and she knew that the duchess had noticed. Turning on her heel, she strode to her dressing table. Seating herself, she reached for her hairbrush, a pretty ivory-handled object that had been a wedding gift from her mother. "Really?" she said coolly. "What about?"

"I've spoken to your mother," Emma said quietly. "She told me you are thinking of leaving your husband."

Julia half turned in her seat, her eyes glittering with hatred. "You'd like that, wouldn't you? You'd like it if Nicky and I were divorced. Then you could have him all to yourself!"

"No," Emma said firmly. "Absolutely not. I assure you, any feelings I may have had for your husband vanished in a puff of smoke when I learned how he's been treating you. I am on your side, Julia. I would like to help you."

"You would like to help yourself to my husband!" Julia accused her.

Emma sighed. "No, Julia. A thousand times, no."

"How he has been treating me," Julia muttered, turning away. She laughed bitterly, pulling her hairbrush through her hair with rough, jerky movements. "You know perfectly well he's never touched me. I'm sure it was all your doing. You would not marry him yourself, but you could not bear to think of him touching his own wife. Did you make him promise to be faithful to you? Is that it?"

Emma sat stunned. "What?" she said faintly. "What are you saying, Julia?"

"He's never touched me," Julia hissed. "My marriage has

never been consummated, and it's all because of you! How dare you sit there telling me you're on my side!"

Emma was on her feet. "What do you mean he's never touched you?" she cried in disbelief. "You told your mother he never let you alone! You described a living nightmare!"

"What was I supposed to tell her?" Julia said sullenly. "That my husband doesn't want me? That he is in love with another woman? A woman *ten years older* than he?"

Emma shook her head. "That is not true."

"You were with him all morning, ma'am! Do you deny it?"

"There is nothing going on between your husband and me, Julia," Emma said firmly. "That was finished long before he married you. I am shocked—*shocked*—to hear that your marriage has not been consummated."

"Shocked, and saddened, I am sure," Julia said sarcastically. "Pardon me, ma'am, if I don't believe a word you say! Now, if you don't mind, I should like to dress for dinner."

"Yes, of course," Emma said mechanically. "I beg your pardon for the intrusion."

Julia loudly summoned her maid, and Emma hastily left the room. Reeling from the unpleasant scene with Julia, she went back to her sitting room. She sat down at the pianoforte and began fingering the keys for relief, her thoughts racing.

"There you are," Colin said, breezing in. "I heard your noise. Shall we go down together? What do you think of my cravat this evening? My man is trying something new."

Emma closed the instrument with a bang. Within moments, she had poured out the whole story to her twin brother.

Colin was obliged to sit down. "Not consummated?" he repeated in astonishment. "Well, there is one bright feature, at least. They will require no divorce. They can simply have the marriage annulled."

"Julia blames me. She thinks Nicholas is in love with me, that he loves me still. Do you think it might be true?" Emma asked him quietly. "He told me he loved me last year, of course, but I never took him seriously! But if he's been in love with me all this time—I mean, *really* in love with me! How he must be suffering."

"And how you long to *relieve* his suffering," Colin drawled.

"But I cannot," Emma whispered. "Even if the marriage were to be annulled, I—I could not *marry* him."

"Why not?"

"I am as good as thirty-one," she explained. "He is twenty-one. When I am forty, he'll be thirty. And when he is forty, I shall be—"

"Don't say it! I forbid you."

"And, of course I have my children to think about," she said.

"They need a father figure, don't they?" Colin said.

"No," said Emma. "They would hate it. At my age, a woman should live for her children, shouldn't she?"

"Oh, absolutely," Colin agreed. "You are Cornelia, mother of the Gracchi. You cannot marry again. You should kill yourself for even thinking of it."

"I am *not* thinking of it," Emma said firmly. "Oh, Colin! How could he let me believe that he'd brutalized Julia? The things I said to him—!"

"Did he admit it?"

"He didn't deny it."

"But that's not the same thing," said Colin. "Aunt Harriet taught me that."

"But why would he let me go on thinking it? Why didn't he tell me the truth?"

Colin pronounced himself equally bewildered. "You'll have to ask him for an explanation. *I* never let people think the worst of me."

Emma shook her head. "I don't think I should talk to him. It's too dangerous."

"Dangerous for whom? You or him? *Are* you in love with him, Emma?"

"Of course not." Emma rose from the pianoforte. "I don't

know. In any case, it doesn't matter. Even if I loved him, I could not marry him. It would be cruel to excite his expectations."

"It would be cruel to let him think you do not care for him," said Colin.

"I never said I cared for him," she said sharply. "I—I am not indifferent to him, but that is not the same thing, you know. It's hopeless. Oh, why cannot he be a normal, selfish, heartless, promiscuous man?"

"Ah," said Colin, "but, then you would be indifferent to him."

Emma frowned at him. "I think your cravat looks ridiculously complicated," she said petulantly. "It looks like it took you all afternoon."

"Thank you," he said, pleased. "I like it, too."

At dinner, Charles Palafox was seated to Emma's immediate right. The conversation turned on the planned visit to Wingate. "The duke has proposed that we make the excursion on Sunday, the seventeenth. Would that be convenient for your grace? If not, I fear it will have to be postponed until after Christmas Week."

Emma could think of no excuse, and on the day after the hunt took place, a large party, comprising three vehicles, set off for Wingate at an early hour. Mr. Palafox gallantly drove his fiancée and her mother in his smart black-lacquered phaeton. Colin drove his nephew Grey in his curricle. Princess Elke, Julia, and Augusta Fitzroy were to go on horseback with the duke and Major von Schroeder. Emma and Flavia Fitzroy were just settling into the duchess's barouche, when Nicholas appeared.

"Forgive my tardiness," he apologized, climbing into the barouche and taking his place opposite the two females.

Emma could not meet his eyes, but she said pleasantly enough, "I did not think you were coming with us, my lord. We nearly left without you."

"Julia will not be happy until she has seen the place,"

Nicholas answered. "She fears it may be grander than Camford Park."

"Oh, dear," Flavia said in dismay. "This makes us a party of thirteen! That is an unlucky number," she explained.

Nicholas smiled at his sister-in-law. "You forgot to factor in the servants, Cousin Flavia."

The plainest of the Fitzroy sisters blinked at him. "My lord?"

"They are people, after all," he told her. "Let's see. The duchess has her driver and her postilions. Three or four grooms are with us on horseback. Lord Colin has his tiger with him, as does Mr. Palafox. I'd say we are at least a party of twenty, and that is a safe, comfortable number, is it not?"

"I suppose so," Flavia said uncertainly.

Wingate was a spacious, though not palatial, mansion of pale gray stone, built in the Palladian style that had been so much in vogue at the turn of the century. The housekeeper greeted them at the door, and they spent the better part of two hours going over the rooms of the house while the servants drove on to a pretty stone pavilion some distance from the house to lay out the picnic the duke's party would be enjoying later.

In her determination not to be alone with Nicholas, even for a second, Emma kept her arm firmly linked with Flavia's, but he outflanked her as they stopped to admire the view of the lake from the tall french windows of the morning room.

"Cousin Flavia," he called from the doorway. "I believe your mother is looking for you. You will find her in the drawing room."

Emma resigned herself to the confrontation she had been dreading.

"You have been avoiding me," he accused her, the moment they were alone.

"Not at all."

"I waited two hours for you yesterday at the stables," he said.

"The stables?" she repeated, frowning. "Oh! Your riding lessons." She laughed nervously. "I assumed it was understood, my lord, I-I cannot be your teacher."

Again, he blocked her way. "You laid some heavy charges at my door," he said. "I was so shocked, I could not defend myself. Let me do so now."

"There is no need," she said quickly. "I have spoken to Julia."

"To Julia!" Anger kindled in his eyes.

"She has told me the truth, Nicholas."

His voice rasped as he tried to keep from shouting. "The truth? That I am some rapacious animal? Julia is incapable of speaking the truth. The truth so rarely serves her purpose, you see."

"She told me that your marriage has not been consummated."

"Ah," he said, after a brief pause. "She has recanted her lies, then? Well! I am all astonishment."

"So am I!" said Emma. "How could you let me think you were capable of—of hurting Julia on purpose?"

He raked his fingers through his hair. "I could not believe you said it to me! I thought—I thought you knew me better than that, Emma."

"I did not want to think ill of you," cried Emma. "It broke my heart. But you seemed to confirm it. Julia *is* unhappy, and you *are* the cause, but it is not what I thought. Oh, Nicholas, what do you think you are playing at with that poor girl? She is near the breaking point. She is the sort of person who withers without affection, or, at least, admiration."

"Always, you take *her* side," he complained. "She *tricked* me into marrying her. Can you not understand how that makes me feel? She has no right to expect marital bliss. It was always my intention to annul the marriage."

Emma stared at him. "Your intention! What do you mean?"

"Just because she caught me in a trap doesn't mean I can't

climb out of it!" he said. "If her victory is hollow, she has no one to blame for it, but herself. As long as this farce of a marriage remains unconsummated, it is no marriage at all. In the eyes of the law, I am still a bachelor, and she is yet a spinster."

Emma shook her head in disbelief. "Are you mad?"

"I don't think so."

"You mean to marry again?"

"Perhaps."

"But of course you must marry again," she said impatiently. "It is your duty to provide Camford with an heir."

Nicholas shrugged. "My cousin, Lady Catherine, is married. Her son could be my heir."

She looked at him in amazement. "You would be content to let someone else's son inherit *your* title and *your* estate?"

"I don't really regard it as *my* title or *my* estate, you know," he replied. "I never did. I'm just a sort of placeholder. It seems fitting to me that Catherine's son should inherit. I don't suppose I will ever marry again. There won't be any need to. Once my nephew is born, I think I'll return to the sea."

"Of course," she said faintly. "Your first love."

"If I could build myself a yacht, I'd like to sail around the world. I don't suppose," he went on, "that *you* would be interested in sailing around the world with me? I still love you, Emma. I always will."

The simplicity of his words took her breath away.

"Oh, Nicholas," she said sadly.

"I know you don't want to marry again," he said quickly. "I'm not asking you to. I just want to be with you. I should prefer to be your husband, of course, but I believe I could be content with something—with something less."

Emma shook her head. "I'm afraid I'm not a good sailor," she said, trying to make a joke. "I get horribly queasy just crossing the Channel. If Paris were not on the other side, I shouldn't bother at all."

"We could live in Paris, then," he said quickly. "I don't care. As long as I am with you, I don't care about anything else. I have tried to forget you, Emma. I thought I was close to success, but the moment I saw you again, I knew it was no use. I have never felt like this about anyone in the whole course of my life."

Emma felt tears gathering behind the bridge of her nose. "I'm sorry, Nicholas."

Without another word, he dragged her over to the window, paying no attention to her protests. Taking her face in his hands, he forced her to look at him. Sunlight fell directly on her face.

"What do you think you're doing?" she complained.

"I'm going to ask you a question. I want to see your eyes when you answer. Do you love me, Emma? Do you feel anything for me? Am I a fool?"

"That is three questions."

"Here's a fourth," he said roughly, giving her a shake. "Is this a game to you? Because it is life and death to me."

"I am sorry, Nicholas," she said. "I cannot return your feelings. And I have a lover already," she added. "I don't need another."

"No, you don't," he said, frowning. His hands released her face. "You have no lover."

"Of course I do," she insisted. "I always have a lover."

"Who? Palafox?"

"Certainly not," she said sharply.

He laughed. "Who else is there?"

Emma looked him square in the eye. "Can't you guess? It's Major von Schroeder, of course."

# Chapter Twenty-One

To her considerable annoyance, Nicholas snorted.

"Is it so unbelievable that I should have a lover?" she said, bristling. "I have not been lonely this past year, Nicholas, I can assure you."

"Oh, yes! But where were all your lovers when Napoleon returned to France?" he demanded. "They left you to your fate, did they not?"

"It's true they deserted me," she admitted. "But they were all French. Fritz is German."

"Fritz!" He shook his head. "Your sons' tutor? I don't believe it. You would not give yourself to a servant."

Emma arched her brows. "Have you become a snob, Nicholas?" she asked him.

Nicholas flushed.

"I like Fritz," said Emma. "He's a good man. The boys respect him. They will listen to him where they will not listen to anyone else."

"Then he is not your lover. He is your bear-leader," Nicholas said.

"He's versatile," Emma said, tight-lipped with anger. "He is both."

Nicholas sniffed. "If you ask me, he's more interested in

your brother's wife, the Princess Elke. He seems to live in her pocket. The man's a gigolo, Emma."

"Not at all. I asked Fritz to look after her highness," Emma said primly. "He speaks her native language, you know. Fritz is very obliging."

"Oh, very," Nicholas agreed.

"Are you insinuating that Fritz has betrayed me with the princess?" she demanded.

Nicholas shrugged.

"Well, perhaps I have been neglecting him," said Emma. "I'll be sure to pay more attention to him from now on. Thank you for your . . . observation, Nicholas."

Curtseying, she excused herself and went to find the others.

Colin, who knew Wingate at least as well as the housekeeper did, was leading the rest of the party up the grand staircase, pointing out the elegance of the carved marble bannister. Emma slipped into place next to her son Grey, who was bringing up the rear.

Octavia, clinging tightly to the arm of Mr. Palafox, paused at the landing to study the handsome stained glass window. "The house seems so singularly perfect for you, Lord Colin," she said, "that I wonder you never bought it for yourself."

A puzzled frown appeared on Colin's face. "Yes, so do I."

"I believe it was the bells that put you off," Emma called up to her brother.

Colin widened his eyes at her. "Ah, Emma! There you are! You disappeared. Where did you go? And Camford disappeared at the same time. 'Tis very strange."

Emma glared at him.

"But you're quite right about the bells," her brother went on blithely. "All these old houses are built shockingly close to the village churches. One doesn't like the thought of the bells crashing into one's head at the crack of dawn, after all.

And, then, of course, there's the location. It's halfway between Chilton and Warwick."

"I should think that would make it perfect for you," said Octavia.

"Hardly," he retorted. "I have no need of an estate halfway between my brother's and my nephew's. If I want to stay at Chilton, I stay at Chilton; and if I want to stay at Warwick, I stay at Warwick."

"I am much obliged to you, Uncle!" said the Duke of Warwick, laughing.

Colin gave a weary sigh. "It's so dreadfully hard having all this money and no home to call one's own. To be a here-and-there-ian—it's no kind of life."

"You're too particular," Emma told him. "If you found fault with people the way you do with houses, you would be a hermit."

"Instead, I am a vagabond," he sniffed. "I believe I shall buy Aylescourt, after all. It is close to Oxford University; Harry and Grey will like that. To have a rich uncle scarcely twenty miles away is always a great boon for a young man."

"And, of course, *I* would be able to visit my sons any time I like," said Emma.

"Lord!" said Harry. "A man don't want his mother around when he's at University! You'll make me a laughingstock, Mama!"

Emma laughed to hide the fact that his rejection stung. "Well, Grey will be glad to have me nearby," she said, ruffling her younger son's hair.

"I daresay!" Harry retorted. "For he is a mother's boy."

Scowling, Grey swatted Emma's hands away. "I am not a mother's boy!" he howled.

Harry laughed at his younger brother. "If you say so," he said shrugging.

"I am not! You take that back, Harry!"

"I won't," said Harry, continuing up the stairs with Julia on his arm.

Grey tore loose from his mother and launched himself at his elder brother, but Harry reacted quickly. By simply placing his hand on Grey's forehead, he held him at arms' length while the younger boy pummeled the air.

*"Was ist das?"* Major von Schroeder demanded, pulling Grey to one side. "Is this how young gentlemen behave in the presence of ladies? I think not. Both of you will apologize at once."

There was a long pause. Then Harry drew himself to his full height.

"You are quite right, Major," he said, to Emma's relief. "Ladies, I do apologize, and the fault was entirely mine. It was very wrong of me to tease my brother. Do let us go on and see the rest of the house."

The tour went on, but, after his brother's insults, Grey would not even look at his mother, let alone walk with her or speak to her. He walked ahead, insinuating himself between the major and Princess Elke. Nicholas rejoined the party, offering his arm to Lady Anne. After a while, Major von Schroeder looked back, and seeing Emma quite alone in front of a painting, took the opportunity to console her.

"It is a difficult age, your grace," he said kindly, looking up at the painting with her so that to a casual observer it might appear they were simply discussing the artist's merits. "When I reached that age, I wanted nothing to do with women. I did not want to be . . . how do you say . . . tied with the apron strings? You must give them their heads and let them gallop. They will come back to you in time."

Emma was obliged to turn her face away as tears pricked her eyes. "I am fully aware they are growing up, Major. I just didn't think it would happen so quickly," she added, crumbling as he silently passed her his handkerchief. Hastily, she dabbed her eyes and returned it to him. "Thank you," she said, pulling herself together.

"I am always happy to be of service to your grace," he answered with a little bow.

"I wonder if you really mean that, Fritz," she said, as they began to walk together. The party had split up and smaller groups were exploring the upstairs rooms at whim. Emma and the major walked the long length of the hall.

The major laughed. "Put me to the test," he invited her.

"The fact of the matter is . . ." Pausing at a curio table, she pretended to study the miniatures displayed under the glass top. "I've done something very foolish, and I need your help," she went on quietly, switching to German.

The major bent over the curio table as a flurry of people came out of one of the rooms. "Ah! These little miniatures, they are so lifelike!" he said loudly in English.

"I believe they are painted on ivory," Emma shouted. When the hall was empty again, she went back to German. "There is a certain married gentleman," she began delicately. "I'm afraid he fancies himself in love with me."

"Ah, the Lord Camford," the major said immediately.

"My dear Major!" Emma rebuked him.

"I'm afraid I saw you at the window," he apologized.

"This gentleman, I'm afraid, has lost his wits," said Emma. "In a moment of weakness, he has declared himself. He seems ready to abandon his wife. In short, he has had the temerity to ask me to run away with him."

He nodded wisely. "You want me to get rid of him?"

"Yes," Emma said gratefully.

"I'll do the job for a hundred British pounds sterling," he said amiably. "His body will never be found."

"What?" cried Emma, horrified as she caught his meaning. "No! Good Lord, Major! I don't want you to *kill* him."

The major looked surprised. "No? But . . . the gentleman is a nuisance, *nicht wahr?*"

"You are not to kill him," she said firmly.

"What then?"

"I'm afraid I told him that you and I—that we are lovers. I just want you to pretend to be my lover, that's all. You don't have to kill anyone. I'll pay you, of course."

"Ah!" he said, enlightenment clearing his countenance. "You want me to be your lover."

"No! No, I want you to *pretend* to be my lover," she corrected him firmly.

He chuckled. "This has been quite a day for me," he declared. "I put this day in my memoirs, I think."

"I'd rather you didn't," Emma said sharply. "Thank you all the same."

"No names," he assured her.

"Oh, well, in that case," she muttered. "No one will ever scry who the Duchess of W—is, I am sure! No one will ever be able to fill in the blanks."

The major chuckled. "Today a certain gentleman asked me to be correspondent in his divorce. Then a certain lady asked me to be the father of her child. And, then, another lady asks me to be her lover! I have never had such a day."

Emma gaped at him. "My brother asked you to be correspondent? And Princess Elke asked you to be the father of her child?"

The major held up a hand. "Please, no names," he said virtuously.

"But I shall look ridiculous if my lover is making love to somebody else! You will just have to tell the princess no."

He sighed. "Unfortunately, I have a war wound that makes it impossible for me to comply with the princess's request. I can give a woman pleasure, you understand, but I cannot father a child. Her highness will have to find someone else for that task, I fear. But I shall be more than happy to be your lover, madame."

"Pretend lover," Emma reiterated.

"Of course."

At the conclusion of the tour, Octavia seemed inclined to take the lease at Wingate, but Mr. Palafox, exercising one of the few powers remaining to him, declared he was not persuaded. The bells, he said as they were enjoying their luncheon on the sunny terrace, worried him very much.

"Nonsense," Octavia said impatiently. "It is a very big house, Charles, and the bedrooms are situated quite far away and opposite to the church. You will never hear them."

"You will allow me to make up my own mind," he said coldly.

"Of course," she said coldly, and nothing more was said on the subject.

The return to Warwick was accomplished without incident, and the next few days were taken up by preparations for Christmas. For Christmas week itself, mourning was suspended. The black bunting was taken away, and the dining hall and the main drawing room were decorated with arrangements of tinsel, balsam, and sugared fruit. While the ladies were engaged in the house, the gentlemen busied themselves out of doors, busily shooting birds for the table. Their activities culminated in the annual stag hunt, which some of the ladies attended, Emma included. She rode out with Princess Elke, Julia, and Augusta.

Augusta quickly moved to the forefront to be closest to the action. Julia instantly attached herself to Mr. Palafox, leaving Emma alone with her sister-in-law.

Princess Elke eyed her coldly. "The major is to take the shot, is he not?" she asked in German.

"Yes, I believe so."

"Do you not mean to be at his side?" said Elke, her mouth pursed in disapproval.

"I don't care about the hunt," Emma confessed. "I'm just here for the fresh air . . . and the venison, of course. I do enjoy my Christmas dinner. Is that not hypocritical of me?"

Princess Elke grunted. "If you truly loved Fritz, you would be at his side," she said contemptuously. "A woman in love is not squeamish, even if she is English."

"But I am not in love with Fritz," Emma told her. "He is only pretending to make love to me to keep Lord Camford away."

Princess Elke scowled. "To keep Lord Camfurt away? Princess Elke saw you with him at Wingate. Princess Elke was walking in the garden, and she happened to look up. There you were, with him, in the window. You did not see Princess Elke, but Princess Elke saw you. I think, perhaps, Lord Camfurt doesn't have the pox at all."

"You accuse me of lying?"

Princess Elke made a guttural sound of disgust. "These games! Princess Elke does not like games. I want only one thing: a strong, healthy man. Together we give Hindenburg a strong heir. There is no need for games. Does the man have the pox or not?"

"Look here!" Emma said crossly. "Lord Camford is not interested in you. You're not his sort of woman at all. Spare yourself the humiliation of rejection, and just leave him alone."

"Ha!" said Princess Elke. "You English are not to be trusted."

"Quite," Emma said tartly. "But we did save your arses from the French. Your highness might show a little gratitude."

Princess Elke bristled. "It was the Prussians who secured the victory at Waterloo!" she snapped.

Emma hid a small yawn behind a gloved hand. "If you say so," she said. Kicking her horse, she galloped off to catch up to the others.

The hunters chased the unfortunate stag from one end of the duke's demesne to the other, until finally, after nearly six hours, the beast was brought to bay in the middle of a stream. The major strolled into the stream and casually took the shot, felling the stag at once. The company, most as exhausted as the stag, applauded, but, Emma could not help but shudder, remembering how cheerfully the major had offered to kill Nicholas for a mere one hundred pounds.

The duke promised that the major should have the head for his wall, and, cold and wet, they all rode back to the house, where a nasty shock awaited Charles Palafox: his aunt, the rich and vulgar Mrs. Allen, had arrived unexpectedly. When her presence was revealed to him, he looked rather like the stag brought to bay, Emma thought, almost feeling sorry for him. Discreetly, she went up to her room to bathe and change.

She had scarcely completed her toilette when Colin burst into the room. "I suppose you've heard Palafox's aunt has come to stay," he said, ignoring her furious protests against this invasion of her privacy. "Pshaw! If I can't invade your privacy what good are you to me? Besides, I peeked through the keyhole to make sure you were decent first."

"I heard she was here," Emma said, relenting. "I don't think she's come to stay. I don't think Charles will allow it."

"What has Charles to say about anything?" he asked, chuckling as he followed her from her bedroom into her sitting room. "'Twas Lady Anne who invited the aunt. Put up to it by Octavia, no less."

"I don't believe it," said Emma as he helped himself to a large glass of brandy. "Octavia is the biggest snob who ever lived, and Mrs. Allen's money comes from Trade. Octavia's marriage to Charles will wash the stink off, to be sure, but the bride would never stoop to associating with Mrs. Allen herself."

"Oh, but she wants Wingate," Colin explained. "She's brought the aunt here to force Charles's hand. No Wingate, no marriage. No marriage, no money."

"That's ghastly!" Emma said indignantly. "Charles may be a cad—in fact, I know he is! But he don't deserve *this*.

This is slavery, blackmail. Charles must be furious, livid! And I don't blame him one bit if he is," she added.

"You will admit it adds a dash of interest to an otherwise crashing bore of a holiday," said Colin. "I'm sorry, Emma, but I've been bored to flinders since Monty left."

"I'm so sorry you've been bored, dear," Emma said tartly. "I myself have had just the right amount of excitement! I daresay I should have devoted more time to your entertainment, but I should think that hiring a man to seduce your wife so that you may divorce her with a clear conscience would be enough to keep you interested in life."

"Oh, my own affairs always bore me," Colin answered. "Now yours are beginning to bore me, too, I'm sorry to say."

"I beg your pardon," Emma said coolly. "But who's to say that Mrs. Allen will be at all interesting?"

"Did you see the look on poor Charles's face when he heard you-know-who was here?" Colin demanded. "*I* only heard about it secondhand from the second footman, and I am persuaded she must be *very* interesting indeed."

"He did seem rather dismayed," Emma admitted.

"Do put her next to me at dinner," Colin begged. "I feel instinctively that Mrs. Allen is the sort of person from whom boredom runs away screaming."


Mrs. Allen did not disappoint. She was a short, squat woman, swarthy of skin, with a mustache bristling on her upper lip, but the eye was not permitted to dwell on her many physical defects. Instead, the eye was walloped by the incredible, enormous lemon-yellow turban she had smashed down on her head in the mistaken belief that it was all the kick, as she put it. She carried a pop-eyed pug dog with her everywhere, even to the dinner table. Colin very quickly discovered that her attachment to her pet was more practical than sentimental. In fact, Pug was the widow's necessity.

Mrs. Allen, owing to her vegetarian diet, no doubt, suffered from agonizing waves of flatulence, and Pug's chief purpose in life was to take the blame for his mistress's unscheduled emissions.

"Good God! What is that smell?" the duke cried at dinner, as a strong odor of cabbage made its way to his end of the table.

"I don't smell anything," Mrs. Allen said, glaring around the table.

Emma had granted Colin's wish to be seated next to the new arrival. Colin's eyes filled with tears. More than one person was obliged to breathe through the filter of a damask napkin.

The scent of her aunt-to-be had not yet reached Octavia, who sat in safety on the opposite side of the table. She smiled and said, "Aunt Allen, you will be glad to know that Charles and I have found the perfect estate, a most eligible house. It belongs to my cousin, Lord Grey, but the duchess has offered us a very reasonable lease. We would very much like to take you to see it, wouldn't we, Charles?"

Mr. Palafox, seated at Emma's elbow, simply pretended not to hear. Sympathetic to his plight, Emma did her best to keep him engaged in conversation.

At last, unable to endure any more of Mrs. Allen's company, Colin abruptly scraped back his chair and fled the room. Emma immediately rose from the table. "Ladies? Shall we adjourn for coffee?"

The next morning, Emma received a letter from her elder brother, the Duke of Chilton. She read it aloud to Colin as they sipped their morning chocolate. Cecily, Duchess of Chilton, had given birth to a son and heir. Lord Scarlingford was to be christened James Stephen Grey on Sunday, December 31.

"I suppose we shall have to leave the day after Christmas,"

said Emma. "After Harry opens the alms box, of course. Harry will not be pleased," she went on, setting aside Otto's letter. "He wanted me to give a small party on New Year's Eve. But we shall have to be at Chilton for the christening. Perhaps we could have a small party on Christmas Eve, after all. That doesn't give us much time, of course. And I shall have to speak to Armand."

She groaned, dreading the interview with her temperamental French chef.

"That doesn't give *me* much time either," Colin said bitterly. "A pox on Cecily! She could have had that baby any time. She did it on purpose."

Emma burst out laughing. "What is the matter with you?"

"If we leave Chilton, the Hindenburg will probably leave too."

"Don't you want her to go?"

"Not without giving me grounds for a divorce, I don't!" said Colin. "With what I'm paying Schroeder, I should have had *ample* evidence by now! Instead, he seems to be paying more attention to *you,* Emma."

"Only when Nicholas is around," Emma protested.

"Then where the devil is my evidence?" Colin wanted to know. "Methinks the major doth double-cross me!"

Emma bowed her head. The major had told her about his war wound in confidence, and, as close as she was to Colin, she could not, in good conscience, tell him.

"You'd better talk to him, Emma."

*"Moi?"*

"Yes, you," he said. "He is your 'lover,' after all. You brought him here. He is in your employ. Get him to come to the point—and soon. He must rendezvous with the Hindenburg, and they must be discovered in flagrante delicto."

Emma made a face. "*I* would not want to be the one to find them together."

"Who else?" said Colin. "You're perfect. You, Emma, must find them together and give evidence at the trial."

Emma shook her head vehemently. "I shall do nothing of the kind," she said firmly.

"Emma, you must. I saved your life. It's the least you can do."

"When did you save my life?" she demanded.

"How quickly we forget!" he complained. "When we were born, I let you go first, even though there was no air to breathe in my mother's womb. I could have died giving you life."

"However, you did not."

"Emma, please! I didn't mind being married to the woman, as long as she stayed at home. But now she's *here*. I cannot stay married to her another year! Come, now, you don't want her for a sister-in-law, do you? She's already ruined your beautiful rug. Who knows what she'll do next?"

Emma stood firm. "No, Colin. If I find them together, people would probably come to the conclusion that Fritz *is* my lover. It would be insupportable. Harry and Grey would be humiliated. I've just been granted a pardon by society. I've just been reinstated at the Court of St. James. I can't risk being involved in a divorce."

Colin scowled at her. "You never cared about society before," he pointed out. "You never cared about the Court of St. James."

"Harry would never forgive me if my name were dragged into it. I can't be linked to his tutor. I'm sorry, Colin. I cannot help you."

"I shall have to ask Aunt Harriet, then," he said grumpily, climbing to his feet. "You disappoint me, Emma."

"I will talk to Fritz, of course," Emma offered. "But that is all I can do."

"Well, if it's too much trouble . . ."

"I got involved in one of your schemes last year," she

reminded him. "That turned out beautifully, didn't it? No, thank you."

"Never mind! I shall see to the matter myself," he said coldly.

"What are you going to do?" Emma asked nervously.

"Perhaps you'd rather not know," he said caustically. "Don't you have things to do? Christmas Eve is the day after tomorrow, you know. One would think the Duchess of Warwick might have a thousand things to do."

"Quite," said Emma. "I must speak to the chef, the housekeeper, the wine steward, Carstairs, of course—"

"If you're too busy to talk to Schroeder, I understand."

Emma threw up her hands and left the room.

Colin brooded for a moment. He finished his chocolate. Then, seating himself at his sister's escritoire, he pulled out a sheet of paper. He began to write.


Emma had no luck finding Major von Schroeder, but she did find Nicholas and Palafox in the billiard room. With them was her younger son. Grey was watching the two men play the game. As she came into the room, the two gentlemen stopped their game and bowed.

Grey did not stand on ceremony, however. "Mama! Lord Camford says he will take me sailing anytime I like." He spoke before Emma could open her mouth.

Emma frowned at Nicholas. "You've never spoken of sailing before, Grey."

"Yes, I have," the twelve-year-old argued. "Next year, for Christmas, I would like a yacht, please."

"It's a bit early to think about next year," Emma said, chuckling. "Anyway, I have just bought you an estate, young man. Now you want a yacht."

"I shan't be able to live at Wingate, not for years and years!" said Grey, twitching his head to one side to get his hair out of his eyes. "Anyway, you're giving Wingate to Mr. Palafox and Cousin Octavia! I could go sailing *now,* Mama, if I had a yacht."

"We'll discuss this later," said Emma. "Right now, I'm looking for Major von Schroeder. Have you seen him?"

Grey scowled at her, his red hair falling into his eyes again. "It's winter recess, Mama. I don't have lessons at the winter recess. No one does."

"I am not accusing you of anything, Grey, " Emma said impatiently. "I am just looking for the major. Your Aunt Cecily has had her baby; a boy."

Nicholas and Palafox offered their congratulations, but Grey said merely, "High time!"

Emma sighed. "We leave for Chilton on St. Stephen's Day, and I need to speak to the major about—about the arrangements."

"Well, he's not here," said Grey. "I haven't seen him."

"Perhaps he is with your brother. Do you know where your brother is?"

"I have not seen a glimmer of his grace all morning," Grey replied.

"Well, if you see him, will you tell him I am looking for him?"

Grey shrugged. "If I see him."

"That is all I am asking!" she said. Exasperated, she left the room.

"Emma!"

To her dismay, Nicholas was striding down the hall to her. She turned on him furiously. "Have you taken leave of your senses?" she demanded. "I do not give you leave to use my Christian name. Grey probably heard you!"

"I don't care if he did," he replied. Forcing her against the wall, he brought his mouth down hard onto hers. He kissed her clumsily and passionately. After a moment of shock, Emma shoved him away.

"I should have done that when we were at Wingate," he panted. "I have been kicking myself ever since."

"My son is in the next room," she hissed at him.

"Is that your only objection? Schroeder doesn't love you, Emma," he went on, as she stared at him. "He's gone out riding with Princess Elke. I am sorry if you care for this—this gigolo—but he does not love you. Not as I do. I love no one but you. I shall never love anyone but you."

Emma was trembling. "I don't have time for this," she gasped.

She hurried away from him.

# Chapter Twenty-Two

The fir tree in the drawing room that Christmas Eve was a far cry from the huge *Weihnachtsbaum* that had graced the Great Hall the year before. "We shan't need any special rigging for this one," Harry said regretfully, when the gentlemen rejoined the ladies after dinner. "Even if it *did* fall over, who would notice?"

"I am sorry I could not manage a better celebration," Emma apologized. "Lady Gresham had so graciously offered to give a ball at Norwood when we cancelled ours. I could not steal her guests from her at the last minute. Or even her musicians."

Harry laughed. "It's quite all right, Mama. We've had a splendid dinner anyway. If Cousin Flavia will play for us, we can sing Christmas carols."

Delighted by the request, Flavia ran to the instrument. Mrs. Allen, however, did not approve of merriment on the solemn occasion of Christmas Eve, and she soon commanded her nephew to escort her to her room. Octavia compelled her mother and sisters, with the exception of Julia, to follow Mrs. Allen's example.

Princess Elke sat down to cards with Lady Camford, Lady Harriet, and Lady Susan. Major von Schroeder danced attendance on the ladies, bringing them cups of coffee, tea, and chocolate. Colin reluctantly agreed to give Nicholas a game of chess.

Rather to Emma's surprise, her boys remained with her on the sofa.

"I shall be glad when Mrs. Allen goes away," Harry said angrily, "and that ghastly pug of hers too!"

"Next year, my love," Emma told Harry. "We'll have an even bigger tree than we did last year. We'll have a Christmas Eve Ball *and* a New Years' Eve Ball."

"And next year will be *my* stag hunt," Grey put in. "May I invite some friends from school, Mama?"

"Of course, my darling. You may invite anyone you like. Next year it will not be so dull at Warwick, I promise. We'll have games and music. I might even hire a troupe of actors to give us a play! And we shall have the biggest *tannenbaum* the world has ever seen. Your friends from school will be quite amazed."

The corner of Grey's mouth twitched faintly. "I suppose *that* would be all right."

"But right now you must go to bed," Emma said sadly.

"Mama!"

"It's half past ten already. The *Kristkindl* will not come if you are awake."

"I mean to stay up all night," Harry announced. "And you needn't bother with any surprises for *me,* Mama. I don't believe in the Christmas Angel. I never did. I only pretended to for your sake. It's just another one of Grandmama's German fairy stories."

Grey frowned at him. "If there is no *Kristkindl,* who puts the presents under the tree every year?"

"Your mother does, of course," his brother answered, laughing.

"Harry!" Emma said furiously.

"I'm only joking you, Grey!" Harry said quickly. "Of

course there's a *Kristkindl*. You don't really think *our mother* stays up all night wrapping presents, do you? Come on. Let's go to bed. We can always sing Christmas carols tomorrow."

Emma bade everyone good night and followed her sons from the room.

Julia yawned at the card table. "I'm so tired. I think I'll go to bed, too. Nicky?" she called to her husband. "I'm going to bed. Shall I wait up for you?"

"No, madam. The game is at a very delicate stage," Nicholas replied. "Lord Colin is on the verge of winning. If I do not apply myself, I may find myself at *point non plus*. I'm afraid this could take all night."

With a shrug, Julia departed.

Colin studied the chess board rather doubtfully. "No offense, Camford, but I don't even want to do anything *pleasant* all night. And, if I'm on the verge of winning, I don't see it."

"I may have exaggerated a bit," Nicholas admitted. "You're not a very good chess player, I'm afraid."

"I am not a chess player at all," Colin answered with a sniff. "I am more intuitive than strategic, you understand. Wist is more along my line."

"Perhaps we'd better leave it, then," said Nicholas. "Go and play cards."

"No, they're playing at loo," Colin said, grimacing. "To be honest, I'd rather go to bed."

"Then go to bed," said Nicholas, already putting the chess pieces away.

"I shall, if Carstairs ever returns," Colin answered. "It's as though he's staying away on purpose! I need my beauty sleep. I'm not eighteen anymore."

"What do you need Carstairs for?" Nicholas asked him.

"I need him to deliver a little note to the major," Colin answered.

Major von Schroeder had taken Julia's place at the card table.

"He is right over there," Nicholas pointed out.

"Discretion, Camford," Colin chided him. "It's a billet-doux from a . . . a certain lady."

Nicholas sat very still. "Billet-doux," he repeated dully.

"A love letter," Colin translated. "I can't just walk over there and give the man a love letter. It's got to be done discreetly, by a trusted servant."

"Leave it with me," Nicholas suggested. "I will give it to Carstairs when he returns."

"I say! That's a very good thought," Colin said gratefully. Taking a small envelope from his pocket, he tossed it to Nicholas. "You don't mind?"

"Not at all," said Nicholas, pocketing the note.

Pleading a headache, Colin bade everyone good night. Nicholas did not remain in the room for very long after his departure. Princess Elke sighed as he left the room. "Lord Camfurt, he is manly for an Englishman, *nicht wahr?* But Princess Elke has heard he has the pox."

"Camford has the pox?" shrieked Lady Susan. "No wonder Julia won't sleep with him!"

"Don't be ridiculous," Lady Harriet scoffed. "Camford don't have the pox. That was just a story Lord Colin made up last year. It's completely untrue."

Princess Elke frowned, puzzled. "Princess Elke's husband tells this lie? For what purpose?"

"General mischief and mayhem, I should think," Lady Harriet said dryly. "But who told your highness that Camford had the pox?"

"The duchess," the princess answered. "She lies to Princess Elke?"

"She wants him for herself, I should imagine," Lady Harriet replied. "She knows perfectly well he don't have the pox."

"The shameless strumpet!" cried Lady Susan. "Emma has

told Julia that Camford has the pox! That is why Julia wants a divorce." A footman jumped forward to help her as she struggled to get out of her chair. "I must go to my niece at once and tell her the truth! The marriage must be saved!"

She ambled out of the room.

Princess Elke stood up. "Princess Elke will go to bed now. *Guten nacht.*"

The major gave her his arm, and they left the room together. "And me, your highness?" he asked her quietly when they were in the hall. "What would you have of me?"

Princess Elke paused to look him over. "Nothing," she decided. "You may go to bed. Your services will not be required, after all. Princess Elke has no more time to waste with you."

"But, your highness! Give me another chance, I beg of you."

"Princess Elke has spoken," she said coldly.


When the Duke of Warwick and his mother returned to the main drawing room a few minutes later, the room was empty but for a few servants who were putting the card table away.

"Where is everyone?" Harry wanted to know.

"They have all gone to bed, your grace," the servant told him.

"Bugger!" said Harry, throwing himself down on one of the sofas. "I wanted to stay up all night. I only pretended to go to bed so that Grey would go to sleep."

"I know, darling," Emma murmured.

"You know, Mama, he's going to find out sooner or later that there is no *Kristkindl*. If he starts going on about it next year, in front of his school friends, he'll be a laughingstock."

"Oh, let me have one last year," Emma pleaded. "You can tell him after Christmas. Come and help me wrap his presents," she added. "It will go faster."

Harry did not budge from the sofa. "Next year will be very different," he announced. "Next year, I shall have lots of friends with me. We will each drink a bottle of wine a day, and we will play cards all night."

"It sounds perfectly dreadful," said his mother.

He sat there, sulking and making plans, while Emma wrapped the presents. Within minutes, Harry was asleep.

Armed with a branch of candles, Lady Susan strode directly to Julia's room. "My dear niece," she cried, throwing open the door, and sailing over to the big four-poster bed, "why didn't you tell your Aunt Susan? Why didn't you tell your mother? Your husband does not have the pox! The duchess lied!"

No sound emerged from the bed. The curtains had been drawn tightly.

"Did you hear me, Julia?" Lady Susan demanded. "Are you awake?"

"She'd have to be dead not to hear you," said a sulky voice from the doorway. Octavia stood there in her nightgown, her auburn hair in curl papers. "Do be quiet, Aunt. You will wake Mrs. Allen."

Frowning, Lady Susan threw open the bed curtains. For a moment she could only stare.

"What is it, Aunt?" Octavia demanded, holding up the bedroom taper she had carried with her down the hall. "Is Julia ill?"

"Go and get your mother," Lady Susan commanded. "And find me Carstairs!"

Octavia did not obey. Instead, she ran to the bed to see what Lady Susan had already seen. Julia was not there. *"Charles,"* Octavia breathed.

Turning, she ran out of the room.

\* \* \*

In another part of the house, Colin crept along a passageway, shielding his candle with one hand. "Quiet, you old fool!" he growled to Lady Harriet, who was following him so closely that from time to time she bumped into him. "The idea is to catch them in the act. If they hear you coming like a herd of cattle, the advantage of surprise will be lost."

"You can't talk to me like that," the old lady snapped back. "I'm doing you a favor, remember? I'd much rather be in bed. Anyway, there's no doubt we'll catch them in the act. They're so brazen, they left the drawing room at the same time. Your silly little note was completely superfluous."

"Silence, hag."

As they drew near the major's door, Colin pressed his ear against the wall, listening. "It's awfully quiet in there," he complained.

Lady Harriet pulled her shawl tightly around her thin body. "What did you expect?" she asked sourly. "Howls of ecstasy? They're German."

Colin cursed under his breath. "Perhaps we're too late to catch them in the act."

"It's not been twenty minutes since I saw them leave the drawing room."

"Some men are quicker than that," Colin said dryly.

"I'll take your word for it, dear boy," the spinster replied virtuously.

Colin gave her a little push. "You'll just have to go in, old girl, and hope for the best."

"I?" she protested. "I ain't going in first!"

"You'll have to, Witch of Endor. I'm ever so squeamish."

"For heaven's sake," she said impatiently, brushing past him to try the door. To her surprise, the latch was not engaged. She went into the room, swallowed up by the darkness.

Colin remained in the hall. He tapped his foot impatiently. "Well?" he called. "Am I betrayed or not?"

*"Wer ist das?"* the major demanded from within. A candle blossomed in the darkness.

"He is here," Lady Harriet called to Colin, "but he is alone, I'm afraid. Sorry to trouble you, Major," she added briskly.

"What?" Colin cried furiously, striding into the room. "After all my hard work? Have you checked the bed?"

"Of course I checked the bed," she snarled. "The man is alone."

"I know she's here," he declared, beginning a search of the room. "I can hear her breathing!"

"That is I," Lady Harriet said coldly. "I have a slight cold in the head. She's not here, little lamb."

"This is all your fault," he raged at her. "I'll bet you didn't even give her the major's letter," he accused her.

"I did," she said indignantly.

"What letter?" the major demanded, getting out of bed. His snow-white nightshirt hung just past his knees. "I do not write letters, except for blackmail, of course. I am very careful."

Colin ignored him.

"Then why isn't she here, Aunt Harriet?" Colin demanded.

She sighed. "Perhaps your wife suspected your letter was a forgery. I didn't want to say anything at the time, but do you think it was a good idea to write these letters in English? Surely these two would communicate in their native language."

"Yes, but *my* German isn't all that good," Colin explained.

"What is going on?" the major demanded.

Colin turned on him. "You double-crossing snake! We were supposed to find you with my wife in a compromising position. Instead, here you are alone. And you have the temerity to ask me what is going on? I might well ask you what is going on! In fact, I will. What is going on? My spy here saw you leave the drawing room with my wife."

"I resent being called your spy," Lady Harriet said frostily.

"We'll compare resentments later," he snapped back. "Well, Major?" he asked, tapping his foot. "Why aren't you in bed with my wife?"

The major threw up his hands. "Because your wife, she is in the bed of the English milord. She finds out he doesn't have the pox."

"Oh," said Lady Harriet. *"Oh."*

"As long as she's in bed with someone," Colin muttered. "What room is he in?"

"I don't know," said Lady Harriet said. "Carstairs took care of him."

"Don't just stand there!" said Colin, frantically. "We must find Carstairs at once."

"I beg your pardon, Lord Colin," said Carstairs from the doorway. "Does your lordship require my assistance?"

Colin stared at him in awe. "You must be clairvoyant. How did you know I was here?"

"I didn't, Lord Colin," Carstairs replied. "Lord Camford asked me to deliver this note to the major personally and discreetly. I am here to complete the errand."

"Never mind all that," Colin said impatiently. "Tell us where we can find Lord Camford. Quickly, man!"

Lady Harriet pushed him aside. "Take us to Lord Camford's room at once," she commanded the butler. "There is not an instant to lose. He is about to commit adultery with Princess Elke, and we should very much like to catch him in the act."

"Certainly, Lady Harriet," said Carstairs, at his most accommodating.


Emma put the finishing touches on the last of the Christmas presents, then stood up, rubbing the back of her neck. She was debating whether or not to wake up Harry and send him along to bed, when Lady Anne flew into the room in her nightgown and bare feet.

"Have you seen Julia?" she gasped, as she nearly collided with a tall Chinese vase.

"Have I seen Julia?" Emma repeated stupidly. "Why, what is the matter?"

Harry sat up on the sofa. "What's this?" he asked, yawning so hard that tears stood in his eyes.

"It's Julia, your grace," Lady Anne answered, sketching a rather confused curtsey. "She is not in her bed. Have you see her?"

"No, of course not," Harry said rather crossly. "I have been here with my mother. She needed me to help her wrap presents," he added.

"Perhaps Julia is with one of her sisters," Emma suggested.

"She did not summon her maid to help her undress," said Lady Anne, "and her best cloak is missing! My other girls are in bed."

Emma frowned. "Julia would not leave the house, surely. The dogs—"

Breaking off, she ran to ring the bell.

"Oh, no! The dogs!" Lady Anne began to cry hysterically. "The dogs will tear her apart!"

"I will go and speak to the groundsmen at once," said Harry, but, at that moment, Lady Susan came into the room, still wearing the black gown she had worn to dinner. With her was Mrs. Allen, sans pug, in a nightgown and lace cap. Between them, they supported a very pale Octavia.

"There is no need to speak to the groundsmen," said Lady Susan. "They have run off together. Julia and Mr. Palafox. They have eloped. Poor Octavia has found a note in Mr. Palafox's room."

"I don't believe it," Harry declared. "Julia? And Palafox? Why, it must be a joke."

Emma brought Octavia a glass of brandy. "Charles is gone," Octavia whispered, staring. "He has eloped with Julia! It's true! Oh, how could they do this to me?"

"Drink this, Miss Fitzroy," Emma said gently. "Harry is right. It must be a prank. Charles has far too much sense to run off with your sister."

Mrs. Allen snorted. "No, he don't!"

"I beg your pardon, ma'am," said Emma. "But he would not risk displeasing you. He depends on your fortune."

"Which he thinks he has already," Mrs. Allen replied. "I told him I'd made my fortune over to him, and that it was irrevocable. I showed him some very pretty papers made up for me in London. Not even slightly legal, but Charles doesn't know that. I wanted to see how he would behave if he were independent of me. Now I know," she added dryly. "He wasted no time, I must say. I only told him this very night!"

Octavia began to sob. "I cannot be jilted again! This cannot be happening to me!"

Lady Susan helped the distraught young woman to a chair.

"I shall leave all my money to an orphanage," Mrs. Allen declared.

"No!" cried Octavia, starting up from the chair. "Please, Mrs. Allen! Have pity on me! You must bring Charles back and make him marry me! I am sure he will be good from now on. I will *make* him good. I cannot be jilted a third time. I do not deserve this!"

Wildly, she appealed to Harry. "Sound the alarm, your grace! Send the servants after them. They cannot have gotten very far. They may even still be on the estate!"

"Calm yourself, Octavia," said Emma. "The damage is done."

"To Julia," she agreed. "But *Charles* can still be saved. He cannot marry Julia, after all; she is married already. But he can still marry *me,* if Mrs. Allen will only forgive him.

When he realizes he has no money, Charles will give Julia up very readily."

"Mama, this is dreadful," said Harry. "Mr. Palafox must have abducted Julia! She would never go of her own free will."

"Show him the letter!" cried Lady Susan. "'Twas Julia herself who wrote it."

Octavia produced the incriminating page, but Harry was too embarrassed to look at it. "What are we to do, Mama? Should I—? Will I go after them?"

"No!" Emma said sharply. "Where is Julia's husband?"

Lady Anne gasped. "Nicholas! Someone will have to tell him," she whispered, wringing her hands.

"I will tell him," said Emma. "Someone must go after Charles and Julia, and he is by far the most proper person."


At that moment, Nicholas was thrashing in his bed, in the throes of a nightmare. He was in a dark, hot, humid place, the West Indies, perhaps. He was being devoured by an immense, powerful python. The evil beast had pinned him to the ground, its incredible weight squeezing the air from his lungs. He could feel his bones cracking as the serpent slowly engulfed him.

Opening his eyes, he screamed, his cry lost in the damp, mounded flesh encircling his face. A large, muscular female had planted herself on top of him, and the mounds of flesh were her very large, sweaty breasts.

"Hush, *liebchen*," said a low, guttural voice. "It is I, Princess Elke von Hindenburg."

"Oh, my God!" he said, throwing her off of the bed by main strength. In the process, he discovered that he was entirely naked, the princess having relieved him of his nightshirt as he slept.

The princess landed in a heap on the floor, but sprang

up hissing. "You wish to wrestle with Princess Elke? Very well, puny Englishman. We wrestle."

"I'm dreadfully sorry, your highness," Nicholas said, stumbling out of the bed as she threw herself down onto the spot where he had been. "You startled me. Obviously, there's been some sort of dreadful mistake," he added, edging to the door.

"No mistake," she said stoutly, stomping toward him in all her naked glory. "Princess Elke has chosen you to be the father of my child."

Nicholas began to stammer. "Thank you for the compliment, madam, but I—I'm a married man, you know. My wife—"

"But English husbands do not sleep with their wives! This I know already. You will make love to Princess Elke now," she commanded.

"What about *your* husband?" cried Nicholas, grabbing a pillow to cover himself.

She snorted. *"Er ist ein Schwul,"* she said. "He does not make love to Princess Elke."

"I am sorry to hear that," said Nicholas. "But . . . I do not make love to Princess Elke, either. So sorry."

"You English!" she spat. "You are all the same."

Babbling angrily in German, she scooped up her clothes.

"I'll wait for you outside while you dress," Nicholas offered civilly.

Going out into the corridor, he came face-to-face with the duchess.

"Emma!" he exclaimed, startled.

Emma was equally startled. "You're awake," she murmured. "You're naked," she added.

"Sorry," he mumbled, adjusting his pillow. "Were you—did you want to see me?"

"No, of course not," she answered quickly.

"Oh," he said. Taking another step into the hall, he closed

the door behind him. "You look upset," he said. "Has that gigolo done something to upset you?"

"No. No," she repeated. "Nicholas, I'm afraid I have some very bad news for you."

"What is the matter?" he asked sharply.

"It's Julia," Emma began, but before she could get any further, the door to Nicholas's room opened. Princess Elke stood in the doorway wearing only her long honey-blond hair.

"You will dress Princess Elke now," she commanded Nicholas. "Princess Elke does not dress herself."

"Nicholas!" said Emma, shocked. "What is she doing in your room? Why is she naked? Why are you both naked?"

"I know how this looks," Nicholas began.

"You told Princess Elke that Camfurt has the pox," said the princess. "You lie to Princess Elke."

"I don't have the pox," said Nicholas. "I never had the pox. You told her I have the pox?"

"Don't you *dare* try to change the subject," said Emma. "You were in bed with her, weren't you?"

"What if I was?" he shot back. "What do you care? You have a lover. Where is your gigolo, by the way? I trust he got your billet-doux!"

"I don't know what you are talking about," said Emma. "Major von Schroeder was never my lover. I only said that so you would go back to Julia. Instead, I find you with— with this bitch in heat! She's desperate for an heir. Did she tell you that?"

"She mentioned it, yes."

Princess Elke exploded. "Princess Elke thinks you are a bitch in heat, too!" she snapped, slapping Emma across the face. Focused on Nicholas, Emma hardly noticed.

"I don't believe this," said Emma, blinking back tears. "After all those things you said to me! You've broken my heart, Nicholas."

She slapped him hard across the face.

"I did?" Nicholas said faintly. "Emma, what are you saying? Are you saying you love me?"

"I am not saying *anything*. I am not *speaking* to you."

Princess Elke slapped Nicholas across the face. "Princess Elke is not speaking to you either!" She retreated back into the bedroom and slammed the door.

Carstairs appeared at the end of the hall. Colin pushed past him, followed closely by Lady Harriet. "Emma? What's going on?"

"Julia has eloped with Mr. Palafox," Emma answered dully. "I was just coming to tell Lord Camford the terrible news, and *I found him in bed with Princess Elke!*"

Colin heaved a huge sigh of relief. "Thank the gods! I am betrayed! With witnesses!"

"But nothing happened!" Nicholas protested. "Emma, please believe me. I never touched her."

"Don't say that," Colin pleaded.

"I know what I saw, Nicholas," Emma said wearily. "Are you going after Julia, or not?"

"Why should I?" said Nicholas. "Palafox is welcome to her. She can have an annulment any time she likes. Emma—"

"But Charles isn't going to marry her," Emma said impatiently. "Mrs. Allen only pretended to settle her fortune on him. When he finds out he's as poor as he ever was, what do you think he will do?"

"I will make him take responsibility," said Nicholas. "He will have to marry Julia."

"You'd better get dressed," Emma said tartly. "No one takes a naked man seriously, you know."

"Yes," said Nicholas. "I should get dressed. But I will speak to you another time, Emma. This conversation is not over."

"Yes, it is," she said, retreating back down the hall. "Good-bye, Nicholas."

# Chapter Twenty-Three

*December 1816*

The following year, Colin was three days late in arriving at Warwick Palace.

Shivering in the cold, Emma went out to scold him as he alighted from his carriage. In his coat of glossy brown otter fur, Colin looked as elegant as ever.

"You're late," his twin sister rebuked him. "I was worried you'd met with some accident. You could have sent word, you know."

"Nag, nag, nag," he growled at her, shaking out his stiff legs. "*You* never send word when *you* are late. Anyway, I have the most excellent excuse. I have been up all night with a colicky baby. I'm dead on my feet."

"Baby!" Emma exclaimed, startled.

As she spoke, a nursemaid stepped out of her brother's carriage. She carried a small bundle of fur in her arms. "Is that—is that a puppy or something?" Emma asked curiously. Colin was just absurd enough to hire a nursery maid for a puppy, she thought. Since being named Royal Consort of Hindenburg, he had become increasingly eccentric and self-important.

"A puppy!" Colin said indignantly. He snapped his fingers and the maid gave him the bundle. Marching up the steps, he dumped the bundle into Emma's arms. "Call that a puppy, do you?"

Emma stared down at the tiny pink face of a baby in a brown rabbit fur bunting, complete with long, velvety soft ears. The infant could not have been more than a few months old. "I stand corrected," she murmured. "It's a rabbit, not a puppy. Colin, where did this baby come from?"

"Must I tell you indeed?" said Colin. "I should have thought you of all people would know where babies come from. May we go inside, please? This cold wind is not good for little Mimi. And it ain't good for little Colin, either."

The child in Emma's arms began to cry. Hastily, Emma followed her brother into the house. She stood shushing the baby while a servant helped Colin out of his coat of glossy brown otter fur. "Mimi," Emma repeated, looking at the babe curiously. "Is that her name?"

"Better give her back to me," Colin said, reaching for the baby. "I seem to be the only one who can comfort her."

Emma turned away from his grasping hands. "No, she's settling down beautifully," she protested. "I *have* had some experience with babies, you know."

"Not like this one," Colin retorted. "Mimi is quite unique. She listens to no one but me. She won't even nurse if her Papa isn't in the room. We have a special connection."

Turning, he caught sight of himself in the gilt-framed hall mirror. There were dark circles under his steel-blue eyes. The sight of these imperfections caused him to grimace in pain.

"Papa?" Emma repeated incredulously. *"You?"*

Colin scarcely heard her. "Look at me," he said brokenly. "I haven't slept in weeks, Emma. I stand before you in ruins and shambles. There are bags under my formerly sparkling eyes. My formerly rosy cheeks are sunken. Before the baby came, I was beautiful. Now I've gone all hollow. If this keeps up, I shall have to resort to rouge."

"Colin! The baby?" Emma snapped.

"Oh, that's right. You've not yet met your niece. You were too busy to come to Hindenburg for the christening," he added coldly. "Your Highness, may I present my sister, the Duchess of Warwick. Emma, this is her royal highness, the Princess Wilhelmina."

"This is Elke's child?" Emma asked in surprise.

"Yes, but we don't hold that against her, poor little thing," Colin replied. "She comes from good stock, on her father's side, after all. Now, where did I put her little silver rattle?" he went on, absently patting his pockets. "It sometimes amuses her."

Looking down at the infant's face, Emma caught her breath as she realized that she was holding Nicholas's daughter, the product of his liaison with Princess Elke last Christmas Eve. She had already noticed that the baby had sparkling blue eyes and rosy cheeks. A few pale gold wisps of hair had slipped out from under the hooded bunting. She was perfect and beautiful, like her father.

"I had my reasons for staying away," she said. "You call her Mimi, do you?"

Colin grimaced. "She was christened Wilhelmina Griselda Margarethe Ottilie, after her maternal grandfather—which, if you ask me, is a damned peculiar name for a grandfather, maternal or otherwise, and an even worse name for a princess. Of course, no one *did* ask me. I wanted to call her something cheerful like Robina or Iphigenia, but no one in Hindenberg ever listens to *me*." Colin shrugged his shoulders helplessly. "To the Hindenburglars, I am a person of no importance whatsoever, merely the royal consort. They christened her out from under me, so to speak. But when we're alone, I call her Mimi, and, thus far, she has not objected. She looks like a Mimi, too, don't you think?"

"Yes. It must be the bunny ears."

"Aren't they adorable?" he said, his enthusiasm sparked. "A very clever young man in Drury Lane makes all her costumes for me. She has a little bear suit, an owl, a froggie, of course, and a badger, and, oh, all sorts of things. *This* is but one of several bunnies we own. I thought Brown Bunny looked the best with my otter coat."

"Ah! Here you are!" Otto, Duke of Chilton came jogging down the stairs toward them. "Another day, and you would have missed me, Colin," he added, embracing his younger brother.

"Yes, I thought you'd be at Chilton by now," Colin replied.

"We meant to stop here but three days, but Cecily was feeling a little poorly, so we stayed longer than expected," Otto explained. "Is that your baby?"

"Yes, this is Mimi," Colin said proudly. "Hasn't she grown?"

Otto glanced at the child in Emma's arms. "Possibly. You should see my boy. He's just starting to walk." Beckoning to the nursemaid, he added, "Go and fetch Lord Scarlingford from the nursery."

"Baby Otto couldn't possibly compare with my beautiful little Mimi angel."

"Not without a significant handicap," Otto retorted. "My son is a gentleman, after all."

"Gentlemen!" Emma rebuked them, laughing. "Boys! Children! It's not a competition!"

Quickly, she led the way to the drawing room. As she had hoped, Colin was instantly distracted by the changes in the decor. "Emma!" he exclaimed in dismay. "What have you done? This used to be a very pretty yellow room. Now it's all sad and dark. Who advised you on your colors?" he went on, glaring at the green-on-green damask panels that lined the walls. "Persephone? Hecate? Aunt Harriet?"

The green velvet curtains blocking most of the windows were so dark they looked almost black. The furniture was big and dark and overstuffed. The paintings were all of hunting scenes, dogs, and horses. Even the rugs were hunter green. The beautifully carved white mantelpieces had been replaced with black marble.

Emma shrugged helplessly. "Harry insisted," she explained. "He wanted something more masculine, I suppose. I was doing so much work at Wingate this year, I could hardly refuse him. It *is* rather dreary, isn't it?"

"It's the smoking room at Brooks's," Otto complained.

"I was going to say waiting room at the undertaker's," Colin said, shuddering. "This isn't masculine; it's mausoleum. I'll give you some names, Emma."

Emma sighed. "Harry likes it. His friends like it, too. All seven of them," she added resentfully as she rocked the baby in her arms. "The spotty little beasts. We're overrun with Harrovians this year, I'm sorry to say."

"Eight fifteen-year-old boys?" Colin was appalled. "Under one roof? Why, it must be pandemonium." Quite overcome, he strode to the liquor cabinet and poured himself a large brandy. "It reminds me of the nightmare of my school days."

"*And* four thirteen-year-olds," Emma told him. "Grey has invited three friends to his first stag hunt. But, at least, *they* are staying with the harbourer at his hut. I don't have to put up with *them* staring at me with their mouths open while I try to eat my dinner."

"Well, that's Harrow for you," Otto sniffed. "No manners. You should have sent them to Eton," he told his sister. "Young Etonians are taught not to stare freely at a woman's breasts. At least not at dinner."

"It's been a challenge keeping them out of the wine cellar, too," said Emma. "Mind you, ever since they knocked down poor Aunt Harriet and broke her arm, they have been *slightly* more civilized. So that's good anyway."

"Aunt Harriet!" Colin exclaimed. "Broken? I wondered why she did not come down to see me. I will go to her."

"She'll be down in a moment," Emma assured him, settling onto the sofa with the baby in her arms. "Her legs are not broken. She was working in the garden when you arrived. She wanted to wash up. Sit down," she urged him. "I haven't seen you in almost a year. Not since Princess Elke bribed you not to divorce her. How do you like being a royal consort?"

"I am bearing it as best I can," he replied, with a martyr's sigh.

"Oh, I can see that. I must say, I'm amazed her highness let you bring her daughter to England for Christmas."

Colin gaped at her. "Lord, don't you read the newspapers? The political situation in Hindenburg is hardly stable. The economy's in a shambles. The peasants are constantly on the verge of revolting. The Treasury is all but empty, and there are some very impertinent people who seem to resent the enormous allowance they are paying me. Austria's moving to annex the whole sorry place. It has been decided that Princess Mimi will be better off with her papa in England. You'd know all this already if you took an interest," he added.

"I'm glad you mean to stay in England," Emma said quickly. "And Mimi is adorable. I'm sorry I did not meet her sooner. I'm afraid I've reached that age when I cannot hold a baby without wanting one of my own," she added.

"Yes," Colin said smugly. "Mimi does has that effect on people."

"It'll pass," said Lady Harriet as two sturdy youths carried the chair in which she was seated into the room. Harry, Duke of Warwick, trotted behind the trio carrying a velvet cushion. "Easy now, boys!" she rasped, as her assistants cautiously lowered her chair to the floor. "You mustn't jostle me! I'm an old woman!"

Harry gently positioned the cushion beneath his great-aunt's right arm, which was in a sling. Lady Harriet groaned piteously.

"Sorry, Lady Harriet!" the boys chorused, wincing in sympathy.

"So I would think," she barked at them. "You may go. I'll call you if you are needed again."

The two boys ran from the room.

"Ambrose and Carter really are sorry, Aunt Harriet," Harry told her.

"They should be sorry," she retorted. "Running through the house like a pack of wild Indians! I feel lucky to be alive. You might say hello to your uncle, young man," she added, glaring at him. "Duke of Warwick or not, you should show a little respect for your elders."

"I'm not that much older," Colin said indignantly.

"Hello, Uncle Colin," Harry said obediently. "How are you, sir?"

"Not bad," Colin answered, "for an elder, I suppose."

Emma brought the baby for Harry to see. "And this is Princess Wilhelmina. Isn't she pretty? Would you like to hold her?"

Harry backed away. "Must I?"

"No," Colin said firmly. "And you needn't hang about here with your *elders* either. Go and be with your friends."

Harry did not have to be told twice. He darted from the room as if his feet were on fire.

"Would you like to hold the baby?" Emma asked Lady Harriet.

"Certainly not," said Lady Harriet. "Can't you see I have a badly sprained arm?"

"I thought you said it was broken," said Emma.

"It isn't. But *they* don't have to know that," Lady Harriet answered.

Emma bit back a laugh. "Aunt Harriet! That is horrible."

"A bad sprain is quite painful, you know," Lady Harriet said defensively. "It just doesn't inspire as much guilt as a *broken* arm. And guilt is so very useful, you know."

Lady Aleta Grey came into the room, leading her little brother, Lord Scarlingford, by the hand. Not quite twelve months old, Lord Scarlingford was already walking, and his father was justifiably proud of his tottering, wobbly steps. "Let him go, Aleta," he commanded the girl. "He can walk on his own."

After a brief struggle, Aleta managed to free her hand from the grip of Lord Scarlingford's little fingers. "See how he grips her hand?" Otto said proudly. "He has the grip of a blacksmith. Look at that."

"He must get it from Cecily," said Colin. "That's nothing. You should see Mimi with her rattle. Now *there's* a grip!"

"Speaking of blacksmiths," said Lady Harriet, turning to Colin as Lord Scarlingford staggered about the room at his father's insistence. "Whatever happened to that big, ugly Scotsman of yours? I suppose he crawled off and died of a broken heart?"

Colin gave a weary groan. "Oh, I do hope it's not going to be one of *those* Christmases," he said, "where we all sit around asking whatever happened to so-and-so? Such a bore! I may as well ask you where Aunt Susan is this year. Or ask Emma where Lord Camford is hiding these days."

"Susan is visiting her eldest daughter this year," Lady Harriet replied, shrugging. "Emma?"

"What?" Emma said sharply.

"Your brother is asking about Lord Camford. She has not seen him since last year," Lady Harriet answered, when it became clear that Emma would not.

Colin stared at her. "I confess I am amazed! I thought for certain he would come flying back into your arms the moment he received his divorce decree."

"Annulment," Emma said coldly. "It was an annulment, not a divorce."

"Whatever. I should have thought he'd seek you out the moment he was rid of poor Julia."

"I don't know why you call her 'poor Julia,'" Emma said crossly. "The scandal was of her own making, and she came out of it better than she deserves. Harry has given her the use of his Lincolnshire estate. She lives there with her parents and her two unmarried sisters, rent free."

"Julia in Lincolnshire?" Colin shook his head. "I repeat: poor Julia! Only two unmarried sisters? So Octavia got Palafox, after all?"

"Oh, yes," Emma said. "She persuaded Mrs. Allen to forgive him. He married Octavia, and the three of them live quite comfortably in Bath. Four of them, including the pug."

"You would not give them Wingate?" Colin laughed.

"They knew better than to ask me."

"Did you see that?" Otto cried, spinning around. "Isn't he brilliant? He walked right to me. It must have been a dozen steps."

"Bravo!" Emma said, even though she had missed the whole thing.

Colin could not pretend to be impressed. "Mimi can smile and blow bubbles at the same time," he said, "with nothing but her own saliva."

Otto frowned at them. "Come, Aleta," he said, hoisting Lord Scarlingford onto his shoulder. "Let us go and show Mama what Baby can do."

"I think I will invite Augusta to come and live with me," said Lady Harriet, when the Duke of Chilton had left the room. "I don't think Harry would deny me anything while my arm is broken. I'll invite your Scotsman too, if you like," she offered civilly. "Not to live, of course. Just to Christmas."

"You go too far, old woman," said Colin. "I believe I'll go to my room now," he told his sister, climbing to his feet. "I think I need a nap."

"What about Mimi?" Emma asked.

Colin yawned. "What about her? She looks very content in the arms of her aunt."

Mimi was still in Emma's arms when Colin joined them in Emma's sitting room before dinner. "Have you been holding her all this time?" he asked her. "You really *do* want one of your own."

Emma laid a finger across her lips to shush him. "She's sleeping so peacefully, I didn't want to wake her," she whispered. "I have been thinking, Colin," she went on softly, when she was sure the baby's rest had not been disturbed. "Don't you think that little Mimi should see her father. He probably wants to see her."

"All right," he said, stretching out his arms for the child. "I'll take her off your hands. You must go and dress for dinner. That's a lovely spot of drool on your bosom, by the way."

Emma relinquished the baby and climbed stiffly to her feet. "I'll just come out and say it, shall I?" she breathed. "Colin, I think you should write to Lord Camford and ask him to spend Christmas with us. I think it's the right thing to do, don't you?"

Colin frowned slightly. "Why don't you write to him yourself?"

Emma shook her head vehemently. "I couldn't! It would be better coming from you, don't you think? Nicholas and I didn't exactly part on the best of terms. But you've never had a quarrel with him, have you?"

"No. We've always gotten on very well," Colin agreed. "I suppose I *could* write to him, if you want me to. But if you can't even write the man a letter, won't it be difficult for you to see him again?"

Emma laughed faintly. "Why? Because he didn't seek me out after his annulment? He had no reason to. He's at Camford House in London," she added. "You should write to him soon."

"I'll write to him now," Colin answered, carrying Mimi over to Emma's writing desk, "if you will but lend me pen and paper."

"I'll hold her for you," Emma offered as he seated himself at the desk, but he waved her away.

"As you can see, I'm perfectly capable of holding my daughter with my left arm while I write with my right hand," he told her. "Go and get dressed. If I run into trouble, I'll summon the nursemaid."

When Emma returned twenty minutes later, the letter was written, the envelope sealed, and Mimi had been removed to the nursery. Colin brought the letter down with him and gave it to a servant. "Do you know," he said, as he led his sister into the lounge, "I can't help but feel a tiny bit responsible for that young man's unhappiness. If I hadn't been so determined to win my bet with Aunt Harriet, he might be safely married to Octavia."

Emma snorted. "It doesn't get any safer than that, does it? We need only ask Charles Palafox."

"Well, perhaps Nicholas will have a happy ending, after all, in spite of everything."

"Yes," said Emma. "He's young. I'm sure he will rally again."

"I'm sure you're right," said Colin.


A light, feathery snow was falling on the morning that Nicholas arrived at Warwick.

Emma was sitting in the window of her sitting room with Aleta playing Fox and Geese. Colin and Cecily were playing piquet, and Otto was sitting next to the fire reading his newspaper.

"There's a carriage coming up the road," Aleta said suddenly, drawing the attention of the rest of the room. "Who do you suppose it is, Aunt Emma?"

"I don't know," said Emma, squinting at the vehicle as it came to rest outside.

"It might be Camford," said Colin, coming over to the window for a look. "I can't make out the crest on the door."

Emma found her spectacles and put them on. "It can't be,"

she breathed. "It's too soon. You only sent your letter two days ago, Colin."

"By special messenger," said Colin. "I think it is he."

"He's a tall gentleman," Aleta reported. "He wears a blue coat. There is a lady with him, and a baby."

That was enough to bring Cecily to the window. "Why, it *is* Lord Camford," she said. "He always did favor a blue coat, I recall."

"Never mind his coat," Colin said impatiently. "Who is the lady?"

Lady Harriet came into the room to inform them that Lord Camford had just arrived. "That is no lady; it's a woman. He has a woman with him—and a baby," she added, brushing past Emma.

"You're right," said Colin. "It is a woman."

"Definitely a nursemaid," said Lady Harriet. "Foreign, by the looks of her. The child has red hair. Could it be Julia's?"

"Nonsense. What would Nicholas be doing with Mr. Palafox's baby?" Colin argued. "Besides, it's walking. Julia's baby couldn't possibly be walking yet."

"Uncle Colin!" Aleta complained. "I'm not supposed to know anything about Julia's baby, remember? It's a terrible secret."

"And you still don't know anything about Julia's baby," he answered. "*That* is not Julia's baby."

"Aleta, go to the nursery at once," Otto commanded.

An argument ensued. Otto prevailed, of course, but by the time eleven-year-old Aleta reached the door, the butler had already opened it to announce Lord Camford. "Go on," Otto commanded, and Aleta obediently left the room.

Emma hastily removed her spectacles and went forward to meet Nicholas. He had removed his hat and gloves, but he was still wearing his greatcoat. The snow on his coat had melted, leaving dark speckles on the blue wool.

"Good morning, Lord Camford," Emma said clearly, offering him her hand. "I believe you know everyone here."

Nicholas bowed over her hand, "How nice to see you again, your grace, your grace, and . . . your grace," he said, addressing Emma, Cecily, and Otto, in turn.

"Oh, never mind all that," Lady Harriet said impatiently. "Just tell us about the baby! We're all dying to know."

"Yes, of course," said Nicholas. "I saw you looking at us from the window. I completely understand your curiosity."

"Then do us all a favor and cure it!" Lady Harriet snapped. "Is it your child?"

"Mine?" Nicholas was astonished. "Well, of course the child isn't mine! What would I be doing with a child? Who would his mother be?"

"That's entirely up to you, I should think," said Lady Harriet.

"Tell us!" Emma said. "Who is the child?"

"It's Michael Fitzroy," Nicholas answered.

Emma stared at him. "Michael!"

"The younger, of course," Nicholas said quickly. "His mother came to see me in London. She has married again, you know."

"Yes," said Emma. "I knew that."

"Her husband, the Conde da Fonseca, is a very . . . interesting . . . gentleman," Nicholas went on, looking rather grim. "He refuses to accept the child, in no small part because he has red hair—the child, I mean, not the Conde. The Conde has black hair, like most Portuguese. He has taken his wife back to Portugal, but he will not allow her to keep the boy, I'm afraid. The poor lady came to me in tears. She pleaded with me to bring the child to his father's family. I have done so."

Otto was the first to speak. "If, by *interesting* you mean the man is a thorough blackguard, then yes! I think the

Conde very interesting indeed! She simply left the child with you?"

"It was her husband's idea to leave the boy with an attorney," said Nicholas, "but he indulged the Condesa in her wish to leave him with me. I suppose there was no one else to ask, really. The rest of her acquaintance had already left London to go home for Christmas."

"That was very good of the Conde, I'm sure," Lady Harriet said acidly. "To indulge the poor woman!"

"How she must be suffering," Emma murmured. "To be separated from her child."

"Yes," Nicholas agreed. "It was very sad to watch. However, given the way his stepfather feels about him, it is probably for the best that the child be with his father's family."

"We will take him, of course," Emma said quickly. "Let him be brought in," she ordered Carstairs, who had not left the room. "And send someone to find the duke and bring him here. Tell his grace it is urgent family business. And Lord Grey should be here, too. This concerns him as well."

"There are some legal papers that were handed to me," Nicholas said, when Carstairs had gone. "They are sealed, as you can see," he went on, taking a leather pouch from the inside pocket of his greatcoat. The pouch was stitched closed. He handed it to the Duke of Chilton. "The child has one trunk, containing a few items of clothing, and a small box filled with letters and keepsakes from his mother. And this."

He brought a flat velvet box out of his pocket. "The nurse gave it to me in the carriage," he said, handing it to Emma.

Even before she opened it, Emma knew what the box would contain. "These are the emeralds I gave her," she said sadly, "as a wedding present."

"I doubt the Conde approved the return," Otto said. "Was there anything else, Camford?"

Nicholas shook his head.

"Surely, the man gave you some money," Colin said

indignantly. "Enough to cover the expense of bringing the boy here!"

"I would not have accepted the offer of money," Nicholas told him, "had such an offer been made. However, it was not."

"This is unforgivable!" cried Emma. "The man should be whipped at the cart's tail!"

"You will be reimbursed, my lord," Otto told Nicholas. "I will see to it myself."

"That will not be necessary," Nicholas said quietly but firmly.

Otto knew better than to insist. "I believe we can safely assume that the child has been left on our hands without a penny to scratch himself with. Those emeralds are all he has."

"But Michael did not die a poor man," Emma objected. "His widow was very well provided for."

Otto shook his head. "When Lord Michael died, his fortune became his widow's property. When she remarried, unfortunately, that fortune became her husband's. I shall be very surprised if the Conde bothered to make any provision for his stepson. And now," he added, "Lord Camford must feel he is intruding upon a very private conversation. Perhaps someone would be good enough to show him to his room."

"Thank you, your grace," Nicholas replied. "However, I think I should stay with you a little longer. As far as I can tell, neither the nurse or the child can speak a word of English. Two years of disuse have not improved my Portuguese, but I may be helpful. I can make the introductions, anyway."

"That is very good of you," said Emma. "Thank you."

Carstairs returned to the room alone. "I have sent runners to fetch his grace and Lord Grey," he told Emma. "However, in the case of the child, he was in such a state of anxiety, I thought it prudent to let his nurse take him to the nursery."

"Oh, of course," said Emma. "Thank you, Carstairs. I should have anticipated as much. The other children will be of more use in comforting him than any of us could possibly be. I'm sure it would be overwhelming for him to meet us all at once, but, perhaps, Lord Camford, you might introduce him to me? I am his aunt, after all. I suppose I shall be the one to raise him."

"I should be happy to make the introduction," he said instantly.

"How does one say 'welcome' in Portuguese?" she asked, leading him from the room.

# Chapter Twenty-Four

*"Bem-vindo,"* he answered. "And then you might say, *Eu sou sua Tia Emma.* I am your Aunt Emma."

The rudimentary Portuguese lesson soon wore itself out, and they walked in silence. As they came to the door of the nursery, Emma said to him, "You, of course, have a special reason for wanting to see the nursery." She tried to sound cheerful.

Nicholas looked at her blankly. "I do?"

"Yes, of course. Mimi is here, you know. Did you not get my brother's letter?" she asked, as he continued to look confused. "Colin's letter?"

Nicholas shook his head. "I have not had the pleasure of receiving any communication from your brother. I did, however, receive *your* letter."

Emma stared at him. *"My* letter!" she exclaimed.

"As I was leaving London, my manservant put the afternoon post into my hand. I went through it on my way here. Your letter—I believe I have it committed to memory, I have read it over so many times these last two days. 'My dearest Nicholas,'" he recited, closing his eyes, "'it has been almost a year since I last had the pleasure of seeing you, and almost two years since I have had the pleasure of holding you in my arms.'"

He opened his eyes and looked down at her warmly.

"*I* didn't write that," she said, horrified.

Nicholas frowned. "It was your paper," he argued. "It was your handwriting. It was your signature. I suppose this really isn't the time to discuss it," he added, changing his tone. "You must have other things on your mind at present. I understand that. But do not deny that you wrote to me. Do not deny that you still love me."

"As you say, this is not the time to discuss it!" said Emma. "I must see to the child."

"When?" he insisted, catching her hand as she began opening the door to the nursery. "May I come to your room after tea? Before dinner? After dinner? Emma, we must talk about this letter of yours. I will not let you me push me away again."

"After tea," she heard herself whisper. "You remember the way, I presume?"

"Yes, very well."

They went into the nursery. Little Michael Fitzroy was sound asleep in bed with his watchful nurse sitting beside him. Emma spoke briefly to the nurse, with Nicholas translating as best he could. Then Emma brought Nicholas to see the other children. Lord Scarlingford was playing with blocks on the rug, and Princess Mimi was nursing.

Nicholas immediately got down on the rug to play with the boy and Emma brought Mimi to him. "Would you like to hold her?" she asked. "You could sit in the window seat; it's nice and warm."

"All right," he said agreeably. "I'm not very good with babies. My cousin, Lady Catherine, had a little girl earlier this year. All I do is make her cry. The baby, I mean. Not my cousin. I've not yet made *her* cry."

When he was settled in the window seat with the child

in his arms, he looked down at her. "So small! How old is she?"

Emma sat down beside him, touching the baby's hand. "About three months."

"She would have been conceived at Christmas, then."

"Yes, of course. Isn't she sweet? Colin just adores her. He's had all these funny little costumes made for her."

"She looks like her mother," Nicholas said warmly.

"Oh, no, she looks like her father," Emma argued, smiling. "Definitely."

Nicholas frowned. "She doesn't look anything like von Schroeder," he objected.

"Schroeder!" Emma repeated. "But he is not her father, Nicholas. You are!"

Nicholas shook his head. "As much as I would like to think so, I know that isn't possible, Emma. You and I have not been together in two years."

"What has that to say to anything?" Emma wanted to know. "*I* am not the child's mother. You think that *I* am her mother?" she exclaimed.

His eyes widened. "Aren't you? If you're not her mother, then why am I holding her?"

"Nicholas, this is Elke's child! *Your* child."

"No," he said, giving the baby back to her. "Absolutely not. That is quite impossible, I can assure you. If this is Princess Elke's baby, von Schroeder must be the father. *I* never touched the woman."

"You forget that it was I who discovered you together," said Emma, keeping her voice low and pleasant as Mimi began to fuss.

"She imposed on me," said Nicholas, "but I declined to impose on her. That is not my child, Emma. It must be the major's. I warned you he was a gigolo."

"No, she can't be the major's," Emma said. "The major

has a very serious war wound that prevents him from—from fathering a child."

"Oh," Nicholas said, looking rather smug. "Not much of a gigolo, then, was he?"

"He could do other things that were highly satisfying," Emma said.

Nicholas snorted. "Like what?"

Emma sighed. "The point is, Nicholas, *he* could not be Mimi's father. It has to be you."

"Well, it isn't," he said stubbornly.

"But there's no one else."

"Obviously, there is. I am not a liar, you know!"

As he raised his voice, Princess Mimi began to cry. From his seat on the rug, Lord Scarlingford stared at them, wide-eyed.

"I did not mean to accuse you of anything," Emma began, rocking the baby.

"Forgive me," Nicholas said brusquely. "I am worn out from the journey. It is making me short-tempered. If your grace will excuse me, I will go to my room now."

Emma could hardly refuse. After he had gone, she remained in the nursery until she was summoned downstairs. Harry and Grey had returned to the house.

"How do we know Lord Camford did not receive any money?" Harry was shouting at the top of his voice as his mother reentered the drawing room. "He might have pocketed it, for all we know."

"Harry!" Emma said, appalled. "How can you make such an accusation? We are indebted to Lord Camford. Another man might have refused to bring the child to us. The poor babe would have been left with lawyers."

"Poor babe is exactly right," Harry yelled. "According to these documents, the child has been left on my hands—*my* hands, Mama!—without so much as a penny. If it weren't for those emeralds, he would have nothing."

"The emeralds were a wedding gift to his mother. I'm sure, when he grows up, he will want to give them to his bride."

"Then we cannot even sell them to raise money," Harry complained.

"No, of course not," said Emma.

"In that case, his upkeep, his education . . . I shall have to pay for everything, I suppose! It must all come out of *my* pocket."

"You do not resent the child, surely," Emma protested.

"Of course not, Mama," he said angrily. "I know I must sound petty and ungenerous! It is the principle of the matter, Mama. How dare this man take my uncle's fortune, but leave my uncle's child behind, penniless? And my uncle Chilton tells me there is little we can do about it. The Conde, as he calls himself, has skipped off to Portugal, beyond the reach of English justice. It could take years to bring a case against him, in any event. By then my uncle's money will all be gone anyway. I daresay he's spending it as fast as he can! And, of course, if I pursue the matter, people will call me a nipcheese, a miser, a mean penny-pincher."

"Worse than that," said Emma. "If the child learns of it, he may think that *no one* wants him. Your cousin must never be allowed to feel that way."

"I know my responsibility, Mama," Harry said. "I bear no ill will toward my cousin. It's just so bloody unfair that *I* should be the one who has to pay! I'm always the one who has to pay. I have to pay for Aunt Harriet's allowance."

"I beg your pardon," Lady Harriet squawked indignantly.

"I have to pay Uncle Hugh an allowance, too!" Harry went on. "After all he's done to me, I still have to pay him a thousand pounds per annum. This mess with Cousin Julia has cost me, too. I could have tenants in my Lincolnshire house, you know. Tenants who pay rent! Instead, I have to house my unfortunate relations and their illegitimate babies!

Now *this!* I shall have to be generous to the boy, of course, generous to a fault, or people will say I am selfish, no doubt. And, of course, I want to be generous."

"Of course you do, darling," Emma said soothingly.

"But there are things that *I* would like to do, you know! For example, I would like to build a hunting box. The harbourer's hut is far too small for all of us. But how can I? When disaster may strike at any time? When I may be called up to lay out huge sums of money at a moment's notice? Wouldn't it be selfish of me to build a hunting box?"

"Oh, Harry," said Emma, reaching out to him. "You know that I will help you with Michael. Money has never been a problem for us."

"This is a Fitzroy matter, Mama," he told her, exasperated. "You are a Grey. I cannot take Grey money for a Fitzroy matter. My father would never have done so."

"That is true," Emma admitted. "Once my dowry was in his possession, your father never touched my accounts."

"So you see? I am stuck with it all."

Grey spoke up from the other side of the room. "I'm glad *I'm* not the duke. I've got plenty of money, and I don't have to spend it on anyone but me."

"I have a broken arm, you know," said Lady Harriet, glaring around the room. "I think it very bad of you, Harry, to start talking of stopping my allowance when my arm is broken."

"I never said I would stop it!" cried Harry. "I'm just saying, it is not fair!"

He ran from the room, knocking over the tall Chinese vase beside the door as he went. It crashed to the floor, breaking into pieces.

"That was probably worth more than ten years' allowance," Lady Harriet grumbled.

"You should go after him," Colin told Emma, giving her a sharp nudge in the ribs.

"I will," she said crossly. "Presently. He'll be too upset to talk now. Anyway, I have a crow to pluck with *you*."

She dragged him out of the room, saying, "What do you mean by writing Nicholas that—that beastly love letter? You signed my name to it, didn't you?"

"You're hurting me," he complained, rubbing his wrist after she released his arm. "You asked me to write to him. I was only doing your bidding. You were too cowardly to write to him yourself."

"But you signed my name to it!"

"I thought he should know the invitation came from you," Colin replied.

"You told him I loved him."

"I only told him the truth," said her twin. "Didn't I? It's why you wanted him here in the first place, isn't it?"

"No. I thought—I thought he was Mimi's father. I thought he should know her. But he says he is not her father."

"Of course he's not her father," Colin said indignantly. "*I* am her father."

"I mean her real father," said Emma.

"I *am* her real father! She is my daughter. Ergo, I am her father."

"You?" Emma said. "You and Elke?"

"Why do you say it like that?" Colin said, frowning. "As if you doubted me?"

"She would have been conceived at Christmas," said Emma.

"I know perfectly well when she was conceived! I was there. I felt sorry for Elke," he explained. "You'd just ruined her chances with Camford, and that gigolo Schroeder couldn't cut the mustard. The poor amazon was in tears. She said she couldn't go back to Hindenburg without an heir. The Hindenburglars wouldn't stand for it. As her husband, I felt slightly responsible."

"*You* felt responsible?"

"Oh, all right," he said impatiently. "It was Aunt Harriet's idea. She thought it would be a real shame if someone as wonderful as me were to live out his days without taking the trouble to reproduce. I felt the sense of her argument. I am fairly wonderful, after all. So I did it. It was not very pleasant, but now I have Mimi, so I do not complain. She is perfect."

"She is really my niece, then?" Emma groaned in dismay. "And I didn't go to her christening!"

"You're the worst aunt ever," he told her.

"Oh, Colin, I am sorry." She touched his arm. "You forgive me, don't you?"

"No."

Emma sighed. "Well, I can't help that. I have to go to Harry now," she added impatiently. "He needs his mother."

"What a good thing you're not his aunt!" Colin called after her.

"Go away, Mama!" Harry shouted through the door of his bedchamber. "I don't want to talk about it anymore."

"I will go away," Emma answered, "if you will stop breaking things."

"All right," he agreed.

Silence ensued.

"You haven't hurt yourself, have you?" Emma called through the door. "I heard glass breaking. Are you sure you haven't cut yourself?"

Harry came to the door and opened it a crack. "I am fine, Mother," he said. "As you can see. Just let me alone for a while. I'll be all right."

Emma could not resist touching his cheek. "Of course, darling," she said softly. "But I'm right down the hall, whenever you're ready to talk. I'm always here for you, Harry. You know that."

"I know that, Mama." He nodded glumly and closed the door.

Emma went back to her own room suffering from a bad headache.

"I could not wait until after tea," said Nicholas, striding toward her as she was closing the door. "Emma, what can I do to convince you that I am not Mimi's father? As you can see, I have nothing to hide. I have no secrets. I am yours."

Emma caught her breath. Except for a strategically placed bunch of hothouse flowers, Nicholas was completely naked.

"Are those nasturtiums?" she asked curiously. "You took them from my vase, didn't you? You're dripping on my carpets!"

"I'm sorry," he said. "I was trying to make a point. Emma, I did not have sexual relations with that woman."

"I believe you," she said.

"You do?" he said eagerly.

"You have an honest face," she explained. "Now let's put my flowers back where they belong," she went on. Moving toward him, she pried the wet stems from his fingers and tossed the flowers away. "Everything in its place, would you not agree, my lord?"

Nicholas shuddered as she took hold of him firmly. "It seems I am in no position to dispute you, ma'am," he said, red faced.

"Then let us find a better position," she gently suggested.

They did not quite make it to the bed. As he had two years before, Nicholas entered her without preliminaries, and took his pleasure almost immediately. While he was recovering, Emma began to undress. Her progress was interrupted by another attack, this one of much longer duration. It was some thirty minutes before she was able to join him in complete nakedness. By that time, she was too exhausted to do anything but collapse into his arms.

Nicholas was ready for more, but he cheerfully accepted

her silent refusal to permit him a third time. "You are a brute," she complained, snuggling closer to him. "An animal."

"No," he said. "It was lovely. Wasn't it? Better than the last time."

Emma propped herself up on her elbows to look at him. "I'm sorry, my dear. If anything, it was worse. It was dreadful. *You* are dreadful."

"If I am so dreadful, then why are you smiling?" he countered.

Emma laughed softly. "I am smiling *because* you are dreadful," she explained. "It's obvious you have not been with anyone else. You have never been with anyone but me, have you? Not Lady Bellingham. Not Lady Caroline Arbuthnot. *They* would not put up with your bad habits. They would have taught you better."

"Are you going to teach me better?"

"Perhaps," she said. "Eventually. I think I will. But for now, I think I'll keep you in a state of helpless innocence."

"I don't feel innocent," he said.

"But you do feel helpless," she laughed.

"Only because I love you from the depths of my being to the heights of my soul," he answered, tugging at a loose curl of her hair until she took the hint and brought her mouth down to his.

"Very poetic," she murmured.

"Don't you recognize your own words?" he said, laughing.

"Did I write that in my letter?" she said.

"You're not going to deny it," he said.

"No," she assured him. "I won't deny it. I meant every word."

Reaching down between their two bodies, she gave him a hard pinch on the thigh. "That," she said as he yelped in surprise, "is for making me write it at all! You should have come to me the moment your marriage was annulled. Why didn't you?"

Nicholas sat up and rubbed his thigh. "I couldn't. By the time I was free of Julia, there was another . . . entanglement. I am still not free of it, Emma."

Emma drew away from him. "What are you talking about? You are not free of what?"

His shoulders slumped. "You know my cousin Lady Catherine gave birth to a daughter this year," he began, not looking at her. "I told you that already. It was a difficult birth. The doctors—it is a certainty that she will never bear another child. It will be up to me, after all, to produce an heir. She has asked me to marry again, as soon as possible. Emma, I gave her my word."

"Is that all?" said Emma, almost ready to laugh. "You cannot break your word to Lady Catherine. I understand."

Nicholas glanced at her. "You understand? It means I will have to go to London after the first of the year and select a bride from amongst the eligible debutantes. It means I will not be able to see you again, Emma. It wouldn't be fair to the girl."

Emma recoiled as though he had struck her a blow to the chest. "Is that what it means?" she said coldly. "You don't want to marry *me*? You think I am too old to give you a child, is that it?"

Her voice reeked of bitterness, but she could not help it.

"Of course I want to marry you," he said, pulling her roughly into his arms. "I have always wanted to marry you. You've always said no."

Emma laughed shakily. "I said no two years ago, Nicholas. A lifetime ago. Well, to be perfectly accurate, I never said no because you never asked the question!" she went on. "Two years ago, you simply announced it at dinner, without talking to me first. Last year, you only mentioned marriage to exclude it. You asked me to sail around the world with you as your concubine."

"Concubine! Who do you think I am? The Sultan of Baghdad? Emma, I am asking you now."

"That's not a proposal," she said.

"Emma, will you marry me?"

"Are you sure you wouldn't rather marry some seventeen-year-old debutante?"

He shuddered. "Please don't make me go through all that again."

"Very well," she said primly. "Since you *ask*. Is there anything else you would like to ask me?" she went on, climbing on top of him and nuzzling the side of his face. "I'm in a very generous mood at the moment. You could probably ask me for anything, and I would give it to you, provided, of course, that we do not leave this bed for another hour at least."

"That is generous indeed," he agreed breathlessly as she began to touch him.

A hour later to the moment, Harry went to his mother's room. Giving it a smart rap with his knuckles, he strode in. "There's something I have been meaning to talk to you about, Mama," he announced, strolling over to the window with his hands clasped behind his back.

On the other side of the room, Nicholas dove under the bed. Emma came running out of her dressing room. "Harry!" she cried, pulling her dressing gown around her.

Harry looked at her in surprise. "You look like a madwoman, Mama," he said. "Your hair's all tumbled. I thought you were in the bed just now," he added, puzzled.

"No, I was just about to have a bath," Emma said quickly. "I tried to have a nap," she went on, making an effort to smooth out the bed, "but I couldn't sleep."

"I've upset you, Mama," the young man said contritely. "I'm sorry."

"You said there was something you'd been meaning to

talk to me about," Emma reminded him gently. "Something besides little Michael, you mean?"

"Yes, Mama," he said, allowing her to lead him over to the window seat. "I tried to before, but it just felt so awkward. I don't really know how to talk to you about it, but now I must. I can't put it off any longer."

"Is it a girl?" Emma asked, delighted.

"A girl!" he said scornfully. "I hope I don't need to talk to my mother about a girl!"

Disappointed, Emma folded her hands in her lap. "All right then. What is it?"

"Well," he said, "to peel the bark from the tree, it's your dower portion."

Emma met these words with a look of blank astonishment. "My dower portion?" she repeated. "What about it?"

"I might have mentioned it earlier when I was talking of Aunt Harriet's allowance, but I didn't want to embarrass you," said Harry. Standing up, he began to pace back and forth in front of her. "As you know, it's twenty thousand pounds a year. You're thirty now, or thereabouts, but you're very healthy. You could live to be eighty."

"Thank you," said Emma. "I hope so."

"So do I, naturally," said Harry, with a brief frown. "But that would be fifty years, if you see my point. Twenty thousand pounds a year for fifty years. Why, that's a million pounds, Mama. A million pounds!"

"Harry, I will gladly forego the money," said Emma. "You know I don't need it. I'll give it back to you, every penny. You can make little Michael a very handsome settlement at no real cost to yourself."

"It's very tempting," said Harry, "but I can't let you do that, Mama. I'm the Duke of Warwick. How will it look if I don't pay my mother her dower portion?"

"All right, then. Pay me, and I will give it back to you."

"I'm not a charity case, Mama!" he said angrily.

"What is it you want from me, Harry?" Emma asked quietly.

"I was just thinking," he muttered. "If you were to marry again, there would be no question of a dower portion. Have you . . . have you ever thought of marrying again?"

He looked at her sheepishly.

"I have, as a matter of fact," said his mother.

"You have?" Harry was delighted. "I wouldn't ask you to go to London, of course," he went on quickly. "You would not want to be in competition with a bunch of silly young debutantes."

"No, indeed. It wouldn't be fair to the debutantes."

"I have someone in mind for you. You wouldn't want to go through a lot of courtship and nonsense, after all."

Emma folded her arms and looked at him with stern frown. "What do you mean, you have someone in mind for me? That is presumptuous, Henry Fitzroy."

"Oh, but he's someone you like, Mama. At least, I think you like him. He's practically a member of the family. He is a bit younger than you, I suppose. I'm not really sure how old he is. But I'm sure he will suit."

"He is twenty-two," Emma said, amused. "And he will suit very well."

Harry grinned at her. "You do like him, then? Good. I suppose we've only known him a couple of years, but it seems longer, doesn't it?"

"Yes," Emma agreed.

Harry knelt at her feet, taking her hands in his. "Does this mean you'll do it, Mama?"

"For you, Harry," she told him gravely. "I'll do it for you."

"Thank you, Mama," he said, throwing his arms around her and hugging her fiercely. "I—I'll let you have your bath now," he added, his nose wrinkling.

"Thank you, Harry," she said.

"We'll make the announcement at dinner," he said, "if that's all right."

"I must speak to Grey first, of course," Emma replied, "but I don't see why not."

He went out quietly, closing the door.

"Did you think it would be so easy?" Nicholas asked, sliding out from under the bed.

"I confess I did not. It must be a Christmas miracle," Emma said, beginning to laugh.

# Chapter Twenty-Five

It was six-thirty in the evening when Lord Ian Monteith and his wife arrived at Warwick. The Westphalia had been made ready for him.

"That will never do," Lady Ian said indignantly. "Not for a married man, Carstairs."

"No, indeed, Lady Ian," Carstairs readily agreed.

"We must have a suite! The St. Petersburg, I suppose, is occupied?"

"Yes, Lady Ian. By their graces, the Duke and Duchess of Chilton."

Lady Ian's dark eyes sharpened. "But their graces must be quitting it soon," she said shrewdly. "They will be leaving for Chilton within a day or two, I should think. I rather wonder at their being here now! You may put us in Westphalia, for now, Carstairs," she decided. "But Lord Ian and I will move to St. Petersburg when the Chiltons quit it."

Carstairs coughed gently. "I fear, Lady Ian, that Lord Camford is to take the St. Petersburg tomorrow, when their graces depart."

Lady Ian gaped at him in astonishment. "Lord Camford? Lord Camford! Lord, what is *he* doing here? Never mind!

We shall go straight to the drawing room. You may announce us, Carstairs."

"Should we not take the baby to the nursery ourselves?" Monty said.

Lady Ian frowned at him. "Lord, why? The servants will look after him. Announce us, Carstairs. Lord, I cannot *wait* to see the looks on their faces!"

"The family are not assembled in the drawing room at this hour, Lady Ian," Carstairs apologized.

Lady Ian pouted. "No, of course not," she said crossly. "They will be dressing for dinner. Come, Monty. We must dress for dinner, too. I suppose Westphalia will have to do for now. We must *not* be late for dinner. Not *too* late, anyway," she added with a laugh. "We will want to make an entrance, naturally. I believe I will wear my yellow satin, with my amethyst parure. Thank you, Carstairs. I know the way."


Colin was in his dressing room, studying his cravat in the cheval glass. Bored by the effect, he frantically motioned to his valet to start over. The offending neckwear had just been removed, when he heard Lady Harriet's voice in the next room, his bedroom.

"Just set me down here, boys. Mind the arm, Mr. Carter!"

"Yes, Aunt Harriet. Thank you, Aunt Harriet."

"Wait outside," she commanded her adolescent slaves as Colin strolled out of his dressing room.

Lady Harriet was in a foul temper. "Why didn't you tell me your Scotsman was coming?" she demanded. "You didn't even tell me you'd invited him!"

Colin was appalled. "Monty! Monty is here?"

"He only just arrived. Didn't you know?" She looked at him curiously. "He's brought a Lady Ian with him, too. I've not seen *her* yet, but I caught a glimpse of the baby as it was being whisked off to the nursery."

"He's married?" Colin snorted. "And with a baby, too! *What* a hypocrite!"

"So you didn't invite him," Lady Harriet said, grunting with satisfaction. "Well, hurry up! Get yourself together. I want to get a look at this Lady Ian."

"She isn't likely to be anyone *we* know," said Colin. But he went obediently back into his dressing room to finish his cravat.

They went down together, Lady Harriet on her throne and Colin on foot. They arrived at the lounge almost simultaneously with the Duke and Duchess of Chilton. The Duke of Warwick and his friends had already taken over the room. They made a loud, boisterous group at the fireside while Lord Camford stood quietly in the corner.

Lady Harriet directed her boys to set her down in a spot commanding an excellent view of the doorway. She sat with her lorgnette at the ready.

"You may go." Colin dismissed the boys. "I'll look after the old harpy."

"Has anyone seen her?" Cecily inquired. "Lady Ian, I mean? We saw the baby in the nursery before we came down. He has no hair and he's called Charles. I think he must be about Mimi's age," she added.

Colin shrugged to show his complete disinterest. He went to join Nicholas in the corner.

"You're very late this evening, Mama," Harry complained as his mother came into the room. He seemed completely oblivious to the way his friends all stopped talking at once and regarded the duchess, openmouthed.

"Well, I'm here now," Emma answered, smiling as she took his arm. "But I see we are still waiting for Lord Ian and his wife, so I'm afraid you must wait a little longer."

"Lord Ian's not married, Mama," Harry told her. "If he *were,* it might excuse his tardiness," he added impatiently. "Why can we never have dinner on time?"

"I believe he is married," said Emma. "Carstairs tells me he is married, and, you know, Carstairs is never wrong. Has anyone seen her yet? Is she a Scotswoman?"

"We have not seen *her* yet," said Cecily, "but the baby is as bald as an egg."

"There's a baby, too?" Harry cried in dismay. "Mama, I swear to you—if I had known he was married already, I would never have invited him here!"

Emma blinked at him. "*You* invited him? Why, I just assumed that my brother had invited him."

"I assume by *brother* you mean Otto," Colin said coldly. "Because I have no desire to see Lord Ian ever again, I can assure you. And even less desire to see his wife."

"But, Harry, why would you invite Lord Ian here?" Emma asked. "You are not friendly with him. Are you?"

"You know why, Mama," he answered, lowering his voice. "You needn't put on a brave front with me. If he's married already, we can hardly ask him to marry *you*."

"What?" Emma said sharply. "I'm sorry. What did you say?"

"Lower your voice, Mama," he pleaded with her. "Please don't embarrass me in front of my friends."

"How could you possibly think that *I* would marry Lord Ian?" Emma whispered. "He's one of your uncle Colin's friends, you know. You know what that means, don't you?"

"But that is *why* you would want to marry him, of course," Harry answered. "Another man might expect you to be, you know, a wife to him. You wouldn't want *that*, would you? Don't worry, Mama. Uncle Colin has a lot of friends. We'll find someone for you."

Emma had not decided how best to reply to this when Lord Ian and his lady were announced. Lady Ian was immensely pleased by the general amazement that met her arrival.

"Good evening, everyone," she said, giving them all a dazzling smile. "We are not too dreadfully late, I hope?"

Harry was thunderstruck. "Cousin Julia!" he stammered.

Lady Ian moved down the room to him in yellow satin, amethysts glittering at her throat. "Good evening, Cousin Harry. I think I know everyone here, except for these handsome young men," she added, eyeing his friends with great interest. "Will you be good enough to present them to me?"

"But what are you doing here?" Harry demanded. Taking her roughly by the arm, he propelled her toward the door. "You are in disgrace in Lincolnshire!"

Lady Ian twisted away from him. "What do you mean, what am I doing here? Did you not invite my husband to spend Christmas here at Warwick?"

"No," said Harry. "Camford came on his own. He had . . . business."

Lady Ian threw back her head and laughed. "Camford? He was no more a husband to me than *you* were, Cousin Harry. I am married to Lord Ian now."

"No!" said Colin.

"That is impossible," said Harry.

"Did you think I would be content to be buried alive in Lincolnshire?" Julia asked, her dark eyes flashing. "Of course, I found myself a husband. And *you* said I was damaged goods, and that no respectable man would take me! Ha! You said I wasn't fit to be married. You said the best I could hope for would be to become *your* mistress!"

Harry paled. "Mama, I never said that," he cried. "I swear it. I may have said she was only fit to be someone's mistress, but not mine."

"I know what you meant," said Julia.

"Then the child in the nursery . . ." Cecily began. She trailed off, her mouth forming a perfect, soundless O.

"It's Palafox's!" Colin said angrily.

"That's right," said Monty, turning on him. "You have *your* wife and *your* baby, and now I have mine. At least, there's no reason the next one won't be mine. No reason at all."

"No, indeed!" said Julia, reclaiming her husband's arm.

"And, just for the record, Lord Ian is quite twice the man you are, Nicky."

Nicholas made her a stiff bow. "I am glad to hear it, ma'am."

Bewildered, Harry looked at his mother. "What are we going to do, Mama? All my friends are staring. I'm sure nothing like has ever happened before."

"But this is good news, Harry," she told him, smiling. "You will now be able to lease the Lincolnshire house to some paying tenants." Moving forward, she surprised Julia by kissing her warmly on both cheeks. "You are very welcome, Julia. Congratulations on your marriage. I am certain you will be happy. And Monty," she added, turning to the gentleman, "you are very welcome, too. Shall we go in to dinner?"

Much of Harry's anxiety had already passed by the time she returned to him. "I'm beginning to think you had a narrow escape there, Mama," he whispered to her. "If Lord Ian is twice the man Camford is, you would not have been very comfortable married to him."

"There is a silver lining to every cloud," Emma answered cheerfully.

"I wonder," said Harry. "I think we all know that Lord Camford couldn't cut the mustard. It's why Julia ran off with that blackguard Palafox in the first place. Do you think Lord Camford would marry you, Mama?"

"Oh!" Emma seemed quite surprised. "I don't know, Harry."

"We could ask him, couldn't we?" Harry whined. "Of course, if it's too embarrassing for you, Mama, I'll ask him for you."

Emma took her place at the other end of the long table. "I will marry Lord Camford," she said, "on one condition."

"Of course, Mama. Anything."

Emma pointed to her cheek. "You must kiss me."

"What! Here, Mama? In front of my friends?"

"I *could* live to be ninety, you know," she told him sweetly.

"That would cost you one million, two hundred thousand pounds."

"I suppose it's worth it, then," he grumbled. Leaning down, he pressed his lips to his mother's cheek.

"It's worth it to me, darling," Emma said softly.

And she meant it.

# GREAT BOOKS, GREAT SAVINGS!

When You Visit Our Website:

## www.kensingtonbooks.com

You Can Save Money Off The Retail Price
Of Any Book You Purchase!

- All Your Favorite Kensington Authors
- New Releases & Timeless Classics
- Overnight Shipping Available
- eBooks Available For Many Titles
- All Major Credit Cards Accepted

Visit Us Today To Start Saving!

## www.kensingtonbooks.com

# Romantic Suspense from
# Lisa Jackson